ALSO BY DAVID BALDACCI

DAVID BALDACCI

THE ESCAPE

GRAND CENTRAL
PUBLISHING

LARGE PRINT

Grand Central Publishing
Hachette Book Group
1290 Avenue of the Americas
New York, NY 10019

Printed in the United States of America

Grand Central Publishing is a division of Hachette Book Group, Inc. The Grand Central Publishing name and logo is a trademark of Hachette Book Group, Inc.

The publisher is not responsible for websites (or their content) that are not owned by the publisher.

ISBN: 9781455530175 (large print)

In memory of Kate Bailey and Ruth Rockhold:
You will be greatly missed.

THE
ESCAPE

CHAPTER

I

THE PRISON LOOKED more like the campus of
a community college than a place where men
were kept in cells for ten years or longer for
offenses committed while wearing the uniform
of their country. There were no guard towers,
but there were two staggered twelve-foot-tall
security fences, armed patrols, and enough surveillance cameras to keep an electronic eye on
virtually every millimeter of the place. Situated
at the northern end of Fort Leavenworth, the
United States Disciplinary Barracks sat next to
the Missouri River on nearly forty rolling,
forested Kansas acres, a mound of brick and razor wire cradled by a green hand. It was the
only maximum-security military prison for
males in the country.

America's foremost military prison was called
the USDB, or the DB for short. The Leavenworth federal penitentiary for civilians, one of
three prisons on the grounds of Fort Leaven-

worth, was four miles to the south. Along with the Joint Regional Correctional Facility—also for military prisoners—there was a fourth privately operated prison in Leavenworth, which raised the total inmate population among the four prisons to about five thousand. The Leavenworth Tourism Bureau, apparently seeking to capitalize on any bit of notoriety to lure visitors to the area, had incorporated the prison angle into its promotional brochures with the phrase "Doin' time in Leavenworth."

Federal dollars rolled through this part of Kansas and jumped the border into Missouri like a flood of green paper locusts, boosting the local economy and filling the coffers of businesses that provided the soldiers with smoked ribs, cold beer, fast cars, cheap hookers, and pretty much everything in between.

Inside the DB were about four hundred and fifty prisoners. Inmates were housed in a series of escape-proof pods, including a Special Housing Unit, or SHU. The majority of inmates were here for sex-based crimes. They were mostly young and their sentences were long.

Approximately ten prisoners were kept in solitary confinement at any one time, while the remaining inmates were housed in the general population. There were no bars on the doors; they were just solid metal, with a slot at the bottom for food trays to be shoved through. This also allowed for shackles to be fitted like a new pair of iron shoes when a prisoner needed to be transported somewhere.

Unlike at some other state and federal penitentiaries around the country, discipline and respect were demanded here and given. There were no power struggles between the incarcerated and their watchers. There was the rule of military law, and the primary responses from those being held here were "Yes sir," closely followed by "No sir."

The DB had a death row on which currently sat a half dozen convicted murderers, including the Fort Hood killer. It also had an execution chamber. Whether any of the death row inmates would ever see the lethal injection needle would be something only the lawyers and judges could determine, probably years and millions of dollars in legal fees from now.

* * *

Day had long since passed to night and the lights from a civilian Piper plane lifting off from the nearby Sherman Airfield were almost the only evidence of activity. It was quiet now, but a violent storm front that had been on the radar for a while was howling in from the north. Another system that had sprung up in Texas was barreling toward the Midwest like a brakeless freight train. It would soon meet its northern counterpart, with devastating results. The entire area was already hunkering down in anticipation.

When the two rampaging fronts met three hours later, the result was a storm of shattering proportions, with jagged lightning slicing sideways across the sky, rain bucketing down, and winds that seemed to have no limit to their strength or reach.

The power lines went first, snapped like string by tumbling trees. Then down came the phone lines. After that more trees toppled, blocking roads. The nearby Kansas City International Airport had been shut down ahead of time, all planes empty and the terminal full of travelers riding out the storm and quietly thanking God they were on the ground instead of up in that maelstrom.

Inside the DB the guards made their rounds, or sipped their coffees in the break room, or talked in low whispers, exchanging scuttlebutt of no importance just to get through their shifts. No one thought anything of the storm outside since they were safely inside a fortress of brick and steel. They were like an aircraft carrier confronted by gale-force winds and heavy seas. It might not be pleasant, but they would easily ride it out.

Even when the regular power failed as both transformers at a nearby substation blew up, plunging the prison into momentary darkness, no one was overly concerned. The massive backup generator automatically kicked on, and that machine was inside a bombproof installation with its own underground power source of natural gas that would never run out of juice. This secondary system came on so fast the short lapse did nothing more than cause jittery fluorescents and a few pops on surveillance cameras and computer monitors.

Guards finished their coffees and moved on to other gossip, while others slowly made their way down halls and around corners and in and out of pods, making sure all was well in the world of the DB.

What finally got everyone's attention was the total silence that came when the foolproof generator with the endless supply of energy in the bombproof installation made a noise like a giant with whooping cough, and then simply died.

All the lights, cameras, and consoles instantly went out, although some of the surveillance cameras had battery backups and thus remained on. And then the quiet was replaced with urgent cries and the sounds of men running. Communication radios crackled and popped. Flashlights were snatched from holders on leather belts and powered up. But they provided only meager illumination.

And then the unthinkable occurred: All the automatic cell doors unlocked. This was *not* supposed to happen. The system was built such that whenever the power failed, the doors automatically locked. Not so good for prisoners if the power failure was due to, say, a fire, but that's the way it was, or the way it was supposed to be. However, now the guards were hearing the clicks of cell doors opening all over the prison, and hundreds of prisoners were emerging into the hallways.

There were no guns allowed in the DB. Thus the guards had only their authority, wits, training, ability to read prisoners' moods, and heavy batons to keep order. And now those batons were gripped in hands that were becoming increasingly sweaty.

There were SOPs, or standard operating procedures, for such an eventuality, because the military had procedures for every eventuality. The Army typically had two backups for all critical items. At the DB the natural gas backup generator was considered a fail-safe. However, now it *had* failed. Now it fell to the guards to maintain complete order. They were the last line of defense. The first goal was to secure all prisoners. The secondary goal was to secure all prisoners. Anything else would be deemed an unacceptable failure by any military standard. Careers and along with them stars and bars would fall off like parched needles from a Christmas tree still up in late January.

Since there were far more prisoners than guards, securing all of them involved a few tactics, the most important of which required grouping them in the large open central areas, where they would be made to lie facedown. This seemed to be going well for about five minutes, but then something else happened that would make every guard dig deeper into the Army manuals and more than one sphincter—whether attached to guard or prisoner—tighten.

"We've got shots fired," shouted a guard into his radio. "Shots fired, undetermined location, unknown source."

This message was repeated down the line until it was ringing in every guard's ears. Shots fired and nobody knew from where or by whom. And since none of the guards had guns, that meant one of the prisoners must. Maybe more than one.

Now things, already serious, morphed into something bordering on chaotic.

And then the situation became a lot worse.

The sound of an explosion flooded the interior of pod number three, which contained the SHU. Now the borderline chaotic leapt right into utter meltdown. The only thing that could restore order was an overwhelming show of armed force. And there were few organizations in the world that could do overwhelming armed force better than the United States Army. Especially when that gunned-up force was right next door at Fort Leavenworth.

Minutes later, six green Army trucks swept through the powerless boundary gates of the DB, whose high-tech intrusion detection systems had been rendered inoperable. Military police in SWAT gear and carrying shields poured off the trucks, their automatic weapons and shotguns racked and ready. They charged straight into the facility, their fields of vision bright and clear owing to their latest-generation night-vision goggles that made the blackness inside the prison look as fresh and vibrant as anything on an Xbox.

Prisoners froze where they were. Then those who were still standing immediately lay face-down, their hands behind their backs and their limbs trembling in the face of superbly trained soldiers loaded for war.

Order was eventually achieved.

Army engineers were able to restore power and the lights came back on and doors could lock once more. In the meantime, the MPs from Fort Leavenworth turned the facility back over to the guards and left the way they had come. The prison commander, a full colonel, grate-fully exhaled as the weight of the world, or at least a sudden wall appearing between him and his next promotion, was lifted.

Prisoners shuffled back into their cells.

A head count was done.

The list of prisoners accounted for was com-pared to the official list of inmates. Initially, the numbers tallied.

Initially.

But on further inspection that did not turn out to be the case.

There was one prisoner missing. Only one. But he was an important one. He had been sent here for life. Not because he had fragged an officer or otherwise killed one or many. Or because he had raped, slashed, burned, or bombed. He was not on death row. He was here because he was a traitor, having betrayed his country in the area of national security, which was a term that made everyone sit up and look over their shoulder.

And even more inexplicably, on the cot in the missing prisoner's cell was someone else—an unidentified dead man lying facedown under the covers. This was the cause of the initial miscount of heads.

They searched every corner of the DB, including the air ducts and any other crevices they could think of. They raced outside into the now dying storm to search there, marching in methodical columns, leaving nothing unexamined.

But this plot of Kansas soil did not yield what they were looking for.

The inmate was gone. No one could explain how. No one could say how the dead man had come to be here. No one could make sense of any of this.

There was only one obvious fact.

Robert Puller, once a major in the United States Air Force and an expert in nuclear weaponry and cyber security, and also the son of one of the most famous fighting soldiers of them all, the now retired Army lieutenant general John Puller Sr., had escaped from the inescapable DB.

And he had left behind an unknown dead man in his place, which was even more inexplicable than how he had managed to break out.

Informed of this seeming impossibility turned stark reality, the prison's commander lifted the secure phone in his office, and in doing so kissed his once promising career goodbye.

2

JOHN PULLER HAD his M11 pistol pointed at the man's head.

A fancied-up Beretta 92—known in the military as an M9A1—was pointed right back at him.

It was a twenty-first-century duel that promised no winners and portended two fatal losers.

"I'm not taking the fall for this," roared PFC Tony Rogers. He was a black man in his twenties with the image of a "terrible towel" and the Pittsburgh Steelers logo inked on his forearm. He was about five-nine, and had a shaved head, dumbbell shoulders, ripped arms, and beefy thighs mismatched with a high-pitched voice.

Puller was dressed in khaki pants and a navy blue windbreaker with the gold letters "CID" stenciled on the back. Rogers wore his Army Combat Uniform, or ACU, pants, regulation boots, and an Army T-shirt, with a patrol cap on his head. He was sweating though the air was crisp. Puller was not sweating. Rogers's gaze was erratic. Puller's eyes did not lift from Rogers's face. He wanted to exude calm, hoping to graft it onto the other man.

The pair of soldiers had squared off in an alley behind a bar outside of Lawton, Oklahoma, home to Fort Sill and also the grave of the Indian leader Geronimo. Puller had been to Lawton a couple of times before, and his father had been briefly stationed there once during his Army career. He was here now in his capacity as an agent in the Criminal Investigation Command attempting to arrest an alleged killer who wore the same uniform he did, and who was now pointing his Army-issued sidearm at him.

Puller said, "So tell me your side of the story."

"I didn't shoot anybody. You hear me? You are out your damn mind saying I did."

"I'm not saying anything. I'm just here because it's my job. You have defenses to the charges, then good for you. Use them."

"What are you talking about?"

"I'm talking about you getting a kickass JAG lawyer to defend you and maybe you beat the charge. I know some good ones. I can refer you. But doing what you're doing right now is not helping your case. So put the gun down and we forget all about you running away and then drawing down on me."

"Bullshit!"

"I have a warrant for your arrest, Rogers. I'm just doing my job. Let me do it peacefully. You don't want to die in a crummy alley in Lawton, Oklahoma. And I sure as hell don't."

"They're gonna put me away for life. I got a momma to support."

"And your mother wouldn't want you to end it like this. You'll get your day in court. They'll hear your side. You can bring your mother in as a character witness. Let the legal system do its thing." Puller said all of this in an even, calming voice.

Rogers eyed him cagily. "Look, why don't you just get out my way so I can walk out this alley and out the damn Army?"

"We both wear the same uniform and I can try to help you, PFC. But I can't do that."

"I will shoot your ass. I swear to God I will."

"Still won't be happening."

"I don't miss, man. Top marks on the damn range."

"You fire I fire. We both go down. It's stupid for it to end that way. I know you can see that."

"Then let's just call it a truce. You just walk away."

Puller gave one shake of the head while his gaze and gunsight held on Rogers. "I can't do that."

"Why the hell not?"

"You're in the artillery, Rogers. You have a job to do, right? One that the Army spent a lot of time and money drilling into you, right?"

"Yeah, so what?"

"Well, this is *my* job. And my job doesn't let me walk away. Now, I don't want to shoot you, and I don't think you want to shoot me, so put the gun down. It's the smart thing to do. You know that."

Puller had tracked the man to this location after finding more than enough evidence to put him away for a long time. However, Rogers had spotted Puller and made a run for it. That run had ended in this alley. There was no way out other than the way they'd entered.

Rogers shook his head. "We both gonna die, then."

"It does not have to end like that, soldier," retorted Puller. "Use your brain, Rogers. Guaranteed death, or a trial where you might get some time in DB—or where you might even walk away? Which sounds better to you?

Which would sound better to your mother?"

This seemed to strike a chord with Rogers. He blinked rapidly and said, "You got family?"

"Yeah, I do. I'd like to see them again. Tell me about your family."

Rogers licked his chapped lips. "Momma, two brothers, and three sisters. Back in Pittsburgh. We're *Steeler* fans," he added proudly. "My daddy was there when Franco caught the Immaculate Reception."

"So put the gun down and you can still watch the games."

"You ain't listening, dammit! No way I'm going down for this. See, that dude drew down on me. It was self-defense."

"Then make that claim at your court-martial. Maybe you walk away free."

"That's not gonna happen and you know it." He paused and studied Puller. "You got stuff on me or you wouldn't be here. You know about the damn drugs, don't you?"

"My job is to bring you in, not pass judgment."

"This is the middle of nowhere, man. Need some juice to get by. I'm a city guy. I don't like cows. And I'm not the only one."

"You've got a good record in the Army, Rogers. That'll help you. And if it was self-defense and the jury believes you, you're home free."

Rogers shook his head stubbornly. "My ass is gone. You know it, I know it."

Puller quickly thought of some way to defuse the situation. "Tell me something, Rogers. How many drinks did you have in the bar?"

"What?"

"Simple question. How many drinks?"

Rogers tightened his grip on the pistol as a bead of sweat ran down his left cheek. "Pitcher of beer and a shot of Beam." He suddenly yelled, "What the hell does that matter? You messin' with me? Are you *messin'* with me, ass-hole!"

"I'm not messing with you. I'm just trying to explain something to you. Will you listen to what I have to say? Because it's important. It's important to *you*."

Puller waited for him to answer. He wanted to keep Rogers engaged and thinking. Thinking men rarely pulled triggers. Hotheads did.

"Okay, what?"

"That's a fair amount of alcohol you've had."

"Shit, I can drink twice that and still drive a Paladin."

"I'm not talking about driving a Paladin."

"Then what?" demanded Rogers.

Puller continued in a calm tone, "You're about a hundred and seventy pounds, so even with the adrenaline spike I'm guessing that your intoxication level is about a point one, and maybe higher with the shot of Beam. That means you're legally too drunk to drive a moped, much less a twenty-seven-ton howitzer."

"What the hell's that got to do with anything?"

"Alcohol impairs fine motor skills, like the kind required to aim and fire a weapon properly. With what you've had to drink, we're talking a serious degradation of marksmanship skills."

"I sure as hell ain't missing your ass from ten feet."

"You'd be surprised, Rogers, you really would be. I calculate you've lost at least twenty-five percent of your normal skill level in a situation like this. On the other hand, my aim and fine motor skills are perfect. So I will ask you once more to put down your weapon, because a twenty-five percent reduction pretty much ensures that this will not end well for you."

Rogers fired his gun at the same time he yelled, "Fu—." But he was unable to complete the word.

3

JOHN PULLER DROPPED his duffel on the floor of his bedroom, took off his cap, wiped a bead of sweat off his nose, and dropped onto the bed. He'd just gotten back from the investigation at Fort Sill. The result had been his tracking down PFC Rogers in that alley.

And when Rogers, despite Puller's requests for him to stand down, had started to squeeze the trigger of his Army-issued sidearm, Puller had stepped slightly to the right while narrowing his target silhouette and firing at the same time. He hadn't actually seen Rogers start to pull the trigger. It was the look in the man's eyes and the curse that had started coming out of his mouth—only half finished because of the M11's punch. Rogers was true to his word—he wasn't leaving the alley without a fight. Puller had to admire him somewhat for that. He was no coward, although maybe it was just the Jim Beam talking.

Rogers's round had slammed into the brick wall behind Puller. The slug's impact chipped off a sliver of brick that shot out and ripped a hole in Puller's sleeve but drew no blood. Uniforms could be mended with thread. Flesh could too, but he'd take the hole in the uniform over one in him.

He could have killed Rogers with a headshot, but while the situation was dire, he had been in worse. He pointed his gun downward and shot the PFC in the right leg just above the knee. Shots in the torso allowed someone to fire back because sometimes they didn't completely incapacitate. Shots around the knee region, however, reduced the toughest men to screaming babies. Rogers dropped his weapon, fell to the ground, and shrieked, clutching his damaged leg. The man would probably walk with a limp for a long time, but at least he would be alive.

Puller had triaged the man he'd shot, called in the paramedics, ridden to the Army hospital with the wounded man, and even let Rogers try to crush his hand when the pain got too bad. Then he had filled out the requisite mountain of paperwork, answered a slew of questions, and finally jumped on a military transport flight for home.

The man Rogers had shot down in the street

after a drug deal gone bad now had some semblance of justice. The Rogers family back in Pittsburgh had a son and brother to support and cry over. The Steelers would still have a fan to cheer them on, albeit from an Army stockade. It shouldn't have happened. But it had. Puller knew it was either him or the other man. Still, he always preferred to put the cuffs on instead of pulling the trigger. And shooting a fellow soldier, criminal or not, didn't sit well with him.

All in all, a pretty crappy day's work, he concluded.

Now he simply needed some shut-eye. All he was asking for was a few hours. Then it was back on duty, because at CID you were really never off duty, though he would be confined to a desk while an incident investigation was performed over his use of extreme force in that alley. But after that he would just go where they told him to go. Crime did not keep a schedule, at least to his knowledge. And because of that he had never punched a time clock during his Army career, because combat wasn't a nine-to-fiver either.

Puller had barely closed his eyes when his phone buzzed. He looked at the screen and groaned. It was his old man. Or, more accurately, it was the hospital calling on behalf of his father.

He dropped the phone on the bed and closed his eyes once more.

Later, tomorrow, maybe the next day, he would deal with the general. But not now. Right now he just wanted some sack time.

The phone started buzzing again. It was the hospital. Again. Puller didn't answer it and the phone finally stopping ringing.

Then it started buzzing again.

These pricks are just not going to give up.

And then his next thought was jolting. Maybe his father had…But no, the old man was too stubborn to die. He'd probably outlive both his sons.

He sat up and grabbed the phone. The number on the screen was different. It wasn't the hospital.

It was his CO, Don White.

"Yes sir?" he answered.

"Puller, there's a situation. Maybe you haven't heard."

Puller blinked and then tied his CO's ominous statement to the calls from the hospital. His father. Was he really dead? It couldn't be. Fighting legends didn't die. They just…were there. Always.

His voice dry and scratchy, he said, "Heard what, sir? I just got back in town from Fort Sill. Is it my father?"

"No, it's your brother," said White.

"My brother?"

His brother was in the most secure military prison in the country. Now Puller's mind turned to other possibilities involving his sibling.

"Has he been injured?" Puller didn't know how that could be. There were no riots at the DB. But then again, one of the guards had slugged Bobby once, for a reason he had never shared with his brother.

"No. It's a little more serious than that."

Puller drew a quick breath. *More serious than that?* "Is he…is he dead?"

"No, apparently he's escaped," White answered.

Puller drew another quick breath as his mind tried to come to terms with this statement. But one didn't escape from the DB. It would be like flying to the moon in a Toyota. "How?"

"No one knows how."

"You said 'apparently.' Is there some confusion on the point?"

"I said 'apparently' because that's what DB is saying right now. It happened last night. I can't imagine they wouldn't have found him by now, if he were still on the premises. DB is big, but it's not *that* big."

"Is any other prisoner missing?"

"No. But there's something else. Equally troubling."

"What could that be, sir?"

"That could be an unidentified man found dead in your brother's cell."

An exhausted Puller could barely process these words. Even with ten hours of sleep behind him he doubted he could have done much with them.

"An unidentified man? Meaning not another prisoner, guard, or other person working at the prison?"

"Correct."

"How exactly did he escape?" asked Puller.

White said, "Storm knocked out the power and then the backup generator failed. Reinforcements from the fort were called in to make sure order was maintained. They thought everything was fine until they did the head count. One head was missing. Your brother's. And then another head was added—the dead guy. The Army Secretary, I'm told, just about had a coronary when he was briefed."

Puller was only half listening to this as another disturbing thought pushed into his tired mind. "Has my father been informed?"

"I didn't call him, if that's what you're asking. But I can't speak for others. I wanted you to know as soon as possible. I was just informed myself."

"But you said it happened last night."

"Well, DB didn't exactly give a shout-out that they had lost a prisoner. It went through channels. You know the Army, Puller. Things take time. Whether you're trying to storm a hill or bang out a press release, it all takes time."

"But my father could know?"

"Yes."

Puller was still in a daze. "Sir, I'd like to request a few days' leave."

"I thought you might. Consider it granted. I'm sure you want to be with your father."

"Yes sir," said Puller automatically. But he preferred to be involved with his brother's dilemma. "I suppose CID is handling the case?"

"I'm not sure about that, Puller. Your brother is Air Force. *Was* Air Force."

"But DB is an Army prison. No territorial fights there."

White snorted. "This is the military. There

are territorial fights over the men's room. And considering your brother's crime, there may be other interests and forces at play here that might trump all the usual interbranch bullshit."

Puller knew what the man meant. "National security interests."

"And with your brother on the loose any number of responses might be triggered."

"He couldn't have gotten far. DB is smack in the middle of a military installation."

"But there's an airport nearby. And interstate highways."

"That would mean he'd need fake IDs. Transportation. Money. A disguise."

"In other words he'd need outside help," added White.

"You think he had that? How?"

"I have no way of knowing. But what I do know is, it's quite a coincidence that both the main power *and* the backup generator failed on the same night. And how a prisoner was able to simply walk out of a max military facility, well, it makes one wonder, doesn't it? And tack on the fact that a dead guy was in his cell? Where the hell did he come from?"

"Do they have a cause of death?"

"If they do, they haven't shared it with me."

"Do they think Bob—my brother killed the man?"

"I have no idea what theories they're entertaining on that score, Puller."

"But you think he had *inside* as well as outside help?"

"You're the investigator, Puller. What do you think?"

"I don't know. It's not my case."

Don White's voice rose. "And rest assured, it will *never* be your case. So during your leave, you stay the hell away from this sucker. You do not need that over your head. One Puller in trouble is enough. You hear me?"

"I hear you," said Puller. But he thought, *I don't necessarily agree with you.*

Puller put the phone down and watched as his fat tabby, AWOL, glided into the room, jumped up on the bed, and rubbed her head against Puller's arm. He stroked AWOL and then picked up the cat, holding her against his chest.

His brother had been at the DB for more than two years. The trial had been swift and he'd been convicted by a panel of his peers. That was just the military way. You were never going to take years to try a case like that, nor were there endless appeals. And the media had been kept largely at arm's length. Fancy civilian lawyers more interested in million-dollar pay-offs and selling book and film rights than actually achieving justice had no place at such a trial. The uniforms had handled it all and the wagons had circled early and effectively. Sure, you had dirty laundry in uniform, but it was never going to be hung on a clothesline for all to see and smell. It was going to be buried in a landfill masquerading as a prison.

Puller had not even been at the trial. He'd been thousands of miles away on CID deployment in the Middle East, where half the time he was playing soldier again and toting a rifle against the enemies of the United States. The Army didn't care about his family problems. He had a mission to perform and perform it he would. By the time he'd gotten back stateside his older brother was already at the DB, where he would be staying for the rest of his life.

But maybe not now.

Puller stripped off his clothes and took a shower, letting the water beat down on him as he rested his forehead against the moist tile wall. His breathing was usually slow and steady, like the tick of a clock. Now it was erratic and too fast, like a wheel freed from a car, bouncing crazy-ass down an embankment.

He could not accept that his brother had escaped from prison, for one compelling reason—that meant he truly was guilty.

This was something that Puller had always been unwilling to believe or accept. It just wasn't apparently in his DNA to do so. Pullers weren't traitors. They had fought, bled, and died for their country. Puller had relatives going back to George Washington's day who had taken musket balls to the chest to be free from England. Corporal Walter Puller had died repelling Pickett's charge at Gettysburg. Another ancestor, George Puller, had been shot down while flying a British Sopwith Camel over France in 1918. He'd parachuted out and survived, only to die four years later in a training accident while flying an experimental aircraft. At least two dozen Pullers had served in all military branches in the Second World War, with many not coming home again.

We fight. We don't betray.

He turned off the water and started to towel off. His CO had a good point. It did seem like an amazing coincidence that both the main power and backup generator would go out on the same night. And how could his brother have escaped without help? The DB was one of the most secure prisons ever built. No one had ever escaped before. No one.

And yet his brother apparently had.

And left a dead man in his wake whom no one could identify.

He dressed in clean civilian clothes and headed out to his car after letting AWOL out to run around a bit in the sunshine and fresh air.

Now Puller had to go somewhere, a place he did not want to go.

He would almost rather have returned to combat in the Middle East over where he was headed. But go he had to. He could imagine the foul temper his father would be in, if he even truly understood what had happened. Puller imagined that being around his old man when he was not happy was like being around another military legend, George Patton, when he was pissed off. It was not going to be a pleasant ride for anyone within earshot.

He climbed into his Army-issued white sedan, cranked the engine, rolled down the windows to help dry his short hair, and drove off. This was not how he planned to spend his first day back after shooting a fellow soldier in an alley. But then again, in his world nothing was predictable except that each upcoming moment could be the challenge of a lifetime.

While driving to see Fighting John Puller Sr., USA Ret., he decided he would dearly love to have the tanks of Patton's Third Army as an escort. He might very well need both the armor and the firepower.

CHAPTER

4

THE STORAGE UNIT'S overhead door was thrust up, the rusted wheels and track groaning in protest. The man flitted inside and closed the door behind him, exchanging the darkness of the night for the deeper obscurity of the unit's interior. He reached his hand out and flicked on a light, illuminating the ten-by-ten room's concrete floor and sheet metal sides and ceiling.

Two walls were covered with shelves. There was an old metal desk and matching chair set against the other wall. On the shelves were neatly stacked boxes. He drew closer to them, examining their labels. His memory was good, but it had been a while since he had been here—well over two years, in fact.

Robert Puller was dressed in Army fatigues and combat boots with a cap covering his head. This had allowed him to blend in well in what was clearly an Army town. But now he needed to completely change his appearance. He opened a box and pulled out a laptop. He set it down and plugged it in. After more than two years he knew the battery would be dead, but he was hoping it would still charge. If not, he would have to buy a new one. He actually needed a computer more than he needed a gun.

He opened another box and took out a pair of hair clippers, a mirror, shaving cream, a towel, a gallon of water in a sealed plastic jug, a bowl, and a razor. He sat down in the metal chair and set the mirror on the desk. He plugged the clippers into an outlet on the wall and turned them on. Over the next few minutes he shaved off his hair, right down to the stubble. Then he coated his scalp with shaving cream, poured the water into the bowl, and removed the stubble with the razor, dunking the blade periodically in the bowl to clean it and then wiping it off on the towel.

He studied the results in the mirror and came away satisfied. The human head had nine basic shapes. With a full head of hair his looked more moon-shaped. With no hair his head appeared bullet-shaped. It was a subtle but distinct change.

He slipped a length of moldable soft plastic in front of his upper row of teeth. This caused a slight bulging and broadening of the skin and muscle there as he flexed his mouth and jaw, changing the shape of the plastic insert until it rested comfortably in place.

Keeping out the mirror, water, and the towel, he put the other things away in the box and replaced it on the shelf.

Another box held articles of a more technical nature. He pulled them all out and set them up neatly on the desk like a surgeon lining up his instruments before commencing an operation. He covered his shoulders and front with the towel and then sketched out what he wanted to do on a piece of paper. He applied spirit gum to his nose and tapped it with his finger to make it sticky. He then quickly added a bit of a cotton ball to the surface before the adhesive dried out. He used a Popsicle stick to remove from a jar a small quantity of nose putty mixed with Derma Wax. He rubbed the putty into a ball, warming it with his body heat, making it easier to manipulate. He applied the putty to sections of his nose, all the while looking at his work in the mirror, first face on and then from the profile. He smoothed out the putty using KY Jelly. The smoothing and shaping took a long time, but he was patient. He had just spent more than two years in a prison cell. If nothing else, that taught you considerable patience.

Once he was satisfied with the shape, he used a stipple sponge to add texture and sealed it all. Then he let it dry. Finally, he applied makeup over his entire face, highlighting and shadowing and then using transparent powder to finish up.

He sat back and looked at himself. The changes were subtle, to be sure. But the overall impact was significant. Few things on a person were more distinctive than the nose. He had just made his unrecognizable from the original.

Next he used the spirit gum to pin his normally slightly protruding ears against his head. He looked at himself once more, scrutinizing every detail, looking for any mistake or imperfection caused by the changes, but came away satisfied.

He scanned a few more box labels and then pulled out another one and opened it. Inside was a fake goatee. He applied spirit gum first and then positioned the goatee while looking in the mirror. When that was done he used a comb to smooth some of the synthetic hairs into place. Facial hair was not allowed in the military—for prisoners or soldiers—so this was a good disguise tactic.

Next he removed his shirt and undershirt and drew out two tat sleeves from the box. He slid one on each arm and once more examined the results in the mirror. They definitely looked like the real thing, he concluded.

Tinted contact lenses were next, changing the color of his eyes.

Then he trimmed his eyebrows, making them much thinner and narrower.

He sat back once more and looked in the mirror, again first face on and then from his right and left profiles.

He doubted even his brother would recognize him.

He went through his mental checklist: *Hair, nose, ears, mouth, goatee, eyes, tats, eyebrows. Check, check, and check.*

He pulled down another box and slipped out the clothes. He had kept his weight constant over the last two years, and the jeans and short-sleeved shirt fit him fine. He slipped the sweat-stained Stetson on over his shaved head, careful not to dislodge his pinned ears. Reaching into the box once more, he pulled out and put on one-inch worn boots that increased his height to that of his brother's nearly six feet four. He slid the belt with the two-inch buckle depicting a man on a bull through his jean loops and cinched it tight. His fatigues, cap, and combat boots went into the box and he put it back on the shelf.

The third box contained the documents he would need to accomplish things in the outside world. A valid Kansas driver's license, two credit cards with a year of life remaining on them, and a thousand dollars in cash, all in twenties. And a checkbook tied to an active bank account with fifty-seven thousand dollars in it plus whatever interest had accrued to it over the years.

He had put in automatic purchase instructions for the credit cards with payments tied to his checking account that had been executed before and during the time he had been in prison. That's how he had been paying for this storage unit and some other recurring expenses. Under his fake identity he had also purchased and sent gifts and items to nursing homes, hospitals, and strangers whom he had discovered to have been in low circumstances. It had cost him several thousand dollars, but he had done a little bit of good at the same time. It also ensured that there was activity on his accounts, which built up a credit history with reliable payments. Otherwise financial institutions might have looked suspiciously at a dormant account suddenly active after more than two years. And people were watching, Puller knew, because he used to be one of the watchers.

He hefted the last items. A Glock nine-mil and two extra boxes of ammo. And an M4 carbine with three boxes of ammo. Kansas was an open-carry state, which meant so long as your firearm was in plain sight a license was not required. But one did need a permit to carry a concealed weapon, and Puller had one of those too, issued by the great state of Kansas under his fictitious identity. It was still good for another eighteen months.

He slipped the Glock into the clip holster he'd put on his belt and covered this with a denim jacket he'd earlier pulled from his clothes box. He disassembled the M4 and slipped it into a carrier bag, which he placed in the duffel. Then he put on a watch, also from the clothes box, and set it to the proper time. He put a pair of sunglasses in his jacket pocket.

There would be a wide manhunt going on for him. And while he now didn't look anything like his former self, he also had no margin for error.

He well knew the chaos that must be reigning at the prison right now. He wasn't sure how it had all gone down, but he realized that he was one of the luckiest people on the planet. This was particularly gratifying since over the last few years he had been one of the unluckiest. The massive swing in his fortunes made him feel a bit lightheaded. He had seized an opportunity when one had presented itself. It was up to him now to carry it all the way to its logical conclusion. He was nothing if not logical. Indeed, some would claim he was *too* logical at times. And maybe he was.

It seemed to run in the family, though, for his father surely had that capacity. And his younger brother, John, might be the most logical of the three Puller men.

Brother John, he thought. What would he make of all this?

Brothers on opposite sides of the cell door. Now brothers on opposite sides, period. It didn't feel good, but it never had. And there was nothing he could do right now to change that.

He put everything away and then turned to his laptop. To his delight it came on, though the battery was still charging. He unplugged it and put the computer in a canvas duffel bag. From another box he pulled some more articles of clothing and assorted toiletries and put them in the duffel. Then he slipped it over his shoulder, turned off the light, and exited, locking the overhead door and quickly walking away.

He hoofed it to a diner that was just opening for business as he walked in. Two cops went in ahead of him. They both looked tired, so maybe they were coming off their shifts instead of going on. Puller sat as far away from them as he could. He huddled behind the plastic menu the waitress gave him and ordered coffee, black.

She brought it in a chipped cup and he drank it down in gratifying measures. This was the first cup of coffee outside of prison he'd had in over two years. And that didn't count the time he had been in custody while his court-martial was going on. He smacked his lips appreciatively and looked over the menu.

He ordered pretty much one of everything, and when his meal came he ate slowly, luxuriating over each bite. It wasn't that the food at the DB was awful. It was passable. But food just tasted different when you were eating it in a prison cell after it was slid through a notch cut in the steel door.

He finished the last bit of toast and bacon and had another cup of coffee. He had been eating so slowly that the cops had finished and gone. Which was just fine with him. What he didn't want to see was a couple of MPs take their place, which they did, right as the waitress deposited the bill at his table.

"You have a good one, hon," she said to him.

"Thanks," said Puller, before realizing that he had not changed the tone or cadence of his voice.

Pick up your damn game, Bobby.

"Um, you got Wi-Fi here, shug?" he asked in a twangy voice.

She shook her head. "Honey, all we got is stuff to eat and drink. You want that Wi-Fi thing, you got to get yourself down to the Starbucks on the corner."

"Thanks, shug."

He zipped up his jacket all the way and made sure his gun was covered.

As he passed by the MPs, one of them flicked a gaze his way and nodded.

Puller drawled, "You boys have a good one." Then he tacked on, "Go Army." And then he smiled crookedly.

The man thanked him with a weary smile and returned to looking over his menu.

Puller was careful to close the swing door after him so it wouldn't bang shut and maybe get those MPs to take a second look at him.

In under a minute he was disappearing into a

darkness just about to be broken by the coming Kansas dawn. It was his first daybreak as a free man in a long time.

It tasted first sweet and then turned to vinegar in his mouth.

In another thirty seconds he had turned the corner and was out of sight.

5

JOHN PULLER KNEW something was wrong the minute he stepped off the elevator and onto his father's ward.

It was far too quiet.

Where were his father's baritone shouts that tended to explode down the hall like mortar rounds, reducing men of iron in uniform to lumps of mush? All he could hear were the normal sounds one associated with a hospital: rubber soles on linoleum, the squeaks of carts and gurneys, the whispers of medicos huddled in corners, visitors coming and going, the occasional shriek of an alarm on a vitals monitor.

He strode down the corridor, quickening his pace when he saw three men coming out of his father's room. They weren't doctors. Two were in their branch's standard service uniforms, while one wore a suit. One of the uniformed men was Army, the other Air Force. Both were generals. The Air Force guy was a one-star. As Puller quickened his pace and closed the gap, he could read the Air Force guy's nameplate: Daughtrey. The Army man carried three stars pinned to the epaulets on his shoulders and his plate read Rinehart. Puller recognized the name but couldn't place him. The collection of decorations on his chest ran nine horizontal rows. He was a big man with his hair shaved close to his scalp. And his nose had been broken, at least once.

"Excuse me, sirs?" Puller said, coming to attention. He didn't issue a salute since they were inside and none were under cover, meaning they did not have their caps on.

They all turned to him.

Puller eyed the generals and said, "I'm Chief Warrant Officer John Puller Jr. with the 701st CID out of Quantico. I apologize for being out of uniform, but I just got back from a mission in Oklahoma and was given some news I needed to see my father about."

"At ease, Puller," said Rinehart, and Puller relaxed. "You're not the only visitor your father's receiving today."

"I saw that you were coming out of his room," Puller noted.

The suit nodded and then flipped out his ID.

Puller read it thoroughly. He liked to know who was in the sandbox with him.

James Schindler, with the National Security Council.

Puller had never dealt with anyone from there before. The NSC was a policy group and their people normally didn't go around investigating things. But these folks were also wired right to the White House. It was heady stuff for a humble chief warrant officer. Then again, if someone wanted to truly intimidate him he would need to have placed a gun muzzle against Puller's skull. And even that might not be enough.

Rinehart said, "You received 'news'? I'm sure it's the same news that prompted our visit here today."

"My brother."

Daughtrey nodded. "Your father was not particularly helpful."

"That's because he doesn't know anything about this. And he has a condition."

"Dementia, we were told," said Schindler.

Puller said, "It's beyond his control now. And he hasn't been in contact with my brother since before he went to prison."

"But patients with dementia have their lucid moments, Puller," noted Daughtrey. "And with this case no possible lead is too small to follow up. Since you were next up on our list, why don't we find a quiet place where we can talk?"

"With all due respect, sir, I'll meet you wherever and whenever you want, but only after I see my dad. It's important for me to see him *now*," he added, acutely aware that he was collectively outranked by a country mile.

The one-star was clearly not pleased by this, but Rinehart said, "I'm sure that can be accommodated, Puller. There's not a soldier in uniform today who doesn't owe Fighting John Puller due deference." As he said this he glanced sharply at Daughtrey. "There's a visitors' room right down this hall. You'll find us in there when you're done."

"Thank you, sir."

Puller slipped inside his father's room and shut the door. He didn't like hospitals. He'd been in enough of them while wounded. They smelled overly clean, but they were actually more full of germs than a toilet seat.

His father was seated in a chair by the window. John Puller Sr. had once been nearly as tall as his youngest son, but time had robbed him of nearly two inches. Yet, at over six-one, he was still a tall man. He wore his usual uniform these days—white T-shirt and blue scrub pants and hospital slippers. His hair, what was left of it, was cottony white and surrounded the crown of his head like a halo. He was fit and trim, and his musculature, while not at the level of his prime, was still substantial.

"Hello, General," Puller said.

It was usually around this time that his father started jabbering on about Puller being his XO here to receive orders. Puller had gone along with his father's delusion, though he didn't want to. It seemed a betrayal of the old man. But now his father didn't even look at him and didn't say a word. He just continued to gaze out the window.

Puller perched on the edge of the bed.

"What did those men ask you?"

His father sat up and tapped the window, causing a sparrow to lift into the air and fly off. Then he settled back against the fake leather.

Puller rose and walked over to him, gazing over his head at the outdoor courtyard. He couldn't remember the last time his father had been outside. He'd spent the majority of his military career out of doors, more than holding his own against enemies doing their best to defeat him and his men. Virtually none of them had succeeded. Who could have predicted it would be a defect in his own brain that would finally bring him down?

"Heard from Bobby lately?" asked Puller, being intentionally provocative. Usually the mention of his brother's name sent his father into spasms of vitriol.

The only reaction was a grunt, but at least it was something. Puller stood in front of his father, blocking his view of the courtyard.

"What did the men ask you?"

His father inched up his chin until he was staring directly at his youngest child.

"Gone," said his father.

"Who, Bobby?"

"Gone," said his father again. "AWOL."

Puller nodded. This wasn't technically correct, but he wasn't holding it against his father. "He *is* gone. Escaped from the DB, so they say."

"Bullshit." The word wasn't uttered in anger. There was no raised voice. His father just said it matter-of-factly, as though the truth behind its use was self-evident.

Puller knelt down next to him so his father could lower his chin.

"Why is it bullshit?"

"Told 'em. Bullshit."

"Okay, but why?"

He had caught his father in these moments before, though they were growing less frequent. It was like the one-star general had said: Lucidity was still possible.

His father looked at his son like he was suddenly surprised he wasn't actually talking to himself. Puller's spirits sank through the floor when he noted this look. Was that all the old man had in his tank today?

Bullshit?

"Is that all you told them?" asked Puller.

He waited in silence for a minute or so. His father closed his eyes and his breathing grew steady.

Puller closed the door behind him and headed down to confront the stars and suit. They were seated in the otherwise empty visitors' room. He sat next to Rinehart, the Army three-star, figuring the bond within the same branch of service might be stronger by the physical proximity.

"Nice visit with your father?" asked Schindler.

"In his condition the visits are rarely nice, sir," said Puller. "And there was no lucidity."

"We can't discuss this here," said Rinehart. "You can drive back with us to the Pentagon. After the meeting we'll get you transport back here for your car."

* * *

The drive took about thirty minutes before they pulled into one of the parking lots of the world's largest office building, though it comprised only seven floors, two of which were basement-level.

Puller had been to the Pentagon countless times in his career and still didn't know his way around very well. He had become lost more than once when he had strayed from his regular route. But everyone who had ever been here had gotten lost at least once. Those who denied doing so were lying.

As they were walking down one broad corridor they had to quickly move to the side as a motorized cart sped toward them carrying stacks of what looked to be large oxygen tanks. Puller knew that the Pentagon had its own emergency oxygen supply in case of an enemy attack or attempted sabotage. The attack against the Pentagon on 9/11 had raised security here to unprecedented heights, and no one foresaw it ever being lowered.

In getting out of the way of the cart Rinehart stumbled a bit, and Puller instinctively grasped his arm to steady his military superior. They both watched as the motorized cart zipped past.

Puller said, "The Pentagon can get a little dangerous, sir. Even for three-stars."

Rinehart smiled. "Like jumping foxholes sometimes. As big as this place is, sometimes it seems too damn small to contain everything and everybody."

They reached an office suite where the name "Lieutenant General Aaron Rinehart" was on the door. The three-star led them inside, past his staff, and into an interior conference room. They sat down and water was poured out by an aide, and then the door closed and they were alone.

Puller sat across the table from the three men and waited expectantly. They had not spoken about anything significant on the drive over, so he was still in the dark about what they wanted.

General Daughtrey leaned forward, seemingly pulling the others along, for they all mimicked his movement. "What we got from your father was one word: 'bullshit.'"

"He's nothing if not consistent, then," replied Puller. "Because that's the same thing he told me."

"You read any meaning into that?" asked Schindler.

Puller gazed over at him. "I'm not a shrink, sir. I don't know what my dad meant by it, if anything."

"When was the last time you visited your brother at DB?" asked Daughtrey.

"About six weeks ago. I try to get up to see him as often as I can. Sometimes the job gets in the way of that."

"What did he say during your last visit?"

"Nothing about escaping, I can assure you."

"Okay, but what *did* he say?" Daughtrey persisted.

"We talked about our father. He asked how my work at CID was going. I talked to him about being at DB. Asked him how it was going."

"Did you talk at all about his case?" asked Schindler. "What landed him in DB?"

"It's not a case anymore, sir. It's a conviction. And no, we didn't talk about it. What is there left to say?"

Rinehart asked, "Do you have a theory on what happened with your brother's escape?"

"I've formed no opinion because I don't know all the facts."

"The facts are still evolving. Suffice it to say the situation was most unusual."

"It would seem impossible that he'd be able to escape without some help. The backup generator failed? How likely is that? And who was the dead guy in his cell?"

"So you are in possession of the facts?" said Schindler in an accusatory tone.

"Some, not all. But who could have orchestrated something like that at DB?"

"It is troubling," said Rinehart, quite unnecessarily.

"Has your brother tried to contact you?" asked Schindler.

"No."

"If he does you will of course contact your superior immediately."

"I believe that would be my duty, yes."

"That wasn't what I asked, Puller."

"I would contact my superior, yes."

Schindler handed him a card. "Actually, I'd rather you contacted me first."

Puller slipped the card into his pocket without answering.

Daughtrey said, "I'm sure you've been warned to stay away from this case?"

"My CO made that pretty clear."

"But since you're an investigator, I'm also sure you're quite interested in getting involved in this case, correct?"

Puller gazed at the one-star. This was interesting territory, he thought.

"I didn't think it was up to me," he replied. "A direct order is a direct order. I've put too many years in to torpedo my career over this."

"Over your *brother*, you mean," said Daughtrey.

Puller gazed at the man. "Do you *want* me involved in the investigation?"

"That would go against all applicable military rules," interjected Rinehart firmly.

"Well, that doesn't really answer my question, sir."

"I'm afraid that's as good of an answer as you're going to get, Puller," said Schindler, rising. They all stood.

"I've got leave coming up," said Puller.

Schindler smiled.

"Well, then, I'd use it wisely if I were you." He tapped Puller's pocket where he'd put Schindler's card. "And don't forget to call me if something pops. Interest in this case goes up so high you'd need a tank of oxygen to breathe."

Daughtrey said, "One more question, Puller."

"Yes sir?"

"Did you ever ask your brother if he was guilty?"

The query surprised Puller, and he didn't like to be surprised.

"I did, once."

"And what did he tell you?"

"He was noncommittal."

Daughtrey said, "And what do you think? *Was* he guilty?"

Puller didn't answer right away. It didn't really matter what he thought about his brother's guilt or innocence. It couldn't change reality. Yet it seemed that all three men very much wanted to hear his answer.

"I don't want to believe that my brother was a traitor," he finally said. That was really the best he could do, and he didn't intend to say any more on the subject despite being outranked.

Daughtrey said, "He *was* guilty, Puller. Because the court-martial said he was. Evidence was overwhelming. You may not have been privy to it, but we all were."

Rinehart said, "That's all, Chief Puller. You're dismissed."

Puller walked out wondering what the hell had just happened.

6

HE NEEDED TO think this through, but also talk things out with someone. And there was really only one person he could do that with. He lifted his phone from his pocket and punched in the number. She answered two rings later.

"I heard," Julie Carson said immediately. "You want to talk, right?"

"Yeah. I just saw my father, and then I got a weird sort of third degree from a suit from the NSC and a couple of generals, one Army, one Air Force."

"What was the NSC's name?"

"James Schindler. I've got his card. He's based in D.C."

"Who was the Army guy?" she asked.

"Three-star named Aaron Rinehart, big guy, broken nose, hair shaved close to the scalp. He had about as many decorations on his chest as my father. His name is familiar."

"I've certainly heard of him, but don't know

him personally. Tough, no-nonsense, incredibly well connected, and moving up fast for his fourth star. There's even talk he'll be the Chairman of the Joint Chiefs or Chief of Staff of the Army at some point. How about the flyboy?"

"One-star named Daughtrey. He didn't offer up his first name."

"Okay, I'll see what I can find out. They're all in the database somewhere."

"Thanks, Julie."

"I haven't done anything yet."

"You answered your phone when you obviously knew why I was calling. You could have played ostrich and dodged the bullet. You've got a new command down in Texas that I'm sure is keeping you busy twenty-four/seven. So thanks."

"I don't much care for ostriches. Never saw the point. And I'm getting these folks down here whipped into shape. I'll call you later."

He hung up and sat back. He wasn't thinking about his brother right now and his dilemma. He was thinking about the woman who had been on the other end of that conversation.

When Puller had first met her, Julie Carson was an Army one-star assigned to the Pentagon with designs on at least one and possibly two

more stars before her military career was finished. Puller had run into her during a case he
was investigating in West Virginia. The two had
started out as adversaries and then months later
had ended up sharing a bed while Puller was investigating his aunt's death at her home on the
Gulf Coast of Florida. And Carson had almost
been killed while trying to help him. Though
badly wounded, she'd fully recovered. Puller
still had nightmares about it.

She had gotten her second star and with it a
new command at an Army base in Texas. They
had said their goodbyes over a bottle of wine
and take-out Italian. The Army tended to get in
the way of any permanent relationships among
service members. He knew he might not see
her in person again, at least for a while. After
Texas the odds were she would be headed to the
Pacific Northwest. After that, it was anyone's
guess. He was just glad that she had answered
his call. Right now he needed a friend with stars
on her shoulders.

* * *

Later that day, he had just gotten back to his
apartment near Quantico when his phone
buzzed. It was Carson.

"I hope you don't mind if I eat while I talk,"

she said. "I had time today to either eat lunch or do a five-mile run."

"And of course you opted to run."

"Don't we all?" she replied as he heard utensils hitting a plate and liquid being poured into a glass.

"You cook a lot down there?" he asked.

"Are you giving me shit?" she said in a mock-reproachful tone.

"No, I'm deadly serious," he replied, though his tone wasn't.

"I almost never cook," she said. "My mother would be so disappointed. Well, she *is* disappointed. She could fill the house with what she did in the kitchen. And the smells were like you wouldn't believe. I played three sports in high school and I think part of me did it so I could eat my mom's cooking and not get fat. Maybe that's why I never even really tried to learn my way around the kitchen. I knew I could never be as good as she was."

"A little competitive, are we?"

"Show me anyone in uniform who isn't," she shot back.

He heard her gulp whatever she was drinking, and then her tone turned serious. "So let's talk about your brother."

"I still can't get my arms around it."

"John, how do you break out of DB?"

"How much do you know about it?"

"Mostly scuttlebutt, but there was a lot of it. A storm. Backup power failed. Reinforcements were called in. They restored order. Head count was done. And no Robert Puller in attendance. But there was mention of someone else who shouldn't have been there."

"Then you know about as much as I do. And the someone else was dead and in my brother's cell."

"Holy hell!" she exclaimed.

"Pretty much says it all," he said evenly.

"I definitely hadn't heard that. And no sign of him since?"

"Apparently not. Don White, my CO, filled me in today. Then I went to see my father. I figured he might have heard and even with his condition he might be upset."

"And that's when you ran into the suit and the generals?"

"They asked me the standard questions: my visits to him, what we discussed. Then, if he contacted me, to contact them. But then it got weird, like I said on the phone."

"In what way weird?"

"First, although they never came out and said it, I believe they want me to look into the case."

"How can that be? I'm sure your CO told you not to go near it."

"He did. And then the Air Force guy wanted to know if I thought my brother was guilty."

"And what did you say?"

It suddenly occurred to Puller that he had never really talked about his brother with her. And it also seemed apparent that Carson *wanted* to know if Puller thought his brother was guilty.

"I didn't really answer him, because I'm not really sure what I think about it."

"Okay," she said, though her tone made clear she was not satisfied by his reply.

He said, "Did you find out anything about these guys?"

"Rinehart's assigned to DIA. At a very high level. It's beyond my ability to find out much more than that. The same really goes for James Schindler at the NSC. He wasn't in the military. He came up through the civilian side of NSA before moving on to the Security Council."

"I guess that makes sense. My brother was convicted of national security crimes. That cuts across all branches. And so does DIA. And the NSC has its finger in everything because of the president. What about Daughtrey?"

"Timothy Daughtrey is attached to STRATCOM."

"Bingo! That was where my brother was working when he was arrested." He paused. "It's ironic."

"What is?"

"Bobby was stationed at a STRATCOM satellite facility near Leavenworth when he was arrested and court-martialed. He didn't have far to travel to go to DB."

"And the STRATCOM connection dovetails right into DIA and NSC because spooks all hang around the same playground," she added.

"I guess so," said Puller slowly.

"The FBI is of course all over this," added Carson. "National security issues bring out all the big dogs. I would say your brother is the most wanted man in America right now. I wouldn't think his chances of evading capture are very good."

"I'm surprised the FBI hasn't been by to see me," said Puller.

"I would imagine if they haven't been by they are at least keeping an eye on you. But it might be that Rinehart et al. have talked to them and made it clear they're heading the John Puller piece of this equation."

"Complicated stuff."

"Yes, it is. I read up on your brother's career this afternoon," she added.

"Did you?" he said sharply.

"Hey, don't cop an attitude. I like to be prepared. A lot of it was classified beyond even my clearances, and some of the files seemed to have been deleted, because there were gaps. Some of the pages I saw onscreen were heavily redacted, but from what I saw your brother's career was still pretty damn impressive. I mean, the trajectory was like a rocket. He would have easily gotten his star, and more. I even dug up a white paper he'd written on a next-generation nuclear weaponry design. I could understand about every tenth word, and I don't consider myself stupid. Some of the math equations in the paper looked like Chinese to me."

"He was always the smart one in the family. Officer material. I was just the enlisted grunt in the trenches."

"Did you ever ask him if he did it?" she asked bluntly.

Puller said, "Once."

"And?"

"And he didn't answer me."

"And now he's escaped. You don't escape from DB without help. It's impossible."

"I know."

"And so you probably know something else."

"Yeah, that my brother was guilty. And maybe he killed the guy they found in his cell. So he's a traitor *and* a murderer." As he said these words, Puller felt a sharp pain in his chest, his breathing grew shallow, and sweat appeared on his brow. He knew he wasn't having a heart attack.

But am I having a panic attack?

He had never panicked, not once in his life. Not while bullets were flying and bombs were bursting all around him. He had been scared then, as any sane person would be. But that was not the same as panicked. It was actually the difference between surviving or not.

"John, are you okay?"

"I'm good," he said curtly, though he really wasn't.

My brother, a traitor and a murderer? No, I am definitely not good.

"So I guess that answers my question," she said.

"What question?"

"You thought your brother was innocent, didn't you?"

"Maybe I did."

"I can understand that, John. It's natural."

"Is it?" he said heatedly. "It doesn't feel natural. None of this does."

"So what are you going to do?" asked Carson.

"My CO gave me some leave time."

"And he also told you to stay away from this sucker."

"And I've got an NSC suit and two generals maybe wanting me to take a whack at it."

"But they gave you no direct order to do so, not that they were even authorized to give one. And you might have misread their intent. On the other hand, your commanding officer explicitly told you to stand down. So the answer is easy. You stand down."

"He's my brother, Julie."

"And you're a soldier, John. Orders are orders. You don't really have a choice."

"You're right, I don't. He's my brother."

"Why are you doing this?"

"Doing what?"

"Putting this much pressure on yourself."

Puller took a long breath and then said again more forcefully, "He's my brother!"

"It doesn't matter if he's your brother. That ship has already sailed, Puller. He's an escaped prisoner. The best you can hope for is that he's captured safely and returned to DB promptly."

"So that's it, then?"

"What more could it be? Look, I know how you must feel. But your brother made his choices. His career and life are over. Are you telling me you want to put yours in jeopardy? And for what possible reason?"

"Everything you're saying makes perfect sense."

"But you're not buying any of it."

"I didn't say that."

"You didn't have to." She took a deep breath. "So, again, what are you going to do?"

"I don't know. And I wouldn't tell you if I did know. That would just put you in an even more awkward position."

"I've been in those with you before."

"And you almost died, Julie. I'm never going to do that to you again. Never."

"I showed up in Florida voluntarily. You didn't ask me to come down there."

"But I didn't tell you to go back home either."

"I survived."

"Barely."

"And I don't want anything to happen to you, John. Even if I am in Texas now. I still care about you."

Though they were not face-to-face, Puller

could imagine the look that Carson was displaying right now. Tender and concerned.

"Not worried about fraternization rules?"

"They don't apply to us. They apply to officer and enlisted. We're both officers. I'm a general, and even though you started out in the ranks, you're a chief warrant officer. And you're not under my command."

"So you checked?"

Her voice rose over the phone. "*Yes*, I checked. So you can understand if I feel a little proprietary toward you. You can't tank your career over this. You just can't!"

"I can't sit on the sidelines. I'm sorry."

"John, please think about the consequences."

"I've done nothing but think about them. But it hasn't changed my decision."

He heard her draw a long breath. "Well, then I wish you the very best of luck. And I guess I can't say I'm surprised. After Florida I understand quite clearly that Puller blood is thicker than even the Army green variety."

"Thanks for understanding."

"I didn't say I understood. Just that I'm not surprised. Take care of yourself, Puller. And consider that a direct order from a two-star."

"That means a lot, Julie. It really does."

Puller put down the phone, sat back, and

closed his eyes. He had never thought that Julie Carson would be the *one*. She was a general on the rise. He was a chief warrant officer pretty much topped out. He cared for her, but professionally they were like oil and water. But they could and would remain friends. And he would always care about her. Always.

Loyalty mattered to John Puller. Almost as much as family did. And sometimes they were the very same damn thing.

7

WI-FI WAS UP and working. And so was Robert Puller. While the enormous machinery of the United States military, along with the even bigger intelligence octopus that spread outward from the CIA and the NSA, was searching for him, arguably the most wanted man in America was sipping an unleaded grande Americano with raw sugar mixed in and pounding away on his Apple MacBook Pro with fingers as nimble as a teenager's. And he'd been here doing this for most of the day.

It was a bit tricky, because as most Americans with an Internet connection or cell phone knew these days, *they* were watching. And *they* could come and get you anytime *they* wanted.

But Robert Puller knew his way around computers and every known way to trace, hack, or spy on their users. And his laptop had been expressly programmed and loaded with software and unique protections not available to the public. There were no back doors for the NSA to pixel-creep up on him. There were no back doors period. Except the ones *he* had planted in other databases before he went to prison, and was now exploiting to the fullest. Being at STRATCOM all those years had left him in a unique position to hack everybody. And to do it with *style*, he admitted to himself as he finished off the grande and looked over the other patrons of the Starbucks, where fancied-up java was not merely a beverage but also a way of life. He had already read all the news stories related to his escape. He had been lucky, that was for sure. But it hadn't been all luck.

The news reports were full of facts. No real details on the hunt, beyond the painfully obvious. Checkpoints, house-to-house searches, watching airports, bus and train stations, asking the public for help, etcetera, etcetera. Pictures of him were all over the Web. If nothing else, they were a stark reminder of how much his appearance had changed overnight. The MPs he had passed earlier at the diner would have had his mug imprinted on their genes. And yet the one guy who'd looked directly at him hadn't even troubled himself with a second glance.

Also posted all over the Web was his past

history. The brilliant academic career where he had topped the lists at every institution he'd attended. The meteoric military career. His far-reaching fingers in all the intelligence pies. The systems he'd developed, the software he'd coded, the farsightedness he'd displayed in arenas of which the public only had a vague awareness. And then the tumble from the high pedestal, the arrest, and the charges aimed at him like a fifty-caliber machine gun set to blow him into little pieces. Then the court-martial. Then the verdict. Finally, the imprisonment for life.

And now the escape.

All of this he read and digested, but it was ultimately meaningless to him.

There *was* one angle to the story that had socked him right in the gut.

His father and his brother had both been mentioned throughout numerous articles. The fighting legend now laid low by dementia. And there was dirt dredged up and regurgitated about the reasons why he had never gotten the fourth star, and why the Medal of Honor had never been draped around his thick neck.

And then there was his brother, the highly decorated combat veteran turned CID agent who was building himself into an Army legend.

But underlying the articles were the visits John Puller Jr. had made to the DB. How close they were as brothers. The lawman and the law-breaker. No, the law-crusher, for he wasn't a mere criminal—he had committed treason, saved from the death penalty by who knew what in the military tribunal process.

But are they implying that my brother some-how helped me escape?

He didn't know where John had been yester-day, but he was pretty sure it wasn't in Leaven-worth. That would have to come out in the pa-pers. His brother would have to be fully cleared of any involvement with the escape. He had to be! Still, he knew that even the hint of suspicion could come close to breaking his kid brother, as strong as he seemed. Personal honor meant ev-erything to John Puller Jr.

And what about John Puller Sr.?

Well, despite his affection for the old man, he just hoped that his father was so far out of it now that nothing could penetrate the dense cloud the dementia was solidifying around his once extraordinary mind.

He set all this aside and tapped his computer keys with renewed vitality. It had been part of his life for so long before it had been taken from him. Yet hacking was like riding a bike.

He hadn't forgotten anything. The codes had changed. The security was better. But it wasn't infallible. Nothing was. There were new hacking techniques invented every day and the good guys simply could not keep up.

He was a natural hacker, because part of his duties had been to hack his own side, to test defenses that he had helped create. If he, their inventor, couldn't crack them, it was assumed that no one else could either. Sometimes they'd been right, sometimes wrong. And sometimes Puller had held back just a bit, because he never played the short game.

His gaze trailed off the screen and ventured to the street where a Humvee puttered by. Inside were soldiers in their cammie uniforms, their methodical gazes sweeping the area.

So they still think I might be around here? Interesting.

He really didn't believe this. The Army was simply covering its ass. The DB had just suffered its first setback. A presence on the street was to be expected. He returned his gaze to the screen and kept typing away, creating his version of a symphony, built note by note, measure by measure, and movement by sly movement.

When the contents of the screen dissolved

and then reemerged as something entirely new, he closed his laptop and stood. What he had just gained access to was not meant to be read at the neighborhood Starbucks.

And while he had used plain-Jane Wi-Fi that was basically open to anyone, his laptop was firing off scramblers of such strength that any punk with an electronic mitt trolling for credit card numbers and accompanying PINs would be left with something so garbled that it would look like a trillion-piece digital puzzle without a handy picture to go by.

But still, there were protocols. And though he no longer wore the uniform, Puller intended to abide by these rules to the extent he could. It was part of who he was, who he would always be. They said the uniform made the man. Well, actually, it did. But that statement had nothing to do with clothing. It was all inside of you.

Now was the time for exploration and perhaps a drive. For that he needed wheels. He wasn't going to do a rental. He was going to write a check for a 2004 Chevy Tahoe pickup in the lot of a used-car dealer the next block over. He'd looked at it earlier while taking a break from his hacking.

It took an hour of dickering and filling out the paperwork. Then he climbed into his new ride, started it up—the eight-cylinder power plant sparking gloriously to life—and drove off. He flicked a wave to the salesman, who'd probably cleared enough of a commission to splurge on a nice meal for himself and the missus, photos of whom Puller had been shown during the course of their negotiation, probably to soften him up.

It hadn't worked. Prison did not soften you up. It made you a piece of rock.

Next mission: obtaining quarters. Where he could read in peace.

And then he could get this thing rolling.

Robert Puller dearly hoped it had been worth the years-long wait.

CHAPTER

8

JOHN PULLER KNEW that flying was out, because ticket purchases by credit card could be traced, and he figured a number of computerized eyeballs would be pointed his way. Trains were out of the question for the same reason, not that there were any convenient ones anyway that would take him where he needed to go in a timely manner. A bus might have worked, but he would need wheels locally, and getting a rental left an electronic trail as well. That limited his options to a car—his. Well, his military-issued sedan. But he would pay for the fuel.

His destination in Kansas would take about twenty hours if he stopped along the way, which he intended to do to see if anyone was following him. The suit and stars might have wanted to make him their hunting dog for any number of reasons, ferreting out an escapee instead of a quail. But Puller didn't want to be stupid about it, or put himself at unnecessary risk.

He packed up his duffel and his cat and left at midnight. This was not unusual for him. He often headed out at odd hours, mainly because soldiers didn't tend to commit major crimes on a strict timetable. Most of them, in fact, were done at night, often after too many beers and too many insults. Turning the other cheek had been strictly left out of all Army manuals.

The important point was that any persons tailing him now would have to show themselves by their headlights. He saw none over the first two miles on meandering roads and quickly made his way to the interstate and started his trip due west. He stopped to eat twice, first breakfast at a Cracker Barrel in Kentucky and then dinner at a packed roadside grill named The Grease Bowl somewhere in Missouri.

He was not in uniform and didn't plan to be while he was on leave. He had his ID and official credentials, to be sure. He had his weapons, because if he didn't have his weapons then he must be dead and someone had forgotten to tell him. And he had some investigative tools that had made their way into his duffel, along with some fresh clothes and other travel essentials.

What he didn't have was a good idea of what he hoped to accomplish by going to the scene of his brother's escape.

Escaped prisoners from an Army installation could certainly be within the purview of the CID regardless of which branch they'd been in. Technically, his brother was no longer a member of the military. Along with his conviction had come a dishonorable discharge—standard procedure. Bad guys didn't get to wear the uniform anymore.

Yet because Robert Puller had been convicted of national security crimes, responsibility for his case fell largely to the special agents of Army Counterintelligence and the FBI. However, Puller had worked on parallel investigations with both agencies and considered them highly capable. Good for them, perhaps bad for his brother. But he had to stop thinking that way. What was bad for his brother was good for him and the rest of the country.

Easy to think, harder to execute, because the brothers had been inordinately close all their lives, due to their father's all-consuming military career and a largely absent mother. John Puller had looked to his older brother for advice on all important decisions in his life, from asking a girl out to what position to play on the high school football team, from much-needed help on a physics exam in his junior year of college to the most appropriate way to approach their father about his decision not to go to West Point and become an officer. It was Bobby's advice, all of it good and on point and well-intentioned, that had helped make Puller what he was today, for better or worse. And now that mentor was suddenly his enemy?

The first time he had visited Bobby at the DB it had seemed as though an enormous mistake had been committed, but that it would be corrected in the near future. The two brothers, both tall and well built, though John was the taller and stronger of the two, had sat across from each other in the visitors' room and Puller had talked and Bobby had listened. And then Bobby had talked and Puller had listened. Then as the visits had continued over more than two years, and his brother's status in prison had gelled to a permanency that seemed unshakable, Puller increasingly could think of nothing to say. It was as though the man he was facing had his brother's face but that was all. The person he'd known all his life could not be in there. He could not be in this place convicted of treason. Yet there he was.

When they had last parted company, Puller

had shaken his brother's hand, but had felt no connection to him at all. It was an impersonator, he had thought at the time. It had to be.

This simply could not be his brother.

It was true that Bobby had helped his little brother, via phone, prevent a disaster of enormous proportions during his investigation into the murder of a military family in West Virginia. For that, his brother became the only prisoner at the DB ever to receive a commendation for service to his country. And when their aunt had been found murdered in Florida his brother had offered him both commiseration and counsel. That had thawed their relationship somewhat, but nothing could overcome the fact that one of them lived behind bars.

Used to live behind bars, Puller reminded himself, as he crossed the border into Kansas at around ten p.m. the night after leaving Virginia. It was dark and his options were limited. He didn't want to stay where he usually did when visiting his brother at the DB. That would be too easy for others to find out and follow him from there.

He kept driving and about ten minutes later stopped at a motel that looked like it had been built in the fifties and then forgotten about. The small office proved this observation correct, even down to the rotary dial telephone, thick phone book, and bulky metal cash register. There was not a computer screen in sight. The woman behind the counter looked like she had been here from day one and had forgotten to change her clothes and hairstyle during that time. He paid for two nights in cash and took the old-fashioned bulky room key from her aged, shaky hand.

A few minutes later he was in his room with his cat, AWOL, huddled on a thin mattress with damp sheets because the wall air conditioner was basically a humidifier casting wisps of wet air into the room's atmosphere where they eventually fell back to earth, or at least to the sheets. Puller stretched out on the bed, damp linens and all, and checked his emails. There was one from his CO reiterating to Puller that this case was off-limits. He didn't answer. What would be the point?

Then he did the only thing he could after driving nearly halfway across the country—he fell asleep. He had been able to rest in the middle of both combat and murder investigations. But tonight his slumber was continually interrupted by thoughts of what he was going to do tomorrow.

By the time he woke the next morning he

still wasn't sure. He fed and watered AWOL and then let her out. Then he got into his car and drove to a diner down the street from the motel. It was from the fifties too, but its food was timeless: pancakes, bacon, eggs over easy, and hot tea. He ate his fill and then went back to his car and sat in the driver's seat staring moodily out the window. Wherever he had been deployed, or for whatever purpose, to fight or to investigate, Puller had always been able to devise a plan, a strategy to get the job done. But none of those times had involved searching for an escaped prisoner who happened to be his brother. In many respects he felt paralyzed.

And then a partial answer walked right in front of him. It shouldn't have been surprising, and it wasn't. It was one reason he was sitting where he was. The coffee shop across the street was one frequented by personnel at the DB. He knew this from previous visits. He had met or seen many of them during his time here. They weren't on a first-name basis, of course, but with his size Puller was hard to miss and harder still not to remember.

He waited patiently as uniform after uniform went into the shop and came out with coffee and bags of food. Uniforms he didn't want.

Too many rules and regulations weighed them down like a gangster's concrete booties. Twenty minutes later his patience was rewarded. The woman had parked at the curb and climbed out of her car. She was in her late forties, maybe early fifties, tallish, stout, with blonde hair that was not her natural color, and wearing black slacks and a red sweater with black flats. He eyed the lanyard and ID around her neck and the USDB parking permit on the front bumper of her car. He had seen her at the prison a few times before.

A civilian, she was in admin at the prison. He couldn't remember her name, but he figured she was a good place to start. They had talked once or twice, and he thought if he remembered her, she'd remember him.

He got out of the car and crossed the street, entering the shop at about the time she was placing her order. He got in behind her and asked for a large black coffee. When she heard his voice she turned and looked up at him.

"Puller?" she said. "Puller, right? CID?"

He looked at her with his blankest expression. "Yes ma'am, that's right. Do we know each other?"

"I work at DB. I'm in admin."

"Oh, that's right. Ms.?"

"Chelsea Burke. You came by my office once with a question about your…" Her voice trailed off just as Puller knew it would.

He nodded, his blank expression turning to grim. "Right. It's why I'm here, Ms. Burke."

"Please, just call me Chelsea."

"Thanks, I'm John. Look, now that we've run into each other, you have a minute?"

She got her coffee and paid her money and Puller did the same. She looked uncertain, but he guided her to a small table near the front of the shop overlooking the street. They sat and Puller took a sip of his coffee while she simply cradled hers and stared anxiously at him.

"It was a shock," Puller began. "When I heard the news. Happened at night, so I doubt you were even there."

"I wasn't," she conceded.

"People have already been by to see me," Puller said. "All very hush-hush, but I'm CID. I can see through all that. You probably can too."

"Is CID involved in this?"

"I'm afraid I can't answer that directly, sorry."

"Oh, of course not. I didn't mean to—"

He quickly waved off her apology. "No problem, Chelsea, but I like to hit the ground running, and it might have been fortunate I bumped into you."

"Why is that?"

"Because you're not military."

"I don't understand."

"Uniforms tend to circle the wagons in events like these. CID's only concern is getting to the truth." This was perfectly true, although he had made the statement to cause her to believe that CID—in the form of his presence—was investigating the matter.

"Absolutely," she said, wide-eyed. He was gratified to see that as she took a sip of her coffee she sat back in her chair and looked more relaxed and engaged.

"I'm sure you can understand that things look very peculiar here. Main power goes, purportedly because of the storm. And then the backup generator dies? You must see that is extremely unlikely to have happened just by accident."

She was nodding before he finished. "That's the scuttlebutt, John. It's like a billion to one. Now, I'll grant you it was one helluva storm. But the storm could not have had an impact on the generator. It runs off natural gas lines buried underground."

He sat forward and smiled. "I like how you

picked that right up." He paused. "But you probably see that the generator would not have kicked in and then died if the power hadn't gone off first."

She considered this and her eyes widened in realization. "So you think the main power was tampered with too?"

"Right now, I have no firm answers. But it's certainly possible."

"DB is going nuts right now trying to figure out what really happened." She suddenly looked at him nervously. "And your brother and all. I'm sure you're as worried as anyone."

"It's not easy seeing a family member in prison. But my job is to investigate serious military crimes. And duty trumps family in this circumstance, obviously."

She cradled her cup of coffee and said, "I knew about his commendation. For helping you. I saw the paperwork go through."

"A lot of lives would have been lost without him."

"Seems weird, doesn't it?" began Chelsea.

"What's that?"

"A man is convicted of treason and then helps his country and gets a commendation but is still in prison. And then he escapes from prison. Just seems off."

"I'm sure agents have been in to interview you and the rest of the staff."

"They haven't gotten to us yet, but I'm sure they will. I know they were at DB all day yesterday, and I'm sure they'll be there for a while longer."

"I wonder if my brother had any recent visitors?" said Puller. He wasn't looking directly at Chelsea when he threw this out, but in his peripheral vision he was observing her reaction.

"That's not my department. The log would show that, of course. DB keeps meticulous records of who comes and goes. Well, you know that, as many times as you've come to see him."

"Yes, they do. And I'm sure they've already looked at the visitors' log." He now looked at her expectantly.

She grew pink under his scrutiny. "I wouldn't know about that."

"Aren't things computerized at DB?"

"Absolutely."

"So there would be digital files of visitors?"

"Yes, there are."

He sat forward and tried to choose his next words with particular care.

"Chelsea, something doesn't smell right to me on this. Now, I'm telling you this on the

QT, okay?" She nodded quickly and he continued. "I was approached recently by a couple of
generals and someone from NSC—"

"The NSC? National Security Council? Oh
my God!"

"Yeah, pretty high-up stuff. Anyway, they
approached me with a lot of questions, none of
which I had answers for. But I think they want
me to get answers. And to do that I need information." Puller went back over in his head
what he had just said and came away confident
that he had told her no outright falsehood. Not
that that would help him much if the hammer
came down. However, he did feel guilty for
asking the woman to help him. But her next
words made him forget this concern.

"I don't see how I can help, John. I don't
really have access to much."

He sat back. "Know anyone who might and
who might be willing to talk to me?"

"There's one of the guards. He's actually been
talking to me about applying to CID. Maybe
it could be a scratch each other's back sort of
thing."

"Maybe it could. What's his name?"

"Aubrey Davis, PFC. Nice guy. Young, single. He likes his beer but I hear he's also serious
about getting ahead in his career."

Puller slid his card out and handed it to her. "Tell him to give me a call on my cell, okay?"

She took the card and nodded. "I will. But I can't guarantee he'll help you."

"No one can guarantee that. Most leads fizzle out. I just try to keep plowing through the ones I have and hope they lead to new ones. Thanks again."

He left her there and returned to his car. Okay, it would take some time for that angle to work out, he knew, if it ever did. If he were really unlucky, this PFC Aubrey Davis might report the inquiry and up the line it would go at top military speed, resulting in Puller's getting a call from his CO or probably someone even higher up the chain. If he were calamitously unlucky it would not be a phone call, but a truckload of MPs to haul him in to hear the charges read against him for disobeying an order. But in the meantime he had other things to check out. Namely, how the DB had lost both sources of power on the very same night, letting a highly valued prisoner simply walk out.

And leaving a dead man, who was not supposed to be there, behind.

It was impossible the way he had stated it. So in some way he had to have stated it wrong.

And the only way to get it right was to start digging.

With a very big shovel. Without anyone knowing.

A tall order, he knew.

But this was family, which meant he didn't really have a choice.

9

PULLER DROVE A circuitous route that took him around the perimeter of the DB and Fort Leavenworth as a whole. His gaze ran over the transmission lines. He had no way of seeing the natural gas generator configuration since that was behind cinderblock walls and the lines themselves were located underground.

He observed a power crew working inside a chain-link fence enclosing what looked to be twin transformers that might have been connected to the prison. This was probably the substation where the transformers had blown. But he couldn't officially question them about it. He tapped his fingers on the steering wheel and contemplated what to do. And that's when he noticed the Hummer pulling in behind him.

The MPs had arrived. Puller sighed, slid his ID out of his pocket, and waited.

Two armed men in uniform climbed out of their vehicle. They put on their caps and approached, one on each side of the car. Puller kept his hands in plain sight and made no sudden moves. He hit the window button with his elbow when the MP on the left reached him.

"What can I do for you?" he asked. "I've got my ID here. I'm—"

"We know who you are, sir. And we've been instructed to bring you into Fort Leavenworth for a meeting."

Puller slowly put his ID away. "You want me to follow you? Or would you rather I went in your ride?"

"Ours, if you don't mind, sir. Just pull yours a little farther off the road. We'll make sure it's here when you get back."

Well, at least he didn't say if *I get back.*

Puller rode in the rear seat with one MP next to him. They were both young, in their twenties, ramrod straight, stubborn chins, bulging necks, and eyes that did not see one inch farther than the orders they'd been given. Puller didn't try to talk to them. They were just the hunting dogs retrieving him to the hunter.

They drove to Fort Leavenworth, where he was handed off to a female lieutenant smartly dressed in her Class B Blues.

They exchanged salutes and she said, "Follow me, please, Chief Puller."

Well, it seemed everyone knew who he was.

They walked down a long corridor while Army life went on all around them. Military installations were centers of nonstop activity, and yet Puller wasn't distracted by any of it. He had no idea whether he was walking to his professional death or a stint in the stockade. Or something else entirely. Questions like that got a man to focus.

She opened a door, ushered him in, closed it behind him, and he heard her regulation heels tapping back down the hall. And then he forgot about the lieutenant. Sitting facing him across the small table were the same three gents as before: Army general Rinehart; Schindler, the NSC suit; and the Air Force one-star Daughtrey. Schindler, Daughtrey, and Rinehart, thought Puller. Sounded like a law firm, which didn't make him feel any better at all.

"Enjoying your visit to Kansas?" began Schindler.

"Up until about ten minutes ago, sir."

"Why don't you take a seat and we'll tell you what you're going to do," said Daughtrey tersely.

Puller sat down across from them.

Schindler took a moment to adjust his tie and apply balm to his chapped lips. Then he said,

"We understand that you disobeyed a direct order from your CO."

"What would that be, sir?"

"That would be your driving here through the night with the purpose of investigating your brother's escape from prison."

"Investigating?"

"Well, so far you've spoken with a woman who works in administration at the prison, Chelsea Burke. And you were hoping to talk with a PFC Davis, who might be able to provide you with some leads. And then you were out observing an electrical substation connected to DB."

Puller stared across the width of the table, silently marveling at how quickly they had been able to pounce on all this.

"You know all the stuff in the papers about the NSA spying and all, Puller?" said Daughtrey, a tiny smile playing over his lips.

"I read about it."

"Tip of the iceberg, but ninety percent of an iceberg is hidden underwater. You used your credit card to buy gas and food. We tracked you that way."

"Good to know, sir," Puller said sarcastically.

Schindler said, "Intelligence keeps us all safe."

"So spying on our own people keeps us safe?"

said Puller more forcefully than he probably intended.

Schindler waved a hand derisively at this comment. "You don't think there are Americans working with our enemies? Some of our fellow citizens will do anything for money. Hell, some of the biggest banks and hedge fund concerns in this country have been laundering cartel money and aiding terrorism for decades, and all for the almighty dollar."

"I'll take your word for it. So what now?"

"Well, now you have a decision to make, Puller," said Schindler.

"And what's that?"

"Basically, work for us or face the consequences."

"And how exactly would I work for you?"

Schindler glanced at his colleagues before continuing. "Doing exactly what you want to do, what you're here to do, in fact. Investigate your brother's escape. But the difference is we're kept in the loop the entire way. You step outside that box, your career is over."

Rinehart added, "The decision is yours, Puller. And we'll respect whichever way you choose to go. But if you choose not to work for us, your butt is on a cargo plane out of here. And just to make sure you don't come snooping back around on your own time, your next assignment will be overseas, starting to-morrow. Got a couple of unsolved murders on two different bases, one in Germany and one in South Korea. Army hasn't decided yet which one you'll be assigned to. My vote would be Korea, and my vote will carry great weight."

Puller took all this in but didn't immediately respond. They had him boxed in and both he and they knew it. "Why me?" he said finally. "You've got lots of resources at your fingertips. CID. Military Intelligence. You don't need me."

Rinehart responded, "On the surface a fair and accurate statement, Puller. But you have something none of those resources have."

Puller thought he knew the answer but waited patiently for the man to deliver it.

Rinehart said, "You're his brother. You grew up together. You both served together, albeit in different branches. We know of his assisting you on that investigation in West Virginia. We know you visited him frequently at DB. We know you two talk on the phone. You know him better than anyone else. So we think that you have the best shot to bring him in."

"Alive," said Puller.

"Absolutely."

"If I say yes to your offer, when can I start my investigation?"

"Immediately."

"No strings attached? No conditions?"

"Other than the one stated, that you report to us."

"And what about the other people investigating this? You can't stop them from doing their jobs. There's no way they'll leave this case to one CID agent."

"You'll just have to work around them. We'll leave it up to you."

"And no help from you on that point?"

"We'll see what we can do. But that ball will largely fall in your court, Puller."

"And my CO?"

Schindler said, "You'll get a written directive from him confirming this, of course, with all necessary authorizations. We don't expect you to take it on faith."

"Okay, I accept. And I'll begin my investigation by interviewing all of you."

The three men exchanged glances and then together looked back at Puller.

Schindler said, "We have nothing to do with this case other than the national security interest in bringing Robert Puller back to prison."

"You said no strings and no conditions other

than the one stated. Are you walking that back now?"

"No, but—"

"Because I am a trained investigator and my training and experience have shown that someone may think they have no valuable information to share, but they actually do. But unless I ask the questions and get the answers, that information never comes to light."

Schindler slowly nodded. "Okay, what do you want to know?"

"You said this was a national security case. Why?"

"You know what your brother was involved in with the Air Force?"

"STRATCOM."

"That's right. The United States Strategic Command. It used to be limited to nuclear defense. Now its mission covers space operations, missile defense, cyber and information warfare, WMDs, global command and control, surveillance, reconnaissance, global strike, the list goes on and on. I can't think of another military command more important to this country. Your brother worked both at the Missile Correlation Center in Cheyenne Mountain and also at STRATCOM's HQ at Offutt Air Force Base in Nebraska."

"I knew all that, sir. I'd actually visited my brother when he worked at STRATCOM at Offutt. But then he was assigned to a satellite office here in Leavenworth, right?" said Puller.

Daughtrey nodded. "STRATCOM outgrew its footprint at Offutt. The new facility won't be completely ready for a few more years. Leavenworth was one of many farm-out locations. But everything was wired back to HQ."

"I understand," said Puller.

Daughtrey added, "There was virtually no aspect of Strategic Command that he didn't have his fingers in. He was one of the most brilliant people they've ever had. The sky was the limit for him. Literally. He was being groomed to head up the whole damn thing at some point. He was just getting his next promotion lined up when everything blew up."

Puller asked, "I know you're with STRATCOM. Did you work with him?"

Daughtrey shook his head. "I was assigned to STRATCOM *after* your brother was sent to DB. The assessment I just gave was one based on all who knew and worked with him. To a person, soldier and contractor, he was one of the best."

"I don't doubt it," said Puller. "He was at the

top of every class. From high school to the Air
Force Academy and beyond."

Schindler said, "Except for the little matter of
treason. Let's not forget that."

"I haven't forgotten it," said Puller, turning
his gaze to the suit. "And I'm pretty sure my
brother hasn't. But what does his old job have
to do with anything?"

Rinehart said, "Since he's only been gone for
less than three years, Puller, much of the top secret data that rests in his head is still viable and
important. The security codes and such have
changed, of course. But the underlying technology, strategies, and tactics are the same. You
know the military way. We finally get everyone
to agree on something and Congress has to al-
locate the money. Everyone jockeys for their
piece, the uniforms for their slice of the command and subsequent promotions, and the contractors for their share of the dollars. Once that
is all set, the years-long process of implementa-
tion and execution begins. We are many things,
but nimble is not one of them. It's like changing
course on a *Nimitz*-class carrier using a handheld rudder: It takes time. So, many of the
projects your brother was connected with are
still being implemented or are in operation
right now. He has intimate and detailed knowl-

edge of some of this country's most important security programs that in turn deal with some of the most critical challenges we have."

Puller considered all of this and said, "So he would be very valuable to enemies of this country."

"Without question," said Rinehart.

Puller looked at each man and said, "So maybe he didn't break out."

Schindler looked confused, an expression he shared with his two colleagues. "I don't quite get what you're saying, Puller. He *did* break out. He's gone."

"I'm not saying he's not gone from DB."

"Then what are you saying?" asked Schindler as he tapped his index finger impatiently against the table.

"That the whole thing at DB was staged, and instead of him breaking out, he might have been *kidnapped* by enemies of this country."

10

QUARTERS.

Even now Robert Puller couldn't refer to it as a room, or an apartment, or a flat. It was *quarters*. Military vernacular was drilled into the minds of those in uniform like fingers marking letters in wet concrete that dried to permanency.

His "quarters" was a motel room on the outskirts of Kansas City, Kansas. He had left Leavenworth behind for no other reason than—

I could.

It was a right-angle drive, hands twelve and three on the clock, meaning straight south and then straight east on I-70, the two perfectly equal legs of a right triangle, only awaiting the hypotenuse to complete it, which he might, taking an alternate but no less straight and direct route back to Leavenworth, if necessary. He had always framed things that way, with a reference to math or science or an adjunct of ei-

ther one, placing them into a perspective that
amused some, bewildered others, but was off-
putting to most, he had found.

And which bothered him not at all.

There was a bed, a chair, a table, a bureau, and
a TV on the bureau with lots of mostly useless
channels. The bathroom was barely an after-
thought, essentially a niche in the wall with a
shower stall so claustrophobic it felt more like
a straitjacket than a proper bathing area.

Again, after a prison cell, it bothered him not
at all.

His duffel was on the floor and his laptop on
the desk. He had purchased a disposable phone
along the way, along with a mobile hotspot, set
it all up, programmed in some interesting features, and was grinding his way through the
military database he'd hacked into back at Starbucks.

It was a special database to which only authorized personnel should have been granted
access. Computer security was only as good as
the programmer. The one who had firewalled
this database had been good—but not great.

Puller had also purchased a small wireless
printer and some three-hole paper and three-
ring and spiral notebooks along with pens.
While his entire professional life had been

mostly spent in the digital world, where the language of ones and zeroes dominated, he appreciated the importance of paper, pen, and deliberative thought that working with such old-school items seemed to inspire. And he thought better in cursive. The joined-up writing seemed to spur connective thinking.

He printed his papers, put them in the three-ring, exited the database, and took up his pen and spiral notebooks. He worked methodically for some hours. He didn't stop to drink or eat or use the bathroom. He was oblivious to whatever else was going on in the world, or at least in Kansas. He was no longer, at least in his mind, the most wanted man in America. He was an analyst, a seer, a prognosticator going over his reams of data, moving their pieces, twisting them, testing them, discounting some, fleshing out others, slowly transforming disjointed intelligence into something that made sense.

After six hours of relentless concentration and the light of day having given over to dark, forcing him to take a moment to turn on a lamp, he put down his pen and sat back, folding his arms over his chest and resting his chin there as well. He closed his eyes, slowed his breathing, and counted his heartbeats until they fell short of sixty a minute. He opened his eyes and ran his gaze down one of his tat sleeves, exposed now since he had discarded his jacket.

They were of his creation. They looked like typical tattoos, but if one looked closely enough the eagles and dragons and other creatures resting there were actually composed of tiny geometric images: squares, triangles, rectangles, and their more complex brethren, the dodecahedron for example, which when viewed flat—meaning as a solid—had twelve faces and was an integral part of his dragon's scales.

Puller knew that other than him no one would notice. But that had been how much of his life had gone—his noticing, others not.

Except for his brother. And his father. They were curious. They observed. They remembered. They figured things out. His father had mastered leading enormous numbers of men, grand corps and divisions at a time, into battle on a scale and dimension that was as complex as anything ever seen on a chessboard, with the added pressure of human lives by the thousands being at stake. His brother tracked down wrongdoers with a sense of justice and an attention to detail that would put most others in the field to shame.

The Puller men, prodigies in their respective fields, but whose skills all shared that core attribute of—

Observing.

He turned to page sixty-six of the printed-out papers, because something had just occurred to him. He studied what was written there and compared it to information contained on page twenty-four. Interestingly enough, they did not tally. They did not tally at all. But they had to if the offered and official result was to make any sense.

This was not a smoking gun. But it was something. And something, as his brother often said, usually led to something else.

Brilliant in its elegant simplicity, and he knew exactly what his brother meant. He carried it out to its logical conclusion.

In fact, something always leads to something else.

He drew out a blank piece of paper and conjured the image of the man in his head. It was not easy, because it had been dark. But there had been a light source. The man's own flashlight.

Puller put his pen to the paper and refocused, transferring the image in his head to the cotton fibers, letting the ink bleed into them, fill out what he was trying to achieve. This was not simply important; it was paramount. Because it was something.

And something always leads to something else.

He was an accomplished artist, a fact not many knew about him. He had taken it up years ago to relax from a job whose stakes and pressures were so enormous.

Hence the sketches, lines connecting and intersecting and bisecting other lines to form something that had not previously existed. It was math yet again, geometry transformed into art, a confluence that had made painters like Picasso icons forever enshrined in history. It was cubism building to masterpieces born of another realm of thought and experience.

He had fits and starts and crumpled-up paper, and endured starting over multiple times. Finally the image gained traction, the root system set in, and the features began to grow, like a plant rising, seeking the light. Plants could not survive without sunlight; indeed, photosynthesis was the key to their survival.

Well, Puller would not be living much longer without this image coming to full fruition.

He worked away for another half hour and then reached the point where the heavy lifting was finished. Now he was simply filling in the edges.

He sat back, put down his pen, and held the paper up to eye level.

Staring back at him was a man. A man Puller had not seen until very recently. A man he still did not know.

That man now lay, he was fairly certain, in a morgue at Fort Leavenworth, as investigators attempted to figure out who he was. And what he was doing at the DB the night Robert Puller escaped. And why he was now dead. These were good, pertinent queries.

Puller was fairly certain that he knew what the man was doing there. He clearly knew *exactly* how the man had died.

Yet he didn't know anything beyond that. And he *had* to know. He had to know all of it. This puzzle could not remain unfinished. Not if he wanted to survive.

And because something always leads to something else.

11

JOHN PULLER HAD his marching orders. He had asked Daughtrey, Schindler, and Rinehart a few more questions and gotten a few more answers that might or might not lead to something. But at least he had the authority to operate out in the open. An email had come through from his CO empowering him to work on this investigation with the accompanying and necessary electronic trail of higher signatories. The suit and the stars definitely had the juice they claimed to have. He felt like he had just been rebadged.

He didn't like slinking around trying not to be noticed. He wanted people to know he was on the case. He wanted to intimidate. Intimidated people with a guilty conscience often made mistakes. The only difference here was that the target of his investigation was his brother. Robert Puller was brilliant. Was he going to make mistakes? Didn't he know John Puller Jr. better than anyone?

He knows how I think. How I tick.

But then I know the same about him.

However, these thoughts didn't make him feel good. They made him feel sick.

He cleared security at the DB and walked up a flight of steps to the visitors' room. He asked to see the officer in charge, displaying his credentials and relaying his purpose for being here.

The woman met Puller in her office. She was Captain Lenora H. Macri, in her thirties, short, trim, with salt-and-pepper hair worn in a bun. She looked wound as tight as a coil of wire and her expression did not appear cooperative in the least. This was not particularly good for him, because she was now the DB's acting commander.

"What can I do for you, Chief Puller?" she began curtly.

"I'm investigating the escape of Robert Puller."

"Right. Your *brother*." She left the statement there, with all its inherent complications and insinuations. Then she added, "I find it extraordinary that you're involved in this case in any way at all. I have duly noted my misgivings with the appropriate channels."

"Which you have every right to do."

"And which I don't need you to tell me," she retorted. "Blood is thicker than water, and what we need is objectivity. I fail to see how you can bring an unbiased perspective to this investigation."

Puller shifted in his seat. "I'm a CID agent. My mission is clear, Captain Macri. Bring him back, brother or not. I've been authorized to do this. If you have a problem cooperating with me, I need to hear it now."

She held his gaze. "I have no problems, Mr. Puller. I think any potential problems will rest largely with you. Now, how can I help?"

She had done that rather neatly, thought Puller. Not only covered her ass with the "appropriate channels" but also put the onus on him to disprove her opinion of his being involved at all while at the same time appearing cooperative. Only a captain now, but she must be bucking hard for her next promotion.

Aren't they all?

Puller went over the facts as he understood them and asked for her confirmation of them.

"They're accurate," Macri said. "Except for the shots fired and the explosion."

Puller blinked at her. "Shots and an explosion? No one mentioned that."

"Well, maybe you didn't ask the right questions. I'm volunteering that information in the interest of full disclosure. The shots and explosion prompted the calling in of reinforcements from the fort."

"Did you determine the origins of the shots?"

"No."

"And the explosion?"

Macri said, "I said explosion because that's what it initially sounded like."

"You were on duty?"

"Yes, I was. But many people heard the noises. They were quite distinct."

"So it wasn't really an explosion?"

"As I just said, it *initially* sounded like one. However, we found no evidence of one actually going off."

"Then perhaps it was the same deal with the shots."

"It probably was, because we also found no evidence of any shots fired."

"So just sound effects, maybe?"

"Actually, that's the only explanation that fits. As you probably know, guards do not carry weapons inside the prison. Thus no shots could have been fired by them. All prisoners were searched. No gun or contraband of any kind was found."

"Except for the escapee. You couldn't search him, because he was gone."

"Correct," conceded Macri.

"But then some device had to make those noises."

"I agree with you. We just couldn't find out what it was. But the investigation, as you know, is ongoing."

"Were the guards searched?"

Macri looked blankly at him. "The guards?"

"If the prisoners didn't cause it, maybe one of the guards?" Puller looked at her expectantly.

"Why would a guard do that?"

"Well, if they'd been searched and the device found, you could have asked that question directly."

"I refuse to believe that one of my personnel was involved in this. It's unthinkable."

"Well, Captain Macri, if nothing was found on the prisoners and nothing was found in the prison and unless you're randomly allowing folks in here to plant devices to cause a panic, it had to be one of the guards."

She bristled at this, but said nothing.

"And the status of your CO?"

"Colonel Teague is on temporary leave."

"Meaning he's the fall guy for this?" said Puller.

"Meaning he's on temporary leave."

"Have you done an investigation of your own, Captain?"

"A preliminary one has been conducted. As you well know, there are others here currently doing their own: MI, CID other than you. Some folks from Washington. Lots of cooks in the kitchen."

"And what did your 'preliminary' investigation reveal?"

Macri said, "That Robert Puller escaped in a manner as yet undetermined."

"And the dead man?"

"What about him?"

"Has he been identified?"

"Not yet," replied Macri.

"Anyone missing from the prison? Guards, support staff, civilians? And how about Fort Leavenworth? Everyone accounted for there?"

"A thorough accounting has been done. There are no missing personnel at either place."

"But there's a federal pen here as well. And the Midwest Joint Regional Correctional Facility. All folks accounted for at those locations?"

She seemed taken aback by this query. "I don't see how personnel at those facilities are relevant. If a prisoner had escaped from there we'd know about it. And it's not like guards at those institutions could just walk into the DB."

He stared at her pointedly. "You're with the 15th MP Brigade."

"I know I am."

"Composed of the 40th and 705th MP Battalions."

She said impatiently, "And your point?"

"The 15th MPs are responsible for the operation of DB *and* the Midwest Regional. Colonel Teague was the commandant at DB and also the commander of the 15th. MPs from the 15th responded to the situation at DB and restored order. In addition, the 40th Battalion was largely created because the 705th was deployed to the Middle East to run the prisons over there. So the prison *is* guarded by the 15th and both its battalions. So are you telling me that they don't overlap in guard rotations? That no guard at DB ever works at the regional prison? Or vice versa?"

She seemed flustered now. "No, I'm not saying that or implying it."

"Then the personnel at those facilities *are* relevant to my investigation, correct?"

She finally nodded. "I guess that's correct. I'm sorry if I misinterpreted your request."

"How do you explain the dead man in my brother's cell?"

"I can't explain it. That's why investigations are ongoing."

He decided to change direction. "I'll need to see the body."

She pursed her lips. Puller knew that despite any animosity she might have toward him, Macri could not refuse this request. A murder always carried with it a body. And for him as a CID agent authorized to investigate this murder, an examination of the body was always required and access never denied.

"I'll make arrangements. They have him at Fort Leavenworth."

"Thank you."

"You're welcome," she said curtly.

"I'll also need to check with the crews who restored the electrical power and repaired the backup generator."

"I can also arrange that."

"I'll also need to look at surveillance footage from the night in question."

"We lost power."

"But the cameras have battery backups."

"The ones in hallways and general areas do. The ones in the prisoners' cells don't."

"Why not?"

"It was not designed that way. I can only imagine that if the main and backup power went out, the only problem would be prisoners attempting to flee from where the cameras could monitor them. They weren't concerned that they remain in their cells in such a scenario. As you probably know, at DB it's one prisoner to a cell."

"I know that. But still quite the blind eye when you think about it."

"No design is perfect. And I would imagine from this point on, cameras in the cells will also have battery backups."

"I thought the system was set up so that if the power failed the cell doors automatically locked. And yet you had to call in the MPs. Why?"

Macri's features were suddenly pained. "It seemed we were hacked."

"Hacked? How?"

"As you said, our system is set up such that cell doors automatically lock when the power fails. That didn't happen. The cell doors *unlocked* instead."

"And a hacker caused this? How could that have happened?"

"Unfortunately, some of our personnel bring in their personal devices, phones, iPads, and on their computers here there is occasional breach of protocol as people log on to outside networks. It's not supposed to happen, but people are people."

"Leaving a way for a hacker to get in and rewrite your code so the cell doors opened when the power failed."

"Yes."

"Any leads there?"

"No."

"But you've confirmed the hack occurred?"

"Technically, that is still speculation, but I see no other way for it to have happened."

Puller thought, *Oh, I see at least one other way it could have gone down.* "I'll need to see all the footage you have," he said.

Her lips pursed once more. "I can arrange that as well."

"And the MP reinforcements from Leavenworth? I'll need to talk to the people involved in that."

She gave a curt nod.

"Just to be clear, are you sure you haven't formed any theories, Captain, as to what happened?"

"No, I have not."

"Not even any hunches?"

"I don't like hunches, Mr. Puller. They often lead to mistakes. And mistakes often lead to the end of military careers."

"Well, I'll let you get on with *your* career, then, as soon as you make the arrangements we just discussed."

Macri gazed at him intently and then picked up her desk phone.

12

AN HOUR LATER Puller was leaning against a fifty-gallon oil drum in a workshop facility near the DB. The man he was talking to, Al Jordan, had been the crew chief for the group that had repaired the blown transformers. He was in his early fifties, with pewter gray hair and a barrel chest set atop skinny legs.

"So it was definitely the storm that fried the transformers?"

Jordan wiped his hands on a rag and then lifted his cap and wiped sweat from his brow. "That's sure what it looked like to me. The two transformers were part of a small substation. Encircled by a chain-link fence that was locked. The station had lots of safety devices built in, but that storm had enough power to do just about anything it wanted to. You can't trump Mother Nature."

"And the transformers were connected to DB?" asked Puller.

"Yep. Along with other facilities around here. We got them back up and running as fast as we could. We didn't even wait for the storm to stop."

Puller understood this. The military was mission first, not safety first.

"So anything unusual you might have noticed?"

Jordan considered this. "I can't say that there was. Those transformers just blew. Probably hit by the lightning. They were all burned up."

"Isn't it unusual that they *both* blew?"

"Well, they're connected. One gets hit, there's gonna be an effect on the other as well. Too much juice, anything can happen."

"You said they had lots of safety devices built in. Don't they ground them?"

"Yes, in addition to other protections like an arrestor for secondary induced surges, but none of them are perfect. You get a direct hit with enough power I don't care what you've done to avoid damage. That sucker is going. A lightning bolt can carry one hundred and twenty million volts or more. You slam that into a transformer in a millisecond, well, can you say 'boom'?"

"So, like an explosion?"

"Very much like one."

"Could it have been a bomb?"

Jordan looked at him in surprise. "A bomb? In a transformer?"

"Yes. It could have taken out both transformers."

"What, to knock power out to the prison, you mean?"

"Yeah."

"But they got backups," protested Jordan.

"They failed too. And a prisoner escaped. Which is the only reason I'm here."

Jordan scratched his cheek. "I don't know if it was a bomb. I guess people who know bombs can check it out."

"Have they?"

"Don't know."

"You talked to anyone else who's investigating this?"

"I have. They asked the same sort of questions you did."

"But not about a possible bomb?"

"What makes you say that?" Jordan asked suspiciously.

"Well, you were surprised when I asked you about the possibility of a bomb. If they had asked you as well, I don't think you would have been surprised when I did."

"Oh, right. Well, they didn't ask about a bomb, as a matter of fact."

"Where are the transformers that blew?"

"They took them away."

"Who took them away?"

Jordan shifted his stance a bit. "Some people."

"Those people have names or credentials?"

"They outranked me. That's all that mattered."

"So no names?" Puller persisted. "No releases signed? You had to cover your butt somehow."

Jordan shrugged. "I just took it on faith, I guess."

Puller gave the man an incredulous look. "Then you should reconsider your faith."

* * *

The next stop for Puller was the backup generator. It was housed in a concrete bunker about a hundred yards to the rear of the DB. The gas lines powering it ran underground. The bunker was also partially underground and surrounded by a ten-foot-high fence topped with concertina wire. There was a guard stationed there. Puller had called ahead and two men were waiting for him.

He climbed out of his car and approached. They were in uniform and carried the ranks of E-4 specialists. With their glasses and scrawny builds they looked to him like nerds playing soldier. He gave a detailed explanation of why he was there, and they led him into the bunker and down a short flight of stairs until they arrived at three mammoth generators.

"I thought there'd only be one of them," said Puller.

"The electrical load requirement for DB is very substantial," said one of the E-4s. "These generators are run in parallel but with sophisticated control features. It'll provide the load required but not more, so the waste is minimal."

"What was the cause of the failure?" asked Puller.

One specialist looked at the other, who cleared his throat. "It was a fuel problem."

"Fuel? I thought the fuel it ran on was natural gas."

"These are bi-fuel systems," said the other E-4. "Natural gas and diesel."

"Why two fuels?"

"Natural gas puts us at the control of the utility. Army doesn't like that. Something happens to the gas flow, we're shit out of luck. The way the system works, the main power fails, the diesel fuel component to the generator comes on and runs the system initially. Then the natural gas feed will be introduced by the system's controller into the fuel mix after certain criteria are satisfied—the requisite electrical load acceptance, for example. The diesel also serves as the pilot light for the natural gas, which has an ignition temperature of about twelve hundred degrees Fahrenheit. That way if the natural gas flow is interrupted we have on-site fuel under our control. The system will typically run on a seventy-five to twenty-five gas to diesel mixture."

"So what happened to cause it to fail? You said there was a fuel problem?"

"The best we can tell, there was either a diesel oxidation degradation problem or a microorganism contamination issue."

"In English?" said Puller patiently.

The E-4 explained, "Diesel can degrade over time. Oxidation can occur in the first year of storage, forming sediment and gum. When introduced into the system they can clog fuel filters and injectors, just like gunk in a car engine. Now, microorganisms are introduced via water condensation in the fuel lines, which promotes bacteria and fungi. They feed on the fuel. They can form colonies that clog the lines as well."

"But I presume you have protocols in place that would prevent those problems from happening."

When the men said nothing, Puller exclaimed sharply, "The Army has procedures for toilet paper usage. Are you saying they had none for maintenance of a power system for the military's most important prison?"

The same E-4 said hastily, "No, no, they do. Lots of them. But it might have still happened. There was a lot of rain this year and we got some underground seepage into the bunker. That could have caused excessive condensation buildup. And these generators are very near the end of their useful life. In fact, they should have been replaced about two years ago."

"Sequestration cuts brought the hammer down on that," pointed out the other E-4. "And the Army also bought some bad diesel that's been working its way through the system."

"Okay. So you checked out the generator and found the lines all, what, gummed up, with microorganisms, sediment?"

"That's pretty much what we did find, yes sir."

"And that caused the generator to fail?"

They both nodded. One added, "And without the diesel serving as the pilot light, you can't ignite the natural gas. So, no fuel source connection. That means no power."

"And a prison with no locked doors," said Puller as he stared at both men. "So you two are the principal caretakers of this equipment?"

"Yes sir," they said together.

"Well, you might want to make alternate plans for your future."

"Meaning exactly what, sir?" asked one of them anxiously.

"Meaning that the Army, in its infinite wisdom, must affix blame for this clusterfuck. And you two are as likely candidates as any I've seen so far."

The E-4s exchanged a shocked glance as Puller headed out of the bunker and back to daylight.

CHAPTER

13

PULLER SAT IN the room and stared at the feed from the surveillance cameras' capture of the events on the night his brother disappeared from the DB. The various loops had been compiled so that he could see essentially an all-inclusive feed. He had wanted the room darkened so his focus would be on the screen in front of him. The total feed wasn't long, perhaps two hours or so to record all that happened, and that counted the duplication from the different cameras. If he had been watching the feed from a single camera, the events would have taken less than thirty minutes total. It was remarkable that so much of significance could have taken place in such a short time.

Puller looked through the feed initially to orient himself to the spatial parameters. Corridors, rooms, doorways. When the power went out on the feed, he leaned in closer to the screen and used his controller to take it in frame by frame.

Blackout. Not much to see.

Then the lights came back on, flickered, and then went back off. The cameras had built-in lighting, so he could make out the silhouettes of figures running, the bouncing beams of flashlights. There was audio too, which he isolated. He listened to each individual voice. He doubted that his brother would have spoken, but he couldn't discount the possibility. The frames ran through, and not one time did he spot his brother. One problem was that the camera recording in his brother's pod was placed far away from his cell door. Puller had seen figures running up and down that hall, but none were recognizable. Perhaps the frames could be enhanced or better lighted, but that would probably take time.

Then came the sound of shots that sounded like the real thing. The next sound was so loud that Puller jerked a bit—an explosion going off in the DB? After that came the reinforcements from Fort Leavenworth. They swept down corridors and took charge of the prisoners out of their cells. At least from what he could see.

He sat back and drank down the rest of the bottle of water. This was going nowhere fast. He had transformers that had blown from a lightning strike during a storm that no one could have relied on to knock out the prison's primary power source. Then, according to Al Jordan, "people" had come around and taken the remains of the transformers. He had a generator that had gotten gummed up and two E-4s who were probably going to get shit-canned or at least receive severe professional consequences for letting it happen.

He had gunshots and an explosion or at least the sounds thereof that no one could as yet explain. He had no opportunity, no motive, no leads, and no suspects. He had nothing at all. And yet his brother was out there somewhere doing who knew what, maybe with enemies of this country. Because there was no way his brother had busted out of the DB without help, from inside, outside, or, more likely, both.

He hit some more keys and brought up an image that was crystal clear. This had been taken before the power had gone out. He sat up straighter as he looked at his brother.

Robert Puller was sitting on the bolted-to-the-floor bunk in his cell. The walls were cinderblock, the floor smooth concrete. There was one window. There was a commode and a sink next to it, both built into the wall. There was a metal table and chair, again affixed to the wall. Robert Puller had on his orange prison jumper and sneakers with no laces. Laces could be transformed into rope, which could be used as either a weapon or a way to kill oneself. His brother was reading a book. His back was against the wall, his long legs stuck straight out in front of him. When the sounds of the storm were heard, Robert Puller glanced up from his book but then went back to the pages. And then the power went out and the cell went black. Then the generator kicked on and the lights came back, on and so did the surveillance camera in Robert's room.

Robert Puller was still on his cot but no longer reading the book. His feet were on the floor and he was staring at the door. In just a short time the generator would fail and the blackness would return.

Before that happened, Puller froze his brother's image, leaned closer to the screen, and peered deeply into Robert's features, trying to decipher the thoughts going through that staggeringly complicated mind.

Talk to me, bro. Show me something. What are you thinking? Are you waiting for something to happen? Are you expecting something to happen? Or not?

Puller observed, and not for the first time, how much he resembled his older brother. Both were tall. Both had the same nose, and both shared their father's angular jaw. The eyes were deep-set, giving each man a brooding look regardless of what they might actually be contemplating. But then again all three Puller men tended to be brooders.

His mind went back to when they were children. Bobby, because of his brains, had been the leader of the military brats on whatever base they had been living with their father. His brother had been the most sensitive, honorable person Puller knew, so sensitive, in fact, that the old man had taken to busting his balls about this perceived "weakness." In fact, he had done it so often that Puller had memorized his father's spiel.

"You can't command men in battle if they *like* you, Bob," his father had said. "They have to have equal parts fear and respect. And I would say fear is even more important than respect. Respect only gets you so far. Fear can get you through every damn obstacle devised by the enemy. Men will follow you to hell if they fear you. Because failing you will scare them more than any other thing they will ever face on the battlefield. You remember that, son. You remember that if you remember nothing else I've ever told you."

Bobby had never gotten over this "weakness." Which was probably why he opted for the Air Force instead of the Army. And staked out his career with technology rather than guns and cojones the size of Nebraska.

When Puller had found out from Captain Macri that the prison computer system had been hacked, he had initially thought that his brother, who knew his way around computers better than just about anyone, might somehow have done it. But then they never let his brother near a computer at the DB. And he'd been sitting in his cell and seemed genuinely surprised when the power went out. So if not his brother, who?

Puller was thinking all of this when the door opened and in walked a woman about his age. She was tall, slender, broad-shouldered and narrow-hipped, dressed in a black pantsuit with a white blouse, the collar flipped up in a way that even Puller, who knew nothing of women's fashions, thought looked sort of chic. She had shoulder-length auburn hair, a freckled face, and a flint-sharp nose. She looked like she had been an athlete in college, and carried herself in a confident manner.

"Agent Puller?"

Momentarily thrown by this unusual greeting, he rose and said, "I'm Chief Warrant Officer John Puller, with the 701st CID out of Quantico."

She put out a hand. "Veronica Knox." He shook her hand and she held up her creds, which dangled on a lanyard. "INSCOM," she said, referring to the United States Army's Intelligence and Security Command.

"Where are you based out of?" he asked.

"I'm a floater going to the trouble spots. That's why I'm here."

"Okay. And your rank?"

"Why?"

"It's just sort of standard to know."

"Captain."

"Okay, ma'am." Puller's antennae were tingling.

"CID is already here investigating."

"I know they are," he said.

"You're not part of that team."

"I know that too, ma'am."

"You don't have to call me 'ma'am.'"

"All right."

"And the escapee is your older brother," she pointed out.

"I'm afraid it's three strikes and you're out, Captain Knox."

She ignored this comment, sat down, and

looked at the frozen image of Robert Puller on the screen. She flicked a finger at it.

"The man of the hour. Find any clues?"

"Not yet."

"I know you have authorization to be here. We got that order. But why *are* you here?"

"Same reason you are. Trying to figure out what happened."

"CID has enough free assets to double up on this?"

"No, we're pretty much stretched thin like every other Army element."

"So?" she said expectantly.

"So what?"

"Why are you here?" she asked again.

Puller said, "I've been ordered to investigate. I'm a soldier, so I follow orders."

"So am I. And I've been assigned to work with you."

"By who?" Puller said sharply.

"You just need to know that I have been. If you want to find out the source, feel free."

"And you can't just tell me why?"

"I don't know you. So I don't know if I can trust you. Not yet."

"You're not in uniform."

"Neither are you."

"I will be. At some point."

"Maybe I will be too." She glanced at the screen again. "You sure nothing caught your eye?"

"Nothing."

"Let's hope we can get beyond that."

The way she said this made Puller stare at her strangely. "I've looked into the transformers at the substation and the generator."

She shook her head dismissively. "Lightning overload, and microorganisms, and a pair of dumbass E-4s who're going to get sliced and diced by their CO."

"Exactly the way I saw it," he replied, again watching her closely. "So we're a team?"

She shrugged. "Only because the Army says so. I usually work alone."

"At CID we work in groups."

"Different strokes," she retorted.

"What's your take on the sound-making device? Shots and explosion?"

She looked at the screen. "Maybe your brother had it."

"Where would he get something like that? And there's his cell right there. You see anything like that in there? Because I don't."

She shot back, "I'm sure you know him better than I do. Maybe better than anyone, which might be the reason you're here."

Puller eyed the door. "You gone over the visitors' log yet?"

"Next on my bucket list."

"Shall we?"

She held the door open for him. "After you."

14

As they walked down the hall, Puller said, "You talk to Al Jordan, guy who replaced the transformers?"

"I did," Knox replied.

"And?"

"And what?"

"Did he mention anything that got your antennae up?"

"Like what?" she said.

"Like the people who came and took the blown-up transformers away?"

"No, he didn't."

"Did you ask to see the transformers?"

"No," she said.

"Okay."

She stopped walking, and he did too after a few paces. He turned to face her.

"What are you driving at, Puller?"

"Just asking questions and hoping to get some answers that make some sense."

"What about the transformers?"

"Everybody thinks the storm blew them up."

"And you don't think that was the case?" she asked.

"I don't think anything. I just follow the evidence. But a pretty simple examination of the transformers' debris would have shown whether there was a bomb involved."

"A bomb?" she said skeptically.

"A bomb," he repeated. "Can't blow something up without a few essential elements. The explosive, the detonator, a timer or a remote switch."

"That I know. But your theory is someone blew up the transformers and sabotaged the backup generator in order to break your brother out of prison?" She paused, frowning. "You didn't tell me you were a conspiracy freak."

"And you think a storm just rolled along, blew out the main power, the backup coincidentally failed, and my brother walked out on his own, taking advantage of an opportunity that had occurred in just a few seconds while a company of MPs from Leavenworth was charging in? And for some reason the sounds of gunfire and an explosion just happened to coincide with it all going down? And an unidentified dead body left behind?" He cocked his head and looked at her more closely. "And I can tell from the expression on your face that you've already thought of this, which means everything that came before between you and me was an act on your part."

She registered surprise. "Really? Based on an expression?"

He said, "I interrogate people for a living. Reading faces is part of that. People can lie with words, but their faces, and in particular their eyes, give them away. They always do. And yours just did. So what exactly is going on here?"

She tapped her heel against the floor, her arms folded across her chest. "This is a delicate situation," she said. "Very delicate."

He drew closer. "I can see that. But feel free to elaborate on the point."

"I just know my marching orders were to tread lightly. And to work with you. And that's what I intend to do."

"Nothing more to add?" he asked.

"Not right now. Shall we go see to the visitors' log?"

The visitors' records at the DB were housed electronically. Puller and Knox were given access to them at a computer terminal in a cubicle adjacent to the visitors' room. Puller had decided to go back at least six months and maybe longer if nothing stood out. They sat next to each other, knees occasionally touching because of their long legs and the cubicle's small space.

After a while Knox said, "You were a pretty regular visitor to see your brother."

"You have siblings?"

"No."

"Well then, maybe it's hard for you to understand."

"Okay, but I don't see anyone else who came to visit him, Puller. Again, other than you, that is."

"Neither do I."

"So now what? The log shows no calls came in to him, other than from you."

Puller studied the screen. "But this really doesn't tell us the whole story."

"Meaning what?"

"Meaning computers only regurgitate what someone puts into them."

He rose.

She looked up at him and said, "Now where?"

"To do some real investigative work."

"Such as?"

"Such as talking to people."

* * *

It took the better part of the rest of the day and they had to speak to numerous people and look at paper records and then talk to supervisory officers and then go back to people originally interviewed. When they were done it was nine p.m.

"You hungry?" said Puller.

She nodded. "Breakfast was a long time ago."

"You know Leavenworth?"

"Not that well."

"Well, I do. Come on."

They drove in his car to a diner on the main street where everything on the menu was fried in grease that was probably as old as the building, which said "1953" on the wall over the entrance. They both ordered their meals. Puller had a beer, while Knox sipped on an iced tea heavy on the ice.

"What we're about to eat will mean five extra miles on my morning run," she said, giving a fake grimace.

"You've got some room to spare," he noted. He took a sip of his cold beer. "Crew or basketball in college?"

"Both."

"Impressive. Multiple sports in college, tough thing to pull off these days."

"Well, it was over fifteen years ago and it was a small college. And crew was a club sport at Amherst."

"Amherst. Great school."

"Yes, it is."

"And what brought you to the Army?"

"My mother."

"She was in the Army?" asked Puller.

"No, my father was. He maxed out as a full colonel. Finished up at Fort Hood."

"Okay, I'm not getting the reference to your mom, then."

"She said anything my father could do I could sure as hell do better. They're divorced," she added, perhaps unnecessarily.

"I take it you don't get along with your father?"

"You take it right." She drank her iced tea through a straw and then fiddled with the paper the straw had been wrapped in. "I looked you up, of course. *Your* father is John Puller Sr. *Fighting* John Puller."

"That's what they call him."

"A true legend."

"They call him that too."

"I hear he's in a VA hospital."

"He is."

"Is he doing okay?"

Puller glanced away and then looked directly at her. "He's doing. We all get old, right?"

"If we live that long." She eyed the scar that ran along the side of his neck to the point where it dipped down his back. "Fallujah?" she asked, indicating the mark.

"Mosul. My Fallujah souvenir is on my ankle."

"I did a tour over there too. Nothing on the front lines." She added firmly, "Nothing to do with me. Everything to do with the Army."

"I've heard that before," said Puller. "No mark against you if they wouldn't let you fight at the front."

"Still a mark, Puller."

"But things are changing. And fast."

"Things *had* to change. Twenty-first century. No way around it."

He raised his bottle of Coors in salute. "Agreed. Some of the toughest soldiers I ever served with were women."

They remained silent until their meals came, and they didn't speak as they ate them. When the plates were cleared Puller came back around to why they were really here.

"Did you see what I saw in the interviews and paper trail?" he asked.

"Tell me what you saw and I'll answer you."

"Let's say the visitors' log is accurate and I'm the only one who visited my brother during the last six months."

"Okay."

"If he didn't talk to anyone else on the outside, then we need to look inward."

"Someone at DB?"

Puller nodded. "Wouldn't be the first time a prisoner has been aided by someone on the other side of the cell door."

"I'm pretty sure it would be the first time at DB."

"And the computer system was hacked, ensuring the doors opened when the power blew. Now that definitely smacks of an inside hand."

This was the other option Puller had been considering when Macri had told him about the suspected hacking.

"That makes sense," agreed Knox.

"We need to talk to every guard who was on duty that night."

"That's a lot of guards."

He sat back looking and feeling put off. "You got something else to do with your time?"

"No. So what would we be looking for?"

"An off answer, a look, a hesitation. And we need to comb through their histories, see if anything pops."

"That could take a long time."

Puller slapped the table with the palm of his hand. "I don't care how long it takes, Knox. All I care about is setting this situation right."

"And what exactly does that mean to you? Setting the situation right? Capturing your brother and returning him to prison safely?"

"What else would I mean?" he said slowly.

She studied him. "I wonder. But if this was an inside job, it might involve more than just a guard. And that for me is far-fetched."

"It's not far-fetched if it turns out to be true. Maybe the picture is a lot bigger than we think it is."

"And maybe it isn't."

"Have you been briefed on my brother?"

"STRATCOM."

Puller nodded. "And you know what that entails. That could be the motive right there. Our enemies snatch him for his brains, use what he knows against us."

"So now you've moved on to spies?" she said skeptically. "A mole at DB?"

"Do you have another explanation?" he said tersely.

"No," she admitted. "I don't."

"We still have no idea who the dead guy is or what he was doing there. I've made arrangements to see his body in the morning."

"That is a puzzler," she admitted. "I mean, how do you get into a prison and get yourself killed and no one sees or hears anything?"

"It might be easier than you think," Puller said.

Knox looked at him expectantly, but he didn't elaborate. Instead he said, "And who ordered you to babysit me?"

"I wasn't ordered to babysit you!" she said sharply.

Puller ignored this. "Was it Schindler…Daughtrey…or Rinehart?"

Her face twitched at the last name.

"So, Lieutenant General Rinehart. Three stars do tend to capture a captain's attention. Especially if you want to move up and beat your old man's rank. Might be a nice shortcut careerwise."

She looked away. "Puller, you don't know what you're talking about. You're really off on this whole thing."

He laid down some cash for his part of the meal. "I'm sure Rinehart will reimburse you for your dinner tonight. You were still on duty, after all." He rose. "Hang in there."

"Where are you going?"

"To bed."

She didn't say anything right away, just held her gaze on him. Finally Knox said, "Why don't I believe that?"

* * *

They went their separate ways. Puller had not even asked where Knox was staying. He doubted it was at the same motel. There weren't that many guests there; he probably would have seen her. He pulled into the parking lot and cut the engine, got out, and looked around. There were two other cars parked in the lot, neither of which had been here when he'd left in the morning. They were clunkers, both with out-of-state license plates. That didn't bother him—his was an out-of-state plate too. This was probably a motel where folks traveling east or west, north or south would pull in for a night's sleep before heading on. Being in the middle of the country, Kansas, he knew, got a lot of such traffic.

He jogged up the steps to his room on the second floor and walked along the exterior passage to his door.

The next moment he had pulled his M11 and curled his finger around the trigger guard.

His door was open, not by much but enough. He distinctly remembered locking it that morning after leaving the light on for his cat.

And this motel did not provide daily maid service. You'd never see the maid, because she only showed up when you checked out, if then.

He slid to the side of the door and eyed the gap. Not wide enough to see anything. He nudged it open farther with his foot. He had both hands on his weapon and the next moment was inside the room, in a crouch, his M11 making defensive arcs in the air as he looked for a target to fire on.

He didn't find one. But he saw two things.

First, AWOL was curled up in a ball on the bed. Her slow breathing and languid toss of her tail showed him his pet was just fine.

The same could not be said of the person next to her on the bed.

Puller eyed the bathroom door and cleared that and the shallow closet before coming back over to the bed and looking down.

Air Force brigadier general Tim Daughtrey was quite dead.

15

THE OLD MOTEL probably had never seen so much activity. Local police were clustered around, talking, moving, observing, and otherwise getting in the way.

An Office of Special Investigations, or OSI, team had been flown in to head up the investigation. They were the Air Force's counterpart to Puller's CID. The Air Force had never lost a general in this way before, and as Puller surveyed what was going on he knew that every agent was taking special care to do things by the book.

He had been interrogated four times so far: once by the locals he'd summoned by dialing 911, then by a team sent over from Fort Leavenworth, next by a team of FBI agents in blue windbreakers and caps who looked grim and asked pointed questions and, at least it seemed to Puller, didn't entirely believe his story and were very curious about whether his brother had tried to contact him. When he had said no, the disbelief in one of the agent's eyes became palpable. Finally he was interviewed by the OSI personnel after they'd barged onto the scene and staked their claim as the lead investigative agency. The locals and the Army team had quickly backed down, though the FBI guys had pushed back some. Puller had found that the Bureau did not back down from anyone.

His statement had never varied. He had met with Daughtrey along with two other high-ranking personnel from the government. He had been assigned to investigate the escape of Robert Puller from the DB. He had been working the investigation from morning till night. He had arrived at his room about a quarter past eleven and found the general shot dead in his bed.

Puller had briefly been a suspect until Veronica Knox had shown up and corroborated that he had been with her up until a few minutes past eleven that night. Prelims on the TOD, or time of death, indicated Daughtrey had been killed around eight in the evening. That could change some, plus or minus, but for now Puller was in the clear.

Puller had gotten a text from Schindler about an hour after the news had broken about Daughtrey. The NSC suit wanted to meet.

Puller had lagged that request because people had been grilling him, and he also didn't want to leave the crime scene. He wasn't investigating it, for obvious reasons—he had only been preliminarily crossed off as a suspect, and that status could change. And OSI had made clear it was the lead agency because Daughtrey had been a flyboy. But he still wanted to watch what was going on.

Puller had seen with his own eyes that Daughtrey had been shot once in the direct center of the forehead. There had been no gun evident. No signs of forced entry, though the lock on the motel room door was not complicated. There had been little blood on the bed or on Daughtrey, which told Puller a great deal. At this time of year the sun set a little after seven. It got truly dark about thirty minutes later.

Puller had gotten here about eleven-fifteen. Based on Daughtrey's presumed time of death at around eight, that meant there was a nearly three-hour window, give or take, in which Daughtrey had been killed and then left here. Because he had been left, not shot here.

"I can see the wheels grinding."

He looked up to see Knox standing next to him.

"Exciting evening," she said, surveying the activity in the room.

"A bit more than I wanted, yeah," said Puller.

"So what's your take?"

"He wasn't killed here. He was shot elsewhere and his body dumped here."

"Lack of blood, bodily fluids, and other forensics residue?" said Knox, and Puller nodded.

"And there was a large exit wound on the back of his head. But the pillow wasn't damaged from the fired round, and there was very little blood on the pillowcase. So the heart had stopped pumping a long time before he was dumped here. And the room was clean otherwise."

"OSI figure that too?" asked Knox.

"Yes, at least from the little they've told me. For obvious reasons, they can't share a lot."

"My statement should have cleared you."

"It did. For now. Thanks for giving it."

"Just telling the truth. But why your room as the dumping ground?"

"Putting up a barrier to my investigation? Sending me a message I don't understand as yet? Just messing with me? Take your pick."

"We talked to a lot of people yesterday. They all know you're on the case. Maybe you made somebody nervous."

He shrugged. "Maybe I did. The question is, who and why?"

Knox looked over as they lifted Daughtrey from the bed, put him in a body bag, and carried him out on a gurney. The OSI team was congregated in a corner going over their notes, Puller could see. There was little evidence to be collected here, other than the body. The local cops, with really nothing else to do, trailed the gurney out of the room.

One of the OSI team came over to Puller and Knox.

"Chief Puller, I'd like to know more about your relationship with General Daughtrey."

"I didn't have a relationship. I had an assignment."

"Was he the only one who assigned it to you?"

"As I said before, there were others, but I'm not at liberty to disclose their names."

"Well, I'm going to have to insist that you do. This is a murder investigation, Puller. We've checked you out. You're CID. You know how this works. Murder trumps all."

"Not necessarily," said Knox, and the OSI man turned his attention to her.

She flashed her creds.

"You gave Puller his alibi."

"No, I told the truth. And there were lots of people in the restaurant where we ate. You can get their statements."

"Already working on it. I don't see INSCOM personnel every day."

"I would hope not."

"Is there something bigger going on here that I don't know about? And could it have to do with a high-profile prisoner going missing from DB who was also in the Air Force?" He glared at Puller. "And who happens to have the same last name as you?" He shook his head, apparently at the perceived absurdity of the situation.

Puller said, "I don't want to impede your investigation, because it would piss me off if someone were obstructing mine. Let me make some calls and then I'll tell you all I can tell you. But I take orders too. From a higher authority than either of us."

The OSI agent stared at him fixedly and then nodded. "I look forward to your call." He put a hand on Puller's shoulder. "And you don't plan to leave the area?"

"Not right now," said Puller. "But that could change."

"Don't let it change without contacting me," the man said firmly.

After he walked off Knox said, "You should

make that call, because the OSI guy doesn't look to be of a patient nature."

Puller pulled out his phone and walked outside.

* * *

Thirty minutes later Puller was sitting across from Schindler and Rinehart at a facility just off base from Leavenworth. Schindler looked harried. Rinehart looked calm but subdued.

Puller had given them a succinct report of his investigation so far, but leaving out, for his own reasons, the part about the blown transformers being taken by "people."

"Okay, you're filled in. Now you need to tell me what you want me to do," said Puller. "OSI wants names. *Your* names."

Rinehart shook his head. "That won't be happening, Puller. I'll run the interference on that. They'll back off."

"Right," said Puller, not sounding convinced of this. "You've got the facts. Your guy was shot somewhere else and left in my room. If it was done to try to incriminate me, it was done pretty amateurishly, because I have a rock-solid alibi."

"For God's sake, can we first focus on who would want Daughtrey dead?" interjected Schindler.

Puller noted the man's tie was askew, his hair ruffled, and he kept picking at his fingernails. He'd expected stronger stuff from the NSC.

"Okay," he said. "When was the last time you saw him?"

Schindler and Rinehart exchanged glances. Rinehart said, "Shortly after we left you, Daughtrey left us."

"So around eleven a.m. yesterday?" Puller glanced at his watch. It was now eleven in the morning and he hadn't yet gone to bed.

"Correct," answered Rinehart.

"Did he say where he was going? What he was going to do? Someone he was going to meet?"

"No," said Schindler. "We flew in early yesterday morning, had our meeting with you, and then went our separate ways."

"Where was he staying? At Leavenworth?"

"No. At the Hilton downtown. I did hear him mention he was going to make a run down to McConnell AFB in the next couple of days."

"The Air Force base near Wichita?" asked Puller, and Schindler nodded. "He was a one-star, wasn't he traveling with a staff? Entourage? Security?"

"If so, they traveled here separately," said Schindler, and Rinehart nodded in agreement.

"We flew out together on an Army jet. General Rinehart had his people with him. He's staying in officer quarters at Leavenworth. I'm also staying at Leavenworth as a guest of the general's."

Puller nodded and wrote all of this down. "So who would want to kill Daughtrey? Any ideas?"

Neither man said anything.

"Does that mean you have no ideas, or you can't tell me the ones you do have?"

"Every man of his rank has made an enemy of someone," said Rinehart. "But I wouldn't think to such a degree that they'd blow a hole in his head."

"He was assigned to STRATCOM?" said Puller suggestively. "Maybe the reason comes from there."

"I'll make inquiries," said Schindler.

Rinehart added, "STRATCOM, after all, is why the three of us were interested in this in the first place."

"OSI will be on to that angle as well, you can count on that," said Puller.

"As I said, I will run the interference on that," said Rinehart.

"Different branch of service," Puller pointed out, putting away his notebook.

"I'm not without influence over there," said

Rinehart. "And the Chairman of the Joint Chiefs was the best man at my wedding right out of West Point."

Schindler said, "Puller, your mission is still to find your brother. His escape may not be connected to the death of General Daughtrey."

"Or it may be the reason for it," replied Puller.

"Or," said Schindler, "your brother might have been the one who killed him."

16

PULLER CHECKED INTO another motel about a half mile from the other one. He locked the door and put a bureau against it, pulled the shades, put his phone on silent mode, turned out all the lights, lay on the bed fully dressed, and fell dead asleep for over six hours with AWOL next to him purring and licking her paws.

When he woke it was dinnertime and he had a voice mail on his phone.

It was Knox. She wanted to meet. He didn't call her back, at least not yet, because he didn't know if he wanted to meet. And he also had a few phone calls to make.

Later, he showered and changed into jeans, a windbreaker, and a white collared shirt. He slipped on his shoes and finally called her back while sitting on the bed.

"So where the hell have you been?" she said after two rings.

Already got me on her contacts list, interesting, he thought.

"Sleeping," he said.

"Nice."

"Yes, it was, thanks. What's up?"

"Developments."

"What are they?"

"Let's do it face-to-face," she said.

They met at the same diner where they'd had dinner the previous night. He had a slab of ribs coated in a Jack Daniel's rub, coleslaw heavy on the mayo, a side of salted steak fries, and a vegetable that looked green but was otherwise unrecognizable. He was washing it all down with a Budweiser.

Knox had a chef's salad with dressing on the side and water.

She looked his meal over and said, "You know, you could eat a little better."

"Yeah, and I'm sure the processed meat in that salad and the chemicals in the dressing won't give you cancer in ten years."

She sat back and glanced glumly down at her salad. He quickly looked her over. She was dressed in blue slacks, cream blouse, and a matching jacket. She didn't look remotely military. He had wondered about this before.

INSCOM. INSCOM on the creds.

He figured he had mysteries at both ends of this sucker, and all down the middle too.

He finished eating, downed the last swallow of his beer, and looked at her expectantly. "Okay, let's talk developments," he said in a prompting tone.

"I have info on the people who took the blown transformers."

He wiped his mouth with his napkin and sat back. "How'd you do that?" he asked slowly.

"Made some calls and ran down some leads while you were taking your beauty rest."

"Uh-huh. And?"

"And they weren't with the military."

"You've got my attention, Knox. The bay doors are wide open, so drop the bomb."

"That's all I have on that. They weren't military. I don't know who they are. Yet."

"Al Jordan said they 'outranked' him. That sounds military."

"I checked with him. It was just a figure of speech. Guys were in suits."

"No creds shown?"

"He said they were very intimidating."

"Uh-huh," said a clearly skeptical Puller. "By the way, technical question, do you treat INSCOM as *military* or not?"

She gazed sternly at him. "What exactly are you implying?"

"I'm not implying anything. I'm just asking a question."

"INSCOM is most definitely military. It's based at Fort Belvoir. That's an Army installation, in case you didn't know."

"Know it well. My CID group used to be there before we got shipped to Quantico."

"Well then?" she said, almost daring him to make another provocative comment.

He decided to take up the dare. Maybe it was the Jack Daniel's rub on the ribs, or the little green things masquerading as veggies, which were now simmering uncomfortably in his gut.

"I made a few calls tonight too."

"Calls to who?" she said stonily.

"I've been in the Army long enough to have a pretty deep Rolodex. INSCOM was formed in 1977 at Arlington Hall Station in Virginia. Intelligence, security, electronic warfare all at the level above corps, pretty big footprint."

"Yes, it is."

"You're divided into eight brigades and various intelligence, operations, and support groups and companies, with a CO who's a two-star, same rank as the guy currently heading up CID."

"I know the breakdown of my command, Puller. Feel free to skip the military history lesson."

"Oh, and you have one more function." He paused. "The Central Security Service."

She blinked but otherwise continued to look blankly at him.

"Central Security Service," he said again. "That's what they call INSCOM and its counterparts in the Navy and Air Force within *NSA*. Because the National Security Agency is also part of INSCOM, or INSCOM is part of NSA, however you want to look at it. Funny, you neglected to mention that you were with Central Security."

"I would find it very hard to believe that anyone in your 'Rolodex' would know whether I am or not."

"Are you?"

"Am I what?"

"NSA?"

She held out her lanyard with her creds on it. "It says INSCOM right here, Puller."

"I know what it *says*," he replied, and then said nothing else.

She let the lanyard drop and sat back. "And why would it matter to you where I'm actually attached? NSA, INSCOM, United States

Army?" She shrugged. "We're all Americans, Puller. All on the same side."

He said nothing. He just sat there staring at her with an expression that finally made her look away again.

He dropped some bills on the table for the meal and rose.

She said, "Walking out on me again? It's starting to get embarrassing. People will surely talk," she quipped, but her look was bordering on panic.

"Take care of yourself, Knox."

"Puller, the last time we parted like this, you found a dead body in your room."

"Are you saying you're involved in that?"

"No, of course not. But I have been assigned to work with you on this case."

"Well, *I* wasn't assigned to work with *you*. Now, I can't stop you from showing up, I guess. But here's where the partnership ends. At least on my side."

"You really need to rethink this."

"And you need to rethink whether dishonesty is really the best policy."

"I wasn't dishonest with you," she said sharply.

"But you weren't honest, so what would you call it?"

She folded her arms and looked away. This appeared to be an idiosyncrasy of hers, he noted, though he didn't know if she was truly not conscious of it, or used it to gain an advantage somehow while she thought of another lie.

She glanced up at him. "Can we talk about this in a less public place?"

"Not if you're just going to keep running in circles. I don't have time for that."

"I will be as frank as I can be. How does that sound?"

"I guess we'll find out." He turned and walked off.

She jumped up, dropped a twenty-dollar bill on the table, and hurried after him.

Outside he was already standing at the side door of his car. "I'll drive, you can talk," he said.

She assented to this by opening the passenger door and climbing in.

Puller hung a left at the next intersection and then headed away from town. Leavenworth wasn't that big and they were soon out of the downtown business district and passing residential streets where houses dotted the dark landscape.

She said, "I need to know if I was positively

identified by anyone you talked to as being with CSS."

"Why?"

"Why do you think? It's not like I advertise my position."

"So you *are* with Central Security?"

"*Did* anyone?" she persisted.

"No."

"So it was just a guess on your part?"

"Not entirely."

"What do you mean?"

"Every uniform I've ever met will automatically relay their rank and what unit they're assigned to. I go to the Pentagon or I go to buy groceries and see another soldier at the checkout, I say, 'Hey, I'm a chief warrant officer with the 701st CID based out of Quantico. Before that I was a sergeant first class with 3rd Battalion, 75th Ranger Regiment out of Fort Benning.' Rank plus squad, platoon, company, battalion, brigade, division, corps, it's all just part of the DNA. We're all attached to something. And we want you to know what that something is. Point of pride, point of belonging. It's a fact of being a soldier. There's no getting around it."

"And I didn't give you my rank until you asked, and I told you," she said resignedly. "And didn't specify a particular unit."

"And when we first met you addressed me as 'Agent Puller.' I'm a chief warrant officer. Anyone actually in uniform would automatically address me as 'Mister' or 'Chief.' Never as 'Agent.'"

"Strike two," she said, clearly irritated.

"And you just don't seem military to me, Knox."

"Is that right?" she said in a slightly offended tone, and her body stiffened.

"Oh, you look to be in good shape. But that's not the issue."

"So what gave me away?"

"I've been in the Army for fifteen years. Before that I was an Army brat from the day I was born. I can smell uniforms from under any layer they try to cover themselves with. And with you, I didn't get a whiff." He paused. "Were you really in Iraq?"

"Yes," she said quietly. "But not in uniform. I was gathering intelligence."

He glanced at her. "So you *weren't* on the front lines." She didn't reply. "Knox, I said—"

"Pull over," she interrupted.

"What?"

"Just pull over!"

He steered the car to the side of the road and shifted to park.

She turned on the interior dome light, un-
hitched her shoulder harness, untucked her
shirt, and pulled her slacks and underwear on
the left side down to near the bottom of her left
hip. Puller simply gaped, wondering what the
hell was going on.

Until he saw it.

In the middle of the soft white skin was a
long ugly scar riding on her left hip that carried
around to the fleshy edge of her left buttock.
The scar was a dull red, the suture tracks still
evident. Though the underlying wound it represented was probably long since healed, it still
looked painful.

She said, "I got this courtesy of shrapnel from
incoming mortars and RPGs. I was in a motorcade heading into Basra. Rebels were trying
to retake it. They were closer and better armed
than we thought. Five of my people died. I
wasn't sure I'd walk again. The shrapnel came
really close to my spine and I couldn't feel my
legs for about two weeks. Turned out to be
concussive paralysis due to the inflammation
and swelling. But it finally went away after I
lived on prednisone and the surgeons finally
got all the metal out and I worked harder than I
ever had in my life. And I eventually got all the
way back. Except when it rains. Then my hip

and butt cheek ache like a bitch. All in all I consider myself the world's luckiest person. A lot
luckier than the rest of my team."

Puller remained quiet for a few seconds and
then said, "Just so you know, while I doubted
where you came from, I never doubted your
patriotism. Or your courage."

She slowly pulled her slacks and underwear
back up and tucked in her shirt.

"I can't believe I just did that. Hell, I've dated
guys for months who *never* saw *that*." She
paused and looked out the window. "I just…I
just didn't want you to think I couldn't hold
up my end of the load, Puller. Because I can. I
know this part of the world is still very much a
man's world. But I'm damn good at what I do."

"Like your patriotism and courage, I never
doubted that either, Knox."

She turned to him. "In my line of work sometimes I have to deceive. But I don't like having
to mislead people like you."

"Okay," said Puller. "Anything else you need
to tell me? Or *can* tell me?"

"I had a dual purpose coming here."

"The first was to work with me."

"The second was to watch you, closely."

"Why?" he asked.

"I thought that would be obvious."

"Your bosses really think I'm involved in my brother's escape?"

"No, that's not it. But they think he may try to contact you at some point."

"And why do you think he would do that?"

"Because with your father the way he is, you're the only family he has left. And all reports indicate you two are very tight."

"So you hoped I would lead you right to him?"

She slipped her shoulder harness back on and clicked the latch. "I never thought it would be that easy or clear, but we couldn't simply disregard the possibility. Everyone goes after the low-hanging fruit first."

"My brother is way too smart to make a mistake that stupid." Puller put the car in drive and got back on the road.

"So where are we going?" she asked.

"To see the body of the dead guy left in my brother's cell. I was supposed to go this morning, but as you know, another dead body got in the way."

"It's sort of late."

"Yeah, but if we wait any longer, the body might disappear like the transformers."

They drove along for a few minutes in silence.

"So are we good?" she asked, breaking the quiet.

"For now, Knox."

"You know, you can call me Veronica."

He shot her a glance. "I like Knox better. It seems to suit you."

She frowned. "In what way?"

He pushed the gas down and the Chevy jumped forward. "As in *Fort* Knox."

When he looked over at her again, she was actually smiling.

CHAPTER

17

THERE WERE MULTIPLE possibilities, Robert Puller knew. He was sitting in another motel room staring at his computer.

The sheer arithmetic of the challenge was compelling.

Officially, there were seventeen American intelligence agencies.

Officially.

While much of the recent media attention had been focused, for good reason, on the NSA and the famous or infamous—depending on your position—Edward Snowden, the fact was the NSA was merely one cog in an ever-expanding wheel known under the rubric of the IC, which stood for "intelligence community."

With nearly thirteen hundred government organizations and two thousand private companies in over ten thousand locations spread across the country, employing close to a million people, a third of those private contractors, all holding top secret clearances or higher, the IC employed about two-thirds as many people in the United States as did Wal-Mart.

By Executive Order 12333, the IC had six primary objectives. These were burned into Puller's brain. Yet there was one on which he was especially focused right now. It was catchall that gave titanic power to the executive branch.

Puller recited it in his head: *Such other intelligence activities as the president may direct from time to time.*

Encapsulated in those thirteen words was nearly incalculable discretion, with the only restriction being the size of the sitting president's ambitions. When it ran up against legal restrictions, government lawyers employed that loophole as an end run around the courts. And since Congress did little oversight of this area, the end run usually worked.

When he was at STRATCOM, Puller had not judged whether this was right or wrong. His work had benefited from these legal tactics. Now he had a slightly different perspective on them. Well, perhaps more than slight. The NSA was part of the IC. Legally, the NSA, which was known as the "ears" of American intelligence, could not listen in on the conversations of American citizens without a court order. But now much of what the NSA and rest of the IC collected was digital. And the world's global data streamers had no national boundaries. Google, Facebook, Verizon, Yahoo, Twitter, and the like had data centers, fiber-optic cables, switches and server farms, and other such infrastructure all over the world. And because many solely American "transactions" took them over this foreign-based infrastructure, they were ripe for exploitation.

Sophisticated sweep tools would unpack and decode the data formats used by the global Internet providers, and built-in filters would analyze the content and select information for poaching, directing them into a buffer for three to five days of perusal before it was turned over to open up storage space. And because data collected by the IC overseas was largely unregulated, there was a massive collection of content and metadata from U.S. citizens, including email addresses of the sender and receiver, video, audio, and photos. So anytime you sent data over the Internet, people you never intended to receive this information would in fact get it. And what would they do with it? Well, you'd never know until they knocked on your door one day and pushed their badges in your face and told you that your right to life, liberty, and the pursuit of happiness was officially over.

Puller bent low over the map on his computer and studied the possibilities.

Nebraska, Colorado, Wyoming, Virginia, Maryland. If he really wanted to be all-inclusive he could add in the states of Texas, Washington, and Arizona. That was the footprint, at least the most obvious one, of the IC's guts. One thing he knew he would not be doing—staying in Kansas.

He set that particular problem aside for the moment and refocused on the man in his cell. He had a sketch of him, but a sketch had no value in tracking him down. You couldn't run a sketch effectively through a database.

Or could you?

He left his room, walked to his truck, and drove off.

Two hours later he was back in his motel room with several things: a Samsung Galaxy tablet with built-in camera, glossy paper, a color printer/scanner, and a few boxes of art-related materials.

He unwrapped these tools and set about his task of turning a sketch into something more substantial. He needed to turn it into a face. A face with color and texture and points that a digital scan would better recognize.

It was dark outside when he'd finished the picture. He was so hungry he walked to a nearby McDonald's and gobbled down a Big Mac and large fries, plus a giant diet Coke to counterbalance the fat and sodium he'd just ingested, before going back to his room and moving on to the second part of his task.

He took a picture of his drawing with the Galaxy tablet and downloaded it to the printer. He loaded the printer with the glossy photo paper and printed out a picture. He examined it closely under the light.

Then he took a snapshot of the glossy print with his tablet camera. He downloaded that photo from the tablet to his laptop and brought it up on the screen. It looked more like a photograph now, the pixel images stark against the glossy background. Then he started to work on the photo, adding color to the skin, hair, and eyes. When he was done he sat back and studied it again. Again, he was satisfied.

But the proof of how good it was would come in the next step.

Using the software on his laptop, he hacked into the first database and ran the photo through the files held there. It took thirty minutes but he did not get a hit. He spent the rest of the night running it through every database he could break into.

It was four o'clock in the morning when he conceded defeat. For now.

The unknown man would remain unknown. Again, for now.

He was running a risk doing this. Access to the databases was monitored. Even though he had hacked in through a back door, there would be indications of the breach. They might try to track it back to him. They might succeed. If he had learned one thing spending most of his adult life in the cyber world, it was that there would always be someone better than you coming down the pixel path. There were fourteen-year-old amateur hackers and Xbox players out there whose skill would rival the very best the NSA had. It was just the way this area worked. If your brain was wired that way, you could do pretty much anything. And if you were fearless, as most kids were, you could hack into the Pentagon or Swiss bank accounts. It was all right there for the taking, because pretty much everyone was connected to the digital universe somehow.

Puller slumped back on his bed, his belly grumbling as it still digested his fast-food dinner. He had to sleep because he had to be well rested and on top of his game from here on. But his thoughts dwelled on the man.

He had been someone. And knowing who that someone was would lead to someone or something else. The man had come to the prison for a specific purpose.

Fortunately for Robert Puller, that specific purpose had not been carried out.

Because, he thought, *I'm still alive.*

CHAPTER

18

THE LIGHTS POPPED on, bright and harsh and direct. Puller and Knox blinked to adjust to this and then waited as the door was opened and the body rolled out on a metal freezer bed.

The military medical examiner was a man in his fifties with graying hair, a trim build, and large muscular hands. He looked a little put out because Puller's call had caused him to climb out of his bunk, get dressed, and show up here.

He held a clipboard in one of those hands as he slid down the sheet with the other, revealing the body of a tall man in his thirties with close-cropped hair, a chiseled physique, and no facial hair. Puller noted the Y-incision already carved in the man's chest and the suture tracks that had sewn this massive postmortem cut back together, with the organs placed neatly in the chest cavity.

"Cause of death?" asked Puller.

The ME pointed to the base of the neck. "In laymen's terms, a broken neck."

"Manner of death?" asked Puller.

"Someone broke it."

"So he didn't fall, hit his head?"

"No. It wasn't a compression injury with vertebrae collapsing on each other that you would associate with a fall like that. Nor was it an injury you would see in a hanging where the vertebrae are separated vertically. Here it seems that the neck was snapped horizontally."

Puller looked instantly intrigued by this observation. "Horizontal? Side to side?" He held up his hands like he was gripping a head and then pulled one hand to the right and one to the left. "Like that?"

The ME considered this. "Yeah, pretty close. How'd you figure that?"

"Any other wounds?"

"None that I could find, and I looked for a long time."

Puller looked down at the body, going over it inch by inch, starting at the head and moving to the feet. He bent closer and examined the forearms a second time.

"What do you think those are?" he asked.

The ME looked where Puller was pointing.

There were three slight indentations in the skin. They were uniform and evenly spaced.

"I noted those. It might have been an article of clothing or something else he was wearing that made those impressions. Or he might have even been bound somehow, although I'm not sure how that could have been the case. He certainly wasn't found tied up in the cell."

"What clothes did he have on?"

"Jeans, long-sleeved shirt, and canvas boat shoes."

"So he walked into a max-security military prison dressed like that?" said Knox. "Are you kidding?"

"My job is to check the body and make my report on the cause, time, and manner of death," replied the ME, stifling a yawn. "You guys get to play Sherlock Holmes."

"And what was the TOD?" asked Puller.

"They called me in right when they found the body. He'd been dead at most two hours."

"You got an ID on him yet?" asked Puller.

"Nothing popped on the fingerprints or facial recognition databases, and they usually do for those in the ranks. I took a dental impression and also DNA samples. They'll be sent up to AFDIL in Dover," he said, referring to the Armed Forces DNA Identification Lab.

Puller said, "Can you ask for stat service? Otherwise, it could take weeks. Even with an expedited reply we're looking at one to four days."

"I can. But there's a backlog these days."

"Not as bad as when Afghanistan and Iraq were going full-bore," pointed out Knox.

"No, and thank God for that," said the ME.

"Can I see the flip side?" asked Puller, indicating the dead man.

He helped the ME turn the body over. Puller again started at the top and worked his way to the bottom. And once more he leaned in closer, this time when he reached the calves. The traces were barely visible, but they were also three in number and uniformly spaced.

"Did you see these?" he asked.

The ME leaned in and then used a handheld light with attached magnifier. He pointed to one faint line. "I thought that one might be from his sock line. But I didn't see the other two," he added in a distressed tone. "Although his legs are particularly hairy. You must have great eyesight."

Puller straightened. "I saw them because I was looking for them. Based on what I saw on the forearms." He helped the ME roll the body back to its original position.

"What do you mean?" Knox asked.

Puller didn't answer her. He glanced at the ME. "Will you let us know as soon as you have an ID on this guy? He looks military, but he might not be. Particularly if he doesn't show up in the databases."

The ME nodded.

Puller leaned down and more closely studied the dead man's features. "He actually looks Eastern European. Jawline, nose, cheeks, forehead." He lifted up one of the hands. "Calluses, heavy one on the right index finger's top pad."

Knox bent closer and looked at the finger. "From friction with a trigger?"

Puller nodded. "Maybe. Can I see the teeth?"

The ME used a tool to open the mouth and lever back the lips. Puller peered inside the mouth. "Guy's never been to a dentist. Bad teeth but no metal."

He nodded to the ME, who let the mouth close.

"Can you run an isotope toxicology on the hair? With that you can tell where he's from, or at least where he's been recently, right?"

The ME said, "That's right. Hydrogen and oxygen isotopes transferred to hair from food and water taken in by the person as well as from the air they breathe. His hair is pretty short so it won't give me a broad spectrum to work with. Head hair grows at a rate of about one to one point five centimeters a month. With hair as short as his any answer will be locked in to where he was recently."

"I think that might be good enough."

"Understand that while the U.S. has a pretty good isotope map on water and air differentials, other countries may not. If he's from some obscure third world nation we might not get a hit."

"We'll never know until we try. As soon as you can get it done would be appreciated."

"Roger that, Chief Puller."

"And, Doc?" said Puller. The ME looked at him. "Keep what we just discussed on the QT for now, okay?"

The ME's brow wrinkled. "But I have reports to make and—"

"Just for now, QT, okay? For a lot of reasons. One of the major ones being I don't see how any of this happened without some help on the inside. So that means we might have someone playing against us who we *think* is on our side."

The ME gaped at him and then closed his mouth. He nodded curtly. "Right."

Puller walked down the corridor so fast Knox had to hustle to keep up.

"Where are you going?"

"To look at surveillance camera footage."

"At this hour?"

"Why, you got a date or something?"

"But we've already looked at the feed from inside the prison."

"But we haven't looked at the feed from *outside* the prison."

* * *

"Hold it right there," said Puller, and Knox clicked the key to freeze the frame.

They were sitting in a cubicle at the DB reviewing the surveillance camera footage from the entrance to the prison.

Puller ran his gaze over the trucks that had just rammed the front gates of the prison.

"Now do it in slow motion."

She did so and Puller started to count, jotting down numbers in his notebook. He had her back up the video and repeat the process twice. When he'd finished, he said, "Okay, let's see the exit."

She brought this footage up and then hit the computer keys to make it move forward slowly. She watched as Puller started to count again. He had her repeat the video as he had done before. And he wrote down more numbers. When he was done she stopped the feed and sat back, looking at him expectantly.

"Well?" she asked.

"Fort Leavenworth dialed up an entire company of MPs to take control of DB. They came in six heavy trucks. Four platoons, totaling one hundred and thirty-two men, and the leadership component, a captain and his first sergeant."

"Okay?"

"The six drivers stayed with the vehicles, but I counted one hundred and thirty-three men in riot gear getting off those trucks. Plus the captain and the first sergeant."

"So one hundred and thirty-five men in total."

"When there should have been only one hundred and thirty-four."

"So one extra?"

"And I counted one hundred and thirty-five men coming out of the prison in riot gear. They climbed into those trucks and drove off."

"So the numbers tally? But we still have the extra guy."

"But what if the dead man was one of the platoon members going *in*?"

She shot him an astonished look. "What?"

"The strap marks on the body? The ones on

his arms I think were from hard-shell forearm and elbow protectors. And the parallel marks on the calves were from the straps on the shin guards."

"But, Puller, that's *riot* gear."

He nodded. "The same gear we just saw on the video feed. That means our dead guy might have been part of the reinforcements sent from Fort Leavenworth."

"But obviously he didn't come back out."

Puller observed, "But we have the *same* number of soldiers coming out as went in. What does that tell you?"

Knox thought about this for a few moments, then her eyes widened. "Shit, your brother took his place?"

Puller nodded. "He could have broken that guy's neck, dressed as him, and escaped that way, as part of the MP reinforcements. It was dark, chaotic. They wouldn't do an ID check on a guy in full riot gear. So he climbs back on one of the trucks, which returns to the fort. Four platoons of soldiers climb off, go their separate ways, and he just scoots off the base."

She looked at him, obviously impressed. "Puller, that is some damn fine deducing. I never would have picked up on the number of MPs going in and out."

Puller looked thoughtful. "But it would be difficult to do all that in the dark. Remember, no lights in the prison. My brother would have to kill a guy who was armed and probably armored without anyone seeing or hearing anything. Then he had to get all that gear off the body and then put it on, all in the dark. Lots of potential holes in that theory."

"There was also lots of noise to cover up anything they were doing. The dead guy no doubt had a flashlight in his gear pack. If the cell door was closed, or his team saw him clearing that cell, there would have been no need for anyone else to go in. I think you figured out how it all went down."

Puller didn't respond to this.

Knox, who had been tensed, relaxed. "Look, I know this must be really hard for you."

"Why, because he's my brother?"

"No, because he's your sister. Of course because he's your *brother*!"

"You're wrong. He's not my brother. Right now, he's just an escaped prisoner who may or may not have been involved in the murder of an unidentified person."

"Well, I think you just answered one really big question. How he got out."

"Yeah. And created about a dozen more."

19

PULLER WAS DRIVING and Knox sat beside him staring moodily out the window.

"How did you think of the manner in which the neck was broken?" she asked, turning to him. "A horizontal break? You showed the ME how it could be done."

"The snap-crackle-pop. At least that's what we call it. It's a technique they teach in the Rangers and the Marine Corps. It's used to quickly kill, typically perimeter security of a target you're trying to take. Hand and forearm cups the top of the head. Other hand and forearm rests at the base of the neck. You apply the requisite foot-pounds of force in separate directions, the neck snaps right in two. Clean and quick and silent."

"But they don't teach that in the Air Force?"

"I don't know what they teach in the Air Force other than to tell their people not to jump out of a perfectly good plane. They leave that to us grunts toting rifles and eighty-pound rucks."

"Okay, but did you by chance teach your brother the maneuver?"

Now Puller glanced at her. "Are you interrogating me?"

"No, just asking a simple question."

"I don't remember. That's my simple answer."

She glanced once more out the window. "Looks like a storm is rolling in," she observed.

"Then maybe we'll have another blackout and another prison escape," retorted Puller.

She shot him a glance. "Don't even joke about something like that."

"We need to ID that guy."

"I know."

"And I don't want to wait however long it's going to take the guys in Dover to do it. And since I don't think he's an American, they probably won't find anything anyway."

"And the ME said he didn't get a hit in the military database off the prints or facial recognition. So it's doubtful he's military."

"At least not *our* military. Which leads to another question."

"What's that?"

"Four platoons."

"Right, but now we think your brother might have taken the dead guy's place. After killing him," she tacked on, perhaps just to see Puller's reaction.

He ignored this. "How did the dead guy get into Fort Leavenworth? And how did he manage to join a company of soldiers going to quell a possible crisis at DB?"

"Well, he must've gotten onto the base somehow. And it was chaotic. If he was dressed in riot gear I doubt anyone took the time to do roll call."

"Which means this all was planned out, Knox. The transformers blowing. The backup gas generator breaking down. The sounds of explosion and gunfire. The Army manual is clear on that. You call in reinforcements. Whoever planned this, they knew how the Army would react and they had a guy at Leavenworth ready to join in."

"But why, Puller? What was he going to accomplish?"

"Helping my brother to escape, maybe?"

"But the guy ended up dead."

Puller said, "Maybe the plan changed. Maybe someone else other than my brother killed him."

"How was he planning on getting your

brother out? There's no evidence that he had a second set of riot gear with him. Your brother probably took his gear. In fact, that's the only way he could have gotten out. So, the guy *had* to die. And they were about the same size." She looked at Puller. "Your brother's about six-three? About two hundred pounds or so?"

"Around that."

"So was the dead guy."

"But why go in on a mission like that if you know it's suicidal?"

"Maybe he didn't know it was suicidal," replied Knox.

"Well, if he didn't then he had to believe he was going in there for some reason that had the possibility of him getting out alive. And we have to find out who came and took those transformers." He eyed her pointedly when he said this. "That's what started this whole chain of events. The transformers blowing."

"Puller, I don't know who did that. I'm telling you the truth."

"I did some reading online. INSCOM conducts operations for military commanders."

"No big secret."

"But you're also tasked to do the same for 'national decision makers.' That term is both suggestive and fluid. Could include folks like the president, the secretary of state, Speaker of the House."

"I'm not here on behalf of any of them, I can assure you."

"And the head of NSA also runs the U.S. Cyber Command."

"I was aware of that."

"Interesting."

She shrugged. "There's a lot of overlap. Some claim they're mirror images of each other. Although NSA operates under Title 50 while Cyber Command checks in under Title 10 authority."

"Is that an important distinction?"

"Maybe, maybe not. There's talk that the entities will have different leaders in the future. Fact is they're now both full-time jobs. But they'll always be operationally related."

"And they're both based at Fort Meade."

"Yes."

"Kissing cousins, then."

"Not a term I'd use," she said, sounding slightly offended.

"Somebody came and got the transformers, Knox. And the guy they took them from said they outranked him. But that's all he would say. That tells me he was told to say no more. Even to the official investigators."

"Which tells you what?"

"That there are multiple investigations—both official and unofficial—going on here along with multiple agendas. It's hard enough to solve a crime without all that baggage. And that baggage is definitely coming from spook central. I can feel it in my official Army jockey shorts."

"Well, what exactly do you want me to do about it?"

"We're a team. Or at least that's what you led me to believe. So based on that the answer to your question should be pretty obvious."

"You want me to find out if anybody on the intelligence side had anything to do with the transformers' disappearance?"

He forced a smile. "I'll make you into an investigator yet, Knox."

Ignoring his sarcasm, she said, "Maybe that's what I'm afraid of. Speaking of spooks, any ideas on Daughtrey?"

"If my brother killed the man back in the prison, he could have killed Daughtrey."

"Why?"

"They both worked at STRATCOM."

"So you think that's at the center of this?"

"I have no idea. You know more about that world than I do. And it's a big one. A lot bigger than most people realize."

"Did you know that Cyber Command technically comes under STRATCOM's leadership?"

He looked at her questioningly. "But how does that work with NSA?"

"It's all very incestuous, Puller. NSA operates from under hundreds of intelligence platforms. You never know where the tentacles are going to reach."

"Then how the hell does anybody keep all of it straight?"

"I think that's the point. They don't want anyone knowing enough to keep things straight. Then they might have to start answering some tough questions."

"Makes congressional oversight damn difficult."

"Damn near impossible," amended Knox. "Which, again, is the central point."

He eyed her curiously. "These are puzzling observations coming from someone in the intelligence sector."

"Just because I work there doesn't mean I have to drink all the Kool-Aid. And have you wondered about something else?"

"What?"

"What your brother was sent to prison for."

"He was charged with national security crimes. Treason."

She said in a scolding tone, "And you weren't curious about the *exact* circumstances? That's surprising for an *investigator*."

"I did wonder. I wondered a lot. As soon as I got back from deployment overseas I checked into it. My brother was already in prison. But I did investigate."

"And?"

"And the file was sealed. I couldn't get anyone to even return a phone call or meet with me. Everything was completely hushed up. Not even the media really got wind of anything. It didn't make any of the newspapers and I only saw one item about it on CNN, and then it just went away like dust in a black hole in space."

"So you don't know what he was convicted of?"

He glanced sharply at her. "Why? Do you know anything about it?"

"I think we might want to find out about it."

Puller kept driving as he thought about this.

She said, "Or do you not want to know if your brother is really guilty or not?"

"He was convicted."

"And in your experience an innocent person has never been convicted?"

"Not that many."

"*One* is too many," said Knox.

"But if the file is sealed on my brother's case?"

"You're the investigator. You must have some ideas on how to find out things. And if I'm going to stick my neck out about these transformers gone missing, you can do the same with your brother's case."

And she said no more as they drove along right into the gathering storm that might as well have been inside the car as well as outside it.

20

HE AWOKE AT noon and slowly looked around.

Robert Puller had been dreaming that he had escaped from the DB. So when he woke, he thought he would see the interior of his prison cell.

But I did escape. I am free. For now.

A few minutes later he showered, careful to keep the soap and water off his altered face, and changed into his one other set of clothes. He would have to go shopping soon if he managed to maintain his freedom. He looked at himself in the mirror, if only to confirm that he still didn't look a thing like himself. He just needed to avoid being arrested, because he couldn't change his fingerprints, DNA, or retinal marker. His belly grumbling again, he drove to a twenty-four-hour diner and ate at the counter. Over his scrambled eggs, bacon, and buttered biscuits he read the local paper, a copy of which was sitting on the counter. The story he stumbled on had not made the front page and he wondered why.

Air Force General Found Dead in Motel Room in Leavenworth, Kansas.

He read on. Timothy Daughtrey, age forty-three and a one-star general in the Air Force, had been visiting the area on military business. He had not been staying at the motel. And there was no information on how he got there or the motive for his death, nor were there any suspects. There was a hotline number for people to call with information.

Puller searched his memory. Daughtrey. Timothy Daughtrey. He didn't recall the name, but then again the Air Force was a pretty big entity. It might be totally unrelated or it might be directly connected to what was going on with him.

He finished his breakfast and carried the paper with him back to the motel. He got online and did a search on the dead general. There were numerous references to him, including a Wikipedia page. He ran his eye down the page.

There it is.

He was with U.S. Cyber, a command component of STRATCOM.

Daughtrey had been assigned there just over

four months earlier, well after Puller had gone to the DB.

His career looked pretty straightforward. There was even a YouTube video of the man pontificating about military matters on some obscure show that probably only people in uniform, and only certain ones of those, would bother to watch. He seemed intelligent and straightforward on the video. Stupid people did not get assigned to STRATCOM. But he was assuredly not straightforward. Such people also did not get assigned to STRATCOM. In fact, reading between the lines of the video interview, Puller came away with the impression that Daughtrey had learned more about the interviewer than the journalist had learned about him, or, more importantly, about STRATCOM.

Yet now he was dead and they had no leads. Murdered in Leavenworth while there on military business. And what business would that be? U.S. Cyber Command was headquartered at Fort Meade in Maryland. The closest Air Force base out here was McConnell in Wichita. But if he were doing STRATCOM business in this part of the country he would have likely gone to Offutt AFB in Nebraska. The satellite office that Puller had worked at in Kansas had closed and the operation had been consolidated at the partially renovated Offutt.

So why was he in Leavenworth, Kansas? The answer seemed suddenly obvious.

Because that's where I escaped from.

As he looked at the face of the dead man on the YouTube video, Puller nodded. That had to be the connection. *He* had to be the connection.

He looked at the newspaper article once more. The motel where the body had been found was a relatively short drive away. He was making no progress with his database searches on the dead man back at the prison. He was still debating when to head out of Kansas and on to another location that might yield answers. But he had time for a side trip. In fact, in some respects, he had all the time in the world.

He left his room and got into his truck and drove back to Leavenworth. He found the motel, passed by it, and noted the military guards posted out front to secure the crime scene. The motel was like the one he was staying in right now in KC. Cheap, run-down, as well as off the beaten path.

A one-star's travel allowance would have paid for a much nicer place. Puller also knew Daughtrey could have stayed, as a professional courtesy, in officer quarters at Fort Leavenworth. The various service branches were nothing if not hospitable to each other, if only to show off what they had.

He parked on the street and doubled back, walking slowly past the motel's entrance before heading on. He reached the corner and stepped partway into an alley, keeping the place under observation. He felt his heart beating faster and knew that being out in the open like this was still a new thing for him. He had been on twenty-three and one at the DB: solitary confinement for twenty-three hours before being allowed out of his cage for a single hour. Now to be freely walking the streets and filling his belly in a diner in the middle of dozens of people was a heady change. He refocused on the motel, and moments later his decision to come here paid off in a way Robert Puller could never have imagined.

A white Chevy sedan pulled up to the curb in front of the motel. Puller locked on this ride because the make, model, and color screamed military. A man and a woman got out.

When Robert Puller saw his brother emerge from the car, he froze, yet only for a second. Then he inched more deeply into the alley, but kept his gaze squarely on his younger brother's tall, imposing physical presence.

What the hell was he doing here?

This wasn't a CID case. And even if it were, the Army would never have allowed John Puller to work on it, if only because it might have a connection to his brother's case. The military not only disliked appearances of impropriety, it loathed them.

But there he was, in the flesh, and he was heading past the guards after flashing his creds. The woman with him was tall, slender, and auburn-haired, but Puller did not get a good look at her face.

So my brother is investigating this case. And I wonder what else he's investigating?

Would the military really let one brother go after another?

Robert Puller had thought a lot about his brother and what he would make of his older sibling doing a bunk from the DB and leaving behind a dead body. But never once, with all his brilliance and built-in paranoia from working so long in the intelligence field, had he imagined his brother working an investigation whose one goal would be to bring Robert Puller in, dead or alive, as melodramatic as that sounded.

And certain people might very well prefer me dead.

He waited for his brother to disappear from his line of sight and then left the alley and quickly made his way back to his truck. He was confident of his new face and altered appearance. But he had learned that his younger brother's powers of observation were far beyond the norm. Sometimes they were even scary. So he was taking no chances.

He reached his truck, climbed in, and then just sat there.

His thoughts were now totally focused on one thing, and they had nothing to do with a dead man in a prison cell.

His brother was *here*.

And Robert Puller did not even want to think about where things might end up.

Things were already complicated enough.

Now? What he was trying to do seemed impossible.

Because his little brother might be standing right in the way.

CHAPTER

21

JOHN PULLER SAT in his motel room staring at a wall. He and Knox had slept in after their late night. Then they had driven back to the motel where Daughtrey had been found. Puller didn't know what he expected to find there the second time around. And ultimately he had discovered nothing new or helpful. Then he and Knox had spent the entire day running down more leads, but absolutely nothing had popped on any of them. Now it was night again and their investigation hadn't progressed one iota.

And something Knox had said was sticking in his head like a Ka-Bar knife driven into his skull.

Or do you not want to know if your brother is really guilty or not?

Do I want to know? Or not?

He slipped his phone out of his pocket. It felt like a brick.

He thumbed through his contacts list until he

settled on the one he wanted. He checked his watch. It was late and even later on the East Coast, but the person was a night owl. Puller knew many such night owls; he tended to be one himself.

He listened to the phone ringing. On the third ring he heard the gruff voice.

"Yeah?"

"Shireen?"

"Who the hell is this?" The gruff had moved on to annoyance.

"John Puller."

Puller heard a thump, like a book had been dropped, and a clink, like a glass with ice in it had just been set down. And knowing Shireen as he did, the glass was not filled with water. More likely gin with a splash of tonic, and ice cubes, because as she had once told him, it was important to keep cool *and* hydrated.

A few moments of silence were followed by, "John Puller? What are you doing with yourself these days?"

Shireen Kirk—her full name, Puller knew, was Cambrai Shireen Kirk—was a Judge Advocate General, or JAG, attorney. She'd had her professional shingle out for nearly twenty years and had been involved in several of the cases that Puller had investigated. Each of those cases had resulted in a conviction. She was now forty-four years old, petite and thin, with reddish-blonde hair cut in a bob and bangs that still showed plenty of her freckles—Irish sprinkles, she had called them once. She was based in D.C. and had a reputation for being brilliant, scrupulously honest, diligent, fair-minded, and a woman who would kick your ass if you lied to her, regardless of military rank. And she could drink anyone of Puller's acquaintance—and that included many large male beer lifters of prodigious capacity—under the table.

"This and that, Shireen," replied Puller.

"We haven't worked a case in a while."

"Maybe we're about due."

"Wait a minute, didn't you just shoot somebody in Nebraska?"

"Oklahoma."

"Right, one of those flyover states. Saw something come across my desk about it. You okay?"

"I'm fine. The other guy isn't. I didn't kill him, but he'll be walking funny for a while. Not how I wanted it to go down, but he didn't give me a choice."

"Where are you now?"

"Kansas."

There was a long moment of silence. Puller could almost hear her mind sorting through things and compiling data, with a conclusion soon forthcoming.

"DB," she said.

"DB's here, all right."

"A little surprised you are," she said warily, as though she were being wiretapped and suspected a legal trap.

"I was too. But it's all official and authorized."

She said in an incredulous tone, "You're not saying you're investigating the escape?"

"That's exactly what I'm saying."

"Get off it! You're shitting me."

"No."

"Has the Army lost its damn mind?"

"I can't really answer that."

"Then have you lost *your* mind?"

"I hope not."

"Well, I *hope* your authorizations go about as high as they can go, otherwise I might be prosecuting you for about a dozen violations of military law, Puller."

"I wouldn't be here if they didn't, Shireen."

"In writing. Sometimes a CO's memory sucks when the shit hits the fan."

"Got 'em in writing. Army three-star and the

NSC with trickle down the chain of command to my CO good enough for you?"

"Well sonofabitch, will wonders never cease? Why are you calling? If you're in Kansas it's too far to catch a beer together."

"I'm calling about my brother."

"What would I know about your brother? Other than he's apparently escaped from DB? And you're there, apparently investigating a crime you shouldn't be within a continent of?"

"That word 'apparently' again."

"What about it?"

"You're not the first to use it when talking about what happened."

"Well of course, Puller. Think about it. People don't escape from DB. And do you believe for one second the Army wants to admit to something like that? The bigwigs are probably still praying he got stuck in a ventilation hole and it was all a big misunderstanding."

"So my brother?"

She said nothing, but Puller could hear papers rustling and thought he detected the sound of a pen clicking. She seemed prepared to take notes. Whether this was a good thing or not, he wasn't sure.

"I need to find out about his case."

"His case?" she said.

"His court-martial."

"Find out what?"

"Basically everything."

"You don't already know about it?"

"No."

"Why not?"

"It was sealed. I'm assuming because of the issues involved."

"National security," she said, and Puller could imagine her head nodding and her perhaps frowning at this. He had found that Shireen Kirk did not like secrets on either end of a case. They were a lot alike in that regard.

"Right. But why do you need to know about his case?"

"I'm trying to find him. If I knew what he went to DB for it might generate some leads for me."

He hoped the late hour had reduced the efficiency of her bullshit meter.

"O-kay," she said slowly, skepticism oozing from both syllables.

"I think you'd agree that breaking out of DB is pretty remarkable."

"I think we can agree on that."

"And maybe he had help to do it."

"So you think whoever he was involved with before helped him escape?"

"It's a theory."

"He's been at DB for how long?"

"Over two years."

"Long time to wait to bust somebody out."

"Not really. Not if you have to acquire the tools with which to do so."

"Inside help, you mean?"

"That wouldn't come easily or cheaply. At least I hope it wouldn't, since it might implicate folks in uniform."

"Well, if the file is sealed, I'm not sure there's much I can do. And if you've been authorized to investigate this case you should be able to get it unsealed going through appropriate channels."

"Maybe, maybe not. But right now I prefer not to employ proper channels. And I was thinking that you might know people who could unseal it."

"That would take a court order, Puller," she said sharply. "Because it would have taken a court order to *seal* it."

"Well, I remember from high school science class that for every action there's an equal and opposite reaction."

"Yeah, and I remember from law school that a fool and her license to practice are soon parted."

"I'm not asking you to do anything unethical, Shireen, because I know you wouldn't. All I'm asking is for you to just see if there's any way I can find out about the case. Something I can read. Someone I can talk to. Anything is more than I have right now. The military never throws anything away. There has to be some record of it somewhere."

There was another pause and Puller started to wonder if she had hung up.

"Shireen?"

"Yeah, yeah, I'm still here. I'm just taking a minute to pull my head out of my ass for even contemplating helping you."

"But you *are* contemplating?" noted Puller hopefully.

"I'll make some calls. Anything comes of it, you'll hear from me. If nothing comes of it, you won't. Good enough?"

"Good enough. Thanks, Shireen."

"Don't thank me. This shit stinks so bad it's a wonder you're still breathing."

"I know it's out of the ordinary."

"It's not just out of the ordinary, it's unthinkable. Letting you work on this case violates every rule the Army has. And you better get *your* head out of *your* ass and wonder why they're really letting you do it. Because I can't think of a single reason that would benefit *you*, three-star and NSC approvals notwithstanding."

She clicked off and Puller put his phone back in his pocket.

He wasn't a lawyer, but he had spent enough time around them to know that they could smell a problem and potential downside from the other side of the world. They definitely looked at the glass half empty. And right now, maybe he should too.

Why do they really want me on this case?

Schindler, Daughtrey, and Rinehart had given him reasons for it. They seemed sound and plausible. But after what Shireen had just said they didn't seem that sound or that plausible. And now Daughtrey was dead.

He was still thinking about this when he heard the woman scream.

22

HIS HAND AUTOMATICALLY dipped to his holster and Puller slid out his M11.

It had been a female screaming, no doubt about that. He hustled to the room's single window and peered out. Four figures were there. There were three men and one woman, the one who had screamed. He wasn't speculating. She was screaming right now.

He eyed the men. He couldn't see their faces. The exterior lighting was poor and their backs were turned to him. He *could* see that two were roughly his size. The other was smallish. The woman was the smallest of them all. And a hand was around her throat as she was being dragged down the stairs.

Puller punched 911 on his phone and reported what he had just seen. Then he threw open the door and stepped out in time to see the group disappearing into an alleyway next to the motel.

He slipped quietly down the stairs, his M11 leading the way, and then sprinted across the courtyard. He stopped at the entrance to the alley and peered around the corner. Farther down the darkened alley he heard the woman scream. And he heard struggling.

There must be another exit from the alley. They might have a car waiting there. He picked up his pace.

And then he was sprawling on the pavement, his gun flying from his grip.

He rolled over and looked up. The three men looked back down at him. They were wearing ski masks. The woman was nowhere around.

This was an ambush and the girl was the bait. *And I'm an idiot because I fell for it.*

Three guns were pointed at him, so he had no choice but to get up slowly with his hands raised over his head.

They made him walk down the alley to where an SUV was waiting. He was pushed in, blindfolded, gagged, and his hands bound with a zip tie. The SUV pulled off.

In his head he estimated the drive time at about thirty minutes. That didn't help much in determining direction or destination, because the vehicle could have doubled back to throw him off. Since it was so late at night the normal sounds of the city weren't as evident. But he didn't think they were still in the city.

When they pulled to a stop the door was opened and he was pushed out. His feet crunched gravel. He was led up a short set of steps, through a doorway, and he heard it close behind him. He was pushed down into a chair and the gag removed.

He waited. He wasn't going to open the conversation, for he assumed that was why he was here. Otherwise, he'd be dead.

When the voice came on, it was hollow–sounding, like the speaker was standing in a hole. The person wasn't in the room, Puller knew. This was all being done remotely.

"Very cloak-and-dagger, I have to admit," said the voice, which had clearly been modified electronically. It sounded like Darth Vader, only on an indie film budget. But it might be significant, thought Puller, because he might not want his voice recognized.

He remained quiet, waiting. Whatever the man said, it would be information he didn't have previously. And if he got out of this alive, it could lead to something.

"I'm not here to make threats, Agent Puller. I'm here to appeal to your patriotism."

"You could have done that over the phone."

"That would have been awkward. I prefer this method."

"Kidnapping?"

"Let's call it an aggressive call for a meeting."

"With three guns pointed at me, I guess you can call it what you want."

"You're investigating Robert Puller's escape from prison. You hope to bring him back, alive rather than dead."

Puller kept his mouth shut.

"I want to know what you've found out so far. Do you know where he is?"

"No."

"Do you have any promising leads?"

"I must have missed the part ordering me to report to some voice."

"It would be in all of our best interests if you were to cooperate."

"Not how it works in my world. I'm a soldier. I have chains of command. I don't step outside them."

"So you won't share your investigation results?"

"You'll have to take that up with the United States Army."

"You hope to bring your brother in alive. I tell you that this is not possible."

"Why?"

"This is not possible," repeated the voice. "If you won't cooperate then I am asking you to stand down."

"I was ordered to investigate. I follow orders."

"There are many outs for you on that score," said the voice. "The command for you to participate in this investigation runs against every protocol the military has. You should not be part of this. You will ask to stand down on those reasons. Your objectivity has been compromised, and understandably so. It's your brother, after all. The United States Army is many things, Puller. But it is not unreasonable."

"And you would know this how?"

"Stand down, Agent Puller. That's all you have to do."

"The investigation will continue regardless of whether I'm part of it."

"That is not your concern. Will you stand down?"

"No."

"I will ask again. Will you stand down?"

Puller said nothing, because he had nothing else to add to what he'd already said.

"I can only add as an inducement that this is far bigger than a mere prisoner escaping from custody."

"Care to explain that?"

"To answer that would require disclosures that I am not prepared to make. Suffice it to say, you have my word that I am a patriot. The good of the country is firmly in my mind for whatever actions have been taken in the past or will be taken in the future."

"You didn't say what country. I doubt it's mine."

"You were described to me as stubborn, and tough and honorable. Those are all ideal attributes for those in uniform. But this, I'm afraid, is the exception that *disproves* that rule. Once more, will you stand down?"

"No."

"Then I'm afraid it's out of my hands."

"*Now* you're threatening me?"

"If only it were a threat, Agent Puller. Now, I'm afraid, it is a *fact*."

The voice cut off and the quiet returned.

And then he heard feet moving closer. And the rack on a weapon being slid back. Puller immediately tensed, his quads and calves bracing for what was to come.

The blindfold was taken off and he blinked quickly to adjust to the brightness provided by the overhead light.

A moment later Puller felt a gun muzzle placed against the side of his head.

And then the shots shattered the window and blew out the light.

Puller and the other man froze and then the man with the gun turned toward the window from where the shots had come. That was the only opening Puller needed.

He sprang sideways, thrusting his shoulder into the chest of the man holding the weapon. Bone, muscle, and cartilage met the same. Puller was the bigger man, with a forty-pound advantage on the other. They both flew backward in the direction from which Puller had attacked.

As Puller had hit the other man with his shoulder he'd locked one of his legs around the man's thigh and the other around his upper calf. Now he ripped the thigh one way and the lower leg the other and listened to the man scream as vital parts of his knee went helter-skelter. He and the now disabled man hit the floor and their momentum propelled them along the smooth boards. The other man crashed headfirst into the far wall and was knocked out by the impact.

Puller's hands were still tied behind his back. Very flexible for a big man, he turned the slide into a roll and slipped his bound hands under his legs so they were in front of him. He grabbed the toppled chair, swung it around, and crushed the piece of furniture into the chest of the second man who had just rushed into the darkened room. The man had managed to get two errant shots off before he took the chair to the chest and hurtled in the opposite direction and then flipped over a table. He lay there panting and moaning with pain.

Puller knelt next to the first man, searched his pockets, and found both his M11 and his cell phone. He snatched up the chair once more and flung it through the window. A second later he sailed through the shattered glass and landed outside. He was on his feet in an instant, looked in front of him, and then chose a path in under three seconds. When in doubt with people trying to kill you there was no perfect answer. There was only action.

He sprinted off in that direction and quickly reached a curve in the road that would put him out of the sightline of the house.

A minute later two men came careening out of the building where Puller had been held and looked around for their former captive. Not seeing him, they ran to the SUV, climbed in, and the driver started it up. They started to speed off but the vehicle began to wobble badly. The driver put the SUV in park and they jumped out to stare in disbelief at the four slashed tires.

* * *

Robert Puller watched all of this from the bushes on the right side of the house. He had fired his weapon through the window, shattering the light. It would have been a difficult pistol shot through glass, but the auto weapon he had was both devastating and incredibly accurate at short range. With the light shot out he knew his brother would have the advantage. Still, he had watched until the chair and then his brother came flying through the smashed window before retreating to his present location. He'd slashed the SUV's tires before taking up his sentry post at the window.

He quietly retreated to where his truck was parked. He had kept the engine running because it was quieter than trying to later start it. He'd also backed into the spot so he could now pull straight out. He climbed in, slipped the truck into gear, released the brake, eased out, and then basically let the truck's forward momentum take him where he wanted to go. Once he was sufficiently far away, he hit the gas and sped down the road.

Robert Puller had followed his brother from

the motel where General Daughtrey had been found. Then he had continued to follow him all the rest of the day, ending at the place where his brother was staying. He had seen the men force John into the SUV and he had followed them here. He didn't know what had gone on inside the house. He had heard snatches of a voice, but could not make out what had been said. He didn't know who the men were. He had made a quick search of the SUV, but there was no registration or other identification documents.

He could have charged into the house, but even with the brutally efficient weapon he was carrying he thought the odds of his winning the battle were too low. And he didn't want to jeopardize his freedom or his brother's life on bad odds.

He knew his brother could run a mile in less than six minutes and perform the Army standard two-mile run in a bit under twelve minutes. He checked his watch. John Puller should reach the main highway shortly. He would have found some way to defeat his bindings. He had a gun. He was safe.

Robert Puller pulled off to the side of the road. He did this for two reasons. He wanted to see if anyone was coming after his brother. And he also wanted to give John time to reach the main road. If he passed him in the truck, his brother's CID instincts would kick in, meaning he would memorize the license plate of the truck, the make and model, and every element of the driver that he could see under the current conditions. And Robert was still paranoid that his brother would be able to see through even his elaborate disguise.

He waited eight minutes and drove down the road at a slow pace until he reached the main road. As he pulled onto it his gaze swept in all directions. He saw him about fifteen seconds later. And he eyed with more than a bit of pride his brother walking along the road, his hands free.

Some people one could completely rely on. And his brother was one of them.

As Robert Puller drove slowly along he saw his brother take out his phone and start punching in numbers. Then he turned off the main road, crossed over a berm, and disappeared on the other side.

You're welcome, bro. And keep your head down from here on. It's not going to get any easier. It's only going to get worse. Trust me. If you still can.

Robert Puller punched the gas and sped on.

23

JOHN PULLER CHANGED motels once more.

At this rate he thought affordable lodging op-portunities in Leavenworth might be extin-guished far sooner than he would like. He spent some time with AWOL, who had taken the move better than he had. If only the feline could talk, for AWOL had been the only one other than Daughtrey to see the Air Force gen-eral's killer.

He didn't know if the police had come in an-swer to his 911 phone call, not that it would have mattered. He wasn't planning on report-ing his kidnapping. The local cops would not be able to figure it out and Puller wanted to play all these recent cards very close to his vest.

He did call Knox and asked her to meet him the next morning at the same diner where they'd had dinner.

At seven a.m. he was sitting in the same booth when the door opened and she walked in, dressed as usual in a dark pantsuit with a white blouse. He watched her spot him and walk over. As her long legs ate up the ground Puller knew he had to do one of two things: trust her or not trust her. And despite her seemingly sincere and graphic display of her war wounds, he did not trust easily. That was because his trust had too often been either misplaced, outright broken, or both.

She sat down and ordered coffee from the hovering waitress, and when the old woman had gone off to fill the request Puller leaned forward and recounted to her what had happened. He watched her closely to see if her surprise was genuine.

He concluded that it was. But Puller also knew that whatever he was dealing with was so full of deceit and fraught with peril that even the slightest misstep could be disastrous. He was also beginning to doubt his normally reliable judgment.

After her coffee came and the waitress drifted away she spoke. And Knox's first question intrigued him.

"Who fired the shot that killed the light?" she asked. "Because whoever did that probably saved your life."

"Shots," corrected Puller. "At least six. I'm

thinking an M4A1. The M4 has a max three-round burst option. I've fired enough of them to know the sound it makes. But you're right. The shooter did save my life. And whoever did it had followed us up there."

"So did that person have you under surveillance or the other guys?"

"Fair question. But I don't have an answer."

"An M4 is a standard Army issue," she noted.

"It used to be a mainstay of Special Forces. I carried one when I was a Ranger. All infantry units use it heavily too."

"Do you think these guys are the ones who killed Daughtrey?"

"I don't know. Could be. But something about what the voice said made me think."

"Think what exactly?"

"That he's not simply a criminal," said Puller.

"Because he talked about having the good of the country in mind?"

"Only what country, Knox? Maybe he's in the intelligence field."

"Puller, American intelligence agencies do not kidnap and try to murder federal lawmen."

"You sure about that?"

"I can't believe you're even asking me that."

"Really? After everything that's happened?"

She gazed down, seemingly unable to meet

his eye. She tapped her spoon against her coffee cup. "If the person *is* in the intel field, maybe it's for one of our enemies, like you suggested."

"Maybe."

"There is one thing you should know."

"What?" he said, reading her tone to mean that whatever she was about to say would not be good news.

"Al Jordan, the maintenance guy who had the blown transformers?"

"Yeah, did you talk to him? Find out who took them?"

"I tried to talk to him."

"What do you mean, 'tried'?"

"He's been transferred."

"Transferred! Where?"

"I can't get a straight answer on that."

"He's a maintenance guy. He's been here for fifteen years. I checked his file. There would be only one reason to transfer him, Knox."

"To get him out of the way so he couldn't tell anyone what he knows—as in who took the damn transformers!" she finished angrily. "And I checked the substation. All the debris has been cleaned up. Even if we go out there we won't find anything."

Puller sat back and looked around the diner

before giving her a piercing stare. "And you're jacking *me* around for being paranoid?"

Now she looked up at him. "Maybe I just didn't want to believe it was possible," she said quietly.

"I thought in the intelligence field allies became enemies on a daily basis."

"That is grossly exaggerated by the press and in the movies and on TV."

"I guess I'll have to take your word for it."

"I guess you will. So where do we go from here?"

"Fort Leavenworth."

"And what are we looking for there?"

"How a guy not connected to the United States military ended up as part of the response team to the incident at DB and was found dead in my brother's cell. And I'm not leaving there until I find an answer."

"And the people who kidnapped and nearly killed you?"

"They can only surprise me *once*, Knox. They come after me again, someone's not walking away."

"Well, let's hope it's not you."

He looked at her. "And I can count on you to cover my back?"

"You have to ask?"

"I wouldn't be asking if I didn't think I had to."

"Yes, I'll have your back. Will you have mine?"

"I've had your back ever since you showed up, Knox."

CHAPTER

24

SINCE PULLER AND Knox both had DoD creds they could access the fort through the east or west gates, named Hancock and Sherman respectively, after long-dead Civil War Union Army generals, rather than the main gate, which was how visitors, newcomers, and commercial traffic entered the post.

The fort had been around since 1827, when it was established by Colonel Henry Leavenworth to be a forward base protecting the fragile and highly dangerous Santa Fe Trail. It had been named Fort Leavenworth after then Brigadier General Leavenworth in 1832. The fort had never been attacked by an enemy force, not even during the Civil War. And residing smack in the middle of the country, it never would be, unless the United States had imploded.

They entered through the Hancock Gate. Puller had arranged to meet a representative of the 15th MP Brigade, which had responsibility for securing the fort.

Knox looked around as they drove along the road.

"Nearly nine square miles of Army," she said. "Seven million square feet of space, a thousand buildings."

"Fifteen thousand personnel on post, thousands off post, eighty thousand-plus visitors a year," added Puller.

"Which equals a needle in a haystack," she concluded.

"A needle we're going to find."

"How can you be so sure?"

"Because failure is not an option."

He pointed to a building as they drove past. "Warrant Officer College. I went there when I got the promotion. It's part of the Combined Arms Center."

"Fort Leavenworth, the intellectual center of the Army," said Knox dryly.

"They train almost all of the Army majors here, and all modern five-stars, from Eisenhower to Bradley, have passed through here."

She pointed out a building as they drove along. "That's where the 902d Military Intelligence Group is located—counterintelligence protection of Army assets in a six-state area."

"Any ties to NSA?" asked Puller, glancing at her.

"Do you need to know that?"

"I wouldn't have asked if I didn't," he shot back.

"I'm afraid I can't get into that," she said. "Who are we meeting from the 15th MP?"

Puller frowned and said, "Command Sergeant Major Tim McCutcheon, senior NCO."

"The CSM? I thought they would have rolled out the top dog for us."

"Well, the 15th's commander got his butt canned when my brother escaped, and I guess his replacement was busy."

"Okay. And what do you really hope to accomplish here?"

"Priority one is to identify the dead guy. Priority two is to determine how he ended up in my brother's cell at DB."

"That's a lot to ask for."

"Well, if you don't ask, you sure as hell won't have a chance of receiving."

A few minutes later they pulled up in front of the headquarters for the 15th MP, went inside, and were led down the hall to the office of CSM McCutcheon.

The man himself rose from behind his desk,

dressed in his ACU cammies in the standard UCP, or universal camouflage pattern, which when viewed through night-vision goggles would simply look black. The uniform was very high-tech. It minimized infrared silhouettes and had markers that would identify friendly personnel in combat zones when seen through NV equipment, and that could be covered up when not necessary. Despite all that, the uniform had been a total disaster. Troops called it "pajamas" because it did not ride well on anyone, no matter how fit they were. The gray color stood out under almost all combat environments except for a concrete parking lot—which was not usually where battles were fought—and the Velcro was badly designed and caught on objects as troops were patrolling, a potential fatal flaw. It had been a five-billion-dollar mistake by the Army, which was planning to spend another four billion to create yet another uniform to replace the barely ten-year-old UCP. But for now, until that day came, the UCP was what the Army was wearing, crap or not. They couldn't exactly go naked.

Riding on McCutcheon's left arm was a simple patch with the legend "MP" in black lettering. The branch insignia was two crossed gold pistols representing the Harpers Ferry Model

1805, the first American military pistol. The branch's distinctive unit insignia had the motto "Duty, Justice and Loyalty."

McCutcheon was in his early forties, nearly as tall as Puller, and outweighed him by about twenty pounds, all of it muscle. His hair was cut to nearly his scalp and he looked like he could bench-press a Stryker and squat a Bradley. They all shook hands and Puller pointed to the unit insignia.

"Always thought those were good words to live by."

McCutcheon nodded and smiled. "Heard you came up through the ranks." He motioned for them to sit down and he sat down behind his desk. "What can I do to help you two?"

Puller explained the issue and McCutcheon nodded.

"I've been briefed, of course. The team that responded was made up of all MPs. We pulled from both the 40th and the 705th. It was a full company plus the CO and the first sergeant."

"A hundred and thirty-two soldiers?" inquired Puller.

"Plus Captain Lewis and First Sergeant Draper," McCutcheon added.

"Right, for a total of one hundred and thirty-four personnel." Puller leaned forward. "But what if I were to tell you that on the video feed from that night I counted one hundred and thirty-*five* MPs climbing off those trucks?"

McCutcheon looked stunned. "I don't see how that would be possible. We called up four platoons. At Leavenworth an MP platoon has thirty-three soldiers. No MP would report for a mission unless he was called up. It was a potential crisis situation at DB, but we didn't call for an all-hands response. Four platoons, one company. It's the way the Army works. You know that."

"And yet there was one extra soldier who did show up at DB," persisted Puller.

"Could you have miscounted, Chief Puller?"

"I went over it a dozen times in slow motion. Knox here did the same."

McCutcheon glanced at her and she nodded. "It's true, Sergeant Major."

"So maybe under the circumstances a roll call or head count wasn't conducted," said Puller. "Four platoons on six different trucks in the middle of the night—who would notice if an extra guy covered head to foot in riot gear is along for the ride? And I'm sure everyone was under intense pressure to get the MPs to the prison."

"They were," conceded McCutcheon. "I

wasn't even on duty and I got a call right away. They were scrambling to fill out the response team."

"Who gave the order for four platoons to form the response team?" asked Knox.

"Colonel Teague."

"The 15th's commandant, until he was put on admin leave," said Puller.

"And he was also the head of DB," added Knox. "And he was on duty that night, right?"

"Yes. When the backup failed and everyone heard the explosion and the gunfire, he got right on the direct line here and ordered up the company of MPs."

"And those noises were only heard in pod three?" said Puller, and McCutcheon nodded. "And no source for those noises has been found?"

"No," said McCutcheon.

"When I asked Captain Macri, she said that she had chosen not to search the guards at DB for any device that might have been the source of the explosion and gun noise."

McCutcheon said nothing and neither did Puller. If the command sergeant major wanted a staring contest to see who would blink first, Puller was certainly ready to accommodate him. When Knox started to say something,

Puller flicked his knee against hers. Finally McCutcheon said, "I'm not pointing fingers." He waited for Puller to nod his assent before continuing. "But I'm sure if she had it to do over again the captain would have chosen differently."

"Meaning she would have searched all the guards?" said Puller.

"Yes."

"Water under the bridge now," said Knox. "We can't do it over. But it is possible then that an extra guy was in the mix?"

McCutcheon leaned back in his chair. "If your numbers are right, then yes. I can check to see if an extra man reported for duty, but that's highly unlikely. So you think the dead guy that's unaccounted for was the extra man? A bogey in the mix?"

"Right now I don't see any other explanation," replied Puller. "Unless you have one."

"I don't," admitted McCutcheon.

"We'll need to talk to Lewis and Draper," pointed out Knox.

"I believe that Captain Macri spoke to them about you. I'll make sure you hook up with them today."

Puller said, "Macri also told me that there were no personnel unaccounted for here."

"That's correct."

"But have you had any personnel leave recently?" asked Puller.

McCutcheon said, "This is an active base, sir. Personnel get assigned and reassigned all the time. Other folks come and go. We have soldiers, DoD civilian contractors, foreign military students, reservists, Air Force exchange—"

Puller interrupted. "Back up to foreign military students. I'd forgotten you had that element here."

"Right. At the Foreign Military Studies Office."

"How many students do you have currently?"

McCutcheon turned to his desktop computer and clicked some keys. "As of this morning, forty-five."

"Any recent departures?" asked Knox.

McCutcheon again turned to the screen. A few clicks later he said, "One from Croatia left the day of the incident at DB. He's the only recent one."

"Croatia?" said Puller.

"The country's a member of NATO, and since last year, it's also part of the EU. And Croatia sent troops to Afghanistan. They're our ally in a troublesome region. So one of the bennies they get for that is to come here and learn from the best. Their military is underfunded and their equipment and personnel are not in the best shape. So we're helping them."

"And the Croatian's name?"

"Ivo Mesic."

"How long was he here?"

"A month."

"You know him by sight?"

McCutcheon nodded. "I've met him a few times. Had a beer with him. Seemed like a real nice guy."

Puller took a photo from his pocket and showed it to the sergeant major. "And this is not him?" It was a photo of the dead man back at Fort Leavenworth's morgue.

"No, that's definitely not him."

"He'd presumably be in the database at the fort," said Knox. "Which means we would've gotten a ping if the dead guy had been in it."

McCutcheon nodded. "Absolutely. Full background check conducted and everything. Foreign military personnel are given access credentials. They're not at the level of a CAC," he said, referring to the military's Common Access Card, "but they're issued for people who have a regular recurring requirement to access the post. As Mesic did."

"So he could come in the Hancock or Sherman gates and not the main gate?" said Puller.

"That's right. DoD ID lane."

"And do we know that Mesic made it back to Croatia?" asked Knox.

"I don't know the answer to that, but I can find out." He pointed at the photo. "But that is definitely not him." He spun his computer around so they could see the screen. There was a picture of a man on it.

"That's Ivo Mesic."

Puller read down the file information and nodded.

Knox said, "Definitely not our guy. And the file says he's in his fifties."

"He held the rank of colonel in the Croatian army," said McCutcheon.

"Was his departure date scheduled well in advance?" asked Knox.

McCutcheon looked at his computer screen. "They all are, but now that you ask, he left a few days early. File says he received orders to return."

"What day was that?"

"The day he left."

"So right before the incident at DB?" said Puller.

"That's right, Chief."

Puller and Knox exchanged a significant glance.

"How did he leave?" asked Puller.

"Come again?"

"Was he driven off to the airport or did he have his own ride?"

"Oh, he had a rental."

Knox said, "Presumably we can check and see if it was turned back in."

"But the dead guy isn't Mesic," said McCutcheon. "So what's the point of pursuing him?"

Puller eyed him. "When you clear a house in Kabul looking for the enemy, how many rooms do you check?"

"*All* of them, of course, Chief Puller," answered McCutcheon immediately.

"Same principle in my line of work, Sergeant Major," said Puller.

CHAPTER

25

PULLER AND KNOX were standing at the entrance to the Sherman Gate into Fort Leavenworth. They had already been to the Hancock Gate and had struck out. Mesic had not left that way. However, the two guards stationed at the Sherman Gate well remembered the Croatian officer.

The first guard said, "He wasn't looking too happy. When I asked him what was the matter he said he was sorry to be going. He liked it here."

"Why did he talk to you at all?" asked Puller. "He had an access cred. He could have flashed it and driven on."

"He could have," said the second guard. "But we'd seen him around the base. Even played some pool with him at one of the local bars. He was a nice guy. So he stopped his car and talked for a bit. There wasn't anyone behind him. Light traffic that time of the day."

Knox said, "What exactly was the time?"

The first guard's brow furrowed. "I'd say around twenty hundred hours. Most people who were leaving the post were already gone. Everybody else had finished chow time and were probably back in quarters. He said he had a flight to catch out of KC. He'd be back in Croatia after a few stops in between. At least that's what he said."

"No nonstops between KC and Zagreb," said the other guard, grinning. "He was an okay dude, never had a problem with him," he added.

"Anything out of the ordinary strike you when he was leaving?" asked Puller.

"What do you mean?" asked the first guard.

"Something odd," added Knox.

"No, nothing odd. I mean, he pulled his usual."

"What was his usual?" asked Puller.

"He forgot something," said the first guard. "He was always forgetting stuff."

"And what did he do when he forgot stuff?" asked Knox.

"He'd come hightailing it back here," said the second guard who cracked a smile.

"And he forgot something that night?" asked Puller.

"His passport of all things," said the first guard. "He looked like he was going to throw up. He's not getting out of the country without his passport, right?"

"And you let him back in?" said Knox.

"Sure. He had his access pass."

"How far had he gone before he turned around and came back?" asked Puller.

The first guard looked down the road a bit. "Probably around the curve." He paused and stroked his chin with his fingers. "I mean, he was out of sight. I don't remember seeing him until he came tearing back in here. Said he'd forgotten his passport. Had left it in his quarters. He went back in to get it."

Puller looked down the road where it curved. Any car turning the curve would be out of sight of the post's entrance.

"You didn't search his car, either in or out?" asked Puller.

"No. Vehicles without creds get searched at the Grant Gate at Metro and Seventh. Not here. The main gate is where they do the searches. Most people with CACs don't use the main gate."

"And when he came back out the second time that was the last you saw of him?"

"Yep," said the first guard, and his mate nodded in agreement.

"Thanks," said Puller, and he started walking off down the road toward the curve.

The guards looked at Knox curiously. "So what is all this about?" asked the second guard.

"When we figure it out you definitely *won't* be the ones we tell," she said, and hurried after Puller.

She caught up to him about a hundred feet later and their long legs ate up the distance between them and the curve.

"So what do you think, Puller?" she asked.

He didn't answer until he'd reached the curve and cleared it. Then he turned and looked back.

"Completely out of the sightline of the guard shack. And it would have been fairly dark."

"Meaning?"

"Meaning our guy could have been waiting there and when Misec comes out the first time the guy climbs into the trunk and Misec drives him onto the base. He gets out and lays low with his riot gear until the call comes from DB. Then he joins the four platoons, rides over there, and ends up dead in my brother's cell."

"Where exactly would he lay low on an Army base and not be noticed? Particularly if he were wearing riot gear."

"Probably had the gear in a duffel. This base has thousands of soldiers. To a certain extent they look alike, particularly in uniform. And there are plenty of places here to hide. And I'm sure that Mesic had scoped one out for him and probably drove him right to it. Maybe one of the base churches. That time of night it might have been empty."

Knox looked unconvinced. "This is all quite a leap of logic. We don't even know if this Mesic guy is involved."

"He left early? Orders from home? What could be that important in Croatia to call him back early? And coincidentally on the day the storm was forecast and all hell broke loose at DB?"

"And if the guy did infiltrate the response team, why? What was his motive for going into DB?"

"I've been giving that some thought."

"And?" asked Knox.

"And it seems to me his mission was to kill my brother."

"Whoa, where the hell did that come from? And you said *mission*?"

"That's right. This was all carefully planned with a lot of moving pieces. This guy didn't just walk into this. He was sent here to kill my brother."

"But he ended up dead."

"Because my brother killed him first."

"I don't see where you're getting all this."

Puller said, "Before the power went out my brother was sitting in his cell reading a book. I read his body language. It wasn't hard. For him this was a night like any other night he's spent here. He wasn't tense. He wasn't anticipating anything more than falling asleep once he'd finished reading."

"And then the power went out," said Knox slowly.

"And all hell breaks loose. Sounds of gunfire and a bomb going off, when neither thing actually happened."

"And your brother?"

"He's smart beyond smart. I think he figured out what was coming and was ready when the guy burst into his cell to kill him."

"Snap-crackle-pop," said Knox. "So you *did* teach him that move."

"Yeah, I did."

"But if what you say is true, your brother still willingly escaped from DB. He took the guy's clothes, climbed onto a truck, rode it back to Leavenworth, and then walked away."

"Look at it from his point of view. He's just killed a guy. He doesn't know the man isn't an MP. But he somehow knows the guy was trying to kill him. But who's going to believe that? He stays at DB and they find the dead guy, my brother is probably looking at a guaranteed death penalty. And while they haven't executed anyone there since the 1960s, I think they'd make an exception for something like that."

"But they'd know the dead guy wasn't an MP," Knox pointed out.

"Who cares? He's still dead. And maybe you don't know this, but there were some in the military community who thought my brother should have been put to death for treason after his court-martial. I heard plenty of scuttlebutt afterward. This would give them the perfect opportunity to push for it again."

Knox considered all this and finally said, "I admit, I can't find an obvious flaw in your logic, but there's still a ton that doesn't make sense to me. And how does this tie in with Daughtrey's death?"

"It may not."

"And why would a Croatian military man be involved in sneaking an assassin onto a U.S. base?"

"I wish Mesic were around so I could ask him. If he's even still alive."

"You don't think he made it back to Croatia?"

"Oh, I don't think he was ever headed to Croatia. Now let's take a ride. I have something I want to show you, Knox."

"Is it important?"

"Very."

26

PULLER WAS SITTING on the hood of his car in the parking lot of the Fort Leavenworth National Cemetery. To the immediate east was the Missouri River, and on the other side of the river was the state of Missouri. A bit north of here the river began its long bend, shaped much like a bell curve. Inside this curve were Sherman Airfield and Chief Joseph Loop.

Knox stood next to the car looking curiously at Puller.

"What are we doing here?" she asked, gazing around at the white tombstones under which lay over thirty thousand dead.

"Lincoln established this cemetery back in 1862, when the Union was losing the Civil War. It was the first of twelve national cemeteries he set up."

"Okay, and the reason for this history lesson?"

Puller slid off the hood and his feet hit the

ground. "He knew it was going to be a long and deadly conflict. But losers don't establish national cemeteries. A president presiding over a fractured country doesn't set up a national anything unless he truly believes he's going to win the war and the country will be reunited."

"Lincoln was nothing if not confident, I guess," said Knox, who still looked perplexed by Puller's words.

"People who lack confidence rarely win anything," he noted.

He strode into the cemetery and she followed. He walked the rows of tombstones before stopping and pointing at one.

"Read the inscription," he said.

Knox glanced down. "Thomas W. Custer. Two Medals of Honor. Captain 7th Ohio Cavalry."

Puller said, "He was the first of four double Medal of Honor winners in the Civil War, and one of only nineteen in American history. Both of his medals came from charging enemy positions and capturing Confederate regimental flags. With the second one he took a shot right to the face, but grabbed the regimental colors and rode them back to his line with blood all over him."

She looked up at Puller. "Wait a minute. Custer? Was he—"

Puller knelt on his haunches in front of the tombstone. "He was George Armstrong Custer's younger brother. He died at age thirty-one with his big brother and a battalion of men from the 7th Cavalry at Little Big Horn. Also killed was their younger brother, Boston Custer. From a tactical perspective George Custer blew it. He knowingly split his force and refused additional soldiers and firepower. He went up against an opposing force that dwarfed his in number of men and guns, and also held the better ground. But his brother Tom won a pair of Medals of Honor. He was a good soldier. Maybe a great soldier. He'd been in innumerable battles and he could see what his brother could see. And more."

Knox's brow furrowed as she thought about this. "But he still went into battle with his brother…even though he knew they would…lose," she said haltingly.

"Even though he might've known they were going to be *massacred*," amended Puller.

"So family trumps brains?" said Knox.

"Family just is," replied Puller.

"Are you saying you're Tom and Robert

Puller is George? You're following your older brother blindly to disaster?" Her voice rose as she spoke.

He glanced up at her but said nothing in response to her statement.

She looked at him sternly. "And your objectivity? Your role as investigator searching only for the truth, regardless of where it takes you? Or regardless of who is ultimately held accountable?"

Puller suddenly stood, towering over her. She took a step back as he stared fiercely down at her. "I gave an oath when I put on the uniform, Knox. Bobby is my family, but so is the United States Army. I will follow this investigation objectively and I will hold people accountable. *All* people."

"So what was the point of bringing me here, then?" she asked, looking mystified.

"To remind you that I'm willing to sacrifice my brother or anybody else if it means doing my job and seeing that justice is done." He paused, but only for a moment. "So what are *you* willing to sacrifice?"

Her eyes widened. "What the hell are you talking about? How did this get turned around to *me*?"

"Are you willing to sacrifice your loyalty to

INSCOM, NSA? And whoever else you work for?"

"Puller, I thought we already had this discussion. You dressed me down and I said I'd work with you. So what's the problem?"

In a voice like a drill sergeant he barked, "I asked you whether the 902d Military Intelligence Group stationed here had ties to the NSA. And your response was, 'I'm afraid I can't get into that.'"

"Look, you're pissed and maybe you have a right to be, but bringing me to a cemetery is a little melodramatic, don't you—"

Puller interrupted, "So I'm asking you for the last time, do you have my back under all conditions? Because if you don't then you are useless to me, Knox. And we're just going to go our separate ways."

There was a long moment of silence before she broke it. "Puller, I told you I hate deceiving people like you. And I meant that."

"That's not an answer."

"What do you want from me?"

"All I want is an answer to my question. It's that simple."

"I can give you an answer, just not the one you so obviously…want," she said, her voice dying out at the end.

He said, "Well, that's answer enough." He spun on his heel, marched back to his car, and drove off, leaving her still standing on the final resting place of Thomas Custer, loyal brother extraordinaire.

27

ROBERT PULLER SAT in his motel room and stared down at the image he'd drawn, photographed, and then transferred onto glossy paper. It was the dead man back in his cell. Puller had gotten no hits on any database that he could hack into. He had finally stopped trying. The man was definitely not in the military. He was not in the federal bureaucracy. He was not a government contractor with a security clearance. He was not in law enforcement. He was not on a terrorist watch list. They would all be in a database somewhere. These days everybody was in a database somewhere.

So who the hell was he? And how did he end up in my prison cell?

Puller moved his face closer to the photo. He had spent years of his life examining the smallest details, looking for something of value, sometimes just a speck within a mountain of digital data. He was a twenty-first-century gold prospector, only his equipment was a computer and a bandwidth pipe the size of New Jersey.

Then his eye caught something, transmitted that something to his brain, and his brain retrieved the necessary information from memory. He looked down at the image with renewed energy and a fresh perspective.

I got the jawline wrong. It was dark in the cell, but that's no excuse. I still got it wrong and I can't afford mistakes. It was more angular. And the eyes, they were more sunken, the forehead a bit fuller, the nose a touch sharper.

On a sketchpad he made the necessary adjustments in the face. Finished, he sat back and stared down at the new image.

No wonder he didn't show up in any database. Any American database.

Puller had examined many such faces during his career. He had become an expert at reading people's origins in their features. The man was from Eastern Europe. Maybe as specific as the Balkan region. But clearly not Greek, Turkish, or Albanian. He must be a Slav. Could be a Bosnian, Croat, or Serb. So how did a Slav end up as part of an MP response team to a crisis situation at America's only maximum-security military prison?

He sat back and closed his eyes. In his mind's

eye he took a trip through Fort Leavenworth, a place he had been to often in his career. Even though he was Air Force, his particular specialty made working with the other armed forces branches mandatory. And the 902d Military Intelligence Group was stationed there.

His photographic memory clicking away, Puller kept up his mental stroll until he came to the answer. He opened his eyes.

The foreign military school at Leavenworth. The man had to have come from there. He thought about it a bit more. But that couldn't be right. He had heard nothing in the news about the dead man being identified. If he had been enrolled in the school at Leavenworth his face and prints would be on a database somewhere. Either he had been identified that way and the news not publicly released, or he hadn't been identified, which meant Puller had missed something in his deductions.

He closed his eyes once more. No, there was another possibility. The foreign military student would have an access card to the fort that would allow him to avoid the main gate. That meant no vehicle searches. That meant the student could have transported onto the base the man who had ended up dead in his cell.

The man had been sent to the DB to kill him.

Puller had known this as soon as the cell door had opened. It was dark, to be sure. But he had suspected something was wrong from the very beginning. The main power might go out because of a storm. But the backup power too? He knew it was fed from natural gas lines buried deeply underground and thus invulnerable to the storm's power.

No, the odds of both systems failing at the same time were colossally long. And then there had been the actions of the man. He had come into the cell and closed the door behind him. That was the first suspicious sign. The second was the man taking out a knife. Puller had seen that in the illumination of the man's helmet light.

But Puller had not given the man the opportunity to stab him. He had disarmed him, grabbed him by the neck.

And, well, the end had come quickly.

Thanks to the teachings of his little brother.

Apparently the Slavs had never heard of snap-crackle-pop.

It was fortunate that he was close to my height and build, yet they never thought of the possibilities there. Not for one second. I'm certain of that. They never imagined that I would end up killing him and taking his place to escape.

The questions, though, were numerous, and Puller was not finding any ready answers.

Why kill me now? Who would want to? And who could have orchestrated such an event at DB?

Puller sat back feeling distressed. He knew that the part of the brain that triggered emotions brought on by pain was the anterior cingulate cortex. Interestingly enough, it didn't distinguish between emotional and physical pain. Thus it could be set in motion as easily by a broken heart as by a damaged limb.

He closed his eyes and started concentrating, turning slow-moving alpha waves into beta waves that cycled through his mind at twice the speed of the alphas.

Eastern Europe.

Foreign military student.

Assassination attempt at Leavenworth more than two years after he had been imprisoned there.

What had been the catalyst? Simply the time for planning? He doubted that. It would take time to do so, but hardly more than twenty-four months. What had occurred in the interim?

All the rest, the power outage, the noises of guns and bombs, even the man sent to kill him, were all part of the "effect" of the cause and effect. They were just filler. Now he needed to get past the fluff and zero in on the root of it all.

His initial instinct had been to set out for a location connected to his old position at SRATCOM. That was still his inclination, but he didn't have the luxury of gallivanting off to multiple places. He had to narrow it down.

So what had been the trigger for all this? If he could find that, he could narrow the number of places to which he might have to travel.

While in solitary confinement, he had had access to the news. He had read as many newspapers as they would provide him. He had seen the TV. He had no Internet access but he had listened to the conversations of the guards. And his brother had brought him news as well during his visits.

Daughtrey had joined STRATCOM four months ago. The man was now dead. Had his joining STRATCOM been the reason for what had happened at the DB?

There was also talk that the intelligence community was going to be undergoing some radical structural changes, bringing more order and a streamlined approach to a sector that had been sorely lacking in those areas. Was that the reason for the events at the DB that had nearly claimed his life? But he had no connection to that world anymore.

He kept blasting the problem with cycles of beta waves.

Five minutes later he slammed his fist against the wall in frustration. His brain, the one thing that had never failed him, just had.

CHAPTER

28

JOHN PULLER HAD gone back and checked out of his motel. His plan was to spend the rest of the day following up leads, and then he was going to head back east, check in, and then report his findings to his new "bosses." As he drove along the surface streets of Fort Leavenworth, to his left was the Missouri River, also known as "Big Muddy." He knew that the currents were tricky and drownings all too frequent. And some of them were not accidental. A few years before, a platoon sergeant had dumped his unconscious wife's body in the river late at night after she had discovered his affair with a subordinate. Whether the poor woman had regained consciousness before she drowned was unknown, but her body had eventually been recovered far downriver where it had snagged on a downed tree. Puller had been put on the case and kept on it for a month. The platoon sergeant was currently in the DB for the rest of his life and his two children would grow up without either parent.

That case he had solved. With this one he still seemed to be at the starting gate.

He pulled to the curb and put the sedan in park. About a half mile from here was the DB. The Castle—the old prison—had had its own farm and dairy cattle operation, where "installation trusty" inmates would work. That had all gone away with the demolition of large parts of the Castle and the completion and opening of the DB. No more milk cows were needed. And who said the DoD didn't know how to cut costs?

Although there were no cow teats to pull or tractors to drive, the inmates at the DB could lift weights, play softball or soccer, or run on the track outside. They could play basketball in the indoor gym, which was named after a sergeant major who had collapsed on the court and later passed away. They could visit with family and friends. They could perform jobs and learn skills in the commercial laundry, the barbershop, sheet metal and welding facility, woodshop, textile repair section, graphic arts studio, and even an embroidery shop that made nametapes for various military purposes.

As an inmate in solitary confinement, however, Robert Puller could not lift weights or play basketball or softball or work in any of those shops. He was designated as maximum custody, at the top end of the restricted grade. His existence at the DB was a solitary one. And, truth be known, he probably preferred it that way. His intellect was so advanced that he might have found the conversation of other inmates and the rigidity of the routines at the prison more harmful than beneficial. Puller had no doubt that his brother could lose himself in his own mind. And that might be the best way for him to survive in prison.

When Puller had first visited his brother at the DB, it had been conducted in the noncontact visitors' area, typically reserved for inmates on death row. There a wall of thick glass separated visitor and prisoner and a phone system was used to communicate. Robert Puller had largely been an exemplary prisoner, however, and the more recent visits had taken place in the general visitors' area, which was open and pretty nice for a prison.

Puller knew that he would never again set foot in the DB's general visitors' area if his brother was caught and returned here. He might never be able to visit Bobby again at all, in fact.

He climbed out of the car and looked back in the direction he had left Knox. She was turning out to be a real problem. It had started off bad, gotten better, and after she had shown Puller her scars of war, he thought they had reached some level of détente. But then she'd pulled the "I can't go there" BS with him, which had been the reason for the verbal drubbing he'd given her in the cemetery.

So right now he was going solo on this. He leaned against the hood of his car and went through some mental notes of where he stood now in the investigation.

He needed to follow up on the Croatian Ivo Mesic. He still had to interview the captain and first sergeant who had headed up the response team at the DB. He needed to make some inroads on the sources of the gun and explosion noises in pod three at the DB. If he didn't hear back from Shireen Kirk, his JAG contact, by tonight, he would call her. This was despite her telling him that if he didn't hear from her that was the end of it. Once Puller had a thread to follow he didn't give up on it.

Then there was Daughtrey's murder. And finally, at some point he would have to sit down with General Aaron Rinehart and James Schindler from NSC. It was clear that much was murky at both ends of this case, and he didn't believe Rinehart's and Schindler's explanations for being interested in this case. For that matter, he didn't really believe anyone connected to this case about anything.

And then there was the matter of who had kidnapped him. And who had fired the shots that had saved his life.

As he stared toward the DB in the distance he wondered if his brother would ever return there. He might never be found. Or he might be killed rather than captured.

And if I'm the one who runs him down? What do I do if he doesn't want to go back to DB? What do I do if he puts up a fight?

Puller's thoughts drifted back to the standoff in the alley behind the bar in Lawton, Oklahoma. The result was he had walked out alive and PFC Rogers had gone down with a ruined limb.

Could I pull the trigger on Bobby? Could he pull the trigger on me?

"No" and "hell no" were the answers that readily leapt to his mind. But on the other hand, his brother had been in prison for over two years. He had quite likely killed a man during his escape. If he were recaptured they might sentence him to death for the murder, even if there was evidence it was in self-defense. Under that scenario, his brother might want to go down fighting. Or he might just let his brother kill him. Puller didn't know which one was worse.

Shaking his head clear of these numbing thoughts, Puller decided to do what he did best.

Move forward. Whether it was on the battlefield or during an investigation, if you weren't moving forward then what good were you? He got back into the car and drove off.

He spent two hours with Captain Lewis and his first sergeant. Neither one had counted the soldiers as they formed the response team. The platoons had simply been called up and deployed to restore order at the DB. Both men seemed genuinely surprised that there was an extra man aboard. Once in the prison the MPs had fanned out to each pod, executing orders previously given.

Puller had asked about pod three, where his brother's cell had been. Neither man could give a ready answer as to what had gone down in that pod. They had not known about the dead man until long after the fact. None of their men had reported seeing anything out of the ordinary and certainly did not know that Robert Puller might have left the prison in the uniform of an MP decked out in riot gear. In fact, they were astonished at the possibility. Yet when Puller explained how it could have happened, both men conceded that they could not prove that it *hadn't* happened.

He examined the area where the staging had been for the response team. It was big, open, and on that stormy night probably totally chaotic. He searched the quarters where Mesic had stayed, but a cleaning team had come in to get it ready for the next occupant, so Puller couldn't even find a usable fingerprint. He had already determined that the rental car the Croatian had used had been leased out and was currently somewhere in Montana. Another dead end.

Puller next moved on to the DB. He sat in his brother's cell on the bed where his brother had been reading his book before the power had gone out. He looked around the small room where his brother had spent twenty-three out of every twenty-four hours of his life. Small room, big mind. It was a wonder that one could contain the other. He eyed the door, trying to imagine what his brother was thinking when the lights had been extinguished.

Did he know what was about to happen? Did he prepare for it when the door opened? He had only a few seconds to determine what was

going on. How could he have been sure the soldier who came through that door was there to
kill him? Maybe he hadn't been sure. Maybe
he saw it as an opportunity to make his escape.
Maybe he would have tried to kill whoever had
come through that opening that night.

Puller tried to meet with Captain Macri, but
she was not on duty. Mike Cardarelli, the officer who was at the command desk, agreed to
answer a few questions. There was nothing that
was helpful until Puller asked one last query
about Cardarelli's whereabouts on the night
Robert Puller had escaped.

Cardarelli said, "I was actually supposed to
be on duty that night, but Captain Macri
switched places with me."

Puller came fully alert. "Why was that?"

"She was supposed to be on duty the next
night but had a family commitment that had
changed. So we switched nights. I guess I
should consider myself lucky. Everyone here
that night took a professional hit."

"What was the family commitment?" asked
Puller.

"What?" asked Cardarelli.

"Macri's family commitment that changed?
What was it?"

"I...I don't know. I mean, I didn't ask."

"Does Captain Macri have family here?"

"I don't believe so. I just assumed they were coming in from somewhere else."

"Does she live on base?"

Cardarelli shook his head. "No. She has an off-base town home."

"I'll need that address."

Cardarelli gave it to Puller. As he rose, Puller said, "Any developments on the device that made the gun and explosion sounds in pod three that night?"

"None that I've heard of. It was the damnedest thing."

"Yeah," said Puller. "The damnedest thing."

* * *

A few minutes later he hurried back to his car and accessed a military database on his laptop.

Lenora H. Macri's photo and service record came up along with her personal history. Puller quickly read through it. Nothing struck him. She had a good record, no blemishes. When he flipped to the screens concerning her personal history, though, things became clearer, or more muddled, depending on how you looked at it.

Her parents were dead and she was an only child. So what were the family commitments that had changed?

And Macri had told him that she had not ordered a search of the guards for the noisemaking device. He had thought that peculiar and perhaps a professional gaffe. But by not conducting a search she had actually accomplished something. She had left available hundreds of suspects who could have smuggled such a device into the prison, and there was no way to prove now which of them might have done it. And by doing so, Macri, if *she* had been the one to bring the device into the prison, was also lost among a sea of potential suspects. And she might have had enough skill and access to override the security system at the prison, resulting in the cell doors opening rather than locking when the power went out.

He started the car and piloted it toward the address the officer had given him. He had strongly cautioned Cardarelli against phoning Macri and discussing anything that they had talked about. The real reason for the admonition was to ensure that Macri not be forewarned and possibly try to make a run for it.

Energized by perhaps finally having a lead in the case, he gunned the engine and made it to the subdivision on the outskirts of Leavenworth in record time. He parked in a spot where he could see her end-unit town home.

He killed the engine and waited. There was a car parked in front of her place. He grabbed a pair of binoculars from his duffel and trained them on the car. Sure enough, hanging from the rearview mirror was a parking tag for the DB. This was her ride, a late-model silver Honda Civic.

His plan was to give it some time and see if she came out, and then he would follow her. If she didn't come out he was going to conduct another interview with the woman with the goal of making her as uncomfortable as possible.

He waited an hour, but Macri did not leave her unit. He was about to get out of the car when another vehicle pulled in and parked next to Macri's ride.

Puller's eyes widened when he saw the person get out of the car and head up the steps to Macri's home.

Veronica Knox was obviously no longer cooling her heels at the cemetery.

29

PULLER WATCHED AS Knox rapped on the door and then rang the bell when no one answered. She looked around and Puller saw her hand dip into her jacket. She withdrew something he couldn't see but assumed it was a lock pick. Her hands moved around the knob for a few seconds and then she opened the door and stepped in.

As soon as the door closed behind her Puller was out of his car and hustling down the street. He passed by the side of Macri's house and went around to the back. It was a three-level structure with a deck above and a walk-out basement door below. The door was a slider. There were no curtains on it so Puller could see right inside. It was not built out; concrete foundation walls stared back at him along with stacked cardboard boxes.

The lock on the slider was a simple one and Puller was through the opening and over to the bottom of the stairs in a few seconds. He could hear footsteps above him, probably Knox looking around. And where was Macri? Her car was out front. But she had't answered the door. Was she here or not?

The familiar firecracker pops signifying gunshots caused Puller to pull his M11, crouch down, and pause, listening. There had been two shots, along with other sounds. He had heard the first shot, then a crash of something hitting something, then the second shot, then a scream and finally a thud. Someone had gone down. Was it Knox? Or Macri, if she was even here?

He took the steps three at a time. There was a door at the top of the stairs. Puller eased it open and did a turkey peek.

He saw no one. He sight-cleared the room behind him and then headed forward. He eased around the corner, his gun straight ahead.

Then he stopped.

Knox was kneeling over Macri, who was sprawled on the floor, blood pouring from a wound in her chest.

Knox still held her gun in her right hand.

"Don't move, Knox," Puller called out, but he was prepared for her to move fast, turn, and fire at him.

Instead she held her gun up, her finger clearly off the trigger, the muzzle pointed down. She was surrendering.

"Put it down on the floor and kick it toward me," ordered Puller.

"She needs an ambulance."

"I'm sure she does. Kick the gun to me and then I'll call one."

Knox did as he instructed. He picked the gun up by the muzzle and laid it on the hall table. He punched in 911 on his phone and ordered an ambulance.

"Step away from her," he said. "Lie down on the floor, hands behind your head and your legs splayed."

"Puller, she tried to kill me!"

"I'm sure we'll sort it all out. But for now, just do as I say."

Knox got on the floor with her hands behind her head and her legs spread wide.

Puller knelt next to Macri, who was sprawled on her back on the floor next to a chair, her arms up around her head. He spotted a small bullet hole in her dark blouse, and saw the spread of blood across the cloth. He took her pulse at the neck and found none. Her eyes were open and frozen. Her hands were already starting to cool just a bit.

"She's dead, Knox. Looks like the shot hit her square in the heart."

"I thought she was dead."

"What happened? Why are you even here?"

She started to rise but he barked, "Stay down. I won't tell you again."

She froze and then settled back down on the floor.

"I came to interview her. I was going to do it with you, but, well, you know how that turned out. I had to hike back to my car from the cemetery thanks to you."

"Why interview her?"

"Because she didn't search the guards."

"Explain that."

"I read your interview notes last night. She told you she didn't search the guards for a device that would have made the noise. She said it was because she couldn't believe any of the guards would have been involved. But of course she should have, regardless of that. There would have been no reason for her not to do so. Except for one." She turned her head to the side and looked up at him.

"Which was?" he asked.

"If it wasn't found on the guards then suspicion would have shifted to her. But if she didn't search them, then—"

"It was like she'd provided an alibi for herself," said Puller.

Knox said, "So you thought that too. Is that why you're here?"

"I saw you pick the lock and go in. I went in through the basement. Then I heard the gunshots. Two of them."

"She fired at me first," said Knox. "Look at the wall over there." She pointed with her right hand to the far wall.

Puller looked in that direction. The round had struck the drywall and driven into it, exposing a bit of the stud behind it.

Knox went on. "I fired a split second later. And I didn't miss."

"Why break in here? Do you have a warrant?"

"No."

"Then nothing you found would have been admissible in court."

"I'm not as concerned with the legal niceties, Puller. I have a job to do."

"So you just walked in here and she took a shot at you. She had the element of surprise. She was a soldier. How'd she miss you at this range?"

"Because I saw her a split second before she fired. I kicked that chair at her, hit the floor, and fired from there. When they do the post they'll confirm the trajectory."

Puller looked at the overturned chair lying next to Macri's body.

In the distance they could both hear the sirens coming.

"So if you had gone in first instead of me," Knox continued with a definite edge to her voice, "you might be on the floor on your belly explaining to *me* how it all went down. Or maybe you might be dead."

"No, I wouldn't have broken into the place."

"Well, I can't take it back now."

As the sirens drew closer Puller stepped to the window and looked out. It was an ambulance and two police cars.

Knox said, "So you've got control of the board, Puller. How are you going to play this?"

Puller muttered, "Shit." Then he added, "Get up, Knox."

She rose slowly and looked up at him. He handed her back her gun.

"I have to say I'm surprised," she said. "I thought you'd let them throw the book at me."

"I still might."

"What do we tell the police?" she said. "I did break in here. I had a gun. It might look like

Macri was just defending herself and her home. And I shot her."

"We tell them the truth."

"They might ding us for being here."

"But you did knock and ring the bell first. And you did identify yourself and you had your creds out?"

"Absolutely. She knew who I was. And she still fired."

"Okay, just follow my lead."

The police were skeptical at first, but Puller's demeanor and statement were unshakably professional, as were Knox's. Their credentials carried great weight with the local police, who were well aware of what had happened at the DB. They took the agents' statements. Then one of the cops said, looking down at Macri, "What about the body?"

"She's an active-duty Army captain shot in her home. This is, without exception, a CID investigation. We'll take charge of the scene. Everything will be preserved."

"I'm not sure I'm comfortable with that," said the older cop.

"Then you have your superiors call my superiors and they'll *get* comfortable. For now, the body doesn't leave the house and the crime scene is not touched."

The cop finally nodded and pulled out his cell phone. "Way over my pay grade."

An hour later the cops left and a CID forensics team from Leavenworth showed up, did an examination of the scene and the body, and then slipped the remains into a zippered body bag and rolled it away on a gurney.

Puller had assisted the local CID agents with processing the scene, while Knox, after giving her statement—and under strict orders from Puller—sat in the other room.

When the CID agents had finished they left. Puller and Knox were alone in the house.

"Forensics will confirm everything I told you was true, Puller."

"Forensics can do many things, but it can't do that, Knox, not entirely."

She said heatedly, "I almost got my head blown off. It was either her or me. What else could it have been?"

"That you came here to see Macri because she knew something incriminating. And you killed her to silence her."

"Oh, so now you think I'm both in on whatever this is and also a killer?"

"I don't know you, Knox. You just showed up on my doorstep. You sure as hell haven't earned my trust."

"Well, you haven't earned mine either," she shot back.

"So the fact that I didn't let the cops or CID arrest you carries no weight with you? That I gave you your gun back? That I backed your story with them? That I haven't slapped you in cuffs? None of that earned me even a bit of trust in your eyes?"

The anger quickly receded from her features and was replaced with embarrassment. "I appreciate that, Puller, I really do. Me being arrested would not be good."

"Certainly not good for *you*. And whoever else is behind you at INSCOM. And that could include a *lot* of folks," he said provocatively.

She slumped down in a chair. "I thought a lot about what you said back at the cemetery." She gave him a wry look. "Your Custer brother analogy was original, I'll give you that."

Puller leaned against the wall and waited for her to continue.

"What do you know about your brother's court-martial?"

"Nothing. I told you that already. The file was sealed. And I was overseas when it happened. He was charged with and convicted of treason, that's all I know."

"Your brother escaping has made a lot of people in the intelligence field very nervous, Puller."

"That one I'd worked out for myself."

"I shouldn't be telling you any of this."

"People shouldn't do a lot of things."

"I came here not just because of your case notes but because of something else."

"What?" he asked.

"We traced a series of deposits totaling one million dollars into an account in the Caymans that Captain Macri had set up about a month ago."

"Her payoff for doing what she did?"

Knox nodded.

"Where did the money come from?"

"Untraceable, even by us. We were fortunate to pick it up on her end, but the origin remains a mystery."

"How did you get on to her?"

"INSCOM had been getting chatter, nothing definite, but certainly strange, that made them start to focus on DB. We did a personnel rundown. A few people raised enough concerns to warrant markers being placed on them. Macri was one of them."

"What concerns? I found nothing unusual in her record."

"She was single, no family in the area, and she was ambitious."

"So are lots of military folks."

"And she had considerable personal debt."

"She was an officer. The Army paid for her ride at West Point."

"She also dabbled in the stock market. Options on margin accounts. She was in the hole for about eighty thousand dollars. Her payoff would have taken care of that debt and left her a lot of extra to get back on her feet."

"None of that was in her record."

"No, it wasn't. What she does with her personal finances is not really the Army's business. And the amounts she owed hadn't been called yet."

"But you guys found out about it."

"Yes," replied Knox.

Puller frowned. "So why the hell didn't you tell me about it?"

"I'm telling you now even though it'll probably cost me my job if my superiors find out." She folded her arms over her chest and leaned back in the chair and exhaled a long breath. "We came up through different tracks, Puller. I was bred from day one for clandestine service. That means we trust no one outside our circle and keeping a secret and outright lying are part of the job description. Just as you're trained to investigate a crime scene, I'm trained to deflect and deceive. I've spent years honing those skills, and if they knew I was telling you this, well, I'm not sure what they'd do to me."

Puller relaxed a bit. "So why *are* you telling me?"

She laughed, but it died halfway out of her throat and she quickly turned somber. "Because your honesty and, well, this damn nobleness about you, *shamed* me. I just felt ashamed having to string you along. It was humbling, frankly. When I thought I was well past that emotion. Along with a lot of others," she added, her voice growing very soft.

"So where does that leave us?" asked Puller quietly after a lengthy pause.

"With me asking for a second chance, or what is it now, a *third* chance with you? And even if you give me one I won't blame you if you don't believe me this time."

He glanced down at her hip. "That scar is real enough and the wound underneath. You were limping when you walked in here and I saw you wince when you sat down." He glanced at the other room. "When you fell to the floor to avoid getting shot, I guess you landed right on that hip. Probably hurts like a bitch."

"Yes, it does," admitted Knox. "More than a bitch, actually. I'd kill for a Percocet right now."

"So is the 902d Intelligence Group at Leavenworth under the NSA's thumb?"

"The NSA is pretty much everywhere, Puller. And the 902d is no exception."

He nodded. "I appreciate how hard that must have been for you to say."

"Training is training," she replied. "But I still have a bit of free will left and I mean to exercise it."

"Okay. It's a start."

Puller's phone rang. It was Shireen Kirk.

"Hello, Shireen. Can I call you back in a few minutes? I'm a little tied up."

She said, "No, you can't call me back. Where are you?"

"Leavenworth."

"So am I."

"Excuse me?"

"I just landed and I'm in a cab heading out to find you."

"What the hell are you doing in Kansas?"

"I don't want to talk about this over the phone. Can we meet somewhere?"

Puller glanced at Knox, who was watching him closely.

"Yeah, there's a diner." He gave her the address. "I've got an agent from INSCOM with me. I'd like her to get read in too."

"I'd rather just talk to you, Puller."

"It's going to have to be the both of us, Shireen. I trust her and you can too."

"I'll be there in thirty," Kirk said gruffly and clicked off.

"Who was that?"

"Shireen Kirk. My JAG contact."

"Where did she come in from?"

"D.C."

"Why come all the way out here?"

"She wanted to do a face-to-face. It must be important."

"I appreciate your wanting me to sit in. But if it makes her uncomfortable, I can bow out."

"No, Knox. We're a team now. We stick together."

"You're sure?"

"Let's go."

30

THEY DROVE SEPARATELY back into Leavenworth and met at the same diner they'd eaten at before. Puller held the door for Knox, who was walking stiffly thanks to her banged-up hip.

"Did you get the Percocet?" he asked.

"No," she said through gritted teeth. "But I downed four Advil. Just waiting for the suckers to kick in."

Puller spotted Kirk at a back booth and they headed over.

Kirk was dressed in slacks and a jacket, both of which were ruffled and wrinkled. Her eyes were puffy from lack of sleep, her curly hair was in disarray, she smelled of cigarette smoke, and there was an empty coffee cup in front of her.

Puller introduced the two women. Kirk gave Knox an appraising look and then nodded curtly.

"I don't know you, Knox, but if Puller vouches for you, then okay."

"I appreciate that."

"Don't thank me, I'm not doing it for you." She turned to Puller. "I left last night. I had to fly to Chicago, where my connection was canceled. I slept in the airport and spent today trying to get on another flight, till I snagged a seat on a puddle jumper. I could have driven the whole way faster. Friggin' useless airlines."

"A phone call would have been a lot faster."

"I'm hungry, you guys want to order? Because I do."

They ordered their food and after some chitchat Kirk hunched forward and spoke in a low voice. "You know how a court-martial works, I take it?"

Puller said, "Fortunately, I've never experienced one, but, yes, I know how it works. They're Article 1 legislative courts, meaning Congress controls them."

Kirk nodded. "The convening authority is the commanding officer. He creates the court-martial and selects the panel members."

"And that's the rub," said Puller. "The CO creates the court and picks the jurors."

"There are strict guidelines concerning unlawful command influence. Rule 104 of the court-martial process is very explicit. The CO is banned from punishing or influencing members in any way. The system has survived all attacks for over two centuries."

"That still doesn't mean it's fair. But who wants to rock that boat?"

Kirk spread her hands. "I'm not saying it's an ideal system, but it's the one we have. And it works for the most part."

"I don't think it worked for my brother."

Kirk sipped her coffee and shot glances around the diner, while Puller stared moodily off and Knox glanced back and forth between the two.

Their food came a few minutes later and they waited for the waitress to leave before resuming the conversation.

"I'm going to eat and talk," said Kirk. "Pardon the open mouth full of food." After liberally salting everything on her plate while Knox looked on in disapproval, Kirk said, "There are no hung juries like in civilian courts. You need a three-quarters agreement among the panel for a sentence of ten years or more, and the panel, not the judge, also decides the sentence."

"But I understand that unanimity by the panel is required for the death penalty," said Puller.

"Not always. If he was convicted under Article 106 of spying, then the penalty decision is taken away from the panel. Spying carries a *mandatory* death sentence. There are no exceptions if the conditions are met. The judge will simply announce the sentence."

Puller sat back. "I wasn't aware of that. What are the conditions?"

"Pretty simple and straightforward. The genesis of the language actually dates back to colonial times, although it's been modified from time to time over the years. It has to be during a time of war, which we certainly were when he was arrested."

"But Congress never officially declared war on Afghanistan or Iraq," Puller pointed out.

"You'd make a good lawyer, Puller. And the defense argued that point. But while technically what you say is true, practically, we *were* at war. And your brother was accused of aiding our enemies. When dealing with something like that, the defense is going to lose more often than it wins. And that's what happened when your brother's lawyer argued that point. He lost."

"Okay, go on," said Puller.

"The accused has to be acting as a spy in a place within the jurisdiction and control of the armed forces or any other place engaged in work in aid of that war. There are other elements: acting clandestinely, attempting to collect certain information with intent to convey to the enemy, etcetera, etcetera."

"But was he charged under Article 106?" asked Knox. She quickly added, "But I guess he couldn't have been. He was convicted but he wasn't sentenced to death."

Kirk said, "It seems Article 106 was *originally* on the table, but then it was taken off. He was instead convicted under Article 106a of espionage. It's sort of splitting hairs, because it carries many of the underlying requirements of spying although there is no requirement that it be during time of war. It also carries a capital penalty when the crime involves certain elements like nuclear weaponry, satellites, and communications intelligence."

"All things my brother was involved in," said Puller slowly.

"Right, but as opposed to a conviction of spying, the death penalty is not mandatory. It's also subject to whatever other punishment the court-martial wants to direct. And as you said, that's when all panel members must vote unanimously to impose death. That's a big difference from an *automatic* capital sentence."

"And they didn't have unanimity?" said Puller.

"No. Otherwise he'd be on death row or actually dead. Instead he was given life."

"So there must have been some extenuating circumstances," said Knox.

"I suppose there were, yes, but the whole picture was a little fuzzy from a trial perspective."

"Surely you didn't get that from just a paper trail, Shireen?" asked Knox.

Kirk swung her gaze to Knox. "My first name isn't Shireen, it's actually Cambrai. But it might as well be 'Scorched Earth.' I dug up the prosecutor and the defense counsel and spoke with both of them. They were surprisingly candid. Surprisingly."

She let the word hang out there.

"And why do you think they were so cooperative?" asked Puller.

"Well, it's hard to say," began Kirk cautiously. "They both remembered the case well, though I'm sure they've both handled dozens since. You know there was a PTA but your brother rejected it."

"What's a PTA?" asked Knox.

"Pretrial agreement. The accused can provide a guilty plea in exchange for a more lenient sentence. He apparently wanted no part of that. He consistently proclaimed his innocence in the strongest possible terms."

"Who was the convening authority?" asked Puller.

"The CO at STRATCOM, Major General Martin Able."

"I know Puller was convicted of espionage, but what were the specific charges?" asked Knox.

"As Puller told me earlier the trial record was sealed. And for good reason, because it was full of classified information. MRE 505 is very detailed on that point."

Knox said, "MRE? Not meals, ready to eat, surely?"

"Try Military Rules of Evidence," suggested Kirk.

"But you wouldn't come all this way unless you had unsealed it," commented Puller.

"As I told you before, that would take a court order. Which there was no way I could get, certainly not in the time since I talked to you last."

"But?" prompted Puller.

"But, as I said, the counsels were cooperative. The defense counsel, Todd Landry, especially so. He told me in confidence about the charges."

"Didn't he ask why you wanted to know?" Knox asked.

"Of course. I made noises about Robert

Puller's escape from DB, which they both knew about. It's all over the military pipelines."

"And they just assumed you were part of some group investigating it?" said Knox.

"If they made that assumption, I did nothing to suggest they were incorrect in that assumption," Kirk said smoothly.

"So what were the charges?" Puller said.

"It's fairly well known that NSA has deals in place with major technology companies and cellular phone carriers to allow them backdoor access into those platforms. Well, apparently Robert Puller had devised a back door into STRATCOM's intelligence platform, which, by the way, is tied to pretty much all the other intelligence pipelines, including NSA, CIA, and Army Intel. And that he was in the process of selling off the access codes to that back door to enemies of this country. It would have been catastrophic."

"Selling secrets? That's bullshit!" exclaimed Puller. "He didn't care about money. Why would he do that?"

"Apparently the motive was online gambling debts. In the millions."

"Online gambling?" exclaimed a stunned Puller. "My brother was not a gambler."

"Well, it seems they found evidence to the

contrary on his personal computers and his cell phone. He played under a variety of fictitious names."

"My brother is a super-smart geek. He would know gambling is based on luck, not skill. He's too intelligent to bet."

"I asked that very question."

"And?" said Knox.

"And the prosecutor, Doug Fletcher, informed me that it seems that your brother had devised an elaborate gambling algorithm that was initially extremely successful."

"Initially?" said Puller.

"Before it became unsuccessful. That's where the millions in losses come in. He just kept playing, trying to bet his way out of a hole. Lots of gamblers do that. It's a bona fide addiction. And playing online just opens up that addiction to millions of potential abusers."

"And they had evidence of all this?" said Knox.

"Yes. Apparently clear-cut."

"So—" Puller began, but Knox beat him to it.

"So why did both counsel remember the case so well?" she asked.

"Landry in particular seemed to think that everything was too neat and clean. There was no question that your brother knew his way around technology. And yet they discovered all this evidence on his personal devices without a lot of effort."

"So he thought it was planted. If so, did he raise that as a defense?"

Knox said, "He would have, except your brother testified that his personal devices could not be hacked by anyone. That anything found on there would have to come from him."

Puller slapped his palm against the tabletop, causing both women to jump. "The idiot. He was proud over practical. He didn't want to admit that someone had beaten him. He was the same way growing up. You might kick his butt once in something, but it would be the only time."

Knox said, "A guilty man would never have done that. He would grab at every defense he could get."

"Another reason Landry remembered the case so well. In point of fact, he'd never had an accused purposely torpedo a potential defense like that. Never. And yet your brother did without blinking an eye, apparently."

"Maybe he never really believed he was going to be convicted," said Knox.

"Well, he was wrong."

"But there was an appeal, right?" said Knox.

"Whenever the penalty is the dismissal from the ranks of an officer, the Court of Criminal Appeals—in this case the one for the Air Force—automatically conducts one. Robert Puller's case was reviewed and the lower judgment was upheld. No further action was taken on his behalf. Any other appeal would take some work to initiate, which he never did."

Puller fingered his coffee cup. "So he protested his innocence strongly. He never told me that. I wonder why?"

Knox shrugged. "There could be lots of reasons."

"I can't believe my brother would ever sell secrets."

"But he *would* be in a position to transmit secrets to the enemy. And if he did he might not have done it for money despite the gambling piece," pointed out Knox.

"What, he's like that Snowden guy and wants to transform what he thinks is a bad system by outing it to the world from a safe distance away?"

"Well, he obviously didn't do it like Snowden," said Kirk. "The court found he did it for the money."

Puller put down his cup. "But we can't lose sight of the fact that someone may have been sent to DB to kill my brother. Since then an Air Force general at STRATCOM has been murdered and Knox here had to shoot an Army captain who might have been involved in the attempt on my brother's life. If he was guilty and safely in prison, why all the attention now?"

Kirk nearly choked on her coffee. She stared over at Knox. "You did what?"

"She shot at me first. I defended myself. She's dead, I'm not."

"But what was the reason?"

"We found out she had financial problems, and lo and behold she sets up an account in the Caymans under another name and someone puts a million bucks in it."

"What did she do to earn that?" asked Kirk.

Puller said, "A device that simulated the sounds of gunshots and an explosion played a primary role in the chaos at DB. My take is she brought them in herself. That's why she didn't search any of the guards for it later. That way we could never pin anything on her. And she might have sabotaged the cell door locking software too."

Kirk held up a hand. "Okay, but let's get back to your last question: Why all this attention now?"

Puller looked at Knox and then glanced back

to Kirk. "I'm not sure either one of us can answer that."

Kirk nodded. "I agree that it all looks dicey. And that more investigation is needed. But you have to understand that it unduly complicates the situation now that your brother has escaped from DB."

"Well, he might not have had much choice. Escape or die. Given those options, I'd have cut and run too."

"And the problem with that answer is that the people hunting him won't care about his reasons."

"And another problem is he may have folks after him who aren't part of the official machine," retorted Puller.

Knox said, "After what happened to you, I think he probably does. Kidnapping and then trying to murder you definitely speaks of unofficial involvement."

A stunned Kirk now shot Puller a glance. "First she shoots a friggin' Army captain, and now you're telling me that you were kidnapped and nearly killed?"

"That's pretty much the gist of it. Bunch of guys with guns got the jump on me using a damsel-in-distress act that I fell for. They took me to a place, tied me up, asked me a bunch of questions, none of which I answered, and then they were going to kill me."

"Then why aren't you dead?"

"I had a guardian angel on site. He did enough to allow me to get my own way out."

"And who was this angel?" asked Kirk.

"I hope to find out one day so I can thank the person."

He turned to Knox and his voice dropped even lower. "And you can guarantee to me that you don't know who any of these folks are, or where they might have come from?"

Knox said, "If you're asking me whether it's any of my people, I can assure you that it's not. We may deceive, we may slice and dice the truth, we may conceal. But we don't do crap like this. We do have oversight committees, Puller. And if we tried any of this and it came out, well, everybody could pretty much kiss their asses, pensions, and freedom good-bye. And I'm not sure there's ever a compelling enough reason to do that. We have enough true enemies without turning on ourselves."

He studied her closely for a long moment and then looked away.

Kirk looked at Knox. "Tell me about this shootout with an Army captain. What was her name?"

Puller answered. "Lenora Macri. And she must've been pretty desperate to take a shot at you, Knox. Do you think she saw you coming in?"

"I knocked and rang the doorbell before I picked the lock. I wasn't trying to do it on the sly."

"I know you did. I was watching. So for Shireen's edification, tell us again how it went down."

"Step by step," added Kirk.

Knox sighed and then gathered her thoughts. "I closed the door behind me and called out her name. There was no answer. I called out again and identified myself, full title and everything. The next thing I know she came around the corner from the living room at me. Her gun was out and pointed at me. My cred pack was in my hand and held out for her to see but I knew it didn't matter. The look on her face told me all I needed to know. I had maybe a second. She was going to shoot me."

"Keep going," encouraged Puller when Knox paused.

"I dropped my creds, grabbed the chair, and flung it at her as I went down to the floor. She fired. I felt the round pass over me and hit the wall behind me. The chair had struck her as she fired and threw off her aim. I hit the floor, kicked away, aimed, and fired upward, into her chest. She dropped where she stood. She hit the floor and never moved after that."

"That all coincides with what I heard downstairs," said Puller, looking at Kirk.

"Well, it also happens to be the truth," replied Knox resolutely.

"But attempting to shoot you in cold blood like that," said Kirk. "It's an extreme response. How could she know what you were there for? It could just be routine questioning. If she killed you she's looking at the death penalty. And how was she planning to get away?"

"She had an alias. Same name she used to set up the account in the Caymans, but we traced it back to her. Under that alias she had purchased a series of one-way tickets with the final stop in Saint Petersburg."

"No extradition treaty between Russia and the U.S.," said Kirk.

"Right. And I doubt Russia was her final destination. She was just going there to disappear. After that, it's anyone's bet. She certainly would have had the financial resources to do it."

"What date was the plane ticket for?" asked Puller.

"Today. She was supposed to be on duty, but

called in sick. She was clearly never going back. That's why I went there."

Puller eyed Knox steadily and she returned the gaze. Kirk noticed this staredown and looked back and forth between them, like she was viewing a tennis match.

"I know what you're probably going to say," said Knox at last.

"Really?" replied Puller. "So why don't you tell me what I was going to say."

"That we're a team and I should have told you all of this. And you'd be right. And maybe if you hadn't left me in that graveyard, I would have told you. But you did leave me and I had no idea where you were. And I had to get this done."

Puller studied her for a while more but seemed satisfied by this explanation. He said, "I'm surprised with all the evidence you had against her that you didn't send in a SWAT team. The Army would have."

"That may be how the Army does things, but not us. What we really wanted was for her to cooperate with us and lead us back to whoever she was working with. In the grand scheme of things she was small potatoes. We wanted the others. That's why I went in solo, to talk to her, to make her see reason."

"And you almost got blown away for your troubles."

"I have to tell you, I didn't see that coming. There was nothing in her profile that would have led us to believe that she would have reacted with such violence."

"Well, profiles can be misleading," commented Kirk.

"And now we've lost her as a potential witness and information source. And it's really all on me," Knox added glumly.

Puller said, "So she saw you in her home, figured out who you were from you calling out. She knew the game was up since she was probably upstairs packing for her trip to Russia, and she panicked."

"Well, I'm just glad her aim was off."

"Because of the chair you threw."

"I'm still lucky, Puller."

"Like the hip."

"Like the hip," she agreed as Kirk looked at her quizzically. Knox saw this and said, "Long story." She sipped her coffee and looked thoughtful.

"What?" Puller asked, seeing an ironic look in her eyes.

"I was just wondering when my luck is going to finally run out."

"Don't we all," replied Puller.

"Well, unfortunately for you two, it seems the answer will be sooner rather than later," noted Kirk.

CHAPTER

31

CAN YOU GIVE me a lift to my hotel, Puller?" asked Kirk as they were leaving the diner.

She had a small roller bag with her.

Knox looked at Puller. "I'm going to check in and then I'll give you a call. I'm sure my superiors will have a lot of questions for me after the incident with Macri. And there's always paperwork to fill out. Doesn't seem like all that much, though, for taking someone's life," she added, looking depressed.

Puller said, "You took her life because she was trying to take yours."

He watched as Knox walked off to her car.

Kirk said, "Do you trust her? I mean do you *really* trust her?"

"Yes, I do."

"Well, I don't. That's why I held a few things back."

Puller shot her a glance and said, "My car's over there."

They walked to his sedan and climbed in. Puller said, "Okay, what do you have?"

"Two facts, one from Todd Landry and one from Doug Fletcher, the prosecuting attorney. Which do you want first?"

"Prosecuting attorney."

"In addition to the computer evidence there were two witnesses who testified against your brother at his court-martial."

"Witnesses? Who were they?"

"People he worked with at STRATCOM."

"What did they say?"

"One testified that he saw your brother meeting in a car with a man who was later identified as being an agent for the Iranian government."

"That's not possible."

"And the other witness testified that she saw Robert Puller burn something onto a DVD from a secure area at STRATCOM's satellite facility in Kansas and try to take it with him."

"And why did the prosecuting attorney point these things out to you? They sound pretty damning and certainly wouldn't help Bobby."

"At the court-martial they *were* severely damaging. No, Fletcher pointed them out because of something in both witnesses' written statements."

"What was it?" asked Puller, his gaze steady on Kirk.

"What they said, what they *both* said in those statements." She cleared her throat and recited, " 'It was clear to me at the time that Robert Puller was acting very mysteriously.' "

Puller kept staring at her. "They *both* said that?"

"To the word. What do you think the odds are of that happening naturally?"

"Slim and none. What did the prosecuting attorney do with that?"

"The statements were made available to defense counsel, of course, under the discovery rules for court-martials. But it's not the job of the prosecutor to do his adversary's job. So he didn't do anything about it. But two years later it obviously had been sticking in his craw."

"And Landry did nothing with it?"

"I don't know. I wasn't at the court-martial and the prosecuting attorney didn't elaborate on that point. And who knows if anything would have come of it. The other evidence they had was pretty conclusive. Similarities in witness statements probably wouldn't have carried the day."

"So did Fletcher think the witnesses were lying? That they were told to say that?"

"He wouldn't go that far, and neither would I if I were in his shoes and someone asked me. If they were lying it was a little sloppy of them to say the exact same thing. Whoever's behind this could be a micromanager, but definitely not a lawyer. People do compare witness statements just for that reason." She paused. "And reading between the lines, Puller, I think that's why an Article 106 spying case became an Article 106a espionage case. I think defense and prosecutor came to an agreement on that because they both thought something strange was going on. If your brother was put to death, that could never be rectified. If he were alive, albeit in prison, then maybe one day another explanation would come to light. At least that's what I think happened."

"You said 'whoever's behind this'? So you believe my brother was set up?"

"Let me tell you what the defense counsel told me. And let me warn you that it might not be easy for you to hear. And it's the main reason I flew out here. I wanted to tell you this face-to-face."

Puller stiffened slightly. "Okay."

"Near the end of the court-martial, Landry wanted your brother to testify on his own behalf. The trial was not going well and Landry thought Robert would be a good witness. He was incredibly intelligent, patriotic, and articulate. Landry thought he would present well to the panel."

"Did he testify?"

"No."

"Why not?"

"He refused."

"Why? What would he have to lose if things were going against him anyway?"

"He let something slip to Landry, and the 'let slip' part is defense counsel's observation, not mine."

"What did my brother say?"

"That he couldn't risk it."

"Risk it? He was fighting for his life!"

"He apparently wasn't worried about himself."

"Who then?" demanded Puller.

"This was the 'let slip' part. He said he couldn't risk it because if he was found innocent his family would suffer."

There was a long moment of silence in the car, until Puller said, "My father and I are the only family he has. So he was talking about us? That *we* would be in danger if he got off?"

"Yes."

"Someone threatened him. Unless he takes the fall, we get killed?"

"Landry said your brother changed during the course of the court-martial. Going from confident and indignant to, well, afraid."

"And nobody did anything?"

"What could they do? Your brother never specifically said he had been threatened. Or that someone was going to hurt his family. In fact, when Landry pressed him on it he clammed up, wouldn't say another word about it and swore him to secrecy. That meant Landry could not share it with the prosecutor or the court."

Puller slumped back in his seat. He felt like someone had taken a jackhammer to his skull and then parked an Abrams tank on his chest. He felt as cold as death.

My brother has been rotting in prison to protect me?

Kirk said, "You shouldn't feel guilty, Puller. You knew nothing about it."

Puller stared out the window at a young couple walking past holding hands. "Maybe I didn't want to know," he said at last. "I could have found out. I'm an investigator. I could have found out. That's what I do."

"Better late than never," replied Kirk. "What are you going to do now?"

"I need the names of the witnesses. Do you have them?"

"Yes. But what will you do with that information?"

"Find out the truth. That's what I really do, Shireen. I find out the truth. And maybe this time I can save my brother if I do find it."

"Well, you also might find a lot more than you bargained for."

32

I APPRECIATE YOUR filling me in on this, Puller," said Knox.

They were sitting in the lobby bar of the hotel where Shireen Kirk was staying. Kirk was upstairs in her room getting some sleep. Puller had met Knox here for a drink and then told her all that Kirk had disclosed to him in the car.

"You needed to know."

She sipped on a glass of Prosecco while he nursed a beer.

"I take it Ms. Kirk didn't want to tell me, though. She waited until you two were alone."

"She plays everything close to the vest."

"Well, with this I can't say I blame her."

Knox gazed around the bar. It was active, with lots of patrons, some with dates and some looking for companionship at least for one night.

"What do you intend to do now?"

Puller slipped out a piece of paper. "I intend to talk to these two people."

Knox glanced at the paper. "The pair of witnesses?"

Puller finished off his beer and nodded. "Susan Reynolds is still in government service but works at Fort Belvoir in Virginia. Niles Robinson works for a private government contractor and is based in Fairfax, Virginia."

"So you doing this long-distance or close-up?"

"I don't interview people long-distance if I can help it."

"Interview or interrogate?" she shot back.

"That's largely up to them."

"What do you really hope to find?"

"Answers."

"When do you want to leave?"

"Tomorrow morning. There's an eight a.m. flight out, gets into Reagan National a couple hours later."

He paid the tab and they rose. He hooked her by the arm as they were about to head out. "The witnesses don't know I'm coming, Knox. I'd like to keep the surprise."

"If you're afraid I'll call them, you're free to sleep in my hotel room tonight and keep watch. I got a room here before I met you in the bar."

He studied her silently, his gaze taking in every point of her expression worth evaluating.

"I trust you, Knox."

She said angrily, "No, I don't think you do. So if you don't want to spend the night in my room, I'll spend the night in yours. And then we'll head to the East Coast and see what we see."

"You don't have to do that."

"No, you're wrong. I saw the way you just looked at me. So I *do* have to do it."

"Look, I'll just get my own room."

"I thought you *had* a room."

"I checked out after I left you at the cemetery. My plan was to run down some more leads and then head back to D.C. Obviously, with what happened with Macri and Shireen being here, things changed. We can head back tomorrow morning. I'll get a room here."

"Puller—"

But he had already walked out of the bar and headed over to the front desk while Knox, her arms folded across her chest, moodily watched. Puller spent a long time with the hotel representative and the woman made several phone calls while Puller looked increasingly frustrated. Finally the woman put down the phone for the last time, shook her head, and said, "I'm really sorry. I even tried the downtown Y. Nothing."

"Thanks," said Puller tightly.

Puller walked back over to Knox. She said, "So what's the word?"

Puller was stone-faced. "The word is there's some sort of cattlemen's convention in town. They just rented the last room in the hotel ten minutes ago."

"Cattlemen?" said Knox, a smirk playing over her lips. "I didn't know they had conventions. What do they talk about? The best ways to cow-tip?"

Puller went on as though he hadn't heard her. "Which means there's not a hotel room to be had anywhere."

"You're wrong there, Puller. There's *my* room. Let's go."

* * *

Puller came out of the bathroom in Knox's room dressed in sweats.

Knox passed by him and handed him her phone. "You can check the log. I didn't make a call, text, or email while you were changing. And if you want you can hold on to it until we get to D.C."

"You're really blowing this out of proportion."

"I don't think so," she said tersely. "I think I'm blowing it just right, actually."

She slammed the bathroom door behind her. A minute later he heard the shower start up.

Puller looked around the room. There was only the one bed. And a chair. He grimaced. Contorting his nearly six-foot-four-inch body into a chair for a full night did not appeal to him in the least.

He eyed the floor. Hardwood. *Great.*

He called the front desk and asked about a roll-away bed. None were available. Apparently, several of the "cattlemen" were doubling up.

"We have a crib," the woman said.

"Right," said Puller before he hung up.

Smartass.

He sat in the chair and eyed her phone. She had disabled the auto lock, because he didn't have to input a passcode. She had made no calls and had received none. He checked texts and emails. Nothing. Just like Knox had said. He checked the trash and junk caches. Zip there too.

He set the phone down on the nightstand, stretched out his limbs, and waited. And while he waited, he listened to the water running in the shower, and then he heard Knox singing.

And before he realized it, his thoughts had drifted back to an unlikely person.

His mother.

It had been the rockiest of relationships between his parents. She was a gentle woman, but with a spine of iron when she was pushed into a corner, a place John Puller Sr. had often forced her. Yet she had doted on her boys, until she was suddenly gone from their lives one day.

She had showered. That's what had prompted the memory now. Puller had heard the water running and his mother singing, as she often did. Then the water had stopped. The bathroom door had opened and then closed. Puller had gone outside in the backyard to play. He remembered looking toward the house on the base where his father was stationed. His mother had been at the window, a towel still around her and her long hair still wet. She was looking at him. She smiled and waved. And he waved back.

That had been the last time he had ever seen her. When he had come back inside hours later she was gone. A search was conducted, but she was never found. His father had never spoken her name after that.

Jacqueline Puller had been Jackie to her friends, of which she had more than his father ever would. People feared his father. People loved his mother. Not a day went by that he didn't think of her. Not a single day.

He conjured that face at the window. The smile, the wave. All of it full of love and reassurance, with nothing to predict such a catastrophic and mysterious end.

The image began to fade as the voice intruded. "Puller? Puller?"

Something shook him by the arm.

He came out of this memory, opened his eyes, and looked up. For one vastly unsettling moment Puller thought his long-lost mother was standing in front of him.

But it was Knox standing there draped in a towel, her hair pinned up and damp.

"Are you okay?" she asked, looking genuinely worried about him.

He cleared his throat, gathered his composure, and nodded as he abruptly stood, causing her to jump back as he almost stepped on her bare foot.

"Sorry, just have a bunch of stuff on my mind."

"Gee, I wonder what that could be?"

She smiled and he forced one to his lips. He picked up her phone and handed it back to her. "I think this is yours."

"You sure you don't want to keep it?"

"I'm sure I don't need to."

She set the phone on the nightstand and eyed the chair, the floor, and then the bed. "I guess we better discuss sleeping arrangements."

"Look, I can just sleep in the lobby. There's a couch there."

She said in a mock playful tone, "What, you don't trust yourself spending the night in a woman's hotel room? What about the Rangers' legendary self-discipline?"

He glanced down at her towel-draped figure. Then he abruptly looked up. "I trust myself." He took in a whiff of air. Her hair smelled of vanilla. He felt an odd sensation creep up his spine. He shook it off, with difficulty.

"Then what's the problem?"

"I can sleep in the chair or on the floor."

"You can sleep in the bed, I'll sleep in the chair."

"Knox, it's your room."

"And you're a lot bigger than me. And I've slept in far worse places, trust me."

She grabbed some things from her suitcase and went back into the bathroom. A minute later she came out dressed in shorts and a tank top, her hair down around her shoulders. She snagged a pillow off the bed and a blanket from the closet. She curled up in the chair and put the blanket over her.

"You sure about this?" said Puller, who had been watching her uncomfortably.

"For the last time, yes. Can you hit the light?"

Puller swiped the switch with his hand. Then he got into bed, lay back against the pillow, and lifted the sheet up to his chest.

Knox sat up in the chair. "What were you thinking about when I came out of the bathroom?" she asked. "Your brother?"

"No. Somebody else in the family."

"Your father?"

"No," he said, his tone blunt.

"Okay, I get the message. I'll stop asking."

They lay there in silence for a few minutes, the only sound their breathing.

"It was my mother. I was thinking about her."

He glanced over. Knox was looking at him.

"Is she still alive?" she asked.

"I don't know," he replied.

"What happened to her?"

"She disappeared when I was a kid. She was waving at me from the window of our house while I was outside playing. She was just there and then she was gone. Never saw her again."

"Puller, I'm so sorry."

"I've…I've never told anyone about this. At least not since it happened."

"I can understand that."

"I'd appreciate it if you didn't…"

"Puller, if there's something I can do, it's keep a secret. I would never tell anyone. I swear."

"Thanks, Knox."

"But why did you start thinking of her now? Because of your brother?"

"No. It was your being in the shower. And the singing."

She looked embarrassed. "I was singing in the shower? Jesus, sometimes I don't even know I'm doing it. I'm sorry. I can't even carry a tune."

"No, you were fine." Then he grew silent.

She said, "Is that the last memory you have of your mother, apart from seeing her in the window? She was singing in the shower?"

Puller nodded, because he couldn't speak right now.

"I had no idea, Puller. I never would have—"

"I know," he said interrupting her. "It's okay." He paused. "Some family, huh. Brother on the run. Mother disappeared. And my father's sitting in a VA hospital still thinking he's heading up an Army corps."

She said, "My grandfather had Alzheimer's.

It's a...terrible disease. It wipes everything important away from the inside out."

"Yeah, it does," he said curtly, and then there was silence once more.

"Good night, Puller."

"Good night, Knox."

33

THE NEXT MORNING they descended into an overcast D.C. and landed a few minutes early. Before they'd left Puller had taken AWOL to Fort Leavenworth and left the cat in the care of a vet who maintained a kennel there. Puller had arranged for an Army car to be waiting for him at the airport in D.C. They loaded their bags into it and drove off from the airport.

"Two witnesses," Puller said.

"Two witnesses," Knox repeated.

"You got anything?" he asked.

"I checked into the INSCOM database on the drive to the airport. Susan Reynolds has worked at Fort Belvoir for about four months. At the time your brother was arrested she worked at STRATCOM in Kansas City."

"Where she worked with my brother, or at least knew him by sight," commented Puller.

Knox pulled a notebook from her bag and flipped through the pages. "Shireen Kirk said that Reynolds testified that your brother copied something from a computer onto a DVD."

"I guess that's a no-no at STRATCOM."

"It's a no-no in most secure facilities. But Reynolds said she saw your brother do it, and then he pocketed the DVD and left the facility with it."

"I wonder if they ever determined what files he accessed and downloaded? Or *allegedly* did?" added Puller.

"I suppose they would have had to check that if they introduced it into evidence against him at the court-martial."

"And I wonder what happened to the DVD? If it ever existed?"

"It really would be helpful to get a transcript of the court-martial proceedings," said Knox.

"Shireen said it would take a court order. And it would have to trump national security, which was the reason the file was sealed in the first place."

"Well, your brother has escaped from prison. So if we accept the prevailing argument that he is in fact guilty, then his being on the loose with all the secrets he has in his head constitutes a national security problem. We could argue that if we are going to help catch him, we need to know about the crimes he was convicted of. In detail. For instance, this Iranian agent that he allegedly met with. If we can get a lead on him, it might bring us to your brother."

"He's not guilty, Knox!"

"I understand that. But the point is we need a way to get the files, Puller. And if we have to play the national security angle, well, hell, let's play it."

Puller flashed her an admiring look. "That's pretty clever, actually. How can they argue against that, right? They need to give us whatever they have, to allow us to apprehend him before he hurts this country."

"Maybe Kirk can file a motion?"

"No, that would take too long. We need a shortcut."

"How?"

Puller pulled out his phone. The man answered on the second ring. James Schindler from the National Security Council said, "Hello?"

"Mr. Schindler, John Puller. I need your help, sir. And I really need it right now."

34

PULLER AND KNOX were parked outside of Susan Reynolds's home in Springfield, Virginia.

Knox checked her watch. "She got off work about thirty-five minutes ago. She might've stopped along the way. Fort Belvoir isn't that far from here."

Pulled nodded but said nothing, keeping his gaze swiveling between Reynolds's two-story home in a newer, very upscale neighborhood of Springfield and the entrance to the subdivision.

"What's her position at Fort Belvoir?" Puller asked.

"She works in the Center for Combating Weapons of Mass Destruction."

"Don't they work closely with DTRA?" said Puller, referring to the Defense Threat Reduction Agency.

"There's a partnership there, yes," replied Knox. "In fact the center is located at DTRA's headquarters and a lot of DTRA'S mission supports the center's work."

"And their mission is to wipe out WMDs?"

"At least the bad guys' WMDs."

"Anything jump out in her personnel file?" he asked.

"No. She joined another STRATCOM component at Bolling Air Force Base about the time of your brother's court-martial. And from there she went to the center. But there must be something if she lied about your brother's actions."

"Well, we're about to find out because there she is."

A late-model Lexus four-door pulled into the driveway of Reynolds's house. A tall, fit, good-looking woman in her early fifties with a thick mane of bleached-blonde hair climbed out of the sedan carrying a briefcase and a plastic bag full of groceries.

Puller knew from her file that she had two grown children who no longer lived with her.

She walked up to the front steps, and by the time she got there Puller and Knox had caught up to her.

"What is this about?" she asked when they flashed their creds.

"Robert Puller," Puller said bluntly and then

watched Reynolds closely for any type of reaction. However, she simply stared up at him.
In her younger days she must've been truly a
beauty, thought Puller. She still had head-turn-
ing looks and her tall, lean figure was impressive. The woman clearly stayed in shape.

"I heard that he had escaped from the DB.
Are you worried that he might come after me
because I testified against him?"

Puller gave her another appraising look and
his opinion of the woman changed. She was not
going to simply crack and confess. She must
have anticipated someone might show up on
her doorstep after his brother had gotten out of
the DB. And she was prepared.

"Can we go inside and discuss this?" said
Puller.

"All right." Reynolds glanced at Knox.
"INSCOM? So you're at Fort Belvoir too."

"Yes, but I don't work from there. And I
hardly have any engagement with the center or
DTRA."

Reynolds nodded. "Well, it's not like I would
ever see you anyway. The place is massive."

She unlocked the front door. The house was
alarmed and she blocked their view of the control panel while she keyed in the disarming
code.

"I need to put the groceries away in the fridge. Can you give me a couple minutes?"

"I can do better than that," said Puller. "I can help you while my partner goes over her notes." He inclined his head at Knox and then nodded toward the living room.

She took up a seat there and hauled out her notepad while Puller followed Reynolds down a short hallway to the large kitchen.

"CID?" she said. "I suppose you're investigating the escape. But Puller was Air Force."

"DB is an Army prison."

"I saw you had the same last name."

"Lots of Pullers around," said Puller, quite truthfully.

He slowly emptied the bag of groceries and handed them to her one by one, taking his time.

"So, you like the work at the center?" he asked.

"It's challenging. And what goal could be more important? Getting WMDs out of the hands of terrorists."

"Or stop them from getting WMDs in the first place."

"Even better."

"So how well did you know Robert Puller?"

"Not well. I mean we worked together at the facility in Kansas City when that was open.

They've consolidated everything back at Offutt now."

"What did you think of him?"

"He was incredibly smart and diligent. Everyone knew he was going to end up running the place some day. Made it all the more unbelievable that he did what he did."

"Gambling debts online."

Reynolds put the last of the groceries away and closed the fridge door. "That's what came out in the trial. I guess if you get addicted to something it can end up ruining you. It did him. All very sad. He was a tough one to replace."

"You testified that you saw him copy something onto a DVD."

"That's right, I did."

"Which is prohibited at STRATCOM?"

"Absolutely."

"How did they check for that?"

"Well, they make it hard to do things like that. Like at DTRA, our computers were deactivated for flash drive usage, so you can't steal data that way. But you can use a DVD, as Robert did. They had to allow that for us to do our jobs. The best security is to vet your employees and make sure they're not working for the other side, because you can't totally eliminate the risk of someone stealing sensitive data. Look at Snowden. There are random searches and they have scanners, but if you're badged you don't run through the scanners. I suspect they have other security measures they don't share with us, just in case we do have a traitor in the ranks."

"So he probably knew that as well and couldn't take the chance of just slipping a DVD into his pocket and hoping he gets out. How did he get the device out the day you saw him?"

"He pulled the fire alarm. The facility was evacuated. As you can imagine, there wasn't an opportunity to search people. And I would suppose that any stealth measures they had in place were trumped by the possibility of a fire."

"But you reported what you saw?"

"Immediately. By the time security arrived the fire alarm had been pulled. They caught up to him outside. They found the DVD in his pocket."

"Was he placed under arrest then?"

"Yes. Then he was released on his personal recognizance. But then it was reported that he had previously been spotted meeting with someone who turned out to be a spy for the Iranian government. It was then that Puller was put in the stockade until his court-martial began."

"What was the time lapse there?"

"I'm not sure. Not that long. Maybe a week."

"Surprising they didn't jail him for good after they found the DVD in his pocket."

"I thought so too. But maybe he talked them into it. He could be very convincing."

"But you said you didn't know him that well."

"I didn't. But I heard him make numerous presentations at STRATCOM. He was articulate, a powerful speaker, and had a comeback for everything they threw at him. Probably because he was smarter than everyone else in the room."

Puller had been jotting notes down. He clicked his pen a couple of times while he thought about her last statement. Did he detect a note of jealousy there?

"You haven't noticed anything unusual around here?" he asked.

"Do you mean have I seen Robert Puller lurking in my backyard? No, I haven't. I doubt I'm important enough for that. It was incredible that he broke out of DB. I would think he would already be out of the country."

"Pretty dicey for him to meet with an Iranian spy."

"Maybe we should rejoin your partner. She's probably wondering what happened to us."

Puller led the way down the hall. Knox was sitting in the same chair by the stone fireplace. She glanced at Puller, her features inscrutable.

"Really nice place," she said to Reynolds. "I love the openness and the decoration."

"Thanks. It's a nice neighborhood. Lots of interesting people from all walks of life."

Knox pointed at an array of photos sitting on a console table. "Is that you?"

Reynolds nodded and smiled. "That was taken when I made the Olympic team in the biathlon."

"Skiing and shooting?" said Puller.

"That's right."

"How'd you do?"

The smile turned to a frown. "I didn't end up competing. Medical condition."

"That must have been disappointing," said Knox.

"What's a life without disappointment? Makes you stronger."

Knox pointed to another photo. "Your kids?"

Reynolds nodded. "My son's a lawyer and my daughter runs a clothing store."

"You must have had them young?" noted Puller.

"Adam and I met in college and married in our sophomore year."

"I don't see a picture of him here," said Knox.

"He was killed in a hit-and-run nearly twenty years ago," Reynolds said bluntly. "It's too painful for me to even see his face."

"Did they ever catch the person who did it?" asked Puller.

Reynolds shook her head. "I was out of the country at the time on assignment. Adam was an FBI agent, and a damn good one. He was working a case in D.C. having to do with a drug cartel. I think those devils were behind it, but the Bureau thought it was simply an accident."

"Did you have proof otherwise?" asked Knox.

Reynolds said, "It was a long time ago, so what does it matter? Nothing will bring him back."

"I'm sorry," said Knox. She then pointed to one more photograph. It was a much older one, in black and white. "Is that you?"

Puller looked at it. It was of an older man in a magician's outfit, complete with top hat and tails. He was holding a wand in one hand and a long cloth in the other. Next to him was a tall, slender teenage girl.

Reynolds nodded. "My father was a professional magician. I was his assistant. He was really good. Taught me a lot. Great guy. I miss him. Cancer took him ten years ago." She added brusquely, "Now, is there anything else I can help you with?"

Puller glanced at Knox and said, "She answered my questions while we were putting away groceries. So I think that's it." He turned back to Reynolds. "Obviously, if you notice anything suspicious, please give us a call." He handed her one of his cards.

She looked at the card and then glanced up at Puller. "Just so you know, I can take care of myself. If I had competed in the Olympics I was a lock for a bronze and with a bit of luck the gold was not out of reach. I have lots of guns and I know how to use them. In fact, I would go down to the FBI's shooting range with Adam and take on all comers. I never lost. And at my age, I've never needed glasses of any kind. The doctors say it's remarkable. I say it's just good fortune. So if someone breaks into my home, I doubt they'll be walking out of here. I always stand my ground. And I don't miss."

Puller gave her a long stare and then nodded. "I'm sure. Have a good day."

He and Knox left and climbed into their car. But Puller didn't start it up. He sat there staring up at the house.

"You find anything while I had her in the kitchen?"

"A forty-five Smith and Wesson hidden in the bookcase. The windows are alarmed too. She has motion detectors all over the place. And there's a large floor safe in her bedroom, which is the first door on the right off the main hall. It's locked, but I'm guessing she keeps her long guns and other pistols in there. And maybe all her *cool* shooting trophies."

"You covered a lot of ground in a short time."

"I do my best."

"Anything else?"

"No smoking gun, no pun intended."

"Maybe we're looking at it," he said.

"What do you mean?"

"She came from KC," he said. "Went to Bolling in Anacostia."

"Right."

"Sticker shock. Cost of living in Kansas is a lot lower than here. How much you figure that house cost?"

Knox studied the place and then looked at the homes around it.

"Million-plus."

"That's what I was thinking. And a late-model top-of-the-line Lexus sedan probably set her back about seventy thousand or more."

"And she has two kids and a husband who was killed when they were still young. So that meant she was the sole breadwinner."

"You saw her file. What was she making, say, twenty years ago?"

"About thirty thousand a year," replied Knox.

"And college and law school aren't cheap. Even if they took out loans. She probably had to foot part of the bill somehow."

"But if she was paid off because of your brother, that was only a little over two years ago."

"Right, but I wonder how much of her debt is still out there? Maybe none?"

"And now she lives in a million-dollar home and drives a luxury car."

"What's her salary now?"

"I figure a little over a hundred thousand a year plus benefits."

"Just doesn't add up."

"No, it doesn't."

"But I assume the government checks up on these things."

"Maybe not. Look at the CIA and Aldrich Ames. Big house, luxury cars, none of which he could afford on his salary." She paused. "Maybe she inherited."

"You saw how she practically threatened us at

the end there? She has guns and she knows how to use them? You walk in but you won't walk out? I think she knew that you were searching the place while we were in the kitchen. And she was smooth, way too smooth for a visit like ours. It was like she was expecting us."

"I swear I didn't tell anyone, Puller."

"I know. So if she's been warned, then so has the other witness."

"You still want to go see him?"

"Hell yes. He might not be as prepared as Reynolds was."

Puller's phone dinged not once but twice. He checked the emails.

"Anything useful?" asked Knox.

"Maybe the Holy Grail."

"What is it?"

"The court-martial transcript. Schindler seems to really have a lot of juice. And that's not all."

"What else?"

"The ME at Leavenworth. He got back the toxicology results on our dead guy."

"And?"

"And he's Ukrainian. Or at least he was there recently."

"I didn't think they'd done isotope mapping over there."

"He said we lucked out."

"How?"

"The guy was from Chernobyl. Apparently because of the nuclear disaster they had there all those years ago, the toxicology signature is absolutely unique due to the water and air contamination."

"Lucky for us. Not so lucky for the poor bastards who have to live there. So, Ukrainian? Aided by an officer from Croatia named Ivo Mesic?"

"Not such a stretch. Ukraine was part of the Soviet Union. And Croatia was part of Yugoslavia, which was a communist regime."

"So the big red monster is rearing its ugly head again?"

"Did you expect them to go quietly into the night? Especially with the guy running the show now. He has more testosterone than Arnold Schwarzenegger in his *Terminator* days."

CHAPTER

35

ROBERT PULLER HAD driven twenty-four hours straight, from Kansas to Maryland. He had kept going with hot coffee, loud music, and more cans of Red Bull than he cared to remember. He had discovered through necessity that his bladder was working just fine.

He was just now driving past Fort Meade, which was like a Russian nesting doll. There were many layers to it, which included an Army installation, the NSA, the U.S. Army Cyber Command, and DISA, the Defense Information Systems Agency. There were probably more intelligence analysts and spy hardware on the nearly eight square miles here than any other place on earth.

If National Geospatial was the eyes of the American intelligence empire by virtue of its role in satellite surveillance, then the NSA was the ears of that same intelligence empire, since it was the chief producer and manager of signal intelligence. And as the world, and ordinary Americans, had recently learned, the NSA was listening in on a lot more than foreign conversations.

The NSA was part of the Department of Defense and by law was required to be headed by a military officer. Upon assuming the leadership of the NSA one was automatically promoted to a four-star or an admiral. The deputy director was always a civilian and had a technical background.

Robert Puller knew all this because he had been groomed to possibly head up the NSA one day. It would have been many years down the road and he would have to have carried three stars on his shoulders by that time. There was no guarantee that any of that would have happened. And it was an ambitious goal for a humble major, but his trajectory had been a steep one. He had been on course for his first star in near record time, and when he reached his fifties he would have probably carried at least the requisite three stars.

Upon his conviction Puller had lost his military commission, along with everything else he held of importance. And now he was an escaped prisoner. His personal and professional destruction was complete.

But perhaps not beyond redemption.

He kept his gaze on the perimeter security fence that surrounded Fort Meade. In the distance was an array of satellite dishes that helped scoop information from the digital ether equal to the entire contents of the Library of Congress every six hours. It was a staggering amount of information that not even the NSA, with all its resources, had the manpower to digest. That was cold comfort for those whose communications the NSA *did* capture *and* act upon.

Puller had been to Fort Meade many times. He could go there no more, unless he wanted a quick return to prison. He drove to a motel near the fort and checked in. He carried his bag up to his room, put his things away, and then sat at a small table set against the wall.

There had been a change in command at STRATCOM. The CO while Puller had been there, Major General Martin Able, had earned another star in the last two years and had held one other major assignment before grabbing the brass ring. He had been appointed and confirmed as the director of the NSA four months ago. It was also four months ago that General Daughtrey had been assigned to STRATCOM. He had not been the head of STRATCOM, though one day he might have been. He had been the second in command behind a two-star.

But Martin Able was now the king of the NSA. He was also in the hot seat with all the recent revelations courtesy of Edward Snowden. His agency had become the target of a turbocharged media looking for scandal to sell subscriptions and ratings and also of a United States Congress desperate to look like it was actually doing something. And the conspiracy theorists were out in force.

And maybe this time they had a point.

A change in control. Four months ago. General Able to the NSA at Fort Meade. His last stop, probably. Most officers retired from the NSA top spot. Able was sixty. The mandatory retirement age was creeping close for him, although it could be deferred under certain circumstances.

There were currently thirty-eight Air Force three-stars. Upon his elevation to the NSA, director Able had automatically gotten his fourth star. There were currently only thirteen of those in the Air Force and only thirty-four across all branches. Pretty select company.

Able had also been the convening authority in Puller's court-martial. Puller and Able had worked closely together. The general liked to have protégés that he could haul out and put on display, and he did so liberally with Puller, subtly taking much credit for the younger man's accomplishments. Mentoring talent helped your career, and Able had been a man totally focused on his career. At least that was how Puller remembered it, and he usually remembered things spot-on.

The man had never contacted him again after Puller's troubles had begun. Not that Puller could blame him. Guilt by association. It ran deep in the military. You stayed far away from the shit. If you stepped in it, the stink never left you.

So Daughtrey promoted at the same time as Able? Daughtrey was dead. Able was very much alive. Able now ran an NSA besieged by scandal. He was running around putting out fires and waiting for more to crop up. A busy man.

But maybe not too busy to think about the past.

How long would it take to plan what had happened at the DB? A few months to get everything in order?

The cover-up later?

But did it involve Daughtrey? Had he come to Kansas to make sure the truth was never discovered? Or was he there to try to find the truth?

The fact that he was dead made Puller believe it was the latter. Otherwise, why kill one of your coconspirators?

There had been two witnesses at his court-martial. They had to have been in on it too.

Susan Reynolds had testified about a DVD in his pocket. It had been found on his person after she had notified security, and Puller had no idea how it got there. The files on it had been classified. The clear implication had been that he was stealing secrets.

The other witness, Niles Robinson, had testified that he had seen Puller meeting secretly with a person who later turned out to be an Iranian agent. Puller had never met with such a man, but Robinson had apparently taken pictures showing otherwise.

Both witnesses and the physical evidence had been devastating. Yet he had never actually believed that he would be convicted, simply because he was innocent. Even when the incriminating files about the online gambling had been found on his computer, he had not wavered in his belief that he would be fully exonerated.

He was not naïve enough to believe that innocent people did not go to prison. But in the military he did not believe that was possible. He had maintained hope throughout until near the end of the proceedings. He had been planning to testify in his own defense, to fight back against the allegations and offer some of his own theories for what had happened.

And then it had arrived.

The envelope had been under his pillow in the cell he was in during the court-martial. He had no idea how it got there.

He had opened it and read the brief contents. The message was clear: Do anything to save yourself and your immediate family will suffer. They will suffer the ultimate punishment.

Well, he had only two immediate family members left. His brother and his father.

He supposed he could have taken the letter to the authorities. It would have perhaps been proof of his innocence, although they could easily claim he had written it himself. But he had never considered doing that.

And thus Puller had not testified. He had accepted his fate. He had been convicted by a panel of his peers and been transferred to the DB. His automatic appeal had been unsuccessful and he had never tried to initiate any others. He had been resigned to living out his days in prison. He was an innocent man behind bars for life. Could there be a worse fate? He had sometimes thought the death penalty might have been better.

He had been rotting in prison for over two years. And now they wanted him dead. They had sent a killer inside the prison as part of an elaborate plan to make sure he was dead. They had failed. He had turned their plan to his advantage. And now he was free.

They could not communicate with him now. They could not threaten him with the ultimate punishment for his immediate family.

So Robert Puller had decided that this opportunity had come to him for a reason. What he had put away in the back of his head when the threats to his family had surfaced was the fact that if they were trying to falsely accuse him of espionage, then *true* espionage must have been going on at STRATCOM. And that could do, and might have already done, incalculable damage to America.

Why they had chosen him to implicate was still unknown to Puller. But he was going through the possibilities in his head. And he was certain an answer would emerge.

But he had already reached one conclusion. He had chosen his family over his country, sacrificing himself for their welfare.

Now he was going to choose his country over everything else.

And although his uniform had been taken away from him, he still considered himself a servant of the United States, forever sworn to protect its interests above all others.

And that's exactly what he intended to do now.

And on top of that was an overwhelming desire to make these sonofabitches finally pay for what they'd done.

36

NILES ROBINSON NOW worked at a defense contractor in Fairfax. Puller and Knox had met him at his office the next morning. He was a black man in his mid-forties, tall and spare with intelligent brown eyes. He answered their questions readily. He had worked with Robert Puller and thought of him as a friend.

That is until he had seen Puller talking with a man who turned out to be an Iranian agent.

"So you didn't know he was an agent at the time?" Puller asked.

"No. But I did take pictures of them."

"Why?" asked Knox sharply.

Robinson gave her a benign stare. "Not to be accused of profiling, but the man was Middle Eastern. And they did seem to be acting furtive."

"They were in a car, on a public street?"

"Yes."

"They could have picked a quieter spot," noted Puller.

"Well, it was late at night and there weren't many folks about. And they never got out of the car."

"And it was just a coincidence you were there?" asked Knox.

"No, it wasn't."

"Oh?" prompted Knox.

"As I testified at the court-martial, I had followed Robert there."

"And why was that?" asked Puller.

Robinson shifted his gaze to him. "Because, quite frankly, I had misgivings about him."

"Based on what?" Puller said.

"At STRATCOM you're taught to be paranoid. And I was. I can't tell you specifically what aroused my suspicions, but I had them. That wasn't the first time I had followed him. Other times nothing had happened. But this time, well, I wasn't sure. That's why I took the photos."

"And gave them to your superiors?" said Knox.

"Not immediately. But I did after a coworker caught Robert leaving the facility with a DVD."

"Why not turn him in immediately?" asked Puller.

"I didn't know that the person he was meeting with in the car was a spy. I didn't want to make trouble unnecessarily."

"But then you did turn in the pictures," said Knox.

"That's right. They ran it through a terrorist watch database and out the man popped. A bad guy. A real bad guy."

"So your suspicions were confirmed?" said Knox.

"Unfortunately, yes. Please understand, I thought the world of Robert. He was incredibly bright and hardworking. He was being groomed for bigger and bigger roles. General Able had made him a personal project, in fact. I couldn't understand why Robert had done what he had, until the Internet gambling came to light."

"And that was the motive?" said Knox.

"Millions of them, apparently," said Robinson evenly.

While Robinson was talking Puller had been looking on the shelf behind the man's desk. He registered one thing and then looked at Robinson. "We appreciate your help." He gave the man his card and asked him to call if he had anything to add.

Robinson fingered the card and said, "So any

idea how he escaped? I thought DB was impenetrable."

"Well, apparently it has an Achilles' heel," said Puller.

* * *

Back in the car Puller settled into his seat and closed his eyes.

"Remember, they both used the same phrase in their report, Puller."

"They also worked together. They might have discussed it before they gave their statements."

"So you're now doubting your brother's innocence?"

Puller opened his eyes and looked at her. "No. My brother was protecting me and my father. He took the fall because the real traitors put him in an impossible situation."

"And photos can be altered," pointed out Knox. "Images added or deleted."

"Yes, they can. And these days, it's pretty hard to detect."

"So we struck out with Robinson," Knox said. "I think the guy was forewarned we were coming."

"I'm sure he was. I checked him out. He served his country well. Now he's on the private side making more money, but there was something about the guy. I didn't see it in Reynolds."

"See what?"

"Remorse."

"You think he feels bad for setting up your brother?"

"Did you notice the photo on the shelf behind his desk?"

"There were a few of them. Which one in particular?"

"The one of the kid in a hospital bed. Shaved head, tubes all over him. I think that was Robinson's kid. He looked to be about ten. Then there was another picture of Robinson with the boy. The kid looked older and healthy."

"So his kid was sick. Maybe had cancer."

"And now he's good."

"And your point?"

"Robinson lives in a modest home. He's shown no signs of coming into wealth. So I wonder if over two years ago his health insurance had topped out. Or did it even cover experimental treatments for cancer? Maybe in other countries? I don't think federal government health plans do."

"You think that might be the motive for him to lie about your brother?"

"Watch your kid die or see a coworker go to prison? What would you do?"

"If you're right, then these people really are bastards."

"You think you can dig around and find out if I'm right?"

"I'm on it. What are you going to do?"

"Go over the trial record. And try to figure out the Ukrainian angle."

"Mercenary no doubt," she said.

"But who hired him?"

"Well, if we answer that, we probably answer everything."

CHAPTER

37

A DAY LATER Puller laid aside the last page, sat back, and yawned. He was sitting at a spare office in a former CID building at Fort Belvoir. The trial record he had just finished for the third time had been tedious in nearly all respects, except when it was riveting. He had just had to read through it all to get to those parts.

He rubbed his eyes, drank the last of his lukewarm coffee, and stared out the solitary window where the rain had started to fall gently, although it was forecast to turn into a pretty nasty storm as a front pushed through on its way to the Atlantic.

The door opened and Knox poked her head in.

"They said you were in here. Up for some company?"

He nodded. "I was about to fall asleep. Got started before dawn. Don't even know what time it is."

She came in holding a white bag and a carrier with two coffees perched in it. "Actually, it's almost noon, but I bet you've had nothing to eat yet."

"You'd win that bet," he admitted.

She handed him a coffee and then reached into the bag and pulled out a sandwich and set it in front of him. Next she placed a large box of steak fries between them as she slid a seat up to the desk on the other side.

He stared at the fries and then at her. "French fries? I thought you'd come in with carrot sticks and non-fat yogurt."

She slipped a thick fry from the box, opened her mouth wide, and poised the fry between her teeth momentarily before chomping down on it, causing him to wince slightly.

"A girl can splurge sometimes, Puller. I ran five miles this morning and then did an Insanity exercise routine."

"Then I think you might be entitled to the whole box."

He unwrapped his sandwich and saw that it was a Philly cheesesteak. His smile was wide and immediate.

"Boys are so predictable," said Knox, giving him an amused look.

"In some ways," said Puller, taking a bite of

his Philly and then a drink of the hot coffee.

She glanced at the stacks of papers. "So, anything good?"

He wiped his mouth with a napkin and drew a legal pad covered with notes toward him. "Shireen said they charged my brother with spying under Article 106."

She put down her coffee. "Right, the one that carries the automatic death sentence."

He nodded, sticking a fry in the small tub of ketchup. "But then it just went away and was replaced with the espionage charge."

"Nothing in the court-martial record about exactly why?"

"No, not really. It was just there until it wasn't."

"Pretty big difference," she noted. "Death for certain or life imprisonment."

"Right. I'm sure if we asked why they would just claim national security."

"They always pull that crap out when they don't want to tell the truth," said Knox.

"Well, I guess you would know," he shot back.

She flashed him a scowl. "So why do you think they would have cut the charge down? Did your brother have some juice in high places behind him?"

"He was still convicted of espionage. He still got life in prison. How much juice could he have?"

"But still, Puller. They were originally going for the death penalty. And it seemed like his alleged crimes fit the requirements for spying."

"The defense counsel and prosecutor Shireen talked to would know all about this."

"But will they talk to us? I'm surprised they told her as much as they did."

"She's a fellow JAG. And they didn't tell her everything." He stopped and lapsed into thought for a few moments. "We could always ask them, in our professional capacity."

"Yes, we could. And they could refuse. And we could press the point, go to court, get a subpoena, let the lawyers duke it out."

"And all of that would take time, maybe a lot of time," said Puller.

"Lawyers never work fast, at least that's been my experience."

"We need to work this out from our angle."

"What about talking to the judge?" she asked.

Puller shook his head. "I doubt he'll even see us. And even if he would, he'll never tell us anything. Judges don't talk about cases."

"Well, then the trial lawyers probably won't either."

"I think we have a better shot with them."

"Okay, so where are the lawyers?"

"The prosecutor's in Charlottesville, Virginia, a couple of hours from here. He's no longer doing trial work. He's teaching at the JAG School there. My brother's former lawyer is out of the Air Force and in private practice in North Carolina."

"Okay, do we split up or do it tag-team?" she asked.

"Do you want to split up?"

"No."

"Then let's head to C-ville. Did you find out anything more about Robinson?"

"Your gut was right. His son was very sick. Terminal, actually. They went to Germany desperate for a miracle cure that fortunately worked."

"And how did they pay for it?"

"There was a community fund-raiser that brought in some dollars. But I spoke with folks in Berlin familiar with the medical procedure and they said it easily would have cost a million-plus. I don't think you could sell enough cookies and lemonade to raise that much cash. And Robinson's insurance, good though it was, did not cover that sort of treatment."

"And no one became suspicious?"

"Pretty touchy subject when you're dealing with a sick kid. And it came *after* the trial was over. Maybe people just didn't put two and two together."

"Or maybe they didn't want to. But we did it, pretty quickly. And I know the kid was sick and I'm glad he's better. But my brother lost everything."

"Preaching to the choir," she replied.

"Yeah," said Puller. "Too bad someone didn't start preaching two years ago."

CHAPTER

38

SUSAN REYNOLDS SLIPPED into her car after putting some shopping bags in the trunk. It was thirty minutes to her home and the traffic was light. She reached her house and carried her bags in. She set them down and turned off the alarm. She was about to switch on the light when the voice called out.

"Please don't move. There's a gun pointed at your head."

Reynolds started to turn around.

"Do not turn around," the voice said sharply.

Reynolds froze where she stood.

"Now, walk forward and turn into the living room. Sit in the chair nearest the television."

"You seem to know my house very well," said Reynolds calmly as she began to walk in that direction.

She turned into the living room and sat in the designated chair. When she reached for the light on the table next to her the voice said, "I'll do that."

She slowly pulled back her hand and laid it in her lap while the person behind her turned on the light to its lowest setting.

"How did you get in here? The alarm was on."

"An alarm is only as good as the password, and yours wasn't very good."

"But then you reset it? Why?"

"Well, not resetting it would have given my intrusion away, wouldn't it?"

He moved fully into the room but kept behind her.

Robert Puller had on a hoodie pulled up and a ski mask that covered everything on his face except his eyes and lips. His gun was pointed at the back of Reynolds's head. Across the room he had placed a mirror he'd found in her bathroom on a table. It was angled so that he could see her face reflected in it, while he remained hidden from her. He wanted to see her face, and more important, her reactions to his questions.

He said, "I would presume that you're armed. Take your weapon out holding it by the muzzle or the next sound you hear will unfortunately be the last one you ever will."

She drew out the compact Sig nine-millimeter by the muzzle and placed it on the carpet.

"Kick it behind you."

She did so and Puller reached down and pocketed it.

"What do you want?" asked Reynolds. "I have some money in the study. My credit cards are in my purse. I don't have gold bullion on the premises, if that's what you're looking for," she added snidely.

"Who paid you to lie about what you saw?" Puller asked.

She stiffened and Puller added, "I thought you would have recognized my voice before now, Susan."

"It's been two years."

"Over two years, actually. But still, I remembered *your* voice."

"I've had a lot more to do over the last two years than you."

"Actually, I've had a lot to think about, if that counts."

"And what did you conclude, Robert?"

"That you were well compensated, judging by the size of your house and the luxury car you drove up in. Uncle Sam doesn't pay that well for someone at your level."

"I invested smartly and I had some money to

start with. It's all been checked out. My security clearances justify that."

"Not always, as you well know. Granting security clearances these days is not what it used to be. But I'm not here to discuss your financial circumstances, other than to find out who paid you off."

"Nobody paid me off. I saw what I saw. You stole classified information from STRATCOM. The DVD was found in your pocket. The evidence doesn't get much clearer than that."

"Which is why you put it there, pulled the fire alarm, and then told others to search me."

"Oh, so now it's my fault? Do you have any idea how many people are after you? You killed a man to get out of prison. You didn't get the death penalty for some reason last time, but this time you will. Oh, and your brother was here to interview me. It was clear that he believes you're guilty."

"So you won't tell me who hired you?"

"No one hired me. Being at DB must have made you delusional. And on top of it you're now a murderer. I hope God will have mercy on you after they stick the needle in you, Robert."

"I think God *will* have mercy, but it won't be directed at me, because I don't require any."

"And what about Niles Robinson? Spin that one."

"I don't have to spin it. He lied. Same as you. You were in it together. Bought off by the same party."

"Well, this is obviously getting us nowhere."

Puller said, "How did you end up at the Center for Combating WMDs?"

"How did you know about that?"

"Please, Susan, don't insult my intelligence."

"I'm at the center because it's a job. There, satisfied?"

He studied her face in the mirror. But her expression was inconclusive. And her hands remained in her lap.

"But it's an unusual job for someone like you. Your work in the past had to do with inspection of nukes, but your more recent specialty was not in that arena."

"That's my business."

"But it does make sense in one respect."

Reynolds stiffened once more, Puller noted as he watched her in the mirror.

"To combat WMDs one must know where they are located. Is that why you're working there, Susan?"

"I have expertise in WMDs from when I worked on the START verification program.

Now would you please leave so I can call the police?"

"I'll get to the truth one way or another."

"So, you're going to kill me too? Like you did the man back at DB?"

"He was sent there to kill me. I don't know if you were told that part of the plan or not."

"Have fun explaining that convoluted mess to the MPs."

"If you cooperate with me, I'm sure you can work a deal. You might not have to go to prison for the rest of your life. A good deal, actually."

"I'm not going to prison. You are. *Back* to prison. Or dead, more likely."

She cried out when the needle pricked her neck. She grabbed at the spot a second after Puller removed the hypodermic. He placed it on the table behind him.

She started to turn. He pulled back the hammer on his pistol. "Don't do it."

"What did you inject me with?" she snapped.

"Something of my own concoction. You'll feel your heart start to beat erratically any second now."

She clutched at her chest, which started to heave. "You poisoned me. You bastard, you poisoned me!"

"But I also have the antidote with me. You answer my questions and you can have it."

"I can't trust you!"

"Well, you're going to have to, because I see limited options."

"I will kill you," she roared. She tried to get up, but he put a hand on her shoulder and held her down. She struggled against him but he was too strong.

"I should warn you that physical exertion such as this speeds up the process. Then not even the antidote will work. And your death will not be painless, I can assure you."

Reynolds immediately stopped moving.

"Now, try to breathe normally. Long, slow breaths. Like you're doing yoga. Long and slow."

He waited while she did so.

"That's better." He paused, watching her in the mirror. Now came the real questioning. "Who hired you?"

"How long do I have before the antidote won't work?"

"Five minutes, maybe less now that you let your heart rate spike. The poison has been distributed throughout your bloodstream far faster than optimal."

"Nothing about this is optimal," she snapped.

"Calm yourself, Susan. Let your heartbeat fall and answer my questions. Who hired you to set me up?"

"What's the poison you administered? Tell me!" she demanded.

"An organophosphate. AKA a nerve agent."

"Shit! And the antidote?"

"Two-PAM, pralidoxime chloride. With a little side of atropine since two-PAM isn't great at blood-brain barrier penetration. And some pilocarpine in case there's a reaction to the atropine."

Reynolds started breathing easier. "You've got atropine?"

Puller said, "So named after Atropos, one of the three Fates in Greek mythology. She was the Fate who chose how a person was to die. I thought it appropriate under the circumstances. After all, you had counted on my being put to death by lethal injection for *your* crime. I'm just returning the favor. Potentially, at least." He paused.

"Now, since time is running out, who hired you?"

"I don't know," she replied sharply.

"Not nearly good enough."

"I'm telling you, I *don't* know. The instructions came through a secure coded link on my private email."

"So because of an email you committed treason?"

"It wasn't just that. I did meet with someone."

"The name of the person?"

"He didn't exactly hand out business cards."

"Well, at least I know it was a man. Who was he with?"

"Not our country."

"Which one?"

He focused particularly hard now, awaiting her response as he watched her reflection in the glass.

She lifted her eyebrows and rubbed at her nose. "Russia," she said.

Puller relaxed just a bit. "Okay, and he persuaded you to do what exactly?"

"What we set you up for. Providing backdoor access to our systems."

"But after you set me up they checked for that. Why call attention to the fact?"

"They checked *your* access points, not anyone else's."

"So you threw me to the wolves to throw them off you?"

"Something like that."

"And the back doors are still there?"

"I would assume they are."

"And they've been used?"

"I doubt they paid *not* to use them."

"And now you've been assigned to the WMD Center. Interesting."

"That has nothing to do with anything. The Russians have WMDs. They don't need anyone else's."

"That's if you assume I believe you that it was the Russians behind this. I don't."

"You've poisoned me. Do you think I'd lie?"

"Of course I think you would. That's what you are, a liar."

"You have no chance, Puller. No chance at all. You're going to die."

"The Russians are easy to blame things on. So you mentioning them as your source is not particularly creative. I would have expected better from you."

Reynolds blurted out, "How much time do I have left? Give me the damn antidote."

Puller continued, as though he hadn't heard her, "Niles Robinson said he saw me with an Iranian agent. Again, he wouldn't have said that if Iran had actually been involved. So we can leave that rogue nation out of the mix. I'm just thinking out loud here. Feel free to jump in anytime with the actual answer." He reached his hand into his pocket.

"You asshole! I bet you don't even have the atropine."

He plunged the tip of another syringe into her neck and depressed the plunger. In a few seconds she toppled over in her chair and lay there unconscious from the sedative he'd administered. The "poison" had been a simple saline solution.

He had already searched her house and found her gun cache in the safe. She had made a mistake there, using the same code as her house alarm. One pistol was missing from its box, which was how he had deduced that she was armed. He had taken pictures with his phone of any documents that looked promising. And he had hacked her computer and downloaded files to his portable drive.

He let himself out, took off his mask, walked to his truck parked across the street, and drove off. There had been pluses and minuses to his visit with Reynolds. The plus was she had admitted setting him up. And she had provided him some clues to the truth. The negative was obvious. She would tell others that he had been to her home and threatened her. This would alert them that he was in the area. And this would also increase everyone's conviction that he was indeed guilty. Not that they needed any such convincing.

But in the end, it had been worth it, because for the first time ever he felt like he was finally going to figure this all out.

39

DOUG FLETCHER WAS just leaving the JAG building on the grounds of UVA's prestigious law school when Puller and Knox climbed out of the sedan. He was in his fifties, lean, with hair probably as closely cropped as during his military career, only now it was mostly gray. His jaw was sharply cut and his blue eyes were alert and penetrating, which helped to gain the trust of a judge or jury.

Puller and Knox flashed their cred packs. Fletcher didn't look surprised by their appearance.

"How can I help you?" he asked, his voice firm and low but carrying a throaty rumble that made it perfectly clear.

Puller explained why they were here and Fletcher nodded.

"I heard about the escape, of course." He glanced around. "There's an office space I use back at the JAG School. Perhaps that might be more private."

They walked there in five minutes. Fletcher closed the door to the small space that had a desk in the center with a computer on it. The walls were lined with wooden shelves filled with dusty tomes and stacks of legal periodicals. Fletcher took his seat behind the desk while Puller and Knox sat opposite.

"We understand that you might have had some doubts about Robert Puller's guilt," began Puller.

"I wasn't the only one," replied Fletcher.

"The witness statements?"

"Among other things. I guess that could have happened naturally. But I also learned later that Puller had a potential defense with his computer being hacked."

"Something he wouldn't acknowledge."

"He was too smart for his own good. Too smart in fact to allow himself to be seen loading a DVD and then get caught with it in his pocket."

"And the Iranian spy sighting?" asked Knox.

Fletcher shrugged. "It was very damning testimony. And the witness was credible and had no known grudge against Puller. So what was the motivation to lie?"

"How about a very sick child who needed a treatment that was deemed experimental and thus insurance-proof and also way out of dad's financial range?" said Puller.

Fletcher leaned forward. "What?"

Knox explained, "Robinson's son had a very rare form of leukemia. Traditional treatment couldn't touch it. The experimental option cost over seven figures and was only performed in another country. Before Robert Puller was convicted his son was going to die. After Robert Puller went to DB, Robinson suddenly got the treatment done. And it wasn't for free."

"How do you know all this?" asked Fletcher.

Knox again answered. "Because my partner here noticed two pictures of Robinson's kid in his office. One was of a dying child. The other was an older version obviously doing fine."

Puller added, "So we ran it down and found what we found."

"And there was no other explanation?" asked Fletcher. "Donations, the experimental treatment being done gratis?"

"It was paid for. Over a million bucks two months after Robert Puller went to DB."

"Damn! So if Robinson was paid off?"

"We think Susan Reynolds was too. We interviewed her. And I've done enough face-to-faces to realize when someone is lying. She was."

"And the motivation? Money again?"

Puller said, "For herself. Her husband was killed nearly twenty years ago, leaving her with two small kids to raise. She now lives in a million-dollar home on a government salary."

"And no one discovered this before now?"

"It was all after the fact. Robinson's kid was dying. Susan Reynolds was poor. After the trial who'd go back and dig through that. You didn't, right?"

"No, I didn't," Fletcher said a bit guiltily. "I had a full plate of work. No time to step back after a verdict was in. And it wasn't my job to do so," he added defensively.

"But now we have to know the truth. Puller is out there somewhere."

"But didn't he kill a man to get out?" said Fletcher. "That's what I heard through the grapevine."

"That's one theory," said Puller. "But it may be more complicated than that."

Knox said, "You were obviously somewhat skeptical of the witness statements containing the same phraseology. You didn't follow that up?"

"Again, it wasn't my job. I pointed it out

to the defense, not that they needed me to do that. And the rest of the evidence was very strong. Online gambling, piled-up debts. Means, motive, and opportunity. It was a classic case."

"Well, the motivation could have been fabricated since we suspect his computer was hacked," Puller pointed out.

"I can see that now," replied Fletcher.

"So when did the death penalty get pulled off the table?" asked Puller.

This comment drew a sharp glance from Fletcher.

Puller said, "We know the charge was changed from spying, which carries a mandatory death penalty in times of war, to espionage, which doesn't automatically mandate death. Why did that happen?" He leaned forward. "Because the record of the court-martial proceedings I looked at had you filing the motion for the change in the charges against Robert Puller. It didn't come from the defense side."

Fletcher clasped his hands in front of him and looked to be in deep thought. "That directive came from above."

"How far above?"

"Well above me. But, frankly, I think the genesis for it came from outside the legal side of the military. And outside even the Air Force."

Puller said, "How could that be? Robert Puller was in the Air Force. They would unquestionably have jurisdiction over him and the case."

"You're right in all respects. But I think it was because his father was a legendary *Army* general, if you want the truth. The DoD apparently thought that putting to death the son of such a hero would not be a good thing."

Puller sat back. This hadn't occurred to him.

Fletcher studied him. "He's *your* father too, of course."

"So you made the connection with the last name?"

"No, I knew before. When you're prosecuting someone for a serious crime, you check out his family. I know all about you. And I'm absolutely stunned that you're being allowed to investigate your brother's escape from DB."

"You're not the only one," said Puller. "So you think it had to do with our father?"

"Well, there was the letter he wrote."

Puller didn't seem to be able to process this statement. Knox glanced at him, saw his rigid look, and said to Fletcher, "What letter?"

"From General Puller, pleading for his son to not be tried for spying. It was quite moving."

"When was it sent?" asked Knox, while still glancing nervously at Puller.

"Early on in the proceedings. The judge accepted the motion I filed, and of course the defense had no objection."

Puller finally found his voice and said, "The letter wasn't in the file."

"I'm not surprised about that. It wasn't technically part of the record."

"Do you remember what else it said?" asked Puller.

"I actually kept a copy. If you give me your email I can scan it in and forward it to you."

Puller gave him a business card and said, "Thanks, I'd appreciate that."

"Is there anything else I can do for you?" asked Fletcher.

Knox said hastily, "If there is we'll get back to you."

They left a moody-looking Fletcher sitting behind his desk.

As they walked out Knox said, "You obviously didn't know your father had written a letter."

"He was at the VA by then. I didn't think he had the capacity to even write his own name."

"Well, he might have found the capacity to help a son fighting for his life."

"But it seemed to me that he didn't care what happened to Bobby."

"Maybe your dad didn't want to admit his feelings to you. Some men have a problem with that. You think your father fits into that category?"

"As far as I knew, my father never had any feelings," said Puller tersely.

40

CHARLOTTE, NORTH CAROLINA, was the next stop on their list. They made it from Charlottesville in a little over four hours with Puller driving fast the whole way. He liked to drive because it gave him time to think. And he had a lot to think about, particularly about a letter a father had written in an attempt to save his oldest son from a death sentence.

"I don't have any pennies on me, but I'll fork over folding money to see inside your head."

He looked over at Knox, who was staring at him with a worried expression.

"I was thinking about my dad."

"And why he wrote the letter?"

"It doesn't make sense."

"Despite what you said, I'm sure your father *has* feelings."

"I've heard him go off about my brother when I visited him at the VA. Unless I was somehow misconstruing his shouts and cursing, I'm not sure he was a real fan of what my brother allegedly did."

"Well, knowing what we know now about your brother's motivation to tank his own defense to protect you and your father, maybe you can tell him one day that his son was innocent."

"I'd like Bobby to be able to do that himself."

Knox placed a hand on his shoulder. "I hope he can too."

"I want to ask defense counsel point-blank why he didn't pursue that angle. I mean, if he knew Bobby was being threatened, why wasn't there an investigation?"

"Well, according to what Shireen Kirk told you, there was no evidence to that effect except your brother's statement. And he wouldn't let counsel pursue it, namely because he thought harm would come to you and your father."

"So he lets an innocent man go to prison?"

"No, he put on the defense he had and a panel of his peers sent Robert Puller to prison."

"You know it's not that simple or straightforward."

"What I know is that we need more proof than we have right now."

"Macri was bought off. And Susan Reynolds is lying. And so was Niles Robinson."

"I believe it. But can we convince others? Even with the financial evidence we have? And more important, can we tie it into your brother's case? Because all most people know is that he escaped from DB and left a dead man behind. Whether that man should have been there or not is largely irrelevant for most people. First and foremost your brother is a killer, at least that's what they think. Whatever the truth is, it's complicated, and complicated is not what our information-overloaded society is good at grasping, because they would have to focus for longer than five seconds, which most folks can't do anymore."

"So all this is for shit, then? Everything we're doing?" Puller retorted.

"Of course it's not. But I want you to understand really clearly that what we have now is not enough. It's not even close to enough. I don't see light at the end of the tunnel yet and neither should you. We have to keep plugging."

"That's all I ever do, Knox. I just keep plugging."

* * *

Knox had scrounged up government travel vouchers that would allow them to stay at the Ritz-Carlton hotel in downtown Charlotte for a reduced rate that would not cause a DoD bean counter to slash his wrists. They got rooms on the same floor, on either side of the elevator bank. They made arrangements to meet in the lobby thirty minutes later and then go have a late dinner.

Puller quickly showered and put on a set of clean clothes he'd grabbed from his duffel. He made some phone calls, including one to the VA hospital to check on his dad.

"Resting comfortably," was the reply he got to his question. Puller knew that meant the old man wasn't yelling at anybody.

He left a message on Shireen's voice mail telling her where they were and what they had found out. He knew he would have to report in soon to General Rinehart and Schindler from the NSC. How much he would tell them he wasn't sure.

He checked his watch, gunned up, and headed to the elevator.

Knox was standing there waiting for the elevator car to arrive. She wore a cream-colored skirt that hit right above the knee, an emerald green blouse, and high-heeled, open-toed shoes revealing rose-colored nail polish. Her auburn hair was highlighted against the green fabric and was done up in a way that revealed her long, curved neck. She carried a clutch purse and a wrap was loosely draped around her shoulders. He caught a whiff of her perfume and felt a little lightheaded as he approached.

He looked down at his khakis, polo shirt, and old corduroy jacket. "I'm feeling a little under-dressed next to you, Knox."

She smiled. "You look fine."

"Where to?" he asked when they reached the lobby. "I don't know the town that well."

"I made reservations at a place. Easy walking distance."

He eyed her spikes. "Even in those shoes?"

She smiled. "I have great balance."

He eyed her purse. "Gunned up?"

She nodded. "Compact but good stopping power. I use it as a backup ordinarily."

The air was warm and the dark sky clear. The walk was only two blocks. The restaurant was fairly full at the late hour. The clientele was made up of well-dressed twenty-some-things who looked like lawyers, bankers, techies, and other assorted professionals tak-ing a break from busy lives to play. When Puller saw the prices on the menu he glanced sharply at Knox.

"My per diem doesn't cover this."

"Relax, it's on me."

They split a bottle of wine and Puller had sirloin steak medium rare, while Knox ordered salmon served on a cedar plank. They divided up a piece of carrot cake over coffee for dessert.

They were the last customers to leave the restaurant.

As they walked back, Knox slipped her arm through his. She leaned into him and for some reason he interpreted this as more for support than anything else. When he glanced at her she confirmed this by saying, "I admit, the heels were a bad idea."

"Well, they look great on you. Just like the dress."

She squeezed his arm. "I wasn't sure you had noticed."

"I noticed," said Puller. He paused. "Just like I noticed the four guys following us. Two across the street and two behind us."

Knox kept looking straight ahead. "And they definitely seem interested in us?"

"They were outside the restaurant when we left. They split into pairs and headed our way. And they're still there matching us stride for stride but keeping just back."

"And the next block coming up is pretty isolated. And at this hour we're the only ones out and about."

"Let's hang a left down the alleyway up there and see what happens."

They made the turn and Puller watched as Knox opened her clutch and took out the pistol. She covered it by sliding her hand inside her wrap.

"I hear footsteps coming across the street," she said.

"See the Dumpster up there?"

"Yes," she said.

"When we get there let's fake a little romantic thing."

"You mean like making out?" she said.

"Yeah," he said crisply.

"Okay, but what's the endgame?"

"I want to be able to see the whites of their eyes. And since we're outnumbered two to one I hope it'll make them let down their defenses for the second we'll need."

They kept walking at a leisurely pace until they reached the Dumpster. Then Puller turned to Knox, brushed a strand of hair out of her eyes, circled her waist with his arm, and bent low to kiss her. As his lips rested against Knox's, Puller had not a romantic thought in his head. He was counting off the footsteps in his head. His left hand was coiled around Knox's waist but his right hand gripped his M11.

He moved his lips to Knox's neck and pretended to nuzzle her skin. "Three-two-one," he whispered in her ear.

They whirled, guns pointed at the four men, who were now only ten feet away. From their stunned expressions they had been caught completely off guard.

"Guns on the ground, now," barked Puller.

One man did not heed this warning and raised his gun instead and fired. He missed his target and the round clanged off the Dumpster behind Puller. Knox fired and the man dropped to the asphalt. As he fell the other three shot back and retreated. Puller returned the fire.

"Go! Go!" shouted Knox. "I've got your six."

Puller hustled after them. Knox checked the fallen man, looked behind her, threw off her heels, and sprinted after Puller.

The three men reached the end of the alley and Puller heard the vehicle coming fast on the next street. He increased his speed, but he needed to duck behind some garbage cans when one of the men turned and fired at him. By the time he got to the street the SUV was just turning the next corner.

Knox came running up to him.

"Anything?" she asked breathlessly.

He shook his head. "They're gone. Didn't get the plate."

"Let's check the guy I shot back there. Maybe he has some ID."

But there was no dead guy. There was blood, but no corpse.

They looked everywhere the wounded man could have gone, but found no sign of him.

Knox looked at Puller, dumbstruck. "I hit him right in the chest."

"Were they wearing body armor?"

"I couldn't tell. It was too dark. But there's blood. I hit him." She smacked her palm against her forehead. "Serves me right. I should've aimed for the head."

Puller phoned the police and explained the situation. Then he called his superior at CID. The cops showed up minutes later. After that came the local detectives, and after that two CID agents arrived from Fort Bragg over in Fayetteville. They didn't look pleased at having to make the drive at this time of night. They asked their questions and checked over the crime scene, what there was of one.

One of the agents asked Puller if he had any idea why they'd been targeted. Puller didn't elaborate but told the agents he and Knox were working a case that was classified.

"Well, good luck with that," said the agent as he and his partner walked off.

* * *

After answering innumerable questions from the local cops and looking through mug books at the precinct and giving their official statements, Puller and Knox didn't get back to their hotel until three in the morning.

"Did you get a chance to report in to your superiors?" he asked Knox as they rode up in the elevator.

She nodded. "You?"

"They weren't happy. But it wasn't like I asked somebody to try to kill us."

She slipped off her heels before walking out of the elevator, leaning against the wall and rubbing one of her feet.

"Not exactly the night I had planned," she said, sounding depressed.

"Wouldn't think so."

"Who do you think those guys were?"

"Same ones who jumped me at Leavenworth, maybe?"

"Did you recognize any of them?"

"The guys in Kansas wore ski masks."

"So maybe they followed us across the country?"

"Maybe," he said.

She looked up at him. "You tired?"

"Not particularly. Must be the adrenaline spike from almost getting killed."

"The Ritz has round-the-clock room service. How about some wine and a snack? I'm suddenly starving."

They headed to her room and she placed the order. It came twenty minutes later, and after the attendant left, Knox poured out the wine and handed Puller a plate with some crackers, breads, cheeses, fruit, and a small bowl of nuts. They sat across from each other at the little table the attendant had wheeled in.

"Someone really doesn't want us to find out the truth, Puller," she said between sips of wine and bites of cheese.

"That's usual in my experience. A lot of people lie."

"Do they try to kill you often, *in your experience*?"

"More than I would like," he admitted.

They were quiet for a few moments.

"You're a strange man," she said in an odd tone.

He swallowed a hunk of cheese. "How so? I always thought I was pretty straightforward."

"You're a stand-up guy, all right. Solid, predictable, always looking to do the right thing. You don't seek glory or medals. You're all about getting the job done. That is what defines John Puller. I've come to accept that as the gospel."

"So where does the strange part come in?"

"I'm still trying to figure that out. Just call it my gut for now." She rose. "And now I think we both need some sleep."

Puller stood and headed for the door. He turned back. "Back in the alley?"

"Yes?" she said.

"You're a good shot. And fast."

"I always have been, Puller. Always. That's how I like to live my life. Fast." She snatched a quick glance at the bed, and when she looked back she wouldn't meet his gaze.

"We both need some sleep," she said. "Big day tomorrow." She glanced up and their gazes met for a brief instant. "Good night, Puller."

He interpreted her look as hungry. And not for food. And he thought he might be giving her the same look in return.

She rose and went into the bathroom, closing the door.

Puller stood there for a few seconds trying to dissect what had just happened. Part of it seemed straightforward. Part of it was mud.

He returned to his room, took off his clothes,

and dropped into bed. It was nearly four in the morning. His internal clock was seriously screwed up. His heart was racing from what had just happened with Knox. The woman was complicated. Utterly professional one moment, then sending weird signals the next. It might be that as a spy she tended to use all of her assets, including her sexual side. She was very, well, alluring, as old-fashioned as that sounded. He took a deep breath and wondered if a cold shower would help.

His phone buzzed. He swore under his breath, but automatically picked up the phone anyway. He always picked up the phone even if he didn't always answer it. And maybe it was Knox wanting him to—

A text had dropped into his electronic basket. He read it.

And then he sat straight up. It wasn't from Knox. But it concerned her.

The text had come from a number he didn't recognize.

He called it back. Twice. No one answered.

He read the text again. It was short, to the point, and capable of only one interpretation.

Don't trust Veronica Knox, Puller. She is not what she appears to be.

41

NILES ROBINSON HAD left work early to catch his son's soccer match. The boy had gone from death's door to being a healthy athletic twelve-year-old in less than two years. It truly was a miracle, and one that Robinson never took for granted.

There were a handful of parents watching the match from the sidelines. The day was warm and the boys had already worked up a sweat. Robinson's son was a center midfielder, which meant he had equal responsibilities for defense and attack. Because of this his kid probably ran more than any of his other teammates, but he seemed up to the task.

Robinson shook his head in wonder as his son flashed past him with the ball. A minute later the ball was in the net and his son's team had taken the lead. It was a lead they would not relinquish. After the match was over, Robinson congratulated his son and then headed back to work. The boy would be driven home by a friend.

A tall man in a hoodie approached him in the parking lot. Robinson didn't register on him until the man was nearly upon him.

"Can I help you?" he asked.

Before the hooded man could answer, four men appeared out of vehicles parked nearby and converged on the pair. The hooded man was grabbed and his hood yanked down as his hands were cuffed behind him.

Robinson stared at the man and shook his head. "It's not him," he said. "It's not Robert Puller."

The man in the hoodie was younger and his face was dirty.

"Get your hands off me," he yelled. "I ain't done nothing wrong. Get them cuffs off me."

One of the other men slammed him up against Robinson's van. "Why did you approach this man?"

"Is that a crime?"

"It might be."

"Some dude paid me."

"What dude? Where is he?"

"Just some dude. Paid me twenty bucks. Said to come over here after the match was over."

"What did he look like?"

"I don't know. He was tall as me. Never saw his face."

"Why'd he pick you?"

"How the hell should I know?"

"You hang around this park a lot?"

"Yeah, going through the trash cans. The kids leave full bottles of Gatorades. And the moms throw half the snacks they bring away. Cornucopia, man."

"You're homeless?"

"No, man, I had my private jet drop me off here so I could go through shit in the garbage."

"When did the 'dude' approach you?"

"About an hour ago."

"Where?"

"Over by the basketball courts on the other side of the park."

The man let him go and looked at Robinson. "He faked us out with this idiot."

Robinson nodded. "I told you he was smart."

The man spoke to one of his colleagues. "Take this smartass and see what else you can get from him."

They pulled the man away and pushed him into a waiting SUV, which immediately drove off.

The first man looked at Robinson. "If he contacts you, you get in touch with us immediately. Understood?"

Robinson nodded, climbed into his car, and drove off. When he looked at himself in the rearview mirror he was sweating.

He arrived at his house, having decided against going back to work. He emailed an excuse to his boss, went out into his backyard, and sat on a chair on his patio, his thoughts a whirlwind of mostly cataclysmic scenarios.

His personal cell phone buzzed. He had almost been expecting this.

He looked at the screen.

Sorry for all the excitement at the park. Had to flush the Dobermans.

A few seconds later another text came in.

I'm glad Ian is okay. But now that he's healthy you have to consider what you've done and the damage that it's caused. Because you opened the door for them. You and Susan. We need to meet.

Robinson stared down at the little screen and then, after looking around to make sure no one was watching him, thumbed in a brief response.

How? They're everywhere.

As Robinson read the reply his opinion of Robert Puller was once more validated. He was a very smart man.

* * *

Union Station was busy at this time of day. Robinson parked in the upper deck and rode the escalator down to the station. He walked inside and over to a bank of phones set against one wall. In a world of cell phones, there was no one using these antiquated tools of communication.

Across from him some scaffolding enclosed with a tall curtain had been set up around repair work being done on the ceiling.

Robinson parked himself at the phone farthest from the door he'd come in and waited. A few seconds later it rang.

He picked it up and said hello.

"You're looking good, Niles. Trim as ever."

Robinson didn't bother to look around. He doubted he could have spotted the man.

"How did you get out of DB, Bobby?"

"Nothing planned. Just taking advantage of an opportunity."

"Your brother came by to see me."

"I'm sure."

"I don't think he believed me."

"It's pretty much impossible to lie to him."

"I know you went to see Susan. She said you tried to kill her. That she finally got away and got to her gun and that you ran."

"I'm sure she did. Not exactly how it went down, but that's Susan for you."

"Meaning she's a lying sack of shit."

"That's sort of what I meant, but I like the way you said it better."

"I'm sorry, I didn't want to do it, Bobby. But they had me cornered. No way out. Ian was going to—" Here, Robinson faltered.

"I'm not here to judge you, Niles. Given the circumstances, I might've done the same thing. But now we have to make this right."

"How?"

"For beginners, you need to tell me who paid you off to do what you did."

"I never met anyone. It was all emails and they never deposited any money in my account. They just paid for the medical care in Germany directly. That way no one would be the wiser. We explained away the treatment in Germany as a charity case because the company running the clinical trials needed bodies to try it on."

"Okay, but what exactly did they want you to do? Backdoor them into STRATCOM and from there everywhere else?"

"That might have been their plan. But that's not what they told me to do. I just had to finger you meeting with the Iranian. They provided the doctored photos."

"Okay, Niles, but there had to be some endgame on this."

"You ever wonder why they specifically targeted you out of everybody at STRATCOM?"

"Of course I did."

"And did you ever find an answer?"

"Not a good one, no."

"Well, I asked myself that question many times."

"And did an answer ever hit you?" asked Puller.

"About a year ago, when I was at work."

"And what was it?"

"You were being groomed to go all the way to the top, Bobby. General Able was pretty clear on that."

"So what?" asked Puller.

"There were some who might not have liked that."

"Who exactly are you talking about?"

"I tried to make it right, Bobby. I really did. This has been eating me from the inside out for over two damn years."

"Give me a name, Niles," urged Puller.

The shot hit Niles Robinson right in the base of his neck and severed his medulla. With that core destroyed, so was he. He stood there for an instant, a look of intense surprise on his now bloody face where the round had exited and struck the wall. Then he fell face first into the phone bank and slid to the floor, the wall smeared with his blood, his hand still clutched around the receiver.

The shooter, dressed as a police officer, was behind the enclosed repair site. He had aimed and fired his suppressed pistol through a slit in the curtain. He holstered his weapon, exited out the other side of the work site, and started yelling at people not to panic but to move away from the site of the shooting. Most people obeyed since he was in uniform.

Still, hundreds of people were screaming and fleeing in all directions, abandoning their luggage and trying to get away from the murdered man. Police, guns out, rushed toward him. Union Station was instantly transformed into a nightmare scenario.

Only two people walked calmly out of the station that day.

One was Robert Puller.

The other was the person who had just killed Niles Robinson.

42

AT SEVEN A.M. the next morning Knox and Puller sat at breakfast in the hotel restaurant. Rays of cheery sunlight were coming through the window facing the street. People walked in and out of the restaurant, and cars motored on their way. It seemed improbable that someone had tried to murder them a few hours ago and only a short distance from here, but improbable or not, it had happened.

She said, "I have to tell you I had trouble going to sleep, at least for the three hours of sack time I had."

"Why?"

"I shot a man, Puller. Maybe that's routine for you. Not so much for me."

"Shooting someone is never routine. At least I hope it never becomes routine."

"We're on the same page there. But we must be making some people nervous. That's progress."

Puller paused with his cup of tea halfway to his lips. "We've covered a lot of ground but we have no answers, Knox. That is not progress. Not in my book."

"I disagree. We've discovered that two people were lying their asses off and got your brother sent to prison wrongly. We figured out—well, you did—that some Croatian snuck a bogey into Fort Leavenworth who was sent there to kill your brother. We've accomplished a lot. We really have."

"But we really don't have answers yet. Not for the important questions. Namely, who and why?"

She fiddled with her spoon. "Obviously your brother is out there right now trying to figure it all out."

"You sound like you've been giving that some thought."

"I've been giving it a lot of thought, actually."

"And what do you think?"

"That he's maybe ahead of us on some things."

"Why?"

"He's super smart. He was set up. He was in the intelligence field. And he's trying to prove his innocence. Lots of motivation there."

"I've started to think that he was the one who

saved my butt when those goons snatched me. It's really the only thing that makes sense."

Knox looked at him in surprise. "I hadn't even considered that. But I guess that would make sense. So you might have been a few feet from him that night?"

"I might have been, yeah. As it turned out, it might as well have been a few miles. He's gone, and I'm no closer to finding him."

"You were really tight with your brother, weren't you?"

"For a long time we were all each other had. Our mother was gone and our dad might as well have been." He nudged a roasted potato on his plate. "That may be one reason I never took the plunge."

"What? Marriage?"

"Yeah."

"Why? Afraid you'd be a crappy father?"

"Crappy husband too."

"I don't see that, Puller, I really don't. You'd make a great catch. And a great dad. Teaching your kids right and wrong, how to color in the lines, throw a ball, execute a room breach, fire a sniper rifle, take out four bad guys with a piece of rope and a stick of chewing gum. All good life lessons."

"You ever think of getting hitched?"

"Actually, I did."

Puller hiked his eyebrows. "You mean you *thought* about it?"

"No, Puller, I mean I walked down the aisle, exchanged rings, and got married in front of a licensed preacher."

"When?"

"Long time ago. We were both eighteen. High school sweethearts. It lasted all of fourteen days. Big friggin' shock there, right? I mean, we both knew exactly who we were and what we wanted in life at eighteen, right? Well, turns out we were clueless. So we did a bookend. And got it annulled. So there's no record of it even happening."

"Did a bookend? What does that mean?"

"That means we were married in Vegas and divorced there, all within the span of two weeks. We returned our rings and signed the necessary papers and went our separate ways. I never even told my parents. They thought I was at a college prep retreat."

"Why do I not picture that at all? I mean, you marrying at eighteen in a wedding chapel in Sin City?"

"I told you I liked to live my life fast. But the fact is I was a straight-as-an-arrow, straight-A student, three varsity letters, did everything right back then. Never walked off the line my parents laid down for me. I won all the awards, got into all the best schools. Then something snapped and I went psycho right after high school graduation. Like I said, it lasted for two weeks. After that I got back on track. I got a top-notch education at Amherst while also servicing my athletic side, earned a master's, decided to serve my country on the intelligence side, and the rest, as they say, is history." She gazed over at him. "You ever do anything like that?"

"No."

She looked disappointed. "Always by the book, then?"

"I was an Army brat with an officer for a father. The book was all we ever knew. The Army way or nothing." He said this last part with particular sternness.

"Okay," she said, taken aback by his tone. "I'll just call you 'by-the-book Puller' from now on."

"Okay, but what do people call *you*?" he said, his tone suddenly harsh.

They stared at each other for a long, uncomfortable moment. "What exactly do you mean by that?" she asked.

"It's just a question."

"They call me Veronica Knox. Okay, now

let me ask you one. What changed from a few hours ago to now? Because three hours ago things seemed pretty good between us. I shot somebody who was trying to do us harm. But you're being so cold and distant now I feel like I'm in Alaska instead of North Carolina."

"You're just being a little sensitive, I think."

"No, I'm just someone who wants the truth, Puller. You up to providing it?"

"I've never lied to you, Knox. And I never will."

"I know, you kept pointing out my deficiencies on that score and you were probably right to do so. But I thought by now I had proved to you that I'm on the up-and-up. So, again, what's changed?"

"I like how you put things. You should think about writing a novel. Or a blog."

"And you should think about stopping the bullshit and telling me what's going on."

Puller started to say something, maybe more than he should. An internal struggle ended with him standing up, checking his watch, and saying, "It's time for our meeting with Todd Landry."

She sat there as he walked out of the restaurant. Knox muttered, "Women are supposed to be complicated, not guys!" Then she grabbed her jacket and followed him.

CHAPTER

43

THEY HAD MADE an eight o'clock appointment to
meet with Todd Landry, Robert Puller's former
defense counsel. He was at his downtown office
in Charlotte, only a short walk from the Ritz.

A secretary led them back to a small conference room in the rear of the office space. As
they walked along, Puller took in the blond
wood and tasteful artwork and felt his feet sink
into the thick carpet. He noted the elaborate
layout of cubicles where people looked as busy
as bees in a honeycomb as they toiled away
on whatever legal conundrum they were confronting.

Landry greeted them at the door of the conference room. He was about five-eight, thin,
with a ring of grayish hair encircling the crown
of his head. He wore a dark double-breasted
suit and a paisley tie fronting a light blue patterned shirt. Puller also noted the gold mono-
grammed links on the French cuffs.

A man careful about his appearance.

Landry had retained his military bearing in the ramrod-straight posture, firm handshake, and take-charge demeanor.

"Have a seat. I'm sure you want to get down to it. Coffee, water?"

"No, thanks," said Puller, and Knox shook her head.

They all sat as Landry unbuttoned his suit coat and waited.

"I suppose you know why we're here," began Puller.

"Robert Puller. Can't believe he got out of DB. I thought he was innocent, you know. Can't say that about most of my clients. I guess I was wrong about him."

"Maybe you weren't," said Puller. "We've uncovered enough to make us concerned that an innocent man was indeed sent to prison."

"Then why escape?"

"We really can't get into that, but we can tell you that there are extenuating circumstances."

"Okay, I know I'm not in the military anymore and my need-to-know is pretty nonexistent, but you had some questions nonetheless?"

"We've met with Doug Fletcher already," said Knox.

Landry nodded. "Good guy, good lawyer. He's teaching at JAG now in Charlottesville."

"Right. And you spoke with Shireen Kirk?" said Puller.

Landry smiled. "I hated going up against her. She kicked my ass more times than I care to admit. I hope she never moves to Charlotte and goes into private practice."

"We appreciated your being so frank with her."

Landry nodded in understanding. "Look, it was a strange case all around. None of it made sense. I know the evidence showed online gambling as the motive, and he had the means and opportunity, but I never bought that. That all can be fabricated quite easily. If Robert hadn't been so egotistical about someone hacking his computer the verdict might have been different. Maybe not, but at least we would have had a fighting chance."

"We understand there was a letter from Robert's father," said Knox, drawing a quick glance from Puller.

Landry eyed Puller. "From *your* father too. I know who you are."

"Yes."

"Your brother said you were the best investigator the DoD had. Really proud of you."

"It was mutual," said Puller.

Landry nodded. "The letter carried great weight. And I believe it's the only reason the charge got changed from spying to espionage. Life versus death."

"Did my brother see the letter?" asked Puller.

Landry hesitated. "No."

"Why not?" Puller demanded.

"Because his—your father didn't want him to. Those were the conditions under which the letter could be viewed by the judge to lower the charges."

"So my father didn't want my brother to know of his involvement?"

"I suppose not. I thought it was unusual, of course. But I was powerless to do anything about it. I was a soldier then, Agent Puller. I did what I was told. So did Doug Fletcher."

Puller sat back, digesting this and shaking his head.

"And Robert Puller talked about threats to his family?" prompted Knox.

Landry eyed Puller. "Did you know about that?"

"I was deployed overseas at the time. Combat zone. Didn't make it back stateside until after my brother had been convicted and sent to DB."

"He talked about you a lot with me. Not in connection with the case. Just talked. He was very worried that you would think badly of him. Not because he'd done anything wrong. He believed himself innocent all the way through. But just because, well, it had brought dishonor onto the family."

"I visited him at DB. Quite often."

"I'm sure those visits meant a lot to him."

Knox interjected, "But did he provide you with any more details about the threats?"

"He told me that a letter had been slipped under his pillow in his cell."

"So someone at the prison must have put it there," said Knox.

"One would think so. He showed it to me. It was all block print, so anyone could have done it. That's why the letter would have been dubious to use as evidence. The prosecution could have argued he did it himself. But I never got a chance to try because Robert refused to allow me to do so. That's what convinced me that the letter was legitimate. Someone was using the threat of violence against his family to influence how he was defending himself at the trial. He wouldn't testify. He wouldn't really let me do my job from that moment forward. The conviction was a foregone conclusion. The panel only took an hour of deliberation before returning the guilty verdict."

"I see," said Puller.

"It's curious, though. I mean, with what happened yesterday in D.C.," said Landry.

Both Knox and Puller looked at him strangely.

"What happened in D.C.?" asked Knox.

"Oh, I'm sorry, I thought you would have heard. An old colleague of mine from D.C. called me last night. He'd seen it on the news. There was a brief article about it in *USA Today* this morning, but I don't think it's gotten much media traction yet. Since it was connected to your brother's case, I just thought the timing was odd."

"What are you talking about?" asked Puller.

"Niles Robinson, you know who he is?"

"He worked with my brother and testified against him at the trial. We spoke with him recently."

"Well, that was a good thing, then."

"Why?" asked Knox.

"Only that it would be impossible to speak with him now. He was shot dead at Union Station last night."

Puller and Knox exchanged a quick glance. Puller said, "Niles Robinson? You're sure it was the same man connected to my brother's case?"

"Absolutely. They had a photo of him in the article. It was clearly him. I recognized him immediately from when he was on the witness stand. I spent a long time cross-examining him on his story, but I really couldn't make any headway. For what it's worth, he seemed genuinely sorry to be testifying against Robert."

"I'm sure he was," said Puller tightly.

Knox said, "Did they get the shooter?"

"Not according to what I read. My friend said the news story in D.C. placed Robinson at a phone bank at the train station. Odd, since, I mean, who uses a pay phone these days? I'm surprised they still have them."

"I wonder if he was there to take a train somewhere?" asked Puller.

Knox shot him a curious glance.

"Don't know," said Landry. "I guess if they find a ticket on him that will answer that question."

"Anything else that you can add?" asked Knox.

"Only to reiterate that I always believed Robert was innocent. But the evidence just didn't cut our way. There were the photos provided by Robinson, his corroborating testimony, the computer files showing the online gambling and the debts, the financial paper trail. And then there was the DVD and the other coworker's testimony. What was her name again?"

"Susan Reynolds," supplied Puller.

"Right. She was a rock on the witness stand. But unlike Robinson, she, um—"

"Didn't seem to be bothered by the fact that she was helping to send my brother to prison for the rest of his life?"

Landry pointed at him. "Exactly. In fact, she seemed rather happy about it." Landry shook his head. "Not a pleasant woman. Tough, ruthless even. Definitely not someone I would choose to hang out with. I investigated her, of course, to see if I could find any ammo to hit her with on the stand. But there was nothing there."

"Well, maybe we'll be more fortunate," said Puller. He rose and extended his hand. "Thank you for your time."

"No, thank *you*. And I hope the truth finally comes out," said Landry. "And if your brother is innocent he shouldn't have to spend one more minute in prison."

They said their goodbyes as Knox looked worriedly at Puller.

* * *

A few minutes later they were walking back to the hotel.

Knox said, "Robinson dead. That's a stunner."

"Maybe not so much."

"What do you mean?"

"Why would he go to the train station and be on a pay phone?"

Knox thought for a moment. "He was communicating with someone and they didn't want to be seen together or have their cell phones tracked?"

"So who was he talking to when someone killed him?"

"Could be a lot of possibilities."

"Maybe not as many as you think. He could communicate with the people who paid for his son's treatment any number of ways. The pay phone, on the other hand, would be the perfect way for someone who couldn't afford to be seen with Robinson to communicate with him without the risk that the conversation could be tracked."

"Wait a minute, are you saying—"

"That it was my brother on the other end of that call."

"But why would he talk to Robinson?"

"Robinson felt guilty about what he did. You heard Landry. I'm sure my brother noted that when Robinson testified. Maybe he thought that Robinson would be receptive to the truth finally coming out, if only to alleviate his guilt."

"Do you think he might have figured out Robinson's motive?"

"The sick child? Maybe. I saw the photo in Robinson's office. My brother could have too, because I'm sure it would have been in Robinson's office back in KC. You have to understand that my brother misses nothing. He sees it all. Never forgets anything. Now we need to find out everything about Robinson's death."

"So who killed him? Your brother? Maybe Robinson wouldn't cooperate."

"If that were my brother's plan he wouldn't have picked a place like Union Station. Too many people around. And he's not a cold-blooded killer. He could kill someone in self-defense, like at DB, but not over distance when he was in no personal danger. I think Robinson was followed, and when the follower saw what was going on he took the guy out."

"And your brother?"

"I have no way of knowing what Robinson told him. If he did tell him something that might have led Bobby on to something else."

"What about Susan Reynolds? You think he's going to visit her?"

"Maybe, if he hasn't already."

"Don't you think we would have heard if he had?"

"Not necessarily. If Reynolds is on someone else's payroll then she might not want her official superiors to know because it would direct attention onto her. She might have only told her coconspirators. Or maybe she did tell people and no one bothered to tell us. Or she called Robinson and told him. I guess that's all possible."

As they were walking along, Puller's phone buzzed. He looked at the screen and his demeanor changed.

"Bad news?" asked Knox, who was watching him closely.

"Doug Fletcher was as good as his word."

"What?"

"He just sent me the copy of the letter my dad filed with the court during Bobby's court-martial."

Knox put a hand on Puller's arm. "Look, you go up to your room, finish packing up, read your letter, take all the time you need. I'll check out and be down in the lobby waiting."

Puller looked across at her. "I appreciate that." He hesitated. "And I'm sorry that I was shitty to you this morning."

"Forget it. I'm not a morning person myself. And I can be an asshole too."

"You said you weren't close to your dad, but do you ever see him?"

"That would be kind of hard, because he's dead."

"Sorry, I didn't know."

"He drank too much, withered away, fell into depression, ended up all alone, and ate a round from a Glock without bothering to leave behind a note."

"Damn, that must have been tough."

"Not as much as you might think. We'd been estranged a long time by then."

"Still, he was your father."

"Actually, in my mind at least, he had lost that title. It's not supposed to be simply granted, Puller, because a sperm happened to hit an egg. You have to earn it. He chose not to. And he suffered the consequences. It's incredibly sad, but it wasn't my choice, it was his."

"I admire the fact you can be so…analytical about it."

"That only happens after you spend about ten years of your life crying about it. Once the emotions are gone, analytics are all you have left."

But as she said this Knox turned away from him and stared directly in front of her.

They had reached the hotel by now and she pushed him toward the entrance. "Go do what you have to do. I'm going to run next door to the pharmacy and pick up some things I need. Meet you in the lobby."

Puller looked at her for a moment and then walked into the hotel.

Knox looked frantically around for a few moments and then spotted the narrow alleyway behind the hotel. She slid into it, turned away from the street, and began to cry.

CHAPTER

44

ROBERT PULLER SAT in a seedy motel room next to a strip mall on Route 1 in south Alexandria staring at the beaten-down strip of carpet but not really seeing it.

Last night he had watched Niles Robinson's brains being splattered on the wall at Union Station. He had worked with Robinson for several years at STRATCOM, first in Nebraska and then in Kansas. He had considered Robinson a friend. He had watched the man on the witness stand testifying against him. He had seen that his friend was mired in conflict over what he was doing.

While Puller had been sitting in the courtroom that day when Robinson was on the stand, his mind had visited Robinson's office, going over everything in it. In the odd way his brain worked, once Puller saw something it always stayed with him, safely ensconced in a little corner of his gray matter.

In his mental meandering he had stopped at the photograph of Ian Robinson when he had been sick, head shaven and tubes running all over his frail body. Puller and Niles had talked often about the boy, his condition and dire prognosis. It had been heartbreaking, truly. And while he couldn't agree with what Niles had done, he could understand why he had done it.

But now, while Ian would grow up, he would do so without his father.

And Puller was blaming himself for that. Robinson had been followed. Puller should have anticipated that possibility. Yet he had never envisioned that they would have killed the man in such a public place.

But he could do nothing for Robinson now. And what Robinson had told him was tantalizing. Some didn't like the fact that Puller was being groomed for great things in the intelligence field. But could it be just that? Maybe Robinson didn't know the whole story.

Ruining my career and putting me in prison just because you didn't like me or were jealous? No, there had to be something else. And what did he mean by he "had tried to make it right"? How?

Puller lay back on the bed and stared at the

ceiling now instead of the threadbare carpet. He couldn't make heads or tails of what Robinson had meant, so he moved on.

Puller had headed east because of a change in command at STRATCOM. Daughtrey was moved up and brought on. And then he was murdered. With the reassignment, other changes had taken place in the pecking order of command. Chiefly, Martin Able had gotten his fourth star and become head of the NSA. It was a plum assignment.

Yet maybe not so much now. The NSA was embroiled in controversy after the Snowden revelations. The former NSA operative had accused the agency of conduct that was unprecedented and that had cast a shadow over the whole intelligence community of the United States.

Puller had not been directly involved with the NSA during his time at STRATCOM, though the agencies worked closely together. But the revelations that had come out over the past year or so had not been related to a drastic sea change in how the NSA did its job. The recently publicized and now denounced tactics and surveillance had long been in place.

Many people would not have wanted those revelations to come out, but come out they still had. And that's where Puller had made his miscalculation. He had suspected his old boss, Martin Able. That was why he had headed east. But this could have nothing to do with the issues at the NSA, and by extension, STRATCOM. He was sitting in a cell at the DB and had been for over two years. All during that time no one had bothered with him. No one.

And then recently a man had come into the prison with the task of killing him. There had to be a reason. And if he could just figure out that reason, he could by extrapolation figure out everything else.

So that brought him back to those people Robinson had mentioned, who did not want to see Puller move ahead and eventually land the top spot. That couldn't have included Martin Able. He had been well on his way to heading the NSA. And he had clearly wanted Puller to succeed; his mentoring had shown that.

Now, Susan Reynolds had obviously been no fan of Puller's and had conspired to do him in for money and perhaps a professional grudge. But she couldn't be the leading force behind this. She didn't have the position or brains.

At this point Puller's thoughts turned elsewhere. To the gap that existed between Daughtrey, the one-star, and Able, the now four-star. When he had left STRATCOM, it had opened up the top spot there. A quick Google search had told Puller that an admiral had taken over Able's job at STRATCOM. He had not been promoted internally, but had come in from another command. Below him at the leadership level was a three-star who was deputy commander, a chief of staff who was a two-star, and a command sergeant major who was the senior enlisted leader.

It didn't stop there. There were also the HQ and component commanders, which was composed of a hodgepodge of three-stars, two-stars, and one-stars, rear admirals, colonels, majors, captains, and also civilians. It was a bewildering array of possible suspects, each of them doing the professional dance, hoping to move up in rank and power before the music stopped.

Puller opened his laptop and went online. He studied the professional bios of each of these people, running his eye down the list again and again hoping that something would pop.

He had one critical time point.

The decision to kill me at DB. What happened to trigger that? It would have taken planning, say a couple of months to manage all the neces-

sary details. The trigger for it could have come anytime before that, I just don't know how long before it. But I have another critical point that might lead me in the right direction.

He hacked a secure database to search for Susan Reynolds's internal and nonpublic c.v.

She had had many assignments over a government career spanning more than twenty-five years. Her academic background was spectacular and she held advanced degrees, despite being a young mother. She had worked herself up to a managerial position, though he doubted she had the horsepower or connections to get to the SES level before she retired, but she might. She had had stints overseas and had been in war zones. She had even served on interrogation teams in the field and was an expert on techniques to get information from people who did not want to provide it. Well, he could certainly see her tightening the thumbscrews on someone. And perhaps her affinity for weapons had helped her there. He went back further in her record. She had had stints in Eastern Europe and South Korea, among others. And, as she had mentioned when he was in her home, many years ago she had been part of a START verification team for nuclear arms reduction with the Soviet Union.

She had joined the WMD Center four months ago. Puller could have thought of five far more likely professional homes to which she could have been assigned.

So why WMD?

He looked up the leadership for the center. It wasn't a military person. The current head was Donovan Carter, a civilian and an SES, or member of the elite senior executive service, which roughly paralleled the rank of general or admiral in the armed forces. And Puller knew that Carter also headed up the far larger DTRA, which held a very prominent position in keeping America safe from WMDs.

Puller knew Carter professionally. They had never worked directly together, but they had met on several occasions.

Carter had come on board at the center and DTRA at roughly the same time that Susan Reynolds had been assigned there. So they were at Fort Belvoir together. DTRA employed a lot of people, and Fort Belvoir was vast, and Reynolds was only a small component of this enterprise.

There's another critical time component. They set me up and got rid of me at STRATCOM right before my next promotion.

He was slated to go from a major to lieutenant colonel. From there his trajectory was predictable in rank: colonel, one-star, two-star, and on up. What was unpredictable was the timing. There were standards for how long between promotions, including minimum time in a particular grade, training requirements for duty performance. And there were additional hurdles to jump for special promotions. This was meritocracy at its finest. And Puller had always been a fast riser, marked for the stars on his shoulders almost as soon as he had left the Air Force Academy at the top of his class, the second-ranked classmate far behind.

And then a possibility hit him.

As a lieutenant colonel at STRATCOM he was to be transferred to Bolling AFB in Washington, D.C., and assigned to the Joint Forces Central Command's Intelligence, Surveillance, and Reconnaissance, or ISR, a component of STRATCOM.

Puller knew that all these acronyms would drive most civilians mad. But for most of his adult life it had been all he had known, becoming a language he could navigate as easily as he could recite the alphabet or know the order of medals and ribbons on the front of a uniform.

At ISR he would have been under the tutelage of a two-star. He also would have had a direct pipeline into the intelligence infrastructure of the United States by virtue of the NSA being only a short drive north into Maryland at Fort Meade.

Could it be possible?

He went back to take a look at Donovan Carter's c.v. It didn't take him long to find it. Two years ago to the week, Carter had been assigned to ISR.

Then he checked Susan Reynolds's work history.

And then it all came together like embers finally igniting and producing a flame.

She had been assigned, along with Carter, to ISR. Now Carter was at the WMD Center and so was Reynolds.

So had they set him up so he wouldn't get the promotion and be moved to Bolling, where he would have been working with Donovan Carter? If so, why? And who had taken his slot at Bolling?

Something crept out of a storage place in his brain and marched out in front of his eyes. He checked his laptop just to confirm that he was right. There was no room for mistakes now.

When he saw it come up on the screen the jigsaw pieces started to fit together even more precisely. Carter, Reynolds, and this person.

Puller's slot at Bolling had been taken by a man who then held the rank of colonel. He had since been promoted to brigadier general. A few days ago his career and life had ended in Kansas.

His name was Timothy Daughtrey.

CHAPTER

45

JOHN PULLER WAITED until he got up to his room before opening the attachment on the email. He sat down in the chair and read through the letter once, and then, being the good soldier he was, he read through it twice more, filling in gaps that the prior readings had left.

He set the phone down and stared over at the wall opposite. He never knew his father could be so eloquent through the written word. He could give orders like no one else, concise and incapable of misinterpretation, the Ulysses S. Grant of his generation. But to convey the feelings, the emotions that he had in the letter to the court-martial, well, it was as extraordinary as it was unexpected.

He had never seen this side of the old man. He doubted anyone had, including his brother. Chiefly his brother. Puller hadn't gone the officer route, and his father had never forgiven him. Yet Bobby, who *was* an officer, had gotten the brunt of their father's derision. Puller had been a grunt with a rifle in the trenches. He had fought for his country, been wounded for his country, and been, in his father's eyes, a soldier's soldier. His brother had been, in his father's words, "a g-d flyboy playing typist," the last word being a derogatory reference to his brother's immense talent with technology.

But in this letter Puller Sr. had dug somewhere deep to find the words to persuade a military tribunal to give his son the possibility of life instead of a certain death. He had said things about his older son that Puller had never heard the old man say before. It was like they were two different men, in fact. But there they were, in his father's bold handwriting. How he had been able to do this while his mind was slowly being eaten away by the disease that was diligently claiming him was beyond Puller.

He put the phone away in his pocket and packed his things in his duffel. He checked out and met Knox in the lobby. He noted that her face was red and she looked exhausted.

"What, did you go for a run while I was up in my room?"

"Why?"

"Your face is flushed and your eyes are red. And you look beat."

"Might be coming down with something. And I've got pollen allergies. And I only had three hours of sleep."

"Okay," he said as they walked to the car.

She said hastily, "I'll be fine. I took something. It's why I ducked into the pharmacy."

"Then I'll drive and you can grab some rest."

"Thanks, I appreciate that."

They loaded the car and climbed into the front seats. The clouds had thickened, blackened, and rain was starting to fall.

"Nice time to catch some shut-eye," said Puller. "Just listen to the raindrops beating on the roof and you'll pass right out."

"Yeah." She snuggled down into her seat with her jacket draped over her and said, "By the way, where are we going?"

"Back to D.C."

"Why?"

"Why not? You want to go back to Kansas?"

"Not particularly. I think we've done all we can there."

"I need to go back at some point and pick up my cat."

She smirked at him. "It still surprises me that you have a pet, Puller. And a cat. And it was lying on the bed next to dead Daughtrey like it was no big deal."

"AWOL is cool under pressure. And she's low-maintenance."

"Like her owner?"

"It's probably why we get along so well."

"It's a long drive to D.C."

"Not a problem. I'll take the wheel the whole way. Give me a chance to think."

"So when we get to D.C.?"

"The first priority will be checking out what happened to Niles Robinson."

"Sounds like a plan." She closed her eyes.

"Let me know if you need a food or bathroom break."

"All I need is some sleep."

Puller reached the highway, headed north, and accelerated.

"You asleep yet, Knox?"

"Not now, no."

"Sorry."

"Something on your mind?"

"You have any enemies?"

"Don't we all have enemies?"

"Anyone in particular with you?"

"Not that I can think of right now." She straightened in her seat. "And why are you asking me that?"

Puller tapped the steering wheel as he stared straight ahead. "I got a text."

"About what?"

"About you."

"What about me?"

"That you're not what you appear to be. That I shouldn't trust you."

Knox glanced away, frowning. "Who sent the text?"

"I don't know. I called the number but no one answered. I'll try to trace it, but it might be a burn phone. In fact, I'd be surprised if it weren't."

"So that's why you were acting that way this morning?"

"Yes."

"So you believed the text even though you don't even know who sent it?"

"I'm not sure what I believed."

"That's bullshit. You *did* believe it. Even after we were attacked in that alley and almost killed."

"If I did believe it I would have done something about it. And I sure as hell wouldn't have told you about it."

"But you didn't tell me right away."

"No, I didn't," he conceded. "But I'm not a perfect man, either."

She crossed her arms and sank back into her seat. "Well, I'm not a perfect woman, that's for damn sure."

"Anything bothering you? I've got time to listen."

"Nothing on my end."

They drove a few more miles before Knox said, "I might tell you about it sometime, Puller."

"That's fine."

"And maybe the text was right, maybe I'm not who I appear to be."

"Text or no text, I never thought you were who you appeared to be, Knox."

She shot him a glance. "Then why—"

"Let's just leave it at that for now."

"I don't get you, Puller, I really don't. Every time I think I've got you figured out you throw me a curve."

"You said I was predictable."

"But I'm coming to learn that you're not. At least not in all ways."

"A good soldier never stops learning."

She snuggled back into her seat again and shut her eyes. "Did you read the letter your father had written?"

"Yes."

"And?"

"And it's made me understand that none of us are who we appear to be. Now get some sleep. I'll wake you when we get close."

A few minutes later her breathing became regular and her arms slid to her sides.

The rain picked up and so did the wind. Puller had a job keeping the car straight on the highway but managed it with both of his big hands clamped around the wheel.

Once they were past the worst of it, his mind could wander from the demands of driving in a storm to the written words of a three-star fighting legend who was supposed to have lost his mind at a VA hospital.

If Puller Sr. had meant everything that he had written in that letter maybe there was hope.

For all of them.

And he wanted his brother to be able to read those words.

He wanted that very much.

It could make up for a lot. Perhaps, even in an imperfect world, it could make up for just about everything.

46

As they approached the D.C. area a little over six hours later, Puller woke Knox by gently nudging her in the side. She came to as he would, calm, alert, and ready to go, or pull the trigger, as the case might be.

"It didn't occur to me," he said. "Where are you staying?"

"You can drop me at the W Hotel downtown. It's centrally located. I've stayed there before."

"Right near the White House. You going to have a powwow with the president?"

"It's not on my schedule for today, no."

Puller glanced sharply at her. The way she said it, she seemed serious.

"The W it is."

"What about you?" she asked.

"Heading to Quantico to get some fresh clothes and other stuff I might need. And to check in."

"I'm going to do the same at the hotel."

"So how will they take the fact that you've shot two people and killed one?"

"I think they'll take it rather well considering the alternative. But I know I'm going to have a roomful of forms to file. And I'll have to go back to North Carolina and Kansas to deal with it at some point."

"I'm hoping they can find the guy you shot in Charlotte."

"Yeah, that would help. Maybe he's lying dead in some other alley down there." She added sarcastically, "They can do another follicle test. If there's ice there, he might be from Alaska. Or maybe Siberia."

Puller's phone buzzed again. He checked the screen while they were stopped at a red light. He slipped it back into his pocket.

"Anything important?"

"General Rinehart and Mr. Schindler want to meet."

"Where?"

"They came back east too. Dinner at the Army-Navy Club downtown. Eight-thirty tonight. You up for it?"

"I don't think they want to meet with me."

"I don't care if they do or not. You're on my team. So you get to come and report in too."

"I hear Rinehart can be a bear."

"Any guy busting his hump for the fourth star can be a bear. I'll need to get my dress blues. I can pick you up a little after eight and we can drive over together. Sound good?"

"Sounds good, Puller. And I'm flattered."

"About what?"

"About being included on *your* team."

He pulled up to the W Hotel and she climbed out and grabbed her bag from the trunk. She came around to his side of the car and motioned for him to roll down the window.

She leaned in and smiled coyly. "But then again, I always thought you were on *my* team." She smacked him lightly on the cheek, turned, and sauntered into the hotel lobby.

Puller watched her every step of the way and then rolled the window back up and drove off.

* * *

He stopped by Quantico and met briefly with Don White, his CO. The man was not happy with the situation, particularly since he apparently knew Puller could not tell him everything.

"I know you've got a lot of juice behind you on this one, Puller. But my advice to you is to watch all points on the compass. If this turns into a disaster, and it might, fingers will be pointing so fast it'll make your head spin."

"Roger that," Puller had said.

He had driven home thinking about this warning and the similar one that Shireen Kirk had given him. Nothing good could come out of this for him. But as smart as the woman was, she might be wrong about that.

I just might be able to get my brother back.

He called Rinehart's office and got the okay for Knox's attendance at the dinner. Then he caught up on some paperwork and checked in with the vet back at Fort Leavenworth to see how AWOL was doing.

"What can I say? The damn cat doesn't seem to even know you've left her," was the vet's reply, and Puller could almost see the smile attached to this comment.

"Yeah, well, tell AWOL I love her too."

He didn't have a lot of time before he had to head back to D.C. for the dinner, but he put on his sweats and went for a run. Afterward, he walked back to his apartment, his tired muscles feeling good, the endorphins bumping up his spirits. He quickly showered and then sat in a towel on his bed going over the notes he'd collected over the last few days.

Macri dead.

The Ukrainian dead.

Daughtrey dead.

The missing transformers.

The men who had kidnapped him.

The person who had saved him, possibly his brother.

The lying Susan Reynolds.

The attack in the alley.

The dead Niles Robinson.

A letter his father wrote.

His brother out there somewhere.

And Knox. They'd shared a hungry look and had come close to sharing a lot more. And then there was the text. She wasn't who she appeared to be. The fact was he couldn't fully trust her. He couldn't trust anyone on this. This was not the world of soldiering. That was one he understood fully. You counted on the guy next to you and he counted on you, because that was the only way to survive.

But this wasn't soldiering, though there were uniforms galore in the mix. This was the intelligence field, which apparently came chock-full of lies, dubious allegiances, ulterior motives, changing agendas, and everyone telling you what you wanted to hear while they were sticking the knife deeper into your back and blaming it on someone else. That world, his brother's world, was totally foreign to him. He felt like a buck recruit, set out in the wild all alone to sink or swim, to live or die.

He put on his dress blues and left Quantico to make his way north on Interstate 95 to D.C. Luckily, he was heading against traffic. Going south on 95 it was, as usual, a parking lot. He pulled in front of the W Hotel and was about to text Knox that he was there waiting outside when she walked out in a navy blue skirt, matching jacket, pale blue blouse, sheer stockings, and high heels. Her hair was done up in a braid and she carried a clutch purse. And now he knew there was a gun in there.

He unlocked the passenger door and she slid in with a swish of skirt and a quick glimpse of her long thighs.

"Productive day?" she asked.

"Pretty good. You?"

"Got some things accomplished. Did you settle things for me to be there tonight?"

"All done."

"I'm surprised they'd allow it."

"I'm sure calls were made, emails sent, your record examined inch by inch, inquiries made, and appropriate parties briefed. And there you go. They'll know more about you now than you know about yourself."

He pulled off and headed toward the Army-

Navy Club, which wasn't very far away distance-wise, but at this time of night traffic and myriad intervening lights could make it seem like fifty miles.

"So what's the agenda for tonight?" she asked.

He glanced over to see her staring at him.

"I'm not setting the agenda. They are. Generals and guys with the president's ear tend to do that. I'm just a lowly CWO."

"You need to improve your self-esteem, Puller, or you won't get anywhere fast."

"Slow and steady wins the day."

"Unless someone is shooting at you."

"You feeling better? Gotten over whatever it was?"

She folded her arms over her chest again, something he again noted she did whenever she was feeling defensive or elusive.

"Still working on that."

"Right. Maybe you should try Sudafed. Or a priest."

She turned to look at him. "A priest?"

"Your personnel file says you're Catholic. I figure you might want to try confession. Supposed to be good for the soul."

"Are you accusing me of lying to you again?"

Puller worked his way through late rush-hour

traffic before stopping at a red light. "We've got about ten more minutes until we get there."

"I'm just not following you, Puller."

"You weren't sick or coming down with a cold. Your voice was normal, not scratchy or husky. On the drive to D.C. you didn't cough, sneeze, or even sniffle. At one point I cranked up the AC and you didn't even shiver. And I've got pollen allergies too. And there's none in the air or else I'd know it."

"And your point?"

"Your face was flushed and your eyes were red for another reason. Emotion can do that. Crying can do that, more specifically, although you don't strike me as a weeper. But then again, I really don't know you all that well. But if something did make you break down, it had to have been something serious. And that might come back to explode in my face. If I'm wrong about any of this, feel free to tell me so."

The light turned green but Puller didn't move. A car behind them honked.

"Keep driving," she said. "Like you said, we have ten minutes."

Puller drove through the intersection. About a minute later Knox said, "I told you I wasn't who I appeared to be."

"And I told you that was no surprise to me."

"But what if—" She stopped and looked out the window.

"What if what?" said Puller.

She turned to face him. "Pull over."

"What?"

"Pull over to the curb. We can walk the rest of the way. If we're a little late, I'm sure the general and Mr. Schindler won't mind. In fact, walking might be faster than riding in a car in this traffic."

Miraculously, Puller found a parking spot on the next block, pulling in as another car was pulling out.

They had walked for half a block when she looked up at him and touched the sleeve of his uniform. He had put his cover on as soon as they had exited the car.

"Nice hat. And I meant to tell you that you look really handsome in dress blues. Quite imposing."

"You look really good too, but I'm waiting to hear what you have to say."

"My being assigned to this case was no coincidence. I was assigned because you were assigned."

"And what was your task?"

"To keep tabs on you and report back. Which I have done."

"Is that all?"

She lightly punched him in the arm. "What, that's not enough for you?"

"It's past flirting time, Knox."

She grew serious at once and looked ahead as they walked. "No, it's not all. The transformers?"

"What about them?" Puller said warily.

"I made them go away. Along with the tech, Jordan."

Puller stopped walking, something she didn't realize for a few more steps. She strode slowly back to him, her brow creased with concern.

He said, "You made critical evidence in a criminal investigation go away? That's obstruction."

"It wasn't on my authority, I can assure you. It was on orders."

"From who?"

"My superiors."

"I'd like names, ranks, and serial numbers. And I'd like them right now."

"I'm afraid I can't go there."

"You just admitted to a crime, Knox, a felony."

"I'll never be tried for it, Puller. Just the way things work in my world."

"But not in mine."

"In case you hadn't noticed, you're in *my* world, not yours, because that's where your brother lived."

"Why did you make the evidence disappear?"

"Because it would have shown traces of an explosive device."

"So it *was* sabotaged?"

"They couldn't let that go to chance, Puller. Just like the generator. It was intentionally gummed up."

"And the two techs?"

"Clueless about it. Easy enough to do. Macri and her cronies had no problem with that."

"And you know this how?"

She started to walk again and Puller matched her pace.

"We have a problem, Puller, a big one. We have a traitor in our ranks. Maybe more than one. No, assuredly more than one. Maybe a lot of them. And they are highly placed. They got your brother sent to DB. They have wreaked damage on this nation's security. They are no doubt planning something else, something big."

"So why am I here, then, Knox, if you know all this? Why was I invited to the party?"

"That's the critical question, Puller. Why *were* you invited to this party? I haven't found anyone who can answer that to my satisfaction."

"Generals Rinehart and Daughtrey and James Schindler told me that they thought because of my connection to my brother that I would have insights others wouldn't. They thought it gave the best chance to find him."

"Maybe, maybe not."

"Well, since we're going to dinner with two of them, why don't we ask?"

"That's exactly what you can't do. When I said this goes high, I meant it might go to Mount Everest."

"Schindler is on the NSC. He's the president's man. And Rinehart is in line for the Joint Chiefs. Are you telling me they're traitors?"

"I'm not telling you they are and I'm not telling you they aren't, because I don't know. What I do know is we have to find out the truth before a very large shoe drops somewhere. It might already have for all I know."

"Well, you seem to know a lot more than me."

"In certain discrete parts that may be true. But I don't know the why or who, just like you said before. And until we know those things we might as well know nothing."

"But why take the transformers? Why cover that up?"

"We don't want them to know that we know. If they go deeper underground we may never unearth them."

"And Macri? The men who kidnapped me?"

"I can't explain them, Puller. I don't know if they're part of the conspiracy or another faction that we're not aware of."

"And the guys in the alley?"

"If I knew I'd tell you."

"You sure about that."

"Don't throw that in my face."

He stopped walking again. "You don't think I've earned that right?"

She sighed. "The short answer is, you *have* earned that right." She suddenly gripped his arm. "But I'm pleading with you not to go there, not now. You can kick me in the ass later, after this is all over."

He glanced at her backside. "I can promise you that," said Puller.

47

THEY WALKED UP the front steps of the Army-Navy Club and into the well-lighted foyer. The main dining room was to the right, but Puller was unsure of exactly where the dinner with Rinehart and Schindler was to take place. As he removed his cover his problem was solved by a man in a suit hurrying over to them.

"Chief Puller? Ms. Knox?"

"I'm Puller."

"And I'm Knox."

"Please follow me. You'll be in a private dining area upstairs."

They followed the man to the second floor and then down a long hall.

Three men were waiting when they entered the small dining room. The man who had escorted them left, closing the door behind him. The three men rose. One was Rinehart in his dress blues, his chest looking armored with all the medals. Another was James Schindler in a

black suit, white shirt, and blood-red tie. Rinehart introduced the third man, who was also
dressed in a suit and tie. He was about fifty, fit
and trim, with grayish blond hair cut haphaz-
ardly. One side of his face had sustained some
type of catastrophic damage and had since been
repaired, but not well. The eye socket, cheek,
and jawline on that side looked more than a
bit cadaverous. And it looked like the eye was
made of glass.

Rinehart said, "This is Donovan Carter. He's
head of DTRA."

Puller did his best to keep his features inscrutable at this announcement, though he
found it hard. The head of DTRA was also the
director of the WMD Center. So this was Susan
Reynolds's ultimate boss?

Puller introduced Knox to the men and they
all shook hands.

As soon as they sat down the salads were
served and glasses of white wine poured. When
the servants had left them to munch their let-
tuce and grape tomatoes and sip their chardon-
nay, Rinehart looked at Puller and said, "A lot
has obviously happened. We'd appreciate a full
report."

Puller shot Carter a glance and then gazed
back at Rinehart.

The general said, "He's been fully read in, Puller."

Puller wanted to ask why that was but couldn't think of a way to do it that wouldn't seem insubordinate.

Puller began to deliver his briefing, going point by point. When he was done he avoided glancing at Knox for fear that she might have been staring at him for what he had left out. His kidnapping and his guardian angel. The transformers being covered up by Knox. The hit man coming to the DB to kill his brother. His suspicions about Reynolds. And what they had discovered about Niles Robinson.

Rinehart said, "A captain in the Army was part of some conspiracy at DB? Unbelievable." He turned to Knox. "And you're the one who had the deadly encounter with her?"

"I'm afraid so, sir. She tried to kill me. I had no choice but to defend myself."

"And some men followed you in Charlotte and you shot one of them too," said Schindler. "That's astonishing."

"It could have easily been me making that shot," said Puller. "Knox was just faster."

Knox said, "But I didn't kill him. He wasn't there when we circled back. He might have been wearing armor. Someone might have helped him get away. I don't know which one."

Rinehart cleared his throat. "But who could these people be? Are they all tied to Robert Puller in some way?"

Knox said, "Well, we are investigating his escape. I can't think of another reason why they would be coming after us."

Donovan Carter spoke for the first time. "But surely you have enemies, Agent Knox. We've all read your professional history since we knew you'd be here tonight. You've accomplished extraordinary things on behalf of your country. That comes with a price."

"But there's no disputing the fact that Lenora Macri tried to kill me. And that she was going to flee to Russia and then from there to who knows where. She aided the hit man coming into DB."

"Whoa, whoa," exclaimed Rinehart. "What hit man at DB?"

Puller gave Knox a quick glance. He had been surprised that she had said that, since he had left it out of his report. But he received a barely perceptible nod of assent from her to speak.

He took a few minutes to explain about the extra man in the MP company responding to the situation at the DB, and how Robert Puller had possibly taken his place to escape. Puller added, "Forensic analysis has confirmed that he was recently in Ukraine. Maybe he lived there. And his going to DB to kill my brother is really the only thing that makes sense."

"Well, not really, he could have gone there to help your brother escape," suggested Carter.

"Then why kill him?"

"They had a falling-out? It was an accident?"

"His neck was broken, using a specific technique. I don't think it was an accident."

"Then a disagreement of some sort?" opined Carter.

"I'm not convinced of that," said Puller. "And when you've planned such an elaborate escape from a max prison, it's not like you have a lot of time to stand around talking and arguing about details. You just execute the plan. But I don't see how the plan works if the two of them tried to get out. The guy didn't have an extra set of riot gear on him. And I don't see how my brother could have walked out with a second set of gear and nobody noticed."

Rinehart looked at Puller thoughtfully but said nothing. Carter and Schindler looked unconvinced.

"And what about Daughtrey?" said Knox. "Who murdered him?"

"Again, possibly Robert Puller," said Carter.

"It happened in Kansas where your brother escaped from."

"Why would he target Daughtrey? I don't think he even knew him."

Carter said, "Timothy Daughtrey was the man who took your brother's slot at ISR at Bolling Air Force Base. Robert Puller was being promoted to lieutenant colonel and would have been assigned to ISR. Instead he went to DB for life. I worked with Daughtrey at ISR. I would have worked with your brother if he hadn't gone to prison."

"So you're saying he targeted Daughtrey because the man took a slot that he couldn't fill because he was in prison?" said Knox skeptically.

"It could be more than that," said Carter. "There could have been more between them. They were contemporaries, competitors in the military pecking order. I'm not saying it happened. I'm just saying it was a possibility. And the fact is, while Daughtrey was a rank ahead of your brother, Robert Puller had more gas in the tank. We'd had our eye on him for a long time. He would have passed Daughtrey at some point. Whether between the one- and two-star or the two- and three-star stage, it was only a matter of time. Daughtrey was going to hit the professional ceiling. He was quite talented, but not as exceptional as your brother."

"But of course that all changed when Puller went to prison," said Schindler.

"Maybe unfairly went to prison," said Knox. "And it seems likely now that he was innocent."

"I don't see that," said Rinehart. "Not yet. You've offered no proof of that, not a sliver. And what you have offered can be explained away. For example, if Macri was involved in helping your brother to escape, he might have promised her something in return."

"He had nothing," said Knox.

"That we know of," countered Rinehart. "A smart guy like him might have had assets hidden in the electronic ether. He bribes her and gets away. You discover Macri was paid off, you don't know by whom, and you have a deadly encounter with her. Now she'll never be able to tell us who she was working with."

"And the guys in the alley?" persisted Knox.

Rinehart shrugged. "If Robert Puller was a traitor and was selling secrets to our enemy, then those forces would still be out there. They have every incentive for the truth not to come out. And the fact that the dead man at DB has been identified as Ukrainian bolsters this theory. He might have been working for his country, or the Russians, or someone else, which in turn could be who Puller was selling secrets to."

"So you think he's guilty?" said Puller.

Rinehart bristled. "He was proven guilty at a court-martial. He escaped from prison. Until you or someone can refute or explain that, then yes, I think he's guilty."

"And Niles Robinson?" said Knox.

"He testified against Puller," said Carter. "And there's something else, something you may not be aware of."

Knox and Puller looked at him expectantly.

"As you may know, Susan Reynolds works at the WMD Center. She also testified at Puller's court-martial. She personally informed me that Robert Puller broke into her home, threatened her, and injected her with some poison to try to make her confess to some lie about falsely accusing him. But she was able to thwart him and reach a weapon. But he escaped before she could capture him." He paused and added, "Or shoot him."

Puller simply stared at the man for a few moments. "My brother was in Susan Reynolds's home?"

He nodded. "And she showed us the injection mark. And her blood was tested. Luckily, there was no sign of poison. He must have been bluffing."

Rinehart added, "Which means he's on the East Coast. Or at least he was."

Puller continued to stare at Carter. "When did you find out about this?'

"Just today."

"Have you told anyone else?"

"The appropriate parties. Those looking for Puller, yes."

"Which includes me."

"Which is why I'm telling you now."

Puller said, "She told you he was trying to make her confess to lies?"

"Yes. Maybe he was recording her somehow and wanted to use that as some sort of bargaining chip. But if she did say anything incriminating it was because he threatened her and she was fearful for her life."

Puller started to say something but Knox beat him to it. "What exactly did she say to him?" she asked.

"Between pleading for her life, she said whatever she thought he wanted to hear. He was a convicted traitor who had killed a man to get out of prison. I can't imagine how frightened she was. We've given her protection at her home in case he comes back."

Puller looked at Rinehart and Schindler. "Did you two know about this?"

"Donovan informed us right before you arrived," said Schindler. "It does not paint a picture of an innocent man."

"If it's true," said Puller.

Carter scoffed. "Why would she make something like that up? It would just bring her into this mess when she wasn't involved at all. She would have no incentive to lie."

"Incentives are in the eye of the beholder, at least that's been my experience," said Puller.

"And my experience, Mr. Puller, is to see things as they present themselves. And as opposed to your brother's actions, Ms. Reynolds is by far the more reliable witness. She is a valuable employee and has faithfully served this country for many years."

"I'm just pointing out that we don't have all the facts yet."

"Your bias in favor of your brother is natural." Carter looked first at Rinehart and then at Schindler. "Which makes it very difficult for me to understand why you are even involved in this investigation."

"He's involved, Donovan, because we asked him to be involved," replied Rinehart stiffly.

Schindler added, "With the knowledge he has

of his brother we felt, along with his training as an investigator, that he held a good chance of tracking him down. Maybe the best chance."

"Well, that hasn't happened, has it?" countered Carter.

"I haven't even been on the case for a full week," said Puller, who suddenly realized it felt more like a year.

"And there are other forces pursuing Robert Puller," added Rinehart. "We don't have all of our eggs in one basket."

"Well, I will presume you know what you're doing," said Carter, as their meal was served.

They ate mostly in silence, with only an occasional question and reply. After their coffees and a port for Rinehart had come, Puller glanced at Knox before saying to the three men, "We learned that my brother received a threatening letter during his court-martial. A letter that said if he didn't basically lie down and let himself be convicted that my father and I would come to harm."

He quickly looked at Rinehart, Schindler, and Carter to see their reactions. He was disappointed because none of them seemed remotely surprised.

"We're aware of that, Puller," said Rinehart.

"I was told it was not disclosed to anyone."

Schindler said, "Don't believe for a minute that we are relying on you solely to further this investigation. As General Rinehart said, our eggs are not in one basket."

Rinehart said, "We're employing scorched earth here, Puller. We talked to both defense counsel and the prosecutor in the case. And to the judge. We learned about the letter from Doug Fletcher, among other things."

"I interviewed him, but he didn't mention talking to you."

"That is because my people told him not to disclose the interview. And even though he's no longer in the military, he knows how to obey an order from a three-star."

"And why was it important to keep this from me?"

"It wasn't necessarily done to keep it from you. I wasn't aware you were going to even speak with him. It was done, in a blanket way, to keep this matter in as tight a group of need-to-know as possible."

"And what did you think about the existence of the letter?"

"Robert Puller could have easily written it himself. That's why it wasn't introduced into evidence."

"That's not exactly right. It wasn't introduced

into evidence because my brother wouldn't let it be. I'm assuming Fletcher told your people that?"

"So what? Even if it had been introduced, there was no way to validate its authenticity."

"But that's the point. My brother would have known that. So why would he even bother to make it up? It couldn't help him at all."

Schindler said, "You don't know that for certain. Maybe he had a change of heart after he wrote it, and decided not to use it. Maybe he thought it might carry some weight on appeal. I don't know because I'm not a lawyer. Your brother is by all accounts a genius. Sometimes geniuses do irrational things. Sometimes they are delusional. Perhaps he felt guilty about what he'd done and wrote the letter and invented the story to make up for it somehow, at least in his mind."

"My brother is not some sort of crazy genius. He had no delusions. He's as pragmatic as I am."

Carter said, "But you weren't around him all the time back then, were you, Puller? You were off serving your country. People change."

"Not like that. Not my brother."

Carter finished his coffee, wiped his mouth with his napkin, and turned to Rinehart. "I think we've exhausted the possibilities of this meeting."

Rinehart nodded and took a last sip of his port.

Before the men could stand, Puller said to Carter, "And why have you been brought into the tight circle of need-to-know?"

"Puller, Mr. Carter is the director of DTRA, for God's sake," Rinehart said sternly. "He oversees a three-billion-dollar budget with personnel deployed in over a dozen countries. His specific security clearances are at the very highest level."

"I have no doubt they are. I was just inquiring as to why he's involved in this particular matter."

Before Rinehart could respond, Carter held up his hand. "I'll field this one, Aaron, if you don't mind." He turned to Puller. "As I said, before I was in charge of DTRA, I worked where your brother was headed before he went to prison. There one of my colleagues was the unfortunate General Tim Daughtrey when he was still a colonel. I never worked with your brother back then, but I had met him. I saw as much potential in him as I'd ever seen in anyone. I didn't consider myself a mentor to him, because frankly I didn't think myself smart enough. And Robert Puller had plenty of mentors since everyone was racing to attach themselves to his coattails. I didn't want to believe that he was guilty, but I have to accept facts too. Now, my immediate interest in this? As you know, your brother was at the heart of many programs, which in turn are at the very core of what this country does in both the intelligence collection and nuclear defense fields. In addition to my duties at DTRA, my main objective at the center is to locate WMDs and prevent them from falling into the hands of our enemies. The work that your brother did at STRATCOM has a direct connection to what I try to do at the center. If he's escaped and people that he was selling secrets to are active once more, then I need to know what is going on. This country has many enemies and many issues confronting it, everything from cyber warfare to corporate espionage. But there is no more paramount concern than rogue WMDs being used against us. A crew of cyber warriors can attack the grid, knock out data servers, and hack into millions of credit card accounts. But a single WMD of sufficient magnitude can wipe out a city and kill hundreds of thousands of people. Credit cards can be replaced. People can't. So which do you think is more problematic from a security perspective?"

"Thanks for answering my question, sir," said Puller.

Carter rose, gave a slight bow followed by a tight smile. "You're quite welcome."

48

RINEHART AND SCHINDLER left in a car driven by a man in uniform. Puller was heading out too when Knox gripped his arm, holding him back.

"Just give it a minute, Puller."

Shortly after that Donovan Carter approached them in the lobby.

"Have time for a nightcap?" he asked, looking at one and then the other.

Puller glanced at Knox, who said, "Sounds like an offer we can't refuse, sir."

They walked to the bar on the second floor. There were only a few people left there and they took a table in the back. Carter ordered a whiskey soda, Knox a glass of Prosecco, and Puller a Heineken. When the drinks arrived, Carter extracted a pill from a silver case and swallowed it along with some of his whiskey.

"Painkiller," he explained.

"Should you be mixing that with alcohol?" asked Knox.

"Probably not, but I've been doing it for years with no adverse results. And the whiskey makes it go down a little bit better."

"Painkillers?" said Puller.

Carter pointed to the damaged side of his face. "In case you failed to notice, I've suffered injuries of unfortunately a permanent nature."

"What happened, if you don't mind my asking?" said Knox.

"Afghanistan in 2001."

"Were you in the military?" asked Puller.

"I was there serving my country before the uniforms even showed up. I was captured and tortured. What you see on my face is just the visible marks. There are lots of others under my clothes. The Taliban are quite adept at inflicting pain. And scars."

"Were you gathering intelligence?" asked Knox.

He nodded. "Intel on the ground was vital before we invaded. Afghanistan is a tough nut to crack. Many nations have tried it. The Brits. The Russians. It's fairly simple to win the war over there turning rubble to dust, as they say. However, it's absolutely impossible to win over the country after the tanks stop rolling, as we found to our chagrin."

"How did you get away?" asked Puller.

"I would like to say that I was rescued, but I wasn't. I got away on my own. Not sure how. I was out of my mind with pain. But maybe I was so desperate that I just pushed the agony out of my head. I killed the three Taliban guarding me. If I had had time, I would have tortured them before I slit their throats. It seemed fitting. But I didn't have the option. I dragged myself about three hundred miles across landscape that resembled the moon until I reached safety. Two years of physical therapy allowed me to function physically, walk and talk and use my arms. But the scars are permanent. The pain is permanent. So I take pills and I drink whiskey, but neither to excess. And I serve my country, and I do it well. After my ordeal in Afghanistan people considered me a hero, rightly or not. At least I had the wounds to show for it. And it certainly helped my career path, which was like a rocket launch after that. I jumped back and forth between Capitol Hill and the intelligence field and built up quite an expertise on national security and foreign affairs. Attaining SES status and heading up DTRA and the center are really the highlights for me. I couldn't expect any more. And now you know more about it than you would ever care to," he added with a self-conscious smile.

"So why the nightcap? It struck me that you had said all you wanted to say at dinner," commented Puller.

"I did. But I wasn't sure that *you* had said all you wanted to say. And if not, I'm here to listen. You'll find me a good listener. And without the presence of a three-star and the president's man, I thought you might feel more comfortable in expressing yourselves."

Knox said bluntly, "Okay, let's do this. We really don't think Robert Puller is guilty."

"Based on what?"

"The evidence at trial was shaky."

Carter shook his head as he took another sip of his whiskey. "Two eyewitness accounts? Classified data found on his person? A trail of online gambling debts providing the motive? Hardly shaky evidence."

"The online trail could easily have been fabricated."

"Perhaps. But the testimony of Reynolds and Robinson?"

Puller studied him carefully. "Inasmuch as you think I can't be objective about my brother, it may be true that you can't be objective about Reynolds, since she works for you."

Carter sat back and considered this statement. "Let's go down that road for a moment. Let's assume Reynolds was lying. Why?"

"She was paid to do it," said Knox.

"So she's a traitor, paid to implicate your brother. Again, why? What's so special about him?"

"As you said, he was a very valuable asset to the government."

"Yes, he was. But our government possesses many valuable people assets, so why go after him in particular?"

"Would there be a reason to get him out of the way at STRATCOM?"

"He was getting ready to leave one branch of STRATCOM after his next promotion, as I said at dinner. He was heading to ISR, which, as you know, is also a command component under STRATCOM. I would have worked with him there, as I also mentioned."

"Would there be some reason to prevent him from going there?" asked Knox.

Carter shrugged. "I can't say. ISR has many employees. Was he important enough to pull off such a conspiracy as you've described? It would be difficult to believe."

"You said that you worked with General

Daughtrey at ISR when he was still a colonel."

"That's right."

"Since Daughtrey took my brother's slot at ISR, you implied that might be a motive for my brother to retaliate and kill him. But let's look at it from the other way."

Carter put down his drink and said curiously, "How so?"

"Was my brother the first choice for the ISR slot?" said Puller.

"Yes. Hands down."

"And Daughtrey was the backup?" said Knox.

"Okay, I see where this is going," replied Carter. "You're saying Robert Puller was set up to prevent him from going to ISR?"

"Yes, but it also allowed Daughtrey to take his place," added Puller.

"For what purpose?"

"What did the position entail? What would the person have had access to?" asked Puller.

Carter took another swallow of his drink and rubbed his chin. "Everything, more or less. ISR's work is broad and far-reaching. From space to underwater and really every-thing in between. ISR is, in many vital re-spects, the eyes, ears, and brain of the DoD. Its commander wears dual hats because he also heads up the Defense Intelligence Agency. ISR works with all other major intelligence platforms, NSA, Geospatial, National Reconnaissance. Its responsibilities cross the full military spectrum of requirements, transnational threats, the Global War on Terror, and WMDs. Everything really."

"So Daughtrey would have had access to all of that?"

"More or less, yes."

"And then he was murdered," noted Puller.

"But he had left ISR at that point," pointed out Carter.

"And went to another component of STRATCOM," said Knox. "Which one?"

"U.S. Cyber Command."

Puller nodded. "Another hot spot. How was his work at ISR?"

"I found him extremely talented, hardworking, ambitious."

"How ambitious?" said Puller quickly.

"Most officers seeking to move up in rank are ambitious. You know that."

"I'm not talking about medals and stars."

"Then what?"

Knox said, "Susan Reynolds lives in a million-dollar-plus house, drives a seventy-thousand-dollar car, wears Prada shoes, and has a closet full of Coach bags. And there's an original Joan Miró painting in her library. I looked the price up. There is no way she could have bought it with even twenty years' worth of her salary."

Puller shot her a glance. She hadn't mentioned the Prada, the Coach bags, or the painting.

She noted his look. "I *am* a girl, Puller, even if I do carry a gun and kick ass. I notice bags and shoes. And I saw the painting when we were there. I was an art history major at Amherst."

"Joan Miró?" he asked.

"He was a Spaniard, born in Barcelona. He died decades ago."

"So he's a renowned artist or something?"

"Well, let's put it this way, Puller. One of his paintings sold a couple years back at a Sotheby's auction in London for nearly forty million. So, yeah, I guess you could say the guy was pretty good."

"Damn," said Puller.

Carter seemed intrigued by this information. "I've never been to her home. And I didn't know what kind of car she drives. And, quite frankly, I wouldn't know a Prada shoe if it hit me in the head."

"The fact is she's living well beyond her

means," said Knox. "So what is the source of income? And there's one more thing. She went to work at ISR when Daughtrey did. And now she's at the WMD Center, while Daughtrey was at Cyber Command. But what if they were still working together? Because it's all incestuous, right? Dual hatters, STRATCOM covers everything. The intelligence world is as interconnected as it's ever been."

"That's true. But do you mean working together as spies?"

"Spies, moles, whatever you want to call it. Would they have things to sell?"

"Of course they would. Which is why we have background checks and security clearance procedures and periodic testing, polygraphs, and follow-up. And why everyone is watched very closely."

"Well, you didn't know about her financial status, did you?"

Carter sat back, still looking dubious, but a bit less so.

Puller said, "So how ambitious was Daughtrey? Not for stars. For money. Anybody check lately? Because in addition to Reynolds, we have Lenora Macri. She was only a lowly captain at Leavenworth. But she had an account in the Caymans under an alias packed with cash. So I wonder how much a one-star would have piled up?"

Carter picked up his glass and then put it back down without taking a drink. "Daughtrey did mention to me once that he was thinking of getting out of the military and starting his own consulting group or maybe going into private contracting to the DoD."

"That would be a nice way to launder any money he'd been paid," noted Knox. "Mix it up under consulting contracts and hire a shady CPA to make it look all perfectly aboveboard."

"You've given me a lot to think about. But Daughtrey and Reynolds? Spies?"

"And Robinson?" said Puller.

"What about him?"

"He had a very ill son before my brother went to prison. His insurance would not cover experimental treatments outside of the country. His son was going to die. After my brother goes to prison, his son gets the experimental treatment costing seven figures in Germany and is alive and well."

Carter snapped, "Why didn't you mention this at dinner?"

"I'm mentioning it now."

"So you think Robinson was paid off to lie?"

"Yes. And you were told my brother visited

Reynolds. Why take that chance? Revenge at her testifying against him? If so, why not just kill her? Why leave her alive to tell the authorities he's in the area? If he is a murderer, what's one more murder to him?"

Carter finished the rest of his whiskey soda. "I wasn't sure what would come of this conversation when I invited you for a nightcap, but I can honestly tell you I never anticipated this. You have put together a plausible argument that your brother might have been framed, and that the real enemies could still be out there."

Knox said, "So the question is, what can we do about it? Because most of what we have is conjecture and speculation. That doesn't work in court."

"Let me see what I can do from my end. I'll be in touch. And I'll be in touch soon."

He rose, dropped cash on the table for their drinks, and walked out.

Puller said, "Nice catch on the Miró and the purses and shoes."

"I didn't tell you because we already knew she had a lot more money than she should have. It didn't add anything new to the picture."

"Right. But meeting with Carter like this was a big risk," he said.

"But if we can't make headway in our investigation then lighting a fire in a munitions dump might be the only way to go. In fact, if he hadn't asked for the nightcap I would have. It's the reason I had us hanging around in the lobby."

"We'll know one way or another, soon."

"Yes we will."

He said, "But remember, if the munitions dump does ignite, a lot of folks could get caught in the fireball, including us."

49

PULLER DROPPED KNOX off at her hotel before heading back to Quantico. He stopped to get some gas near the base. Another vehicle swung into the fuel bay next to his. Someone got out to pump fuel.

Puller had put the nozzle in and was leaning against the hood of his car when the voice said, "Don't react, Junior. Somebody might be watching."

Maybe because he was hoping that something like this might eventually happen, Puller didn't even flinch. He pulled his phone out and pretended to be checking messages, with not a care in the world. Out of the corner of his eye he saw the pickup truck parked in the fuel bay next to his. A tall man, nearly as tall as he was, stood next to it, pumping gas. Under the light of the overheads Puller snatched a glimpse of the man he knew was his brother. Yet if the man hadn't called him Junior he might not have recognized Bobby. There were only three people in the world who had ever called him that: his father, his mother, and his brother.

Bald, tatted arms, goatee, totally different nose and ears. There was a rifle rack in the back window and a "Don't Tread On Me" sticker on the side of the cab.

"You've changed a little bit," mumbled Puller.

"Just on the outside. Same nerd on the inside."

Robert opened his wallet and drew out a credit card and swiped it through. He hit the necessary keys and then put the gas nozzle into his tank outlet.

"We have a lot to talk about," said Puller.

"Yes we do, little brother."

"I've found out a lot."

"So have I."

"You were set up."

"Yep."

"We've gotta make it right."

"I plan to," said Robert.

"How do you want to do this?"

"Can't go to your place. Too obvious."

Puller pretended to make a call and held the phone up to his ear and said, "I can lose any possible tail and then meet you."

"I was going to suggest that."

"You staying somewhere close?"

"I will be. Passed it a couple miles back. The Holiday Inn. You know it?"

"I know it."

"I'll park my ride in front of my room. Truck's hard to miss. Kansas plates."

"Right."

"Please make damn sure you're not followed, bro. That would not be in either of our best interests."

"They'll never be able to, Bobby."

"I know, Junior. I know."

John Puller finished fueling and drove away. A couple minutes later Robert Puller drove off in the opposite direction.

* * *

John Puller reached his apartment complex but kept driving until he got to Quantico. He passed the security checkpoint and headed over to the CID building. He walked down the hallway to an office he shared with other agents. It was empty and he spent about twenty minutes doodling on a piece of paper and also trying to get his nerves settled after just running into his fugitive brother at a gas station.

Despite being on the run, his brother had

sounded cool and calm. And Puller had let him dictate the plan going forward, when that was not his natural inclination. Yet between the two boys Robert had always been the leader. Even if he hadn't been older, Puller thought that would have been the case. Robert just had that way about him.

Puller waited another twenty minutes. During that time he changed out of his dress blues and into a set of fatigues he kept in the locker room. He left the building through a rear entrance and walked over to the motor pool. He checked out a four-door sedan and drove out another gate. He drove for twenty miles through rural roads, turning left and right, backtracking, stopping, going fast, then slow, and making it impossible for anyone to have followed him. He then parked a half mile away from the Holiday Inn and hoofed it the rest of the way through both woods and residential areas.

The truck with the Kansas plates was parked in front of room 103. Puller checked the bed and cab of the truck as he passed by it. He knocked on the motel room door and it opened a few seconds later after he had observed the curtain on the window adjacent to the door slide to the side just a bit as someone peered out.

Puller didn't go in immediately. He put a hand on the butt of his holstered M11. "Bobby?" he said softly.

"Coast is clear, Junior."

Puller walked in and closed and locked the door behind him.

There was only one light on in the small room, a table lamp next to the bed. His brother sat in a chair in the corner of the room. Through another door Puller could see the bathroom. A duffel bag was lying on the bed.

Puller sat on the edge of the bed and eyed his brother.

"Any problems getting here?" Robert asked.

"I took my time and if anyone was able to follow me then they deserve to win."

Robert Puller rose and held out his arms. "It's damn good to see you, John."

Puller rose too and the two men exchanged a prolonged hug accompanied by back slaps. When they drew apart, Puller could see the moistness in his brother's eyes and he could feel his own eyes begin to water. It was the most unusual feeling seeing his brother not a prisoner. It felt great. And it also felt fleeting and temporary. And that frightened Puller more than anything had in a long time.

Robert sat back down and Puller retook his

seat on the bed. Neither man spoke for a long moment.

"How did you manage to find me?" asked Puller.

"I wasn't following you, at least initially. I was following someone else and picked up your trail at the Army-Navy Club."

"Who was the someone else?"

"Donovan Carter. I tracked him from Fort Belvoir. Surprised the hell out of me when you showed up."

"Why were you following Carter?"

"I'm trying to do what I'm sure you're trying to do: Solve a problem."

"Of who set you up and why?"

Robert nodded. "Susan Reynolds was in on it."

"We talked to her. She told Carter that you were at her house and threatened her. Injected her with poison."

Robert held up his phone and pushed a button. Puller listened to the exchange between his brother and Reynolds that he'd recorded.

"It proves nothing, of course. She could just say she said it so I wouldn't kill her. And it wasn't poison. I just let her imagination take over and then knocked her out with a sedative."

"Russians?" said Puller.

"A red herring, at least I think it is. You heard about Niles Robinson?"

"It was his kid that was the motivation, right?"

"Yes. He was talking to me on the phone at Union Station when someone gunned him down."

"That's what I figured."

"Did you? Well, I can't say I'm surprised. I recorded that conversation too. The salient point was he said someone might have a problem with me getting the slot at ISR."

"Who?"

"He never got a chance to tell me."

"Daughtrey took your slot at ISR. Then he went to Cyber Command."

"And now he's dead."

"He was found in my motel room back in Kansas."

"I saw you there with a woman. Didn't know he was found in your room."

"The woman is Agent Veronica Knox, INSCOM. Know her?"

"No." He paused, eyeing his brother steadily. "I'm sure you have a lot of questions for me."

"And some answers. DB? A Ukrainian was sent in to kill you after they orchestrated knocking out the power. A Captain Macri was in on it. Knox ended up killing her in a shootout."

Robert fiddled with a pen he was holding. "When the guy came into my cell, I was already suspicious. I knew before I ever went there that DB had backup power that was infallible. But it *had* failed. I also knew that when the power went out the cell doors automatically locked. That didn't happen. They opened. That meant someone had screwed with the software. Now I wasn't sure exactly what was going on or that I was the target. But I decided to stay in my cell and see how it played out. When I heard someone at my cell door I called out that I was on the floor with my hands behind my head. When the guy came through the door he had a knife, when standard operating procedure is a gun in a situation like that. And you would never have only one guy clearing a room. You'd have at least two. This guy was clearly a rogue."

"And by using a knife he can kill you silently, whereas a shot would bring a bunch of other MPs."

Robert nodded. "And a knifing could be attributed to another prisoner who had fashioned a shiv and might have had a grudge against me. That would probably be the explanation when they found my body. No one would suspect one of the MPs."

"And I'm sure they were counting on that. But you turned the tables on them."

"I wasn't on the floor with my hands behind my head. I was behind the door. I disarmed him. When he started yelling at me in what I recognized was Ukrainian I knew he was trying to kill me. So I killed him instead."

"Snap-crackle-pop? At least that's what occurred to me from the ME's description."

"Came in handy, bro. For that I thank you."

"Then you put on his gear and left that way."

"Lucky for me he was about my size."

"So you went back on the truck to Leavenworth and then got away. But how did you change your appearance so drastically?"

Robert smiled and touched his nose. "After I moved to Kansas I rented a storage unit under a fictitious name. Set up credit card and bank accounts under that name and outfitted the storage unit with things I would need to change my appearance and also some other items."

"Why? You couldn't have been expecting to be arrested and then escaping from DB?"

"Didn't figure in the equation at all. But while I was at STRATCOM I would disguise myself and go out undercover to military watering holes around the base."

"But why?"

"When I got to the satellite facility I learned that people stationed there weren't being as tight-lipped as they should be. Classified info was getting bandied about in places it never should have been. I was instrumental in busting up a ring of people that were preying on drunk soldiers and personnel from STRATCOM to get information to sell, or blackmail them with."

"And no one knew about your alter ego?"

"That would have defeated the point. But it came in extraordinarily handy when I got away from DB. I could change my appearance, gun up, have equipment, cash, and a credit card, and be on my way."

"So what have you been doing since you escaped?"

"Trying to work out who set me up." He paused and stared pointedly at his brother. "Look, I'm stunned they allowed you anywhere near this case."

"Three-star named Aaron Rinehart and a guy from the NSC, James Schindler, came to me, along with Daughtrey. They set it up."

"I've met Rinehart. I know of Schindler.

Never crossed paths with Daughtrey. But still, what's their angle?"

"I don't know. A JAG friend told me she didn't see any positives for me in the scenario."

"I'd call that good advice."

"You were following Carter, so you suspected him?"

"Reynolds works at the WMD Center, which he runs. Daughtrey worked with him at ISR. I'm not sure if he was the 'person' Robinson was mentioning, but it seemed a good place to start. I haven't found many leads on this sucker, so I intend to follow up all of them until I hit the right one."

"Is it all about money? I think it is for Reynolds."

"She has a Joan Miró in her mini-mansion," said Robert.

"So my colleague Knox pointed out."

"That painting is worth at least a few million dollars. That's reason enough for STRATCOM to do surprise searches of every sensitive personnel's home. Sometimes we can't see the forest for the trees. But I don't think it's all about money for all of them."

"What, then? If they're traitors then they're selling stuff."

"Maybe, but I think there's more to it than just cash."

Puller mulled this over. "By the way, I think I figured out how Reynolds got that DVD in your pocket."

"How?"

"Her father was a magician. She assisted him. I'm sure she's quite adept at sleight of hand."

"I'm sure you're right."

Brother looked at brother.

"So what now?" asked Puller.

"Tell me what else you've learned," said Robert. "I'm sure it's a lot."

Puller did so, keeping nothing back. He could see that his brother's mind was going a mile a minute, taking it all in and then neatly cataloging each piece.

Finished, he said, "What about you?"

Robert took a few minutes to fill in his brother.

"So you think there's a conspiracy going on?" asked Puller.

"I do. It can't be simply one person."

"I told you about those men kidnapping me?"

"Yes."

Puller studied his brother for a long moment. "Was it you? Did you fire the shots?"

Robert slowly nodded. "I was glad I could be there for you, John. Knowing you, you probably would've made it out okay on your own, but, well, I was glad I was there to help. I haven't been able to do that much with you over the last two years."

"No bones about it, Bobby, you saved my life. But you could have made contact with me then."

Robert looked guiltily at him. "I thought about it, trust me. But it would have put you in an untenable situation. You'd be duty-bound to arrest me."

"But you made contact now. Why?"

Robert sighed. "Because I didn't know if I'd ever get another chance. I know how many people are out looking for me. Highly trained people good at their job. I...I just wanted you to hear things from my side. I wanted you to know that..."

"I never believed you were guilty of anything."

His brother smiled weakly. "Sure you did. Or at least you weren't certain."

"I found out about the threatening letter you got in your cell."

Robert's smile faded. "Who told you that?"

"Doesn't matter. You took a dive to protect Dad and me. Your career, years of your life, everything, Bobby."

"The fact is I was too arrogant. I never thought I'd be convicted because I wasn't guilty. Talk about naïve."

"You still took a dive."

"I couldn't let anything happen to my family," he said quietly. "You two were all I had left."

"Any idea who they might be?"

"No. But you said the voice you heard when you were kidnapped thought of himself as a patriot. That's both interesting and disturbing."

"Why disturbing?"

"Because in my experience, patriotism, while a fine quality, can fuel quite a dangerous agenda if taken to the extreme."

"An agenda as yet unknown," said Puller.

"I think we can cast a little bit of light on it."

"How?"

"If I was prevented from going to ISR and Daughtrey filled my slot, then that's something."

"But what would be the reason?"

"I'm honest and above reproach. I can't be bought. Unusual language coming from a convicted traitor, but it is the truth. Daughtrey, on the other hand, might've been none of those things."

"And they wanted him at ISR. Carter told us

how important that component is to our national defense."

"In many vital ways ISR *is* our national defense."

"So a traitor could do a great deal of damage?"

"Catastrophic."

"What do you know about Daughtrey? How did he get that far in the military without anyone suspecting?"

"If he *is* guilty. We don't have definite proof of that yet. But if he is guilty, who's to say when he went over to the other side, or what the motivation was?"

"If he was a traitor why kill him?"

"You said he was part of the team that recruited you to work on my case?"

"Yes."

"So if he was bad, he was doing that to piggyback on the investigation. He was hoping you would find me and he could make sure I never got back to DB alive."

"But how can you hurt them?"

"I don't know. I was nothing to them while I was sitting in DB, John. Something happened to trigger this."

"Okay, let's say that's true. Let's go back to the question of why kill Daughtrey?"

"The main reason to kill an operative is pretty obvious."

"He decided to defect?"

"Or had a change of heart of some kind. Maybe he had a conscience and drew the line at outright murdering someone."

"Then he signed his own death warrant."

"Yes, he did." Robert rubbed his thighs with his hands. "So how can we work together without anyone knowing?"

"A couple of burn phones?"

"And we can use that code I invented that we used as kids."

"You always said it was unbreakable."

"I guess we'll find out."

"One more thing, Bobby."

"Yeah?"

"I've got a letter for you to read."

His brother's eyes narrowed. "A letter? From who?"

Puller got the document up on his screen and handed his brother the phone. "Just read it."

Robert took the phone, his features curious, and started to read. Though the letter was relatively short, he was still reading, or more likely rereading, five minutes later.

Finally, he handed the phone back to his brother.

"That's why the charges were dropped to espionage from spying," said Puller quietly while watching his brother closely.

"Difference between life and death," Robert said in a hollow tone. It seemed like every bit of energy had been struck clean from him. "No one ever told me about the letter."

"I didn't know about it either, until very recently."

Puller looked at the screen. His father's letter had been extraordinary, if for no other reason than that Puller had never seen this side of his father. Even though his brother had already read the letter, Puller felt he had to do it. He believed he owed it, to both men.

He cleared his throat and read:

I had the honor of serving my country in uniform for four decades. Many people who think they know me would probably believe that such service was the high point of my life. They would be wrong. The crowning glory of my life is and will always be as the father of two extraordinary young men. Indeed, God has shown that there can be no higher purpose for a man. And while I was absent for many important moments in their lives, not a single day ever passed without me thinking about them. I love them more than I have ever loved anything or anyone in my long life. So I write to you today, gentlemen, as a person who does not see a grown man faced with the destruction of his professional life and the loss of his liberty, but rather as a father who sees the young boy with a beautiful mind, a kind and sympathetic nature, and an extraordinary heart, who, I know beyond doubt, is innocent of these charges. And I trust that time will prove me right. And by God, I will await that day with all my strength, all my spirit, and all my love for my son, Major Robert W. Puller.

Puller couldn't go on because his voice was cracking. He stopped reading and looked up.

Robert started to say something but then stopped, put his elbows on his thighs, and hung his head.

When his big brother started to weep, Puller sat next to him and put an arm around his shoulders.

The Pullers sat there for a long time together, big, strong, and courageous men transformed back into two little boys by an old man's loving words that had come a lot later than they should have.

50

PULLER MET KNOX in the lobby of the W Hotel the next morning. Though he tried hard to hide it, she apparently noticed something different.

"You okay?" she asked.

He rubbed his eyes. "Didn't sleep much last night."

She didn't look sympathetic. "Join the club. I don't think I've slept a full night since I met you."

They walked out of the hotel and to his car parked on the street. The air was surprisingly crisp and cool, with a light breeze. A jet overhead made a sharp left bank to avoid flying over restricted airspace after taking off from Reagan National.

"So while you *weren't* sleeping, did you think anymore about our 'nightcap' with Donovan Carter?" asked Knox.

"Carter gave us an excuse to go back and talk to Reynolds again."

"The visit your brother made to Reynolds?"

"Exactly."

"She'll be at work now most likely."

"She works for DoD. I'm a duly assigned military investigator. Nothing prohibits us from interviewing her while she's at work."

"What are you going to ask her?"

"I want her take on the encounter with Bobby. And I want to watch her while she answers the questions."

"Body language cues?"

"They often tell more than what the person actually says."

* * *

Puller had called ahead and Susan Reynolds met them in her office, a modest space that looked, oddly enough, both cluttered and organized. Her security lanyard was around her neck, her features were placid, and she greeted them politely and indicated chairs for them to take.

She sat down and waited.

As Puller lowered himself into the chair he let his gaze sweep her office. He saw no items that were not work-related. The woman didn't even have any plants.

As his gaze came back to her, he found that

she was staring at him. And Puller could tell she knew exactly what he had been doing.

"I like to keep things streamlined and separate," she said. "Professional and personal."

"I can understand that." He pointed at one photo showing a younger Reynolds in a line of all men on what appeared to be an airstrip. "That looks interesting."

She turned to look at it. "Back in the 1990s I was part of a START verification team when the U.S. and the Soviets were whittling down their nuclear stockpiles. As you can see from the photo, I was the only woman on either team, and the youngest by far. Quite a feather in my cap. But I had worked hard for the opportunity."

"Interesting work?" asked Knox.

"Yes. Although by seven o'clock each night the Russians had drunk enough vodka to float an aircraft carrier. So I'm not sure how accurate their verification was. But I never touched a drop and I crossed every t and dotted every i," she added emphatically.

"I'm sure you did," said Puller. "Now, we've been told that Robert Puller—"

Reynolds cut in. "Your brother, you mean. I knew it the first time we met."

Puller continued, "We were told that Robert Puller came to see you?"

"Came to kill me, more likely."

"But he didn't kill you."

"I was able to get away, found a gun, and he ran like the coward he obviously is."

"So he tied you up?"

"No, he put a gun to my head and then injected me with what he said was poison. I couldn't believe the bastard had done that. Maybe prison made him crazy."

"So you were able to overpower him and get to your gun?"

"I didn't say I overpowered him. He's a man and, as you know, he's far larger than I am. But I'm not exactly a weakling. I managed to hit him in the face with a lamp. Before he could recover I got to the bookcase. I keep a forty-five pistol there. I drew it. When he realized I was armed and ready to shoot, he turned and ran. I tried to stop him, but he was too fast. I called the police but they couldn't find him."

"You hit him in the face with a lamp?"

"I did."

"That must have hurt."

"I hope it hurt like hell," she said. "He deserved to be hurt a lot."

"Bruised and bloody probably."

"Yes. He was. And surprised, I'm sure."

"And what did he want?" asked Puller.

"He threatened me. He wanted me to confess that I had done something wrong."

"Why would he do that?" asked Knox.

Reynolds peered at her as though just that minute realizing she was there.

"How am I supposed to think like a nutcase? He's desperate. He's escaped from prison. He's killed a man. Maybe two men."

"What makes you say that?" asked Puller sharply.

"I heard about Niles Robinson. We've all heard about him. Gunned down at the train station."

"Why would you think Robert Puller would be involved in that?" asked Knox.

Reynolds gave her a patronizing stare. "Oh, I don't know, let's think about it. He breaks into my house at gunpoint and threatens me because I testified against him. Then soon thereafter Niles Robinson, who also testified against him, is shot and killed at Union Station. What are the odds of that having been done by two different people when Robert Puller was absolutely in the area? Don't insult my intelligence!"

"So what did you tell Puller?" asked Knox.

"I told him lots of things. To get out. To leave me alone. To never darken my door again. And then when he stuck me in the neck with what he said was poison I of course told him whatever he wanted to hear."

"And why would you do that?" asked Puller.

Now it was his turn to receive a condescending look. "Because I felt sorry for him and wanted him never to go back to prison. And I very much wanted to confess to treason and take his place." She suddenly snapped, "Why the hell do you think? Because he told me that was the only way I was getting the damn antidote to the poison he injected me with."

"But he didn't actually poison you," pointed out Puller.

"Right, I know that *now*. He told me he'd injected me with an organophosphate. Nasty stuff, let me tell you. I was scared out of my wits. I would have said anything to get the antidote."

"So when you hit him with the lamp and got to a gun, what did you expect would happen?"

"That I would force him to give me the antidote."

"And when he got away?"

"I called the police and the paramedics. I literally thought I had minutes to live. I was out of my mind with fright, thanks to that bastard."

"And I guess you were relieved when that turned out not to be the case?" noted Knox.

Reynolds didn't even dignify that with an answer.

They asked Reynolds a few more questions and then left. As Puller turned back around at the doorway he saw Reynolds staring right at him. She wasn't smiling or looking triumphant. She was just watching him. And then she turned and went back to her work.

As they walked down the corridor Knox said, "Every time I see that woman I want to strangle her."

"Not me, I'd just shoot her," said Puller.

She looked up at him. "So did you get any good body cues from the witch?"

"Ironically enough, this time it really was more what she said than how she said it."

"What do you mean?"

Puller knew she hadn't hit his brother with a lamp. He was neither bruised nor bloody. But he couldn't tell Knox that without revealing that he and his brother had met. Yet there was something else.

"I checked the toxicology report that they did on Reynolds after my brother supposedly injected her with poison. Remember that Carter said they had done one? Well, I got a copy emailed to me this morning."

"But it didn't find poison."

"No, but it did reveal traces of a strong sedative. Strong enough to have knocked her out."

Knox stopped, and so did Puller.

"A sedative?" she said. "Why didn't anyone else notice that?"

"Because I think they all stopped looking at the tox report when it showed no poison. Me, I tend to read until the end."

"But why would there be a sedative in her system?"

"My brother could have injected her with one."

"Why would he do that if he wanted her to talk?"

"To allow him to escape *after* they finished talking."

"But why would she lie if she knew it was provable by a blood test?"

"Because she's not as smart as she thinks she is. I don't believe she thought it all the way through. And I think she truly hates my brother and saw an opportunity to really stick it to him. Calling him a coward and trying to make us believe that she was able to fight him off successfully must have really brightened her day. Oh, and she obviously knew you had searched her house and found the gun in the bookcase. That's why she mentioned it. Really good liars always work in something true to make the lie more plausible."

"So that means she was lying about…well, everything."

"I never doubted that for a minute," said Puller.

51

THEY HAD ALMOST gotten to the building's exit when two security personnel stopped them.

"Chief Puller? Agent Knox?" said one, who was dressed in cammies and carried the rank of sergeant.

"Yes?" said Puller.

"Mr. Carter would like to see you both."

Donovan Carter was waiting for them in a room adjacent to his formal office. There was one other person in the room, a man of medium height with a thick head of blond hair and penetrating green eyes. Like Carter he wore a suit, regulation navy blue with a white shirt and muted striped tie.

"This is Blair Sullivan," Carter began, indicating the man next to him. "He heads up our internal security section."

The man gave a curt nod in their direction but said nothing.

"After our conversation last night," began Carter.

Puller's gaze shot to Sullivan, but Carter said, "It's all right, Agent Puller. I've brought him into the circle. He was instrumental in tracking certain things down for me."

Sullivan folded his arms across his chest and did his best not to look at either Puller or Knox.

Carter drew open a file that was sitting in front of him. "Let's first address Susan Reynolds's financial history. I wasn't personally aware of this, but her husband was an FBI agent who was killed many years ago."

"A hit-and-run, she told us," noted Puller. "Never solved."

Carter glanced at Sullivan, who took up the story. "There was a two-million-dollar life insurance policy on Adam Reynolds," said Sullivan.

"Why so large?" asked Puller.

"He was an FBI agent. They had two young children. Ms. Reynolds had a similar policy on her because she traveled a great deal out of the country for the government in some remote places. Thus there obviously was a heightened risk for them both. The premiums had been duly paid up. Ms. Reynolds collected the money. She used it to pay off some debts, help raise her kids, and she invested the rest. I wish I had asked for her investment advice. She did a lot better than my 401(k). Needless to say, the insurance payout has grown substantially over the intervening years." He stopped and stared at Puller.

"And the Joan Miró in her library?" asked Knox.

"It is a Joan Miró, but it's a signed limited edition. Not something I could ever afford, but Ms. Reynolds purchased it some years ago for quite a good deal. And she had the money to do so. It's on her disclosure form and has been for years." Again, Sullivan stopped talking and stared pointedly at Puller.

Carter said, "I apologize that I wasn't aware of any of this last night when we spoke."

Sullivan said, "With all due respect, sir, you run an organization with thousands of employees. It would be impossible for you to know the intimate financial details of each person. That's my job."

"And Niles Robinson?" asked Knox.

"He's not employed by DTRA," said Sullivan promptly. "Mr. Carter has told me of your concern there as well. I suggest you check that out with his last agency." Sullivan paused. "However, Mr. Carter filled me in on what you told him about Mr. Robinson. And since I am also the father of a child who had a serious health issue, I can tell you that a parent will do anything to see them through it. I wouldn't be surprised if Mr. Robinson didn't hock everything he had and take out every loan he could to see that his child lived. But I have to say that I find it repugnant that you jumped to the conclusion that a man would betray his country in such a manner. I really do."

"I don't jump to conclusions, Mr. Sullivan, I investigate matters," replied Puller.

"Well, I think you need to keep investigating, but down a different path. Susan Reynolds is a well-respected member of the DTRA family and has never had a shadow on her record as far as I can find." Sullivan paused again and the next moment his entire body seemed to swell with stark indignation. "Your brother, on the other hand, cannot say the same, can he? And I find it absolutely remarkable that you would accuse one of our people of treason while your own flesh and blood has not only escaped prison, but also killed someone. Have you no shame, Agent Puller?" He rose when he said this last part and looked like he might take a swing at Puller, who outweighed him by sixty pounds and had him by seven inches.

"Sullivan!" Carter said sharply. "You are way out of line. Stand down, immediately."

Sullivan dropped into the chair, folded his arms over his chest, and looked away.

Carter said, "I apologize for my colleague's tone and words, Agent Puller. We can't let our emotions run away with us." He looked at Sullivan and added in a firm voice, "We will talk about this later." He turned back to Puller. "With that said, I do have to agree with his conclusions about Susan Reynolds. Everything seems to be in order. And I have communicated that to her."

"Well, we appreciate your looking into the matter, sir," said Knox, rising and tugging on Puller's sleeve. Puller was staring dead at Sullivan. When the man finally looked at him and found Puller's piercing gaze directly on him, he hurriedly glanced away.

They left Carter's office and were escorted to the exit. Once they were outside, Knox said, "Okay, first Reynolds and now this. Why do I feel like I just got sent to detention?"

When Puller didn't say anything she added, "Do you think this Sullivan character is in on it? He was acting like a psycho."

Puller shook his head and pulled out the keys to his car. "He looked at the file and found what he found. And if he had a sick kid then he probably does think I'm an asshole. And I get what he means about my brother being a traitor and I'm here trying to point fingers at good people. But it still stuck in my craw."

"And Carter?" she asked.

Puller didn't answer right away. "I don't know, Knox. Jury's still out on him."

"I can tell you this, that was no limited-edition Joan Miró. It was an original. I'd swear to it."

"Well, by now it'll be long gone, original or not," said Puller.

"I guess so," Knox agreed glumly.

"I think I was wrong about Reynolds, though."

"What! You mean you believe she's innocent?"

"No, I believe she's a lot more dangerous and a lot more capable than I thought she was. She just kicked my ass. Not to sound full of myself, but I'm not used to that happening."

"Well, neither am I," replied Knox. "She lied about your brother. The sedative was in her bloodstream. She never got her gun and scared him off. We can use that against her."

"She'd have an explanation for that, Knox.

She self-medicated, hoping to slow down the advance of the poison."

She said resignedly, "Yeah, I guess you're right. But we can't let that bitch win, Puller."

"She's not going to win. But it's not going to be easy either."

"If only we had something against her." She looked at Puller, who was now gazing off and obviously not listening to her.

"Puller, where is your head?"

He said, "I just think I missed something."

"Missed something? Where?"

"That's just the point. I don't know where. But something…was off back there. I just don't know."

"Well, that neatly sums up where we stand on everything to do with this case, doesn't it?" she said grimly. "We just don't know."

52

KNOX PARTED COMPANY with Puller at Fort Belvoir, where INSCOM was located. She wanted to check in and she had some paperwork to complete. They made arrangements to meet later at her hotel.

Before driving back to Quantico, Puller stopped at a coffee shop and pulled out a phone he had recently purchased, one of a pair, actually. His brother had the other one. Over coffee he took his time to thumb in a long message and then sent it off.

His brother's unbreakable code would be put to the test, he thought. But then again, he had considerable confidence in Robert's skills.

As he was pulling in to his apartment complex his new phone buzzed. He parked and pulled it out. His brother's response matched the length of the original message. He hurried to his apartment and, using a pad of paper and a pencil, was able to decode the message in about thirty minutes.

His brother had come up with the code when they were boys. He had based it on the concept of a one-time pad key he had read about, but one that could be reused. It really was unbreakable, because it was similar to a substitution cipher but based on a story that Robert Puller had created and then taught, word for word, to his younger brother over and over until even all these years later Puller could remember it in detail. If one didn't know the story, one couldn't break the code. And the only ones who knew the original story were the two Pullers.

Puller had told his brother of the results of their meeting with Reynolds and then Carter and Sullivan and also the facts of Reynolds's financial history. Robert's decoded message was succinct: *She covered her tracks well. Find out what you can on the death of her husband. That fact that he was an FBI agent is intriguing. She never mentioned that to me or anyone else I know that knew her. The more that I understand her hostility to me, the more likely it is that she was the one Niles Robinson was alluding to on the phone call I had with him. But jealousy could not be the primary motivation. It was to replace me with Tim Daughtrey. So*

*you need to investigate him in greater detail.
Everything about his career that you can un-
cover, John. And I mean everything.*

However, the last part of his brother's message was the most surprising, and intriguing:
*Reynolds being part of the START verification
team is also of importance. She told me that
when we "met," but I didn't focus on it then.
But you mentioning her relaying that to you
when you saw the photo in her office brought it
back to my mind. Find out what you can about
that, because it may very well tie into her present assignment. And that may well be the brass
ring we've been looking for.*

Puller stared down at this part of the message
for another moment or two before deleting it
all. He could see what his brother might be
getting at. If Reynolds was a spy, then spies
didn't just spy on one thing over the years.
They went where the most was to be gained by
their treachery.

But it couldn't be just Reynolds. There had
to be someone else who had an ocean of juice.
And there could only be a few at that level.

And one of them might be Donovan Carter.

The head of DTRA could have listened to
them last night during the nightcap just to learn
what they knew. He could have told Reynolds

everything, so that she would be fully prepared for them today. And while her financial picture seemed perfectly logical and would have normally convinced Puller, he knew the woman was a liar.

He wrote his brother a short message and pocketed the phone. He had a lot of work to do and he better get to it.

Starting with the late Brigadier General Tim Daughtrey.

* * *

After numerous phone calls, Internet searches, and a quick trip to Bolling Air Force Base in D.C., Puller had accumulated a great deal of material on the dead man. He sifted through this information while sitting in the W's hotel lobby. He had still not heard from Knox, but expected to at any time. He figured he would meet up with her at the hotel.

Daughtrey's career had proceeded along a tried-and-true formula of nose to the grindstone, checking off all the boxes for continued promotion, and going to where he needed to go and doing what he needed to do at each of those stops in his relentless chase for the shoulder stars. In that regard he was like many men and women who had done the very same thing over the years. His strengths and experiences, however, had not been in the battlefield, but rather in technology, which might be the battlefield of the future. At least that's what everyone at the Pentagon seemed to be saying. The general consensus was that Daughtrey was well liked and his death had been a huge loss to the country's defenses.

Puller collected all of these facts and then sent them in a coded message to his brother.

He next turned to the issue of Reynolds's dead FBI agent husband. He found some old news clippings on the Internet. Adam Reynolds had been an agent in the Washington, D.C., Field Office. He was only in his early thirties when he was hit and killed by a car near his home.

Puller had a contact at the Bureau and made a call to that person, who remembered the case and had actually worked briefly with Adam Reynolds many years before. Reynolds had been one of the few FBI agents ever killed, although it had not been in the line of duty.

"He was walking back from a coffee shop in a strip mall near his house," said the agent.

"How do you know that?"

"If I remember correctly, they found the coffee cup about ten feet from his body. And someone from the coffee shop remembered him coming in."

"Where was this exactly?" asked Puller.

"In Burke, Virginia. His wife said he walked there all the time. Adam liked his coffee, like most of us."

"Was his wife home at the time?"

"No, I don't believe so. No, that's right. She was out of the country. She worked for Uncle Sam too. Don't remember where."

"But they had young kids back then. Who was with them?"

"I'm not sure about that. They might have been old enough to stay by themselves for a few minutes. You know things were different back then. You could leave your kids for a bit without people screaming at you or seeing it posted on Facebook."

"And they never found the driver?"

"Never did. It was pretty late at night. Where he got hit there were no houses, so no one saw anything."

"Did you think he was targeted? That it was work-related?"

"We always think that initially. But the official conclusion was that it was probably some drunk who hit him and then took off. Damn shame, because Adam was a good guy."

"Good marriage? Everything okay on that end?"

"As far as I know. But we weren't best friends or anything. I'd met his wife a few times. Seemed like a nice sort. She was gone a lot, according to Adam. Why do you ask?"

"No reason. Just groping around for a few leads on something."

"Something to do with Adam's death? After all these years?"

"It might tie into something I've got going on. I suppose you don't know where their kids are? I think her son is a lawyer."

"He is. With the Bureau actually. I guess he wanted to follow in his dad's footsteps. At least partly."

"You got contact info for him?"

"I can look it up right now. I'll give it to you on the condition that one day you tell me what the hell this is all about, Puller."

"I promise I will. And thanks."

Puller wrote down the information and clicked off. He called Dan Reynolds, who was in the FBI's D.C. office. When Puller explained who he was and what he wanted to talk about, he expected the young man to either ask a lot of questions or hang up on him. But instead Reynolds said, "In about twenty minutes I can meet you at the Dunkin' Donuts around the corner from WFO."

Surprised by this, Puller quickly agreed and headed to his car. On the way to the parking garage he texted Knox about this development.

The Dunkin' Donuts was fairly busy when Puller got there. But he had no problem spotting Dan Reynolds, for the young man had taken after his mother in height and looks. Puller introduced himself and they bought their coffees and headed outside to sit at a small table on the sidewalk.

Dan Reynolds, in addition to inheriting his mother's good looks and height, had her penetrating gaze. He took a sip of coffee and stared at a car passing by.

"So why is an Army CID agent looking into my father's death all these years later? He wasn't in the military."

"It might be connected to another case of a military nature," Puller answered.

"Mind telling me which one?"

Puller mulled this over. "A former colleague of your mother was murdered at Union Station."

"Niles Robinson," said Dan.

"That's right."

"And that's the case? But Robinson wasn't in the military either."

"No, but he was a witness in a case involving a military member."

Dan turned his gaze directly to Puller. "And how could that be connected to my father's death?"

"I have no idea. That's why I'm poking around trying to find a lead." He paused and then added in a casual tone, "I suppose I could talk to your mother."

Dan made a cutting motion in the air with his hand. "I wouldn't bother with her if I were you."

"Why not? She works in the area."

"At DTRA. But you'll learn nothing from her."

"I don't understand. It was *her* husband."

"Yeah, it was her husband, how about that?"

Puller leaned forward. "I really need to understand what you're saying here."

Dan had looked away again at the passing cars. "I was eleven when my dad was killed. My sister was nine."

"Must've been tough."

"It was hell. My dad left to walk to the store and he never came back."

"His favorite coffee shop."

Dan looked at him. "No, he went to the store to get some things."

"But they found a coffee cup from his favorite shop near the body. At least that's what I was told."

"I didn't know that. I knew he went to the store. He usually didn't leave me and my sister alone like that. But she'd called."

"Who had called?"

"My mother."

"And told him what?"

"To get some things from the store. Stuff she said we needed. At least that's what my dad said. He wasn't happy about it, because like I said he didn't like to leave us. But she had that way about her."

"What way?"

"To get what she wanted. My dad was a tough FBI agent. But around her, well, he just seemed to shrink to nothing. I think he was afraid of her."

"I understand that she's a fine shot."

Dan looked disgusted. "Her guns! She's so proud of her guns. Loved them more than she loved us. I went in and messed up her 'trophy room' one day when I was seven. Threw her hardware all over the damn place. I just wanted to get her attention. I thought she was going to beat me to death. It was lucky that Dad was there."

"She sounds unbalanced. It's a wonder she could pass a polygraph and get her security clearances."

"Jekyll and Hyde, Agent Puller. She could walk the walk and talk the talk when she wanted to. What went on inside our house was a totally different story. But you'll never find a finer actress. Meryl Streep has nothing on my mother."

Puller ran through some possible questions and angles in his mind before saying, "Your dad could have taken you with him to the store that night."

"No, my sister had broken her leg that summer and she was in a cast. In fact, she was already asleep when my mom called. He would never have left her alone. I stayed to watch her."

"Where was your mom?"

"Overseas somewhere. Eastern Europe maybe."

"Well, if it was night where you lived on the East Coast, it would be very early morning over there."

"I guess so. But she called. I heard the phone ring. And I talked to her for a minute or so."

"And then your dad went out?"

"Yeah."

"If he wanted to hurry because you two would be alone, why not just drive?"

"The car wouldn't start. He came back into the house mad as hell about that. So he just grabbed his jacket and went on foot. It wasn't that far."

"And you only had the one car?"

"My mother's was at her workplace. She always left it there when she was overseas."

"So he was on his way back because they found the coffee cup but they didn't find any of the stuff from the store? How do you explain that?"

"I don't know. It was a hit-and-run. At least that's what we were told. We were kids, they didn't tell us much."

"Look, if I'm wrong on this, please say so. It's just the cynical investigator coming out in me." Puller hesitated, choosing his words with great care. "But you seem to have doubts about this whole thing. Am I right or wrong?"

Dan turned to look at Puller again. "If you're asking whether I think my mother set my dad up to be killed, then, yeah, I do."

Puller took this revelation in slowly. "That's quite an allegation."

"I'm a lawyer, I *know* it's a serious allegation."

"So when did you arrive at this conclusion? Surely not when you were a kid."

"No, it was later, when I was grown." He gave a wry smile. "When I became cynical too."

"Okay," said Puller encouragingly.

"Things didn't add up. Why call him that late to go to the store to get stuff? Why couldn't it have waited? And my dad had taken the day off and driven my sister to the doctor for her leg and the car worked fine. So why wouldn't it start later?"

"So he'd have to walk to the store, that's what you concluded?"

"And get hit by a car, yeah."

"Did you ever raise this possibility with anyone?"

"No."

"Why not?"

"My mother can be pretty intimidating for an adult, much less a little kid. And by the time I became really suspicious, what could I do? Years had gone by. The evidence was gone. There would have been no point."

"There was a large insurance payout."

"I know."

"Did you tell anyone about your mother's phone call that night?"

"No one ever asked me. My mother flew home the next day. She handled everything."

"Meaning she kept you and your sister from talking to anyone?"

"Pretty much, yeah. And the cops were convinced it was just a hit-and-run. They weren't looking beyond that."

"I've actually spoken to your mother. She intimated that she thought it might have been connected to one of your dad's cases."

"Did she tell you that she had called him that night?"

"No, she somehow left that out."

"Well, then?"

"I take it you don't get along with her?"

"No, I don't. Even if this hadn't happened with my father, my mother is not the warm fuzzy type. She had her kids but I don't think she had any interest in actually being a mother. I was a lot closer to my dad. And after he died my grandmother pretty much raised us, not her. So now I have nothing to do with my mother. And she seems perfectly fine with that."

"Does she know you suspect her?"

"I've never mentioned it to her. She scares the shit out of me if you want to know the truth."

"I think that's a good thing, actually. I meant the not mentioning part."

"I truly wouldn't put anything past her."

"If she did have a role in his death, do you think it was for the money?"

Dan shrugged. "I would hear my dad sometimes in his little den after he'd been hitting the booze a bit."

"What would he say?"

"He had really bad arguments with my mother about things. And when she wasn't around, he would go to his den and talk to himself."

"And say what exactly?"

"I just caught snatches here and there. And he didn't seem to be making much sense. But it seemed he had a problem with my mother and what she was doing in her job."

"And do you know what that was?"

"I know she spent a lot of time in Russia."

"As part of a START verification team?"

"I think that's right, yeah. At least I found out about that later. She never talked to me about her work."

"Why would that bother him? She was helping to dismantle nukes."

"It didn't seem like he had a problem with that. I think it was more personal."

"Meaning someone she worked with?"

"All I know is I heard my dad once say he'd kill the guy if he had the chance."

"Kill the guy?"

"Yeah. And my dad was a pretty calm person. I don't know what he found or heard, but he was definitely pissed off about it."

"What does your sister think?"

"She was closer to our mom than I ever was. She wouldn't agree with anything I've been saying. They see each other a lot. They're tight. My mom has even helped my sister out financially."

"Where does she live?"

"In Gaithersburg, Maryland. She has a clothing store up there."

"She do well with it?"

"She does okay. Like I said, I know Mom helps her out financially."

"Does that surprise you? I mean, given what you've told me about your mother?"

Dan shrugged. "My sister won't bite the hand that feeds her. So she tells the woman what she wants to hear. But to give our mother her due, if she loves anyone, it would be my sister."

Puller wrote some notes down and said, "She told me about making the Olympic team in the biathlon. She said she might have won the gold."

"Did she tell you she didn't compete?"

"Yeah, some sort of medical issue."

Dan laughed.

"What's the joke?" asked Puller.

"*I* was the medical issue."

"Come again?"

"She was pregnant with me. They wouldn't let her compete."

"Was she upset about that?"

"She was so upset about it that she never mentioned it. I only found out from my dad."

"Hey, it takes two to tango. She knew what she was doing."

"My dad said she claimed he messed with her birth control pills."

"Did he?"

"Who knows? If she wanted to win a medal in the Olympics she knew she couldn't do it while heavily pregnant. Maybe my dad did do it. She was so controlling. Maybe he wanted to give her a taste of her own medicine. And it might be one reason she never really took to me. I guess I represented her missed opportunity at glory."

"It may or may not have been someone's fault, Dan, but it sure as hell wasn't yours. You weren't even born."

"Sounds logical. But some people are not swayed by logic."

They sat in silence drinking their coffees.

Puller finally said, "I'm surprised you've talked to me about all this."

Dan gave a mirthless laugh. "I guess I surprised myself. But when you called out of the blue, I thought, well I just thought—"

"That the truth might come out and justice would be finally served for your father?"

The two men locked gazes. Dan said, "After all, it's why I joined the FBI's legal office. And I really loved my dad."

"Well, I hope I can make that happen for you," Puller said.

And for my brother, he thought.

He thanked Dan Reynolds and headed back to his car. Before he got there his phone buzzed. It was Knox.

"I was wondering when I was going to hear from you," he said. He listened for a bit and said, "Shirlington, huh? Okay, it was definitely worth a shot. Why don't you stay with them and we can hook back up later." He paused, listening, but she broke off in midsentence. His features grew tight. He said, "Knox? Knox?"

He heard her yelling something, not at him, at someone else.

When he heard her words he started to run.

The next sound he heard made Puller redouble his efforts. As he ran full out to his car he screamed into his phone. "Knox? Veronica!"

She never answered.

And then the line went dead.

53

KNOX HAD BEEN sitting in a car she had requisitioned from INSCOM at Fort Belvoir. While she had told Puller that she needed to report in and start filling out voluminous paperwork, her real purpose was to stay behind and then follow Donovan Carter when he left the facility.

He had a black Town Car and a driver. And Knox could see the man accompanying him.

It was Blair Sullivan, the internal security man who had gotten so heated about their investigation of Susan Reynolds.

As they exited out of the DTRA complex, Knox fell in behind them. They got on Interstate 95 and Knox kept a few car lengths back. They exited onto Interstate 395 and headed north toward D.C.

Knox had no idea if this would lead to anything, but there was a chance and she felt she had to take it. She had nothing to lose. They exited at Shirlington and she followed. A few minutes later the car pulled to a stop in front of a small outdoor mall of upscale eateries and shops. The driver parked the Town Car, and Carter and Sullivan went into one of the restaurants.

"Great," said Knox out loud to herself. "An early dinner. Just my luck. And I can't go in because unless they suddenly go blind, they're going to see me."

She backed into an open space across the street and waited. She listened to the radio and answered emails but continually kept her gaze roaming over the street. She was drumming her fingers on the steering wheel when a white van pulled in next to where the Town Car was parked. A burly guy opened the passenger door and in doing so clipped the side of the Town Car.

The window of the Town Car came down and Carter's driver stuck his head out. Knox could hear him yelling at the guy. The guy yelled back.

The driver got out and the two men stood toe to toe, still yelling and jabbing fingers in each other's chests.

Knox was hoping this was not going to escalate into something bad, because she was pretty sure the driver was armed. Her gaze drifted to a teenager rolling down the sidewalk on a skate-board. He had long curly hair, a ball cap turned backward, and was wearing a bulky hoodie, jeans torn at the knee and thigh and sneakers the size of small dogs with no shoelaces. He was riding low, and then he attempted a complicated jump and fell on his ass right next to the Town Car, disappearing from her line of sight.

Knox's gaze drifted back to the two men. They were still arguing, only now Carter's man was showing his creds to the burly guy. She hoped that would put an end to the confrontation.

Knox shifted back to the kid, who was rising up next to the Town Car. He dusted off his pants and looked sheepishly around as he gripped his board.

Not such a hotshot on the board, thought Knox.

As he dropped his board, stepped on it, and pushed off he passed by the two men. Then he gathered speed, turned the corner in a tight curve, and was gone from her view.

The burly guy climbed back into the van, still scowling and yelling, and the van reversed out of the space just as the restaurant's door opened and Carter and Sullivan emerged. His driver yelled one more thing at the van as it pulled away, honking its horn. The driver turned and saw Carter and Sullivan and hurried to open the car door for the DTRA head.

Knox pulled out her phone and called Puller. He answered on the second ring.

She told him what she was doing, and also where she was. He replied to her information in a few succinct sentences.

"Roger that," she said. "But I think that—"

As if someone had pushed a secret button in her brain, Knox started to piece together what she had just seen.

No, not what she had just seen.

What had really just *happened*.

She heard Puller say, "Knox? Knox?"

She didn't even hear him. What she had just seen was a diversion.

The guy in the van bumping the Town Car on purpose.

A kid who wasn't a kid sailing by on a skateboard while the driver was distracted by the van guy.

Then a planned fall that allowed the kid access underneath the Town Car out of sight of anyone.

Then the kid had disappeared.

As if on cue the burly guy had given up on the confrontation and the van had raced off.

She snapped back from these thoughts and saw that Sullivan and Carter were in the car.

The driver started it up.

Still holding the phone, Knox kicked open her car door, leapt out, and started to sprint across the street.

"Get out of the car!" she screamed. "Get out of the car! There's a—"

The ground moved violently under her feet, the pavement seemed to whipsaw like a snake on crack. Everything took on the elements of a world reduced to slow motion. She staggered, braced herself for what she knew was coming and could do absolutely nothing about. Visions of Mosul came roaring vividly back to her. Sitting in an armored Humvee one second. Lying far away in the dirt another second later and having no idea how she had gotten there, not knowing whether people were alive or dead, whether she would die here too. Whether her legs would ever function again.

All of this took a millionth of a second to pass through her mind. And that was good, because even with that, she was out of time.

She had looked away at the last moment, and it was a good thing she did. Looking directly at an explosion of sufficient magnitude could blind a person. But it didn't really matter. People close enough to be blinded by such a flash didn't usually live anyway.

Her last conscious thought was a surprising one to her.

Sorry, Puller. It's up to you now.

The concussive force of the explosion lifted her right out of her shoes, throwing her twenty feet through the air like a pellet from a sling-shot, until she smashed against the plate glass window of a linen shop. She managed to cover her head with her hands right before impact as her phone flew from her, landed in the street, and broke apart. Knox ended up on the floor of the shop in a heap of limbs.

The Town Car had been obliterated. What was left of the three men inside was no longer recognizable. The explosion had shattered windows up and down the street. People were lying on the sidewalks, bloodied, battered, unconscious, and some of them would never be waking up.

Others were moaning, groaning, and staggering around. Some were in shock, others badly injured, and others, though unhurt, could only stare in horror at what had happened.

It was like a street in Baghdad or Kabul, not an affluent area a few miles from Washington, D.C.

Car alarms triggered by the blast were going off up and down the street. People were running now, some toward the blast site, others away from it, no doubt terrified that more explosions were going to take place. A police officer who had been pulling security guard duty in a jewelry shop did his best to help the injured and direct people to a safer area.

Inside the linen shop Knox was lying facedown on the floor in a pile of glass shards, covered with sheets and pillows that she had crashed into after cracking through the window. Her eyes were closed, her breathing was tight and shallow, and the blood was flowing down her face.

In another minute the sirens started to wail, people started to scream louder, survivors tried to help the injured and the dying. Then there were the dead. They had come here for a meal, or to do some shopping or run an errand, unaware that it would be the last time they would ever do any of those things.

Inside the shop, Veronica Knox didn't move. The blood just continued to flow down her face.

CHAPTER

54

WHEN VERONICA KNOX opened her eyes the first thing she saw was a blindingly white light.

That convinced her that she was truly dead. And that somehow, despite having committed a mortal and venal sin or two, she had ended up up rather than down, ecclesiastically speaking.

It's a bloody miracle, she thought. And she was being literal about that.

The second thing she saw were transparent tubes running into her right arm.

That drove the ecclesiastical element and the thought of miracles forcefully from her head.

The third thing she saw was John Puller hovering over her.

That brought her fully back to earth. And life.

She saw him breathe a sigh of relief, and then he flicked his finger against his eye as though to rub something away.

A tear, her groggy mind thought. But no, men

like John Puller did not shed tears. If they did shed anything, it would be blood, not water.

She tried to sit up, but he put a big hand on her shoulder and held her right where she was.

"Just chill, Knox. You took a big hit. Doc says it's a miracle you're still here."

She suddenly looked wildly down at her body. "Am I here? Am I *all* here?"

He gripped her shoulder tighter to calm her. "Two arms with hands attached, though two fingers on your left hand are broken, hence the splints. You have two legs with feet attached. One head with brain intact, though concussed. And a lot of superficial cuts to your scalp, arms, and legs, hence the bandages. And enough blood loss that they had to give you a replacement bag."

"But can I move everything?"

"See for yourself."

She tentatively moved first her right and then her left arm, and then wiggled her fingers, even the ones with splints on them. Drawing a deep breath, she looked down at her legs.

Puller saw tears cluster in her eyes and knew she was thinking back to the Middle East when her legs had not worked. He slipped the sheet up a bit, revealing her feet. He squeezed one of her toes. "Feel that?"

She nodded.

"Now wiggle your toes."

She swallowed, prepared herself, and did so. She felt them, saw them, and sank back on her pillow with a grateful, "Thank you, God."

He put the sheet back over her feet. "Legs are just fine, Knox. With that said, you were lucky as hell."

"I remember flying through…glass," she said slowly and groggily.

"You picked the right store to fly into. A linen shop. You hit the glass, which was hard. But you fell into a display of comforters and very soft pillows. Sort of cushioned everything."

"And Carter?" she mumbled.

He shook his head and said grimly, "Didn't make it. Neither did Sullivan or the driver. Nothing much left of any of them."

"How long have I been here?"

"They brought you in last evening. It's now late afternoon."

"I suppose people want to question me?"

"They do. But I got permission to come in here and sit with you until you came around. The cops and the Feds are all over the crime scene. Lots of people saw things. They've got lots of statements."

"But I bet they don't know what *I* saw."

Puller sat down in a chair next to her bed. "So why don't you tell me what that was?"

Knox glanced at the glass door to her room and saw a police officer, a man in a suit, and a burly MP standing guard there.

"They're not taking any chances with you," he said, following her gaze. "Cops, FBI, and the military."

She turned back to Puller and slowly but clearly told him what she had seen. The van, the kid, everything.

"So it was a deliberate setup the whole way," Puller concluded.

"It appeared to be. But why target Carter?"

"Well, he heads up an important part of our nation's defenses. He's a target just by virtue of that."

"No, I get that. I'm just looking at the timing. Why now?"

"You mean is it connected to what we're doing?"

"It could be."

He looked her over. "You up for some information sharing?"

She smiled and slid her hand around his forearm. "With you here I'm up for anything."

Puller placed his hand on top of hers. "I'm

sorry I wasn't there for you when this happened, Knox. I should've been."

"You had no way to know I was going off half-cocked on my little sleuthing trip."

"You tried to save them. Over the phone I heard you screaming for them to get out of the car."

She shook her head, looked miserable, and put a hand to her face. She let out a sob, her eyes filled with tears, and she moaned, "I didn't see it fast enough, Puller. I should've seen it faster, but I didn't."

"You did everything you possibly could. You had seconds, maybe not even seconds. No matter what you did or didn't do, Knox, they weren't going to make it. They were already dead. They just didn't know it. So while you may want to take the blame for it, please don't. It won't help you or them."

She let out another sob, composed herself, rubbed her eyes dry with her sheet, and focused on him. "I guess that was the weirdest phone call you've ever gotten, huh?"

Puller looked down. "When I heard the bomb detonate over your open line—"

She reached out and cupped his chin, drawing his gaze back to her. "I'm here, Puller. A little banged up and bloodied. But I'm not dead. Let's count that as a victory."

He smiled. "I count it as a lot more than that."

Their gazes held on one another for a few more moments and then Puller reverted to business mode.

"I spoke to an FBI agent who remembered Adam Reynolds, Susan's husband."

"The hit-and-run?" she said.

"Maybe, maybe not."

He went on to tell her about the rest of his conversation with the agent and then his subsequent meeting with Susan Reynolds's son, Dan.

That part made Knox try to sit up again, and again, Puller held her back down.

"I know," he said. "I know. She really is a piece of work."

"That witch gets her husband killed for some reason. Another man? That's what Adam Reynolds thought?"

"Apparently so. And she was working in the former Soviet Union."

"Do we know exactly where?"

"Working on it. But it had to do with the START verification program. She told us that herself."

"Nuke dismantling."

"Right. And she works at the WMD Center now," Puller reminded her.

Again, Knox tried to sit up, and this time he helped her, adjusting the bed control to support her.

"So is that what this is all about? WMDs?"

"Maybe it is *now*. If she's a spy then she's probably covered a lot of territory over the years. WMDs may be the latest on her checklist. But the positions she's held have given her access to lots of valuable information that our enemies would pay a pretty penny for."

"And she just stares at you like you're an idiot for even hinting that she might be involved in something shady."

"If she's been doing this as long as I think she has, her poker face has to be exemplary. And by the way her financial history was conceived and hardened, I'm thinking she was seen as a high-level, long-term asset." He added, "I have to believe the two-million-dollar insurance policy was her idea, not her husband's."

"I need to get out of here, Puller. We need to get back to work."

"Whoa. You need rest. And you need time to heal."

"I don't have time to do either. That can wait."

"No, it can't wait."

She tried to get up and he pushed her back

down. On the third time she said, "Damn it, John Puller, if I had a gun I'd shoot your ass."

"Well, good thing you don't have a gun, then."

She stopped struggling, lay back, and let out a long, resigned sigh. "Okay, so when can I get the hell out of here?"

"I'll check with the docs, but probably within twenty-four hours. And after that, bed rest."

"Shit!"

"It is what it is, Knox."

"And what are you going to do in the meantime?"

"Follow up on all this."

"Without me?" she said, stunned by this prospect.

"I will keep you informed of everything, I promise."

"And you won't get killed?" She said this in a joking manner, but there was no humor in her look. "I almost bought it, Puller. One more step, one more second, no soft pillows at the end of the runway, I'm not here."

"I know that."

"No, maybe you don't know that." She reached up and gathered a fistful of his shirt. "Don't die. Just…don't."

"Okay. I won't."

She slowly let his shirt go and sank back, breathless.

"I'll check in later."

"Yep," she said, not looking at him.

Puller walked out. He had told Knox everything he knew. Now he had to tell someone else.

His brother.

No code.

Face-to-face.

55

HE DID END up sending a coded message first, to advise his brother that he wanted to meet. Then he did what he had done before. Drove to Quantico, swapped cars and left via another exit. He drove the rural roads, doubling back and then doubling back again before setting off for his actual destination. His brother's pickup truck was parked in front of the same motel room door.

He knocked. He saw the swish of curtains and put his hand on the butt of his M11. He said, "Bobby?" And his brother answered, "The coast is clear, Junior."

Déjà vu.

Puller closed the door behind him, crossed the room, and sat down on the edge of the bed. His brother was on the chair he'd occupied at their last meeting.

"Heard the news?" asked Puller.

Robert nodded. "It's all over the place. Carter's dead."

"And two other guys."

"Media said a bomb."

"Media is right. My partner Knox was there. She saw it all. She tried to prevent it. Almost got killed."

"What exactly did she see?"

Puller gazed sternly at his brother. "I said she almost got *killed*, Bobby. She's in a hospital bed right now. She wanted to climb out of it, get back to work on this thing. To help try to clear you."

It seemed to be an unfortunate quirk of his brother's genius that he did not always grasp the personal side of the equation.

Robert looked thoroughly taken aback. "I'm sorry, John, how is she?"

"She'll be okay." He went on to tell his brother what Knox had observed.

"They moved fast, then," said Robert. "And they had operatives who could get it done on short notice."

"How do you know this hasn't been planned for a long time?"

"You met with the man this morning and he's dead by the early evening."

"Could be unconnected."

"We have to deal in probabilities, John. And the clear probability is that the connection is there. A plus B equals C."

"But when we met with Carter and his side-kick, it was clear that they thought Reynolds was completely innocent. The matter was over and done in their mind."

"I read your notes on the conversation. They might have said that, but I don't think they believed it."

"Based on what?"

"For one they played their hand too strong, John. The head of DTRA is not going to meet with you directly the morning after you had a nightcap with him. He is not going to bring in his chief internal security officer. I happen to know Blair Sullivan. He's worked all over STRATCOM. If the guy said more than two words to you, or became emotional in any way, it was an act. That's not what he does. He could see a piano falling toward his head while he was at an outdoor café having lunch and he'd just move to the right and finish his sandwich."

"But why an act? Why try to deceive us? If they believed what we told them then I don't get it."

"Just the act of believing does not mean they wanted to necessarily collaborate with you on this. You're not one of them. DTRA is a critical agency to this country. They would never want it to appear that they could not appropriately control their employees. And if they have a spy in their midst, that would be dirty laundry that they would most assuredly not air in public."

"So what would they do?"

"Clean it up from the inside. That's why Sullivan was there."

"So they thought Reynolds was dirty?"

"I can't tell you exactly what they thought, but I can tell you that for an allegation of spying they would not have done a quick financial search the next morning and concluded everything was hunky-dory. This would take some time to complete and they would have gone back over her entire history. She's at the WMD Center, for God's sake, John. There is no room for mistakes. And if you found out about the suspect circumstances of her husband's death, then they could too. They have a whole department of extremely bright people to work on stuff like that."

"Really? Well, if they were really bright people they wouldn't have let her do what she's been doing for probably the past twenty years, would they?"

"People *have* failed at their jobs on this; I would agree with you there."

"So why did they target Carter so fast?"

"I would imagine at DTRA the scuttlebutt of your meeting with Carter and Sullivan reached Reynolds's ears."

"They told me that they had met with Reynolds and informed her of their conclusions."

"Then there you are. But she must have suspected what I just did. That they weren't satisfied. And that they were going to keep looking into it. So she made contact with her people. The decision was made to pull the trigger."

"Damn, like you said, they don't waste time."

"The fact that they knew his travel schedule leads me to believe that Reynolds has spies everywhere over there."

"Spies everywhere at DTRA? Are you serious?"

"Well, at least exceptionally well-placed ones even if they're not numerous. And if you're really well positioned the few can accomplish what sometimes the many can't. A secretary, a clerk, a data manager. Those positions might seem relatively trivial, but they're at the heart of important information flows."

"I'm glad you can sit here and analyze this so calmly."

"There are more spies here than you would ever want to believe, John. And not just in government. The corporate side is filled with them. And many of those come from our so-called allies. They steal our secrets, use them against us, and smile at us while they're doing it. We're America, the one-ton gorilla. Everybody hates us."

"But what if Carter told someone of his suspicions? Wouldn't his death put a bull's-eye on Reynolds?"

"Possibly. But things don't move that fast in the intelligence field. Carter was never in uniform. He's a scholar and a wonk for the most part."

"He killed three Taliban in Afghanistan to get away."

"Granted, but in the intervening years he's been immersed in academia, for want of a better term. Slow and sure drives the boat. He would have wanted to mull this over, gather and consider additional facts. He brought along Sullivan for his input, surely. Reynolds is at the managerial level at DTRA, with a distinguished record. You do not knee-jerk accuse someone like that without indisputable evidence. Other-

wise you're looking at a lawsuit and a huge
black eye for the agency. And Carter could
have lost his job."

Puller shook his head in frustration. "This intelligence world is beyond me, Bobby. I'm used
to being able to count on the people wearing
the same uniform I do."

"Now DTRA is not focused on Reynolds.
They're looking for who did this to Carter.
And I doubt anyone will seriously believe she
had anything to do with it."

Puller rubbed his temples and said, "We still
don't know why Daughtrey was killed."

"I think we can reasonably speculate that he
was killed because he no longer wanted to play
the game. Niles Robinson committed this same
act of treachery when he came to Union Station
to talk to me. They had followed him, perhaps
surmised that I was on the other end of that
line, and he paid the ultimate price."

"Okay, but how did they bring Daughtrey
into this in the first place? All I found out about
him points to a patriot above reproach."

"Then we have to find a reason why he would
switch sides. It might be very subtle, but obviously enough for a 'patriot' to turn tables."

Puller thought about this. "He has a condo in
Pentagon City."

"Think you can get in there?"

"I can try."

"I'd like to go with you."

"Not going to happen, Bobby. Nothing personal, but if I get caught with you, we're *both* going to DB as fast as they can get us there."

As Puller rose to go, Bobby said, "I *am* sorry about your friend. Sometimes I'm too damn analytical for my own good."

Puller smiled weakly at his brother. "Don't worry about it. Comes with being a genius, I guess."

"Well, that doesn't seem like a good enough reason," said Robert quietly.

56

TIM DAUGHTREY'S CONDO was in an upscale high-rise in Pentagon City. He wasn't married and had no kids. He seemed to be a man totally focused on his military career. It was a secure building and Puller was stopped in the lobby by a security guard. He pulled his creds and the man looked them over.

"Still don't think I can let you up, sir. You know what happened to General Daughtrey?"

"Yeah, it's the reason I'm here. I'm investigating his murder."

The guard glanced at Puller's creds again. "But you're Army, he was Air Force."

"He was also involved in a multiplatform intelligence operation that cut across all branches." He paused and inclined his head toward the man. "Sensitive national security parameters," he added quietly.

The guard looked anxiously toward the elevator bank. "Then maybe I shouldn't have let him up there."

"Who?" Puller asked sharply.

"General Daughtrey's friend."

"This friend have a name?"

"Charles Abernathy."

"And what is he doing up there?"

"Getting some things."

Puller looked incredulous. "I'm not understanding this. Why let a friend up there if you're giving me a hard time?"

"Well, he actually lives there, sometimes. With General Daughtrey."

"I thought Daughtrey owned the condo."

"It's actually held in the name of a corporation, and Mr. Abernathy is an officer of the corporation and entitled to come and go. At least that's what my paperwork tells me. It's all authorized and everything. He's been here more than General Daughtrey, actually."

Puller glanced toward the elevator bank and then gazed down at the guard's nameplate. "Look, Officer Haynes."

"I'm not a real cop, just a rental. Call me Haynie."

"Okay, Haynie. I'm not looking to get anybody in trouble. But an Air Force general was murdered under very suspicious circumstances.

There's a friend up in his apartment doing God knows what. I'm not sure that should be allowed."

Haynes was looking more and more nervous.

Puller continued, "I need to get up there, see what this man is doing, and try to preserve any evidence. Have the police been here yet?"

"They might have come while I wasn't here. We're supposed to write it down, but some of the guards don't give a crap. They're just collecting a paycheck."

"Which makes it all the more critical that I get up there. We are talking national security, Haynie. This is not a game. So what are you going to do?"

Haynie snatched a key off a hook behind his console. "Follow me, sir."

He led Puller over to the elevator bank and used his key card to engage one of the cars. He handed Puller the key.

"His condo is 945. This is a master key. It'll open it right up."

Puller took the key. "Thanks."

"Yes sir." Haynes gave Puller an awkward salute just before the doors closed.

Puller reached the ninth floor and sped down the hall toward Daughtrey's condo. He held the door key in one hand and kept his other hand

on the butt of his holstered M11. He reached
the door of the apartment, glanced up and
down the length of the hall, and found it clear.
He put his ear to the door and listened. He
couldn't hear anything other than the hum of
the air-conditioning.

He slipped the key into the lock and turned
it, easing the door open as quietly as possible
and drawing out his pistol at the same time. He
closed the door behind him, bent low, and listened again.

Nothing.

He looked around. The condo was large and
the tastefulness of the decoration and how everything just seemed to go together surprised
him. He didn't think a hard-charging career-
oriented general would have had the time to fill
a space out like that.

He moved forward, keeping low. He had
thought about announcing himself, but something in his gut told him that would not be a
good idea. If this guy was in on the plot with
Daughtrey, he might panic and open fire like
Macri had done with Knox. Puller didn't mind
using his weapon. But he liked *not* using his
weapon better, just like any soldier.

He passed through the kitchen, which looked
like a place where a five-star chef would feel

right at home cutting up vegetables. His feet sank into thick carpet and his eye was caught by unique pieces of art on the wall and equally imaginative sculptures resting on tables and pedestals.

There were leather-bound books lining floor-to-ceiling mahogany bookcases. The furnishings looked relatively new unless they were obviously antiques, and the finishes—wood, chrome, stone, and bronze—looked very expensive. Too expensive maybe for even a one-star's pocketbook. Had Daughtrey done it, like Reynolds, for the money?

He ducked lower when he heard the sound, training his gun's muzzle down the hallway from where the noise was coming. He scooted forward, keeping low and at an angle to the door he was heading toward.

As he approached the room, the noise took on a more distinctive quality, like a garbled transmission becoming clearer as the frequency grew stronger.

He reached the doorway and decided to do a quick peek in.

It was a bedroom, his fast glance told him. And there was apparently someone in there.

A second look confirmed that the room was indeed occupied. The man sat on the bed. His head was bowed. He was holding something in his hands.

And the sound Puller had heard was quite clear now.

The man was crying.

No, actually he was sobbing.

Puller eased into the room, confirmed that the man was not armed, and then holstered his pistol.

"Mr. Abernathy?" he called out, his hand still on the butt of his weapon.

The man jumped up so fast that what he was holding fell to the floor. Luckily the floor was thickly carpeted, or else it might have cracked.

"Who…who are you?" Abernathy said in a quavering voice as he backed away.

He was a slender man, barely a hundred and forty pounds, and maybe five-six in his shoes. He was dressed in blue slacks, leather shoes with no socks, and a patterned shirt. His sports jacket had a pocket handkerchief that matched the shirt. A Tag Heuer watch was on his left wrist. His hair was thinning but was professionally styled and swept back off his forehead and held there with gel. He was clean-shaven and his light blue, intelligent eyes were streaked with red.

Puller held out his creds. "I'm a military investigator. Chief Warrant Officer John Puller, United States Army, 701st CID out of Quantico."

The man glanced at the CID shield and the ID card but didn't seem to really register on either.

"I...I guess you're here about Tim," he said in a hollow voice.

"General Daughtrey, yes."

"Someone killed him."

"I'm aware of that. And how do you know General Daughtrey?"

Abernathy wouldn't meet his eye. "We were friends...Good friends."

"I understand that you two co-owned this condo."

Abernathy looked taken aback that Puller knew this.

"The guard downstairs told me. That's why he let you up here."

Abernathy slowly nodded, bent down, and picked up the framed photograph he'd been holding.

Puller drew closer and said, "May I?" indicating the photo.

Abernathy said resignedly, "Well, I guess it doesn't matter now, does it?"

Puller took the photo. It was of Daughtrey,

who was out of uniform, and Abernathy in a friendly embrace, their gazes on each other. They looked like a nice couple. Happy, relaxed. Very much into each other.

Puller glanced up at him. "I take it you two were close…friends?"

Abernathy gave a noiseless laugh. "Let's not beat around the bush anymore, okay? I'm really done with that shit, pardon my language. We were a lot more than friends."

"I see."

"Then you can understand why we had to keep things under the radar."

"DADT isn't the law anymore, sir," said Puller, referring to Don't Ask, Don't Tell.

"Isn't it?" Abernathy said skeptically. "Well, for one-stars fighting their way up the ranks it might as well be an elephant chained around their ankles. You're in the military. You know that as well as anyone. How many generals have come out recently?"

"One that I can think of. An Army reservist promoted to brigadier general a couple of years ago."

"A woman," pointed out Abernathy. "Oh, don't get me wrong, I'm thrilled for her. Absolutely thrilled. But I didn't see any male officers rushing to join that gay parade."

"No sir, at least not yet."

"Maybe not ever."

"They're starting to come forward in professional sports, basketball, even football. If it can happen in the NFL, then you never know."

"The military is a different beast. I've certainly learned that lesson."

"So, General Daughtrey and you? Can you tell me about your personal life?"

"Why?" snapped Abernathy. But he quickly calmed. "I'm sorry. That was rude. It's just a very difficult time for me."

"I can completely understand that, sir. And what you tell me will go no further. I'm just asking because it might help my investigation. That's all."

Abernathy nodded and wiped at his eyes, composed himself, and sat down in a chair. "We've been together for about ten years. Ten great years. But all in secret. We even bought this condo under the name of a corporation. We don't appear in public together. I will receive no benefits now that Tim's dead. Not that I care about that. I'm a partner in a large law practice. I've made my pile of money, far more than Tim. Hell, I paid for most of the things in this place, and did the design myself. You see, I didn't really want to be a lawyer. I wanted to be the next Ralph Lauren. But life doesn't always work out how you want it."

He eyed the floor. "But it's the principle of the thing, really. I have no rights whatsoever. I won't even be able to attend his burial at Arlington. No one will present me with a flag. His parents will get that, even though they've had nothing to do with him for years. I helped vet his speeches. Helped him prepare for every promotion review. Cooked for him and looked after him when he was sick. And just so you know, he did as much for me. We traveled together. We vacationed together, but always with the sword of Damocles over us. Meaning we got to the places separately and left them separately. When people asked about my presence, we told them I was his old friend," he added bitterly. "Friggin' old friend." His laugh turned to a sob.

"I can see how hard that must have been," said Puller.

Abernathy looked up at him. "This is 2014, not 1914. It just doesn't make sense to me that other people can dictate who I can or can't openly love. It's disgraceful."

Puller handed the photo back and looked around the space. "Did you come up here to collect some things?"

"Some incriminating things, you mean? Yes, I suppose I did. I never did anything to embarrass Tim while he was alive. I certainly won't do so now that he's gone. I loved him very much."

"I'm sure he would appreciate that."

Abernathy glanced sharply at Puller. "Are you closer to finding his killer? Please tell me you are. Tim was the sweetest guy. I know he wore the uniform, but he was as gentle as they come."

"I think it'll only be a matter of time. And I promise that I will do all I can to catch the person who killed him."

He eyed Puller keenly. "Thank you, I believe you will."

"Can you answer a few more questions for me?"

"Like what?" Abernathy asked warily.

"Did you at any point notice a change in General Daughtrey's attitude?"

"How so?"

"Did he start to seem more nervous? Would he get upset more easily? Did he appear to be holding things back from you?"

Abernathy was nodding before Puller even finished the question. "Hell, all of those things. I kept asking him what was wrong. He just

wasn't himself. But he could never bring himself to tell me. At first I was terrified that he
had found someone else. But that wasn't it. I
would've known. He was just as affectionate.
But there was a wall he'd built that I couldn't
get through. I mean, I was used to his keeping
secrets from me because of his work. That was
normal."

"But this was different?"

"Yes. His work-related secrets were par for
the course. This other stuff, well, it seemed to
me that they were *guilty* secrets. Things he was
ashamed of. That would not have been associated with his work. He was one of the good
guys."

"Did he ever mention any incident that
prompted this? Any names?"

"No, not really. He did say once that there
was a heavy price to be paid for keeping our secret. And that maybe that price was too high."

"Interesting choice of words. Do you recall
roughly when this new secretiveness started?"

"I can tell you exactly because we had a big
argument about it. He had been reassigned to
STRATCOM. A command component of it,
anyway, I think they call it."

"ISR?" supplied Puller.

"Right, that's exactly right. ISR. It was over

at Bolling Air Force Base in Anacostia, so at least the assignment was local. Before that he'd been stationed in Louisiana, and before that in North Dakota where the nearest town had fewer people than live in this condo building."

"So what was the argument about?"

"Well, he had always told me he wanted to go in a different career direction in the Air Force. I thought he had decided to turn this offer down and accept another that he was up for. Tim was a super-bright guy. Lots of folks wanted him in their command."

"But he changed his mind?"

"To tell the truth, I think someone changed it for him. So off he went to this new place."

"So this was about two years ago?"

"A little over, but that's right."

"Did he ever mention a soldier that he was, in essence, replacing in that job?"

"No, he never did. I do know that he hated being at ISR. He traveled a lot. He was meeting with people in out-of-the-way places."

"He told you this?"

"Yes. He never gave me any content or context, but it was like he had this powerful need to just, well, confide something in someone."

"Did he say anything else?"

"Yes, he did. Something strange given all he had done up to that point."

Puller waited expectantly.

Abernathy said, "He told me recently that he wanted to get out of the military."

"Did he say why?"

"He said it had gotten too complicated. And that he didn't enjoy what he was doing anymore."

"Did he give a reason for this sudden unhappiness at work?" asked Puller.

"No, he didn't. When I asked for specifics, he changed the subject."

After giving Abernathy his card and asking him to call if he remembered anything else that he thought was relevant, he said his goodbyes and left Abernathy holding the photo of the man he had loved in life and was now mourning in death.

As Puller rode the elevator back down, he finally knew how they had gotten Tim Daughtrey to turn traitor.

CHAPTER

57

AFTER LEAVING ABERNATHY, Puller took a minute to compose a coded email to his brother telling him what he had found out from the bereaved lawyer. Daughtrey was gay and they had used that to blackmail the man into betraying his country. And maybe they had killed him because he had refused to do so anymore. He might have even threatened to turn them in. That would certainly have warranted a bullet to the head. They seemed to have no problem killing anyone at any time for any reason.

His brother's coded response came swiftly.

Puller had to smile grimly when he read it.

We have to get these assholes. Every single one of them.

Agreed, Bobby. Agreed. But how?

As he was driving along he checked his watch. It was after visitors' hours, but he was confident they would make an exception. He stopped by a Smashburger and bought two burgers with the works, two large fries, and two fountain Cokes containing enough soda to fill a bathtub.

After getting the okay from the guards stationed outside her door, Puller opened the door a crack and peered in. Knox was lying on the bed with her eyes closed. She still had a tube in her arm and she was still hooked up to a monitor. He read her vitals, and all looked good.

He walked over to her bed and sat down in the chair set next to it.

"Knox?" he said quietly.

She slowly opened her eyes. "Do I smell food, Puller?" she said.

"Wow, that's good, Knox. Were you a bloodhound in an earlier life?"

"The food here—they call it food, anyway—sucks."

"It's a hospital. If the food were good you'd want to stay, and that just wouldn't work, would it?" He pulled out the burgers and fries and set everything up on the meal table that he rolled over to her. Finally he powered the bed so that Knox rose up to a seated position.

She looked at the burger and fries and then gave him a skeptical look.

He said a little guiltily, "I know it's not your

usual healthy stuff, nuts and twigs and nonfat cottage cheese. But I thought that—"

"I love you," she interrupted.

"What?" he said, startled.

"Come over here so I can hug you."

He did so, and she embraced him for a few seconds, pushing her face into his chest.

When they pulled apart she said, "When I rowed crew I ate stuff like this all the time. It's only when I got older that I realized I couldn't keep doing it unless I wanted to weigh three hundred pounds."

"Nice of you to share that little secret."

She took a huge bite of burger and a long gulp of the Coke and said, "You're like a knight in shining armor come to save me from a tower filled with limp noodles and stuff here they call meat but tastes like aluminum foil spray-painted brown."

"I'm not so sure how shiny my armor is."

She took another mouthful of burger and then stuffed some fries in after it. She still managed to mumble, "God, so good."

"You might have to run ten miles and do *two* Insanity routines to work this sucker off."

"It'll be worth it."

She wiped her mouth with a napkin and watched him take a bite of his burger. "Did you just come to feed me or do you have something else?"

"I have a lot."

He looked around the room.

She followed his gaze.

"Problem?"

"There might be more than four ears in here," he murmured.

She sat back, ate another fry, then leaned over, opened the drawer of the nightstand, pulled out a pad of paper and a pen, and handed them to him.

"You can swallow it after you show it to me," she said in a low voice.

He wrote it all down and handed it to her.

She read it all, her eyebrows hiking at several spots. She handed him the paper and he crumpled it up and put it in his pocket. "I'll swallow it later, after I finish my meal. But until then—"

He pulled out his phone, dialed up his music library, and cued up a song. The music wafted through the room as Puller drew closer and looked at Knox. If they were being eavesdropped on, it would be very difficult to do so now.

"Damn, Puller," she said. "Daughtrey. Poor guy. I never imagined."

"Yeah. So we have the motive."

"Like Niles Robinson. No winner, no matter what you did."

"But not Reynolds."

"No. She made her choice for reasons that all benefited her."

"So they eliminated Daughtrey because he probably was no longer willing to do what they wanted. And he wanted out of the military. They couldn't allow that."

"That's the way I see it."

She sat back against her pillow and looked anxious.

"What?" he asked.

"Promise you won't get really mad at me?"

Puller looked taken aback by this question, and he was. But then his features softened. "You almost died in an explosion. How mad could I get?"

"I don't know. That's why I'm asking."

"Okay, I promise I won't get mad."

"I think I know why your brother was targeted. And the timing of it too."

Now Puller looked dumbstruck.

She eyed him nervously. "Are you starting to rethink your promise about not getting mad?"

"Just tell me, Knox!"

"We received a warning about your brother."

Puller gazed at her stonily. "You received a warning about my brother?"

"Yes."

"Who is 'we'?"

"INSCOM."

"And who was the warning from?"

"We don't know. It was anonymous."

Puller took a deep breath. He was clearly close to losing it. Knox seemed to realize this, because she sank back into her bed like she was trying to disappear.

"What exactly did the warning say?" Puller asked, his voice tense but under control.

"That Robert Puller had been framed, and that the DoD should take another long, hard look at it."

"When exactly was this?"

"About four months ago. That's what I meant about the timing."

Now Puller did lose it. "Four months! And you're just telling me about this? What the hell is wrong with you, Knox?"

He turned away, embarrassed. "I'm sorry," he said. "Not the time or place for that. I'm sorry," he said again.

She put a hand on his shoulder and tugged slightly. "Look at me, Puller. Please."

He turned back around to stare at her.

She was trembling. And in the bed she looked small and helpless.

"I deserve anything you want to say, Puller. You can yell and curse and even punch me if you want. It's okay."

"I'm not going to do any of those things, Knox. Not now."

"I should have told you before now. I know that. But I didn't. Seems like it's a sickness with me. I can't tell people the truth." She said this last part in a small voice. Her features were full of disbelief, perhaps that she had made such an admission. To him. To herself.

Puller sat back, nodding thoughtfully. "Let's forget about the timing of what you told me and focus on *what* you told me. Four months? It would have taken that long to prep the hit on him. Question is, how did they find out you guys were going to take another look at Bobby?"

Knox looked deeply troubled. "The simple answer is we have a mole in INSCOM, which is astonishing. Remember, I alluded to that before?"

He eyed her appraisingly. "So that's why you were brought on this case? Not just to keep an eye on me."

"Yes," she admitted.

"Would have been nice to know before now."

Her face flushed and her lips trembled. "I should have told you that too, Puller. I know you were spinning your wheels trying to figure out the catalyst for all this. And I just sat back and said nothing."

"I'm not happy about it, Knox. But that's water under the bridge."

Knox looked relieved by this.

He continued, "And maybe we know the anonymous source now."

"Who?"

"Niles Robinson."

"Why?"

He gazed steadily at her. "I have my secrets too."

She looked put out by this, but because of what she had withheld, it wasn't as though she could press the point.

Puller was thinking that that must have been what Robinson had been referencing when he'd told Bobby that he had tried to make it right. He apparently had tried to make it right, by contacting INSCOM, albeit anonymously.

"Any idea who your mole might be?"

"Not a clue. But it's really hampered everything we do. We're not sure who we can bring in on something."

"I can see that."

"And we never even thought that they would plan to kill your brother at DB. If we had any inkling of that we would have taken steps to ensure his safety."

"I believe you," Puller said quietly.

"In fact, it was that attack that made us realize we had a problem in our own ranks. The leak had to come from our side."

She fingered her last fry, looking uncomfortable. "So do you bring all the girls meals like this?"

"I haven't been associated with that many girls."

"That's pretty hard to believe."

"Okay. Only the ladies in hospital beds for bomb-related injuries get this kind of special treatment."

That brought a brief smile to her lips.

She popped her last fry into her mouth. "I am sorry I didn't tell you."

"In your heart you're a spy plain and simple. And they just can't let it all hang out. Now finish your burger. But hands off my fries," he added when he saw her greedily eye his untouched pile.

58

ROBERT PULLER WAS sitting in his pickup truck watching her. The Kansas plates had seemed to stick out here, so he had replaced them with D.C. plates he'd lifted from a car sitting in a D.C. impoundment lot.

Susan Reynolds was eating dinner at a table in the front window of a restaurant on trendy H Street. She looked like she didn't have a care in the world, but looks could be deceiving. And he wasn't going to underestimate the woman. Not again. He had gone back through her professional history multiple times, focusing on parts he had skimmed before. He had taken all of this and built it into a new mosaic, which had presented some interesting possibilities.

She was dressed to entice tonight, that was clear to see. The skirt was knee-length but tight, and the starched white shirt with the two top buttons undone was suggestively revealing.

The shoes were long spikes and the stockings had seams down the backs.

He sank lower in the driver's seat as a D.C. patrol car sailed past. He knew cops everywhere now would be alerted to his possible presence in the metro area.

He had picked up his tail on Reynolds at her home and followed her here. He didn't recognize the man she was with, but he was dressed like a lawyer or lobbyist, which meant he was dressed expensively. Puller had gotten a look at him when he drove up shortly after Reynolds arrived. He had arrived in an Aston-Martin. So there was money there if nothing else. As he watched, she laughed at something the man said.

It must be nice to be able to still find amusement in life when your boss just got blown to dust. Puller could imagine that the rest of DTRA must be mourning their slain chief. And Blair Sullivan. And the driver. Three innocent men who would not get to live one day longer. But not Reynolds. She just trucked on with not one blemish on her. Not an ounce of remorse.

Puller knew that Reynolds had had some part to play in the bombing. He just didn't know how or exactly why. His brother had told him that Sullivan had gone off on him and defended

Reynolds. And Donovan Carter had agreed with his internal security chief's position, though not necessarily his tone. So if Reynolds was off the hook, why kill them? his brother had wanted to know. But Carter had suspected Reynolds. And so had Sullivan, of that Puller was certain. And Reynolds must've realized this or discovered it somehow, and their deaths had swiftly followed.

His brother was a superb soldier and a crackerjack investigator, but he was both an honorable and an honest man. And while he could sniff out when suspects were lying, the intelligence world was a different paradigm altogether. People in that world didn't lie simply to conceal things. They lied for a living. And when you did something over and over you tended to get really adept at it. At least the ones who stuck with it did. The others were either drummed out of the field or perished within it.

That's what was so perplexing about Reynolds. His brother had been convinced she was lying. And when he had questioned her with a gun to her head, Robert Puller had felt the same way. And she *had* been lying. She had also been telling the truth about one crucial fact, but had tried to fashion it as a very clever lie.

She saw the mirror I was using. She knew I

was watching her face. She faked me out. Or at least she tried to.

He could see that now. And that truth was worrying him greatly.

He viewed Reynolds and her guest with his binoculars. There was definitely something familiar about the man. With the camera he had purchased, Puller took a long-range photo of him. He downloaded the image to his laptop and then ran the picture through the same databases he had used to check the image of the man he had killed in his prison cell.

Yet unlike that image Puller got a hit on this search.

Malcolm Aust.

Now he connected the name with the face. Of course.

He was neither a lawyer nor a lobbyist.

He was a chief UN weapons inspector from Germany, greatly respected across the world for both his knowledge and his courage.

Though Puller knew something of the man, he quickly read through Aust's bio. He had been in his position for over twenty-five years and had traveled to pretty much every hot spot on the globe. He was held in high esteem and had also written scholarly papers and appeared often on news programs.

He was cultured, spoke several languages, and was rich thanks to his status as heir to a fragrance fortune. Thus the Aston-Martin didn't trouble Puller. But something else did.

Why would Reynolds be meeting with him? Despite her employment at the WMD Center and many accomplishments, she was not at the level where she would be having a dinner meeting with someone of Aust's stature. Their types of professional circles were tightly controlled by those within the field. They adhered to strict pecking orders like any good hierarchy. The various status levels simply did not associate with each other. Aust might sit down with secretaries of state or chairmen of congressional committees. He might hobnob with generals and admirals and key CEOs or even heads of state. But Reynolds was none of those things.

And yet Aust looked quite engaged with the woman, and Puller started to wonder if it were simply personal on his part. Reynolds, despite what he believed she had done, was very attractive and smart and held an important position in a field that mirrored Aust's own interests.

As he watched they clinked glasses and Reynolds leaned across the table and gave him a peck on the cheek. The look on the man's face—which Puller could see through his optics — made it clear that Aust wanted far more than a brush of the lady's ruby red lips against his skin.

This might get interesting.

It was then that he glanced in the truck's side mirror and saw the man. He was about four car lengths back and casually smoking a cigarette while leaning against a building. He had looked away, only not in time.

The watcher is being watched. I've been made. But I don't think they realize that I know that. At least not yet.

Puller sat there glancing in the rearview mirror from time to time to check the man's movements. Then he gazed around to see if others were back there. There were many cars parked along the street. It could be any one of them. And then he saw a flash of light in a black Mercedes three cars back and on the other side of the road.

A camera flash. Someone had just snapped a photo of him and his truck.

He slipped his phone out and thumbed in a coded text to his brother. It was short but packed with information. He needed John Puller's help. And he needed it now.

He looked across the street to the restaurant.

Aust was no longer at the table, but Reynolds

was still there. She was on her phone. She nodded several times, spoke into the phone, and
then put it away. She swept a hand through her
hair and in doing so glanced outside. The tactic
was done well, and if Puller hadn't discovered
that he was being watched, he would probably
have associated nothing unusual with it.

But as she looked out the window, her gaze
had flickered across him. Just a flicker, but it
was enough. How they could have gotten on
to him was inexplicable. Even his own brother
had not recognized him.

The headlamps of the big Mercedes burst
to life as the engine was started.

Puller glanced in the rearview again and saw
the man who'd been watching him climb into a
coal-black SUV. It too started up.

Puller looked ahead of him. There was a stop-
light at the next intersection. At this late hour
traffic was light, which was both good and bad
for him. His hand slipped to his ignition key
right as his phone vibrated. He glanced at the
screen.

His brother had texted him back.

Like the cavalry, John Puller was on his way.
But it might not be in time. However, Robert
had an idea. His fingers flew over his phone. He
was sending a downloaded program together

with some additional data to his brother, all linked together. He hoped it worked. Otherwise, he was dead.

Finished with that, Robert Puller counted to three, watching the light up ahead, and then turned the ignition key. The truck started up. He shifted into gear.

The Mercedes shot out of its parking spot, but he gunned the truck engine and laid down some tread, beating the German-made car to the open lane. He raced ahead, glancing to his right as he did.

Reynolds was still in her seat and staring dead at him as he sped by.

And then she was gone as the truck blew through the intersection. The light turned red, just as he had planned. Only the Mercedes made it through, simply because it didn't stop. The SUV was blocked by traffic coming from both the left and right. But the driver used his vehicle like a battering ram and broke through the obstruction.

Now the chase was on.

59

JOHN PULLER KEPT his regular phone in his right front pocket and his burn phone in the left pocket. He was sitting at Knox's bedside when the burn phone started to vibrate.

He slid it out and looked at the message. It was short enough that he decoded it quickly. He was on his feet before he had finished reading it.

Knox looked up at him.

"What is it?"

"Gotta go." He was at the door.

"Puller?"

"You can have my fries."

Then he was gone.

Knox stared after him for a few seconds and then pulled off the line running to her arm, leapt out of bed, rushed to the closet, grabbed the bag with her bloody clothes in it, and started to get dressed as the monitor alarm began to wail.

* * *

Puller was on a dead run to his car. He jumped in, started the engine, and slammed the Malibu into drive. He fishtailed going out of the hospital parking lot and hit the surface road.

His brother had given him his last position, but it would still take a miracle to find him. And by then it could well be too late. No, that wasn't an option. He hadn't been there for Knox. But he was going to be there for his brother.

His phone buzzed again. He held it up in front of him as he drove. He gaped at the screen. There was a map on there with a dot. A moving dot. Somehow his brother had sent him a real-time tracking link through the burn phone. He quickly saw where the dot was located, hit a right and then a left, accelerated up the entrance ramp to the interstate, and gunned it. He flew past traffic, heading due east. He raced over the Roosevelt Bridge and into D.C.

He had three choices of direction coming up. As he sped along he eyed the map. Bobby was heading west, which meant he was coming Puller's way. But he was also heading north, which meant he was also moving away. Puller looked ahead. There was a cop car in the far left lane and Puller was blowing way past the speed limit. Road work was backing up traffic in the center heading onto Constitution Avenue. Puller veered all the way to the right, getting waves of honks from other cars, and fought his way to the exit lane leading to Independence Avenue.

He blew through the next several intersections as his eye continued to follow the dot. Then an idea occurred to him. He thumbed in a two-word text.

Go south.

A few seconds later he saw the dot turn. He watched its progress as he raced through intersection after intersection, running lights and blasting past cars with inches to spare. If a cop took up the chase, so much the better. But he didn't see a single patrol car.

He made a quick calculation and next thumbed in *East.*

The dot turned yet again. Puller matched the turn, but went right to his brother's left.

He edged over two more streets and checked the dot.

He thumbed in another text.

Next left.

The dot moved in that direction. Puller looked up ahead as the pickup truck, tires smoking, catapulted onto the street and headed toward him. Puller put the phone down and looked behind his brother's vehicle. Message time was over. It was now execution time.

There were two bogey cars. His brother had described them in the first text.

Black Mercedes S550 and a black Escalade. The Escalade's front end was battered. He didn't know from what. The Mercedes was right on the truck's bumper and looking for an opening to come up alongside. There was no way on a straightaway that the truck could hold it off.

Puller was racing right at this tight group, barely seconds away.

He thumbed in one more text.

Gun it.

The truck leapt ahead, providing a small gap between it and the Benz.

Puller checked his seat belt, noted the air bag sign on the dash, took a deep breath, and pushed the accelerator to the floor. He hoped the Army had enough insurance on this sucker. And he knew he would spend the rest of his life filling out forms. But better that than attending his brother's funeral.

He passed Bobby on his left and cut the wheel hard into the gap. His tires screeching, the g-forces ramming him against the side of the car, he flashed directly behind the S550. His left front fender clipped the left rear fender of the other car. He had timed it perfectly, and the Mercedes did a three-sixty. As Puller sped past he could see the shocked faces of the men in the S550. The Mercedes came out of the spin completely out of control, went airborne, and sailed into a sturdy tree on the sidewalk.

The metal gave, the wood did not, and the S550 was down for the count.

The Escalade avoided this melee by falling back. Now it shot forward like a shark after a seal.

Puller had gone up on the opposite sidewalk and clipped a parked car. He cut his wheel to the left and shot through a gap in the line of parked cars, slamming back onto the street. His brother was up ahead and getting farther out of sight. But the Escalade was now right behind Puller and closing fast.

The driver of the SUV gunned his ride and the bumper of the Escalade rammed into the rear of the Malibu, crumpling it.

Puller fishtailed briefly and then regained control. He looked up ahead. His brother was slowing down. Puller cursed, flicked his headlights, and honked his horn in a precise manner.

The truck sped up again.

Good old Morse code, Puller thought. He had just spelled out *G-O.*

His positive feeling was short-lived as the SUV hit him again and then pulled up beside his car.

He knew what was coming next.

The windows of the SUV slid down. Gun muzzles appeared at the openings.

He already had his M11 out. He hit the window switch for the passenger side. As it came down he fired directly at the driver's window. The window glass didn't break.

Polycarbonate. Great.

Unfortunately, his windows were not bullet-proof.

An instant before they fired he slammed on the brakes, smoking his wheels, and the SUV flew past him. The guns roared and a line of parked cars was suddenly full of bullet holes, hissing radiators, flattening tires, and the sounds of car alarms screaming.

Puller looked around for a cop but again saw not a single one. He expected to hear sirens in the air, but all he heard was his heart hammering in his ears. What, were they all on a break? Was the president out and about in his motorcade and the cops were clearing the streets for the man?

Cars in the lanes ahead had seen what was coming and had pulled off the road, horns blaring.

He cut the wheel to the right and slid in behind the SUV.

They couldn't fire through the glass in the rear of the SUV, but they might fire out through the side windows. He gauged the height of his hood and that of the SUV's bumper. Well, he was about to find out if his math was good or not.

He rammed down the gas and the Malibu surged ahead, hit the SUV's bumper, and stuck there. He kept his foot on the gas and the hood of the Malibu crumpled and then slid downward and under the SUV's bumper. He kept the gas flat to the floor.

The gun muzzles reappeared at the side windows pointing backward. Puller dropped sideways in his seat as his windshield exploded, covering him with shards of glass. But because the two vehicles were now coupled, he didn't really need to see to drive. The SUV was steering for him. He was just providing the horsepower.

He waited for their fire to subside and then popped back up and hit the gas harder. The Malibu slid farther under the rear bumper.

One inch, two inches. His hood was crumpling badly; his front bumper was but a memory back in the road.

But now what he had wanted to happen did. The Malibu's engine chassis, far stronger than the car's hide, started to bear the weight of the SUV's rear.

And then the back wheels of the SUV began to rise slightly. He didn't need them to be completely off the road, just not hugging it.

Then the SUV's rear window started to open. That could only mean one thing. They were getting ready to fire again and the driver was making sure they would get a direct sightline this time.

Well, we can't have that, thought Puller.

He whipped the wheel of the Malibu back and forth and had to grin when the two unbuckled gunmen, who were trying to take aim at him through the rear opening, collided with each other like pinballs. He cut the wheel twice more and their heads thunked together. One of them fell over. The other dropped his weapon and clutched his head, cursing.

The driver of the SUV undoubtedly could sense what Puller was doing, because he heard the SUV's engine slow and he felt the truck decelerate. The only problem with that was that

Puller was running the show now, not the other vehicle. He kept the gas pedal jammed to the floor mat, and the SUV was propelled along by the Malibu's motion.

Puller eyed what was coming up and gauged the trajectory.

He counted off the seconds in his head, hoping that his brother had long since turned off this road and was gone for good. He couldn't see around the SUV to check.

He stopped counting at ten, said a silent prayer, and then ripped the wheel to the right.

The Malibu's front broke free from the SUV's rear. The truck's nose went hard to the left. When its back wheels fully touched down they caught right in the middle of the cut. Neither the driver nor the truck was apparently ready for this wild mix of gravitational and centrifugal forces. The SUV corkscrewed, hit the curb, then a parked car, and then a steel bench anchored to the pavement.

And finally, for an exclamation point, it flipped.

It landed on its top, which caved in, and then it rolled, which crushed the driver's side. It came to a stop on its side after colliding with the corner of a brick-and-masonry town house.

Puller kept rolling and never looked back.

He turned left up ahead, then right, and then checked his dot. His brother was up ahead, two streets over and going fast.

Eschewing any more texts, Puller called him.

"You okay?" his brother said anxiously.

"Both bogeys gone and I'm in one piece, although my car's trashed. You?"

"They made me somehow, John. I have no idea how. I was watching Reynolds eating dinner and then I was suddenly surrounded."

"Kansas plates?"

"Couldn't be. I switched them out."

"They couldn't have recognized you."

"No. When I went to her house Reynolds never saw me."

Then it hit Puller.

"Her house! Bobby, she has a pretty intricate security system. You think she has exterior video cameras?"

"Shit. That must be it. I didn't see any, but I didn't check that closely either. She could have seen the images and known what I look like now. I didn't put my ski mask on until I got to the front door. And I took it off when I left."

"And a surveillance camera could have picked up your truck on her street. That's how they might have spotted it tonight."

"That was a big screwup on my part."

"The lady's good, we have to give her that."

He took a deep breath. "It seems I'm not very good on the ground with this cloak-and-dagger stuff."

"They haven't caught you yet. And it was pretty nifty how you sent me a real-time map of where you were."

"Simple, actually. It's just software."

"Still, I never would have found you without it."

"I saw what you did back there. I'd be dead tonight if you hadn't shown up."

"Then we're only even. Did you see anything helpful tonight?"

Robert told him about the dinner between Reynolds and Malcolm Aust.

"So a big cheese in the WMD world?" said Puller.

"One of the biggest. I just don't how it all fits in. I can't believe Aust is part of any conspiracy."

"Who the hell knows, Bobby? The only person I know I can trust is you."

"So what now?"

"Find a new place to stay and text me with it. Get rid of the truck."

"I need transportation."

"I'll try to find you something. Only after I

turn this wreck in the Army might never let me check out another vehicle. I'll circle back to you as soon as I can."

"They almost got us tonight," said Robert. "And don't say some shit like 'close only counts in horseshoes.'"

"I won't, because this ain't horseshoes. It's combat only without a declaration of war."

"We need to go on the offensive instead of just reacting."

"When you think of a way to do that, be sure to let me know, big brother."

"Yeah," said Robert glumly. "Will do, Junior."

CHAPTER

60

WITH NO WINDSHIELD and a crushed front bumper, Puller decided it would be best to ditch the ride and figure out the paperwork later. Finally he could hear sirens wailing and engines being gunned and he wondered what the cops would find when they got there. Would the guys still be inside the wrecked vehicles? Were they dead? If not, would they answer questions? Would this sucker finally start to unravel?

He hoofed it hard to a metro station and was about to enter the building and hop on a train when a car screeched to a stop directly next to him.

His hand automatically went to his sidearm. The window came down and what he saw truly astonished him.

Knox said, "You need a ride?"

The two stared at each other long enough

for it to get uncomfortable. And also long enough for a car waiting behind her to honk its horn.

He opened the door and climbed in next to her.

"Put on your seat belt," said Knox. "It might get bumpy. But then again it's been a pretty bumpy night for you already, hasn't it?"

"How did you find me? You're supposed to be in a hospital bed."

"Reach in your left pocket."

"What?"

"Just do it, Puller."

He did as she asked and pulled out the small metal object.

"When did you put the tracking device in there?" he asked curtly.

"When I hugged you for the burgers. Susan Reynolds isn't the only one good at sleight of hand."

Puller stared fixedly at her. "So you figured out how she put the DVD in my brother's pocket?"

"Just used a little magic," said Knox as she pulled out of the metro station.

"Should you be driving in your condition?" he asked.

"I feel fine. I'm more worried about you."

"Not sure what you're talking about."

"That was one wicked piece of driving back there. You should be proud. Take ownership of it, Puller."

He dropped the tracking device into her cup holder. "I won't be needing this anymore, and I'm sure you guys like to recycle."

She ignored this and said, "Care to tell me what went down tonight?"

"Sounds like you had a front-row seat."

"Actually I was in the nosebleed section. That's why I'm asking for a recap."

"So do you know who the guys were in the black vehicles?" he asked.

She smiled, but there was no mirth behind it. "And you're asking me this why? I was just a spectator."

"Just thought you might have an educated guess, being a spy and all. This is more your turf than mine."

"Who were you protecting tonight, Puller?"

"Not sure what you mean?"

"You get a text, tear out of my hospital room without telling me where you're going or even touching your delicious fries, and the next thing I know you're playing monster truck derby in the middle of D.C." She pulled to the curb and put the car in park. Turning to him, she added,

"Must've been a really important reason. Or more specifically, *person*."

"I'm not sure what you want me to say, Knox."

"You're all about the truth, Puller. You preach that all the time. You take me to gravestones of long-dead Custers to make your point. You pound it into my head. You throw it in my face. You make me feel like shit for holding back from you. So do I take your position to mean that that standard only cuts one way? And when you told me you never lied to me and never would, what was that? Having a little fun at the spy lady's expense, you sonofabitch?"

She ended this tirade by clocking him in the jaw with her left fist, broken fingers and all. The blow stung because she was strong and knew how to throw a punch, but he didn't feel much of it. Her words were hurting him a lot more.

She rubbed her damaged fingers and he brushed his hand against his chin and then looked out the window.

"If you don't talk, we don't get anywhere," she said.

"Not sure I can do much talking on this one, Knox. Not sure at all."

As he said this, his gut felt like someone had filled it with dry ice.

"I'm afraid that's not going to cut it, Puller. There's way too much at stake."

He looked over at her. She was holding her phone, her finger poised over the send key.

"Who are you calling?" he asked.

"Well, I've got lots of people on speed dial, Puller. And you'd know the names of all of them. You see them in the newspapers and on the news shows. They're the kind that hold news conferences and set policy and move the country in new directions. They keep us safe and they attack our enemies and they will have no problem stripping off your medals and ribbons and uniform and locking your ass up for the next millennium if the person in the truck back there was who I think it was."

"And who do you think it was?"

"Are you doing this to annoy me? If so, don't bother. I don't believe I could be any more pissed off at you than I am right now."

"It's complicated, Knox."

She laughed derisively. "Oh, really? From where I'm sitting it's pretty simple. You came down on me for hiding evidence. Okay, fine. I deserved that. Well, now it's my turn. What's the penalty for aiding and abetting a convicted felon, Puller? You're a military cop, you ought to know that off the top of your thick head."

"I get the point, Knox."

"No, I don't think you do. This is not some little criminal case, Puller. This is not one bad guy out there who's selling drugs on base, or did a little adulterous dance in bed with his CO's wife, or stabbed someone because he just wanted to. This is national security. This is global. These are the highest stakes you will ever run into in your life. We could be talking about rogue WMDs."

He sighed and stared over at her. "Been there, done that, Knox."

Knox's superior manner disappeared. "What?"

"It's classified. But with all your speed dial friends, you'd have no problem finding it out. Bobby could explain it to you better than I can."

Knox pursed her lips. "So it was 'Bobby' in the truck tonight?"

"It was."

"And how long have you known his whereabouts?"

"Not long."

"And you realized that you had a duty to arrest him?"

"I did."

"But you didn't."

"Obviously not."

"You're in a ton of trouble, Puller."

He nodded at this statement, his gaze directed over her shoulder. "Understatement, actually," he said.

"So what am I supposed to do? I've got a duty too."

"Then carry it out, Knox. Make the call. I'll sit here while you do it."

"You're a real bastard for putting me in this situation, you know that?"

"Yeah, I pretty much do."

"Is he filled in on everything?"

Puller nodded.

"Did he have anything to add to the party mix?"

"He did."

When he said nothing else she snapped, "Well, can I hear it too, or is it some secret brother thing?"

He looked at the phone still clutched in her hand. "Aren't you going to make the call?"

She looked at her cell phone for a long moment, as though it were a gun she was debating firing or not, before sliding it back into her pocket.

"Not now. Maybe later," she added warningly. "So fill me in."

When he was done she said, "Malcolm Aust? He's sure it was him?"

"Yes. So do you know Aust?"

"Not personally, no. But I certainly know of him. He's a renowned expert in WMDs. He's rooted them out all over the world. And he's one of the top UN inspectors in recent memory."

"So why have dinner with Reynolds?"

"Your brother said Reynolds was lovey-dovey with him. Could it just be that?"

"Bobby doesn't think so. He said that would never be enough for Reynolds."

"He's probably right about that."

"So what has Aust done over the years?"

"He was outspoken about Saddam having no WMDs, although he was pretty much ignored. He's also done work in North Korea, Iran, Libya, and Pakistan. He also helped oversee the destruction of Assad's chemical weapons in Syria. Although I doubt it was the entire stockpile."

Puller interrupted her. "Did he have anything to do with START?"

"Of course. It was before my time, but I know about it. We had our team, the Russians had theirs, and Aust headed up an independent observation group sent out on behalf of a number of other interested countries."

"To make sure the big boys played by the rules."

"Yeah, and what exactly were they going to do if we didn't? I doubt France would have declared war against the U.S." But then her expression changed. "Reynolds was part of that verification team. Do you think she could have met Aust then?"

"I don't know. I do know what Dan Reynolds told me."

"That his dad was ticked off at some guy on the verification team."

"Right. Only what if it wasn't sexual? Or at least not that alone?"

"Meaning Adam Reynolds might have thought his wife was a traitor back then?"

"And then he dies."

"But Malcolm Aust is as straight as they come, Puller. He's never had a hint of scandal. And he's independently wealthy. He wouldn't be doing it for the money."

"What happened with START?"

"Some nukes were dismantled. But things fell apart. Both the U.S. and Russia have substantial stockpiles left. And because Russia isn't as meticulous in securing nukes as we are, Moscow has the rogue WMD potential. Particularly in some of the former Soviet bloc countries. Those countries don't have much money and their ability to adequately protect their warheads is seriously in doubt, at least in the eyes of the international community."

"You think Aust might be upset about that? After all, he was there observing all of it. And when it fell apart? And now we have potential for nuclear material to get into the hands of terrorists?"

"I guess it's possible."

Something else occurred to Puller. "And if he was really ticked off that everybody ignored him when he said Iraq had no WMDs, this could be a way to get back at them."

"But what would his endgame be?" she asked.

"To maybe teach the big boys a lesson they'll never forget."

61

YOU NEED TO take me to your brother, Puller, and you need to do it now."

"Is that right?" he replied impassively.

Knox had pulled back onto the road. "Where is he?"

"I don't know."

"But you obviously have a way of contacting him."

"I do."

"Then contact him and arrange a meeting."

"Why? You plan on putting the handcuffs on him?"

"I don't arrest people, Puller. I talk to them. I gather intelligence, not fingerprints and suspects."

"Don't take this the wrong way, but how do I know I can trust you?"

"You *can't* trust me, that's sort of the point. But you also have zero options. So you either take me to him or I make my speed dial and you go to the stockade. And I'll still find your brother. But by then I won't be nearly as nice. Am I making myself clear?"

"I get the gist of it," he conceded.

Puller slipped out his phone and sent a coded text to his brother. "I'll have to wait to hear back from him."

"Yeah, well, he better not beat around the bush. And if you sent him a warning in that gibberish I just saw you type, then your military career is over."

"And here I thought you liked me."

"I don't like anybody that much," replied Knox. And she clearly wasn't joking.

Puller heard back from his brother ten minutes later. He *had* included a warning in the text. But his brother had chosen to ignore it.

The message was short and to the point: *Where and when?*

"Tell him to meet us at my hotel room at the W. Number 406. In one hour. That is if he's sufficiently caught his breath from the NASCAR ride."

"Do you think that's a wise meeting place?"

"I doubt anyone would be looking for your brother right down the street from the White House. 'Hiding in plain sight' is the phrase, I think. And I assume he's changed his appearance."

"Yes, he has."

"Well, then?" she said expectantly, lowering her gaze to his phone.

Puller typed it in and sent the message off. He looked at Knox. "You like calling the shots?"

"No. I *love* calling the shots. Now let's get going. I need to prepare to meet the famous, or perhaps infamous, Robert Puller. And I want to look my best."

* * *

Puller sat in a chair by the window. Knox was perched on the edge of her bed. Someone knocked on the door. Knox motioned to Puller. "Probably better if he sees your face first."

Puller rose and answered the door. His brother quickly stepped in and Puller closed the door behind him.

Robert Puller was holding his duffel. He gazed around the room before settling his eyes on Knox. She had removed the bandages and done her hair. She had also showered and changed her clothes. She had on jeans, a blouse, and calf-high boots.

She didn't stand when Robert came in, nor did she extend her hand. She just gazed up at him, an inscrutable look on her face.

No one seemed to want to disrupt the silence.

Both Pullers' faces showed the strain they were feeling. Puller knew that if Knox decided to drop the hammer, his brother would be back at the DB tonight. And Puller would probably be right there with him. And there would be nothing he could do about it. His gaze sought out Robert's and he could tell by his brother's expression that he was thinking pretty much the same thing.

It was Knox who finally broke the silence. She said to Robert, "You could get a job in the hair and makeup department at any studio in Hollywood. And I'm speaking from experience. We use some of their techniques in my line of work."

Robert said nothing to this and Knox pointed to a chair next to the one Puller had been occupying. "Why don't you gents take a seat and we can have a nice chat about things."

The brothers looked at each other and then took their seats.

Knox began without preamble. "I'm in military intelligence, which means I like listening a lot more than I do making speeches. But this time I'm going to make an exception. Point one: I should turn you both in. You have enough charges against you that it would take me six months to fill out the friggin' paperwork. Which is a good enough reason in itself not to. But I'm very much into quid pro quo." She settled her gaze on Robert Puller.

"Point two: Like your brother, I don't believe you're guilty. But you were convicted and sentenced, which means, in the eyes of the military, you *are* guilty."

Robert still remained silent.

"So we get to point three: The real traitors are still out there. And we have to catch them. And I plan on using you as bait to do it. I'm not asking you. I'm telling you," she added. "That's the quid pro quo for me not turning you in right now."

Robert looked at his brother.

Puller said, "Have you really thought this through, Knox? There's a lot more that can go wrong with it than right."

She looked at him incredulously. "Are you really going to lecture me on the pros and cons of risk-taking after the crap you pulled with him?"

Puller shook his head. "I had to do that out of necessity. You have a choice. And you need to make the right one. Meaning the right one for *you*. I made my bed. Don't be concerned about what's going to happen to me."

"You could *both* just turn me in," said

Robert. "In fact, from your perspective that would be the best plan. You'll get a promotion, a medal, and a pay bump."

"I'm not really into promotions, medals, and money," Knox retorted. She looked at Puller. "I'm more into getting my job done. How about you? Or would you rather turn your brother in so they can pin another ribbon on your manly chest?"

"What do you think, Knox?" asked Puller.

"So to be clear, do I take that as a yes?" she replied.

"Just tell us the plan."

She didn't hesitate. "I want to confront Reynolds."

"We've confronted her before," countered Puller.

"Right. But now you guys just left a litter of wreckage across D.C. I'm betting that the cops are going to find somebody alive in either the Benz or the SUV."

"So?" asked Puller.

"So Reynolds won't know whether they did or not. She won't know whether one of her goons has fingered her. We can go in with that leverage and squeeze her until she breaks."

"I'm not sure that will work," noted Puller. "She's a tough nut to crack."

"There's something else," said Robert. They both looked at him.

"What?" asked Knox.

"When I interrogated her I asked her who she was working with."

"What did she say?" demanded Knox.

"That she was working with the Russians. I have it on my phone recorder."

"I believe you. But what's the point?" said Knox.

"When she said it, her micro-expression betrayed her. I was watching her reflection in a mirror I set up."

"How did it betray her?" asked Puller.

"Her eyebrows were drawn upward, causing short lines across the forehead."

"Characteristic of someone lying," said Knox.

"She also touched her nose."

"The nose?" said Knox. "Haven't heard of that one."

Puller said, "When you lie a rush of adrenaline to the capillaries in the nose causes it to itch. So people who are lying tend to involuntarily scratch it."

Robert nodded. "Right. But I checked her c.v. Reynolds worked on interrogation teams in the Middle East extracting intelligence out of people, hardened people who did not want to give it up. She taught interrogation tactics as well."

Puller said, "So she would know the micro-expression and that nose scratching when answering a question would signal a lie."

Robert said, "Correct. And she knew I had training in reading faces as well. Many of us did at STRATCOM. And she must have seen the mirror I was using. But she screwed up, I just didn't see it until later."

"How?" asked Knox.

"Though I knew she was lying to me throughout, this was the only time she exhibited those indicators. She truly has impressive self-control."

Puller said, "So when she answered, 'Russia'?"

"She was actually telling the truth," finished Knox.

"That's what I think, yes. She was playing it too cute, actually. Often people who think they are more intelligent than anyone else do that. It would have been better if she had done the nose touching and micro-expressions throughout, to confuse me."

"So if the Russians *are* involved in this, it must be big," said Puller. "Whatever *it* is."

Knox added, "In fact it seems over the last

several years that Moscow has been able to read our collective minds. They seemed to be always a step ahead of us. In a million different ways."

"Well, if they had Tim Daughtrey as a mole at STRATCOM allowing them a back door into our secure communications that's quite understandable," said Robert.

"I think Reynolds has been spying on us for a long time," said Knox. "Maybe ever since her days on the START verification team. She could have been turned to their side during that time."

"Where exactly do you want to do this?" asked Puller. "Her house is being watched. Donovan Carter told us that. So that's out. If you want Bobby to tag along, we can't confront her at DTRA, for obvious reasons. So that's out."

Knox held up her phone. "I've been having Reynolds followed."

"Since when?" asked Puller.

"Since she got the upper hand on us at her house," said Knox.

"And where is she right now? Did she leave the restaurant and go home?"

"No." Knox stared at her phone screen. "She has another house. A cabin, actually, a ninety-minute ride west of here in Virginia."

"And she's on her way there?"

"She's almost there right now."

"A cabin?" asked Robert. "She must have a purpose for it."

"She may use it as a safe rendezvous spot," noted Knox. "And she might be meeting with whoever she's partnering with on this. If so, I'd love to nail them all."

Puller rose. "Then let's get going."

Knox rose too and put a hand on his arm. "But let's get one thing straight. I'm running this op, not you, certainly not your brother. You will follow my lead at all times. Are we clear on that? Whatever it is, you *will* follow my lead."

The Puller brothers glanced at each other. Robert nodded and then so did Puller.

Knox eyed them both for another long moment, seemed satisfied, turned, and led them out of the room.

John Puller muttered to his brother, "Why do I always end up running smack into the hard-ass women?"

"Heard that," called out Knox.

62

PULLER DROVE WHILE Robert sat next to him. Knox was in the back giving directions while glancing at her phone screen from time to time. It was now quite late and they had left D.C. and the suburbs of northern Virginia behind. They could just make out the foothills of the Blue Ridge Mountains up ahead. Puller turned off the highway and the car continued to roll along on surface roads that grew increasingly rougher and narrower.

"How much farther?" asked Puller.

"Looks to be about ten minutes. I'll tell you when we get close enough to ditch the car. We'll go the rest of the way on foot."

"Where are your folks who are tailing her?" asked Puller.

"Stationed to the north and west of the cabin but a hundred yards back, forming a perimeter."

"How many are there, in case we need some backup?"

"Two teams of three. Loaded."

"Well, let's hope we won't need them," said Robert.

About six minutes later she had Puller stop the car and they pulled over to the side of the road.

Knox's fingers flew over her phone's keys but the text didn't go. She stared at the loading bar on the screen. It seemed stalled halfway through the operation.

"Reception is shitty around here," she complained. She punched in a number on the phone. It didn't go through.

"I've got no bars," said Puller, glancing at his phone.

"I don't either," said Knox. "Okay, we'll just have to wing this. But there are three of us and only one of her."

Puller gripped her arm. "This mission is too important to just *wing* it. We need reliable communication up here or else we could be divided and taken out one by one."

"We'll stick together as long as we can. Then we can figure out a way to communicate."

"I don't like this, Knox."

"Are you telling me whenever you were in combat the conditions were perfect?"

"Of course not, combat is never perfect."

"Then what did you do, soldier?"

"He adapted," answered Robert. "And so will we. Let's go."

They climbed out of the car, their guns drawn. There were no homes on this road, which edged higher into a crevice between two of the foothills where the land flattened out. A fog had started to spread.

"The ground conditions aren't great," said Puller to Knox.

Robert said, "And keep in mind that, as Reynolds clearly pointed out to you both, she has guns and is really good at using them."

"Especially long-range sniping," said Knox grimly. "Olympic-caliber."

"Well, then we can't give her the chance to deploy that particular skill," said Puller.

Knox led the way up the road, staring at her phone screen as she did so. Puller noted this and drew next to her.

"Memorize where we're going, Knox, and then turn the damn phone off. It's like a spotter beacon right into your chest."

She nodded, did a quick but focused study of the screen, and clicked her phone off.

They moved up the road and then Knox led them to the right, over a stretch of ground that was uneven, rocky, and slippery. However, all three were surefooted and made their way across it without trouble.

They had progressed another five hundred yards when Knox held up her hand and stopped. The two men drew next to her. She pointed up ahead. In the distance about another hundred yards to the east they could make out a dim light.

"That has to be the cabin up there," she said, pointing at the light. "It's the only structure around here."

Puller gazed around on all compass points before returning to the light.

His brother looked at him and said, "What do you think, Junior?"

"Junior?" said Knox staring at Puller. "That's your brother's name for you?"

"Well, he *is* a junior," said Robert. "He's named after our father."

"But you're the older son," pointed out Knox. "Why aren't you the *junior*?"

"It's not always the oldest that's called junior," pointed out Robert. "And our mother named me," he added. "Her brother's name was Robert."

Knox gave Puller a quick glance but said nothing. Puller didn't look at her. His gaze was on the target up ahead.

"What I think, Bobby," said Puller, apparently choosing to ignore the discussion around his nickname, "is that the approach to the cabin on all sides is entirely open. The ground is flat; there is no cover. You wouldn't have to be an Olympic-caliber shot to pick us off easily enough."

"But it's foggy and it's dark," pointed out Knox. "That favors us."

"If I were Reynolds I'd have some sort of perimeter security. We trip that and then we're sitting ducks. Later-generation NVGs work just fine even in the fog. I bet she has them in there, and we don't."

"Well, we can't just sit here," retorted Knox. "This is your area of expertise, Puller. Pretend you're back in Kandahar and trying to clear a house. What would you do?"

He studied the area ahead for a couple of minutes. "Okay, what we can do is split up and approach on three sides." He pointed up ahead. "This is the east side, which faces the back of the cabin. I think we should approach from the west, north, and south, meaning the front and two sides, because her natural instinct might be to guard her rear flank."

Robert said, "On the south side the foothills pick up again and the land starts to rise. I doubt she would be expecting someone coming from that direction."

"Well, then let's just hit it from that way," said Knox.

Puller shook his head. "We can't put all our eggs in one basket. Unless she has a bunch of other shooters in there with her, she can only defend one position at a time." He pointed at Robert. "You circle around, Bobby, and approach from the south. I'll go from the west, which faces the front of the cabin, and Knox, you go in from the north."

"How do we communicate and coordinate?" asked Robert. "My phone still has no bars."

Puller said, "We'll be close enough to use a quick flash of phone light to communicate. We'll each do one flash when we get in position. After that, I'll flash twice when I'm ready to approach the cabin. Do a sixty-second countdown from that point. And then we attack."

Knox smiled at him in the dark. "See? You do adapt well to conditions on the ground."

He ignored this and said, "And it's confirmed that she is there?"

"Her car is in the driveway. It's confirmed."

"Roger that," said Puller. "Okay, let's hit it. But keep your head down, move slowly and methodically. And watch for my signal." He looked at his watch. "Five minutes to get in position. That should be plenty for you, Bobby. You have the farthest to go."

Robert headed off. Before she left Puller, Knox said in a joking tone, "So do I call you Junior now?"

Puller said curtly, "No one called me Junior except my brother and my father. And my mother. And my father doesn't call me anything anymore except 'XO.'"

Knox's smile faded, and she gave a curt nod and set off.

Puller gazed around one last time. He didn't like any of this. He had sized up many potential battlegrounds and his instincts had been honed to a fine degree. Everything about this was problematic. Their intelligence about the target was spotty and now the communication chain was broken. They had no idea what awaited them inside the cabin. Knox said it was confirmed that Reynolds was in there, but for Puller there was no real certainty about that.

However, the plan had been set, the forces deployed, the intel was what it was, as was the terrain they were confronting. He checked his M11 and set off, quickly making his way to his designated compass point and then squatting down in the high grass that was situated about fifty feet from the cabin.

He studied the structure in the poor light. One room was illuminated. He was facing the front door. The lighted room was to the left of that. Whether a bedroom or perhaps the kitchen, he didn't know.

Reynolds's Lexus was in the small gravel drive to the left of the front door. At least that much was confirmed to him. The cabin was small, rustic, with a front porch that ran about halfway along the front. The door was wood, the siding the same. It was unpainted. What bothered Puller the most about this was it didn't match what he believed Reynolds to be.

She was a woman who obviously liked fine things and had the money to pursue those likes. So why a crappy cabin in the middle of nowhere? Just as a clandestine meeting place? He didn't think so. And how could Reynolds have allowed herself to be so easily followed?

Everything about this seemed out of whack, but they were ready to execute. He checked his watch and watched the second hand sweep to the five-minute mark. When it reached it, he pulled his phone and gave a quick flash of the light. A second passed and then he saw a corresponding flash from the right and then the left. They were all in position. He immediately started to count off sixty seconds on his watch. At fifty-eight, he tensed his legs and readied his weapon. At fifty-nine he was starting to move. At sixty he commenced a zigzag trek to the front porch, keeping low and to the side, never exposing himself full on to sightlines from the cabin's front.

The light in the house never went off. No other lights came on. No shadows moved in front of that light. He could hear no sounds other than the occasional scurry of an animal in the nearby woods, and his own heartbeat.

Then he was on the porch and standing with his back to the left of the front door. It was a simple door lock. Again, that seemed off. He checked up, down, and along the eaves of the roofline. No surveillance cameras. He had encountered no tripwires. If the porch had a pressure plate embedded in it that would trigger an alarm, it must have been a silent one.

He faced the door and kicked right at where the lock met the frame. The door crashed inward and he was through the opening, his M11 making broad, precise sweeps in front of him.

To the left and right he heard glass crashing inward, then footsteps.

An instant later Bobby appeared in the hall to his left.

"Clear my way," he said to his brother.

They both headed to the right.

They started to run when they heard the shots fired.

"Knox!" called out Puller.

They kicked open doors and cleared rooms until a few seconds later they reached the last room. The door was partially open. And the light was on.

Puller pushed the door open fully and he and his brother filled the doorway, their guns pointed in front of them.

There was glass from the broken window on the floor.

Reynolds was sitting up in her bed, holding her shoulder, and blood was streaming down her left arm.

Knox had her gun pointed at the other woman's head. She glanced at Puller. "I had the misfortune to fall right into her bedroom," she explained.

She pointed to the gun on the floor. "She drew down on me and fired, but I'm the better shot, I guess. Even if I'm not an Olympian," she added, casting Reynolds a snide look. She pointed at the bullet lodged in the wall near the windowsill.

"Never doubted it," said Puller with a grin.

She eyed Reynolds's bloody arm. "You want to triage her? I'm no good at that."

Puller kept his weapon out and walked over to Reynolds.

She looked up at him, pain in her eyes. "She tried to kill me."

"I'm sure she had a great reason."

"You broke into my home."

"Again, with good reason."

"I'm calling the police."

Knox barked, "What you're going to do is confess."

Reynolds swiveled her gaze to her. "You really aren't thinking very clearly. I have nothing to confess to."

Knox said, "It's over, Susan. The goons you sent after Robert Puller got slammed by his little brother. The cops have them in custody. They're talking like you wouldn't believe. Your best bet is to cooperate and get a lighter sentence. But you're still going to prison for a long, long time."

Reynolds eyed Robert Puller, who still had his gun pointed at her. "You really should have just left it alone, Robert."

"How could I? You sent somebody to kill me."

"Then you should have just died." She grimaced, grabbed at her arm, and exclaimed, "Shit. You hit the bone."

"Sorry," said Knox, though her tone was not sorry at all. "Puller, you better tourniquet it so our star witness doesn't bleed to death."

Puller holstered his gun and sat next to Reynolds.

Robert put his gun in his waistband and went to stand next to Knox. "It went down easier than I thought," he said.

"For me too," said Knox.

Puller started to examine Reynolds's wound, drawing up the sleeve of her shirt.

"Uh, Junior?"

Puller was frowning because he couldn't see— He said, "Knox, where the hell did the round go—"

"John!" exclaimed Robert.

Puller turned to his brother. "What is—"

He stopped.

His brother's gun was gone from his waistband. It was now in Knox's hand and pointed at Puller.

In her other hand Veronica Knox had her pistol pressed against Robert's head.

She smiled apologetically at Puller. "I told you that you couldn't trust me—Junior."

CHAPTER

63

REYNOLDS SLIPPED THE bedcovers off and rose, drawing a Glock nine-mil that she had hidden under the pillow.

She was dressed in jeans and her feet were bare. She pointed her weapon at Puller, who had risen off the bed and backed away. Reynolds took a few moments to wipe the red off her arm using the sheet from the bed.

Finished, she looked at Robert Puller.

"Theatrical stuff," she said. "Much like what you have on. Nice job, by the way. Never would have recognized you except for the exterior surveillance cameras at my house."

"So why Russia, Susan?" said Robert. "They don't need any help, do they? The Middle East is where it's at, right?"

She said, "Moscow will always have more staying power than the desert rats. The terrorists will get subsumed into rising economies because they have no clue how to run a country or create jobs. People over there care less about Allah and more about having clean water, electricity, and ways to feed their families. But Russia is a real country. With a real army. With real nuclear capability."

"And you want to side with a country run by a former KGB agent?" retorted Robert.

"As opposed to what? A country run by old white billionaires and their paid lackeys in Washington?"

"The same goes on in Russia. It's just overtly backed by the government there."

She slipped on a pair of shoes that were set on the floor next to the bed. "I'm not going to have a geopolitical discussion with you about the validity of my arguments or positions, Robert."

"You've done incalculable damage to this country's interests, Susan."

"Well, as they say, you ain't seen nothing yet."

"What's that supposed to mean," said Puller quickly.

"Literally what I just said. You think I've been working this hard just to kill your brother? He was a piece, a tiny piece of what's coming." She smiled. "If you're still alive, which I doubt, you'll never forget it." She glanced at Robert. "On second thought, I might keep you alive just so you can see it."

Knox pointed her gun down at Puller's ankle. "Your throwaway. Take it out, muzzle first, and slide it over to Susan."

Puller lifted his pant leg, drew out the short-barreled pistol, placed it on the floor, and kicked it over to Reynolds, who reached down and scooped it up.

When Puller straightened Knox said, "Anything you want to say to me, Puller?"

He just stared at her.

Robert looked at Reynolds and said, "I'd like to know how you orchestrated all this tonight."

Reynolds said, "Easy enough. I came up here. Told Veronica. She informed me that she would have you in hand soon and would bring you to me."

"So you weren't being followed?" said Robert.

"No," said Knox. "That's just what I told you."

"How long have you two been working together?" asked Robert.

"Not that long, actually," said Knox. "But it's been memorable." She glanced at Reynolds and smiled. "She's a great persuader."

Robert said, "But John picked the sides of the

house we were going to attack. So how did you know she'd be in the room you were going to be coming in through?"

Knox shoved Robert toward his brother and then put one of the guns in her jacket pocket. She kept the other one pointed at Puller. She reached into her pocket and held up her phone. "I have bars. I called Susan and told her which side I'd be coming in on after Puller made his decision on that. She just crawled on her stomach to that room. And voilà!"

Robert nodded but said nothing. He snatched a glance at his brother, who had still not taken his eyes off Knox.

"Sure there's nothing you want to say to me, Puller?" asked Knox tauntingly.

Reynolds said, "I don't think he can come up with the words, Veronica. I can see in his eyes that he never saw this coming."

Knox said in an annoyed tone, "You know, you could have told me you were going to take out Carter with a bomb. I almost got blown up."

"Sorry, we had to hurry on that one. And I didn't know you'd be following him."

"But why kill Carter?" asked Robert.

"He suspected me," said Reynolds. "Despite what he might have told your brother, there was going to be an investigation. And that would have been bothersome to me."

Knox said, "Let's go." She shoved Puller ahead of her while Reynolds kept her gun on Robert.

As they walked to the door Puller broke his silence. Speaking in a voice only Knox could hear, he said, "How did you manage that attack in the alley in Charlotte?"

"I thought you might be wondering about that. My gun had blanks. I got you to go running after the others, which gave the 'dead man' plenty of time to disappear, after leaving some of his blood behind, of course."

"Why do it at all?"

"I knew you were still suspicious of me. That was a way to allay that suspicion."

Puller said, "So was it for the money? Just for kicks? Professional envy? Not getting promoted fast enough? Or maybe missing your fast life?"

"Maybe all of the above."

"I don't know about that," said Puller.

As they walked she looked curiously at him. "What, then?" she said in a casual tone.

"I think your old man had twice the guts you had. You knew you could never live up to that. You probably just invented the bullshit about him. Did you kill him and then come up with the lie about the suicide?"

Knox was unfazed by this barb. "Maybe I did. And after I kill you maybe I can make up some bullshit about how you groveled for your life. Or maybe it won't be bullshit. Maybe you will. Maybe you're not nearly as tough as you think you are, *Junior*."

"And maybe you're not as smart as you think."

"Well, I am holding my gun on you." She paused and then gave him a knowing look "You wanted me, Puller. In your bed. I could see it in your eyes."

They were outside the house now and heading to the car. Knox's voice had risen, and Robert, who had heard this part, quickly glanced at his brother.

"I'd rather put a bullet in my head than lay one finger on you," said Puller.

"I *know* you wanted me. You can't deny that. And it's not like I'm unattractive."

"Sure you are, Knox. On the inside. You could be the poster child for 'beauty is only skin deep.' My gut on you was right. I couldn't trust you, because you have no spine."

"I was wounded on behalf of my country," she snapped.

"So was I. But I never let scum like her"—he pointed at Reynolds—"talk me into betraying my oath. You're weak, Knox. Weak. You're nothing."

Now Knox's superior look faded. She stopped walking, turned to Robert, and shoved the muzzle of her gun against his head. "Get on your knees!"

"What?" said a startled Robert.

"On your knees. Now!"

Robert got down on his knees. Knox placed her gun muzzle against the back of his neck and looked at Puller.

"You want to apologize for that comment? Or he'll get a bullet in his head."

Puller looked down at his brother and then back up at Knox. "You really want to do this?" he said quietly.

"I have a better idea. I can shoot him with your throwaway."

She slipped the revolver out of her pocket, pulled back the hammer, and placed the barrel against Robert's skull.

"You have three seconds to say you're sorry to me, Puller, or big brother is no more. One, two—"

"I'm sorry," said Puller.

Knox fired anyway. But she had angled the

muzzle to the left so that the round didn't hit Robert. He yelled out and dropped to the ground clutching his head.

Puller started to rush to his brother, but Reynolds pointed her gun in his face.

Robert sat up and glowered at Knox. "I think you blew out my eardrum."

"Better than blowing your brains out. I hear you've got a big one. Now get up!"

Robert struggled to his feet, still clutching his ear.

When they reached the Lexus, Knox said, "Let's secure them."

Reynolds nodded and used zip ties to bind the Pullers. They all climbed into the Lexus. Knox drove. The Pullers sat in back and Reynolds in the passenger seat with her gun trained on them both.

They headed back into D.C. and, following Reynolds's directions, Knox pulled into an underground parking garage. It was well after midnight and the parking garage was full of cars because it was a residential building.

Knox used a knife to cut the zip ties. "If we meet anyone along the way and you make any attempt to communicate with them, you're dead and so are they."

They rode in an elevator to the main floor,

and then took a private elevator up to the twelfth floor, for which Reynolds had a key card. The car emptied into a wood- and granite-lined vestibule. Knox nudged Puller in the back with the muzzle of her pistol. They walked into the first room of the vestibule, which turned out to be a large space with walls of windows that offered sweeping vistas of the downtown D.C. area. The lights in the room were dimmed.

Puller looked around. So did Knox and Robert.

However, Reynolds was not at a loss. She stared into one corner of the room where there was situated a desk.

Someone was sitting behind the desk. Only his silhouette was visible.

Reynolds turned to Knox. "I wasn't going to bring you here," she said. "Until you did what you did to those two," she added, indicating the Pullers. "You scared Robert shitless and humbled his egotistical brother. What could be better?"

Knox eagerly eyed the figure behind the desk. "May I be formally introduced?"

Reynolds switched on a light. It barely illuminated the room. Everything was cast in shadows. But there was one thing they could see clearly.

Knox gasped. Puller took a step closer.

Robert said nothing, but he stared at the man sitting rigidly behind the desk.

From the shadows, James Schindler stared back at them, his eyes wide and penetrating. He seemed to be silently appraising the situation.

Knox pulled her gaze from Schindler and looked at Reynolds. "I have to hand it to you, your access goes right to the top."

Reynolds smiled. "For what we're planning we needed it."

"And now I can help you execute that plan."

"Which is why we're here. But first things first." She pulled her gun, slid a suppressor on the muzzle, pointed it at Robert Puller, and said, "You can't believe how long I've waited for this."

Before she could fire Knox kicked the gun out of her hand. Then she whirled and clipped Reynolds's legs out from under her. The woman fell hard to the floor.

A moment later Knox tossed two guns. A stunned Puller caught one and Robert the other. The brothers looked confusedly at each other.

Puller said, "Knox, what the hell is—"

Knox yelled out, "I'll explain later. Keep your guns on Reynolds. Don't let her out of your sight."

Robert aimed his gun at Reynolds, who was still on the floor.

When Puller looked over at the desk, Schindler hadn't moved a muscle. He still just sat there. Puller's jaw went slack as the truth hit him.

Knox pointed her pistol at Schindler. "You're under arrest. Get up! Now!"

"Knox!" Puller called out. "Something's way off."

Knox shot him a glance. "What?"

The glass behind Schindler shattered as the high-powered round crashed through it.

The Pullers and Knox dropped to the floor.

"That shot came from the building across the street," yelled out Puller.

Another shot shattered a second section of glass. Then more high-velocity rounds poured through these openings, slamming into walls and the floor. One hit the light fixture and it exploded, throwing them into near-complete darkness.

"What the hell is going on?" shouted Knox from behind the chair where she had taken cover.

"Just stay down," Puller called back.

"Wait a minute, where's Reynolds?" cried out Robert.

They all looked around the darkened room.

"I think I heard the elevator when the shots were going off," said Robert.

They looked around but no one moved. Puller waited for more shots to be fired, but none were.

A moment later Puller rose cautiously and peered at the shattered windows. When Knox started to get up he said sharply, "Stay down. The shooter might still be out there."

Robert had crawled over to the desk to examine Schindler, who still had not moved, even when the shots had started. "John!" he said frantically.

Puller shot across the room to kneel next to his brother. "What is it?"

Robert pulled back Schindler's jacket.

As soon as Puller saw it he grabbed his brother and pushed him toward the elevator. "Go! Go!"

He next shouted at Knox. "Run, Knox!"

The three sprinted for the elevator, but when Knox hit the button it did not light up.

"Reynolds might've disabled it," said Robert.

Puller looked left and then right and spotted the door at the end of the vestibule. It was locked when he tried the handle. He pulled his M11 and shot the lock off.

"What is it?" yelled Knox before Puller pushed her through the opening and then did the same with his brother.

"Move!"

He closed the door behind him and sprinted down the steps toward the first landing. Knox and Robert reached it first, turned, and headed down the stairs to the second landing.

Puller had almost reached the first landing when the detonation occurred. The concussive force blew the door to the stairs off its hinges and the compressed air surged downward like a million-mile-per-hour tidal wave.

When it hit the two-hundred-and-thirty-pound Puller he was lifted off his feet as though he were weightless.

The last thing Puller remembered was tumbling headfirst down the stairs. Then he hit something very hard.

And then there was nothing more.

64

WHEN PULLER OPENED his eyes all he saw was darkness. At first he thought he was dead, but then wondered how he could still see. Or think.

Then the darkness lightened and he was able to make out a silhouette.

Then he heard a voice.

"Sucks being blown up, doesn't it?"

The silhouette slowly transformed into something more solid. And familiar.

Knox was smiling at him, but the concern was evident in her eyes and wrinkled brow. She dabbed his forehead with a wet cloth.

Next to her he saw his brother, looking just as anxious, with no accompanying smile.

Puller tried to sit up, but it was Knox's turn to put a hand on him to hold him down. He was lying on a bed in a small, dimly lit room.

"You got knocked cold, Puller." She held up three fingers. "How many?"

"I'm fine, Knox."

"How many?"

"Three!"

"Okay, your head must be even harder than I thought."

He looked around. "Where are we?"

"In Virginia, near Gainesville. Reynolds left her car in the garage and I still had the keys. We drove back to get my car, left her car there, and then we drove around until we found this place," said Knox. "We've been sitting here waiting for you to wake up."

Puller rubbed his head and winced at the lump on the back of it.

"Couple of times we came close to taking you to the hospital," said Knox. "That would have required some problematic explanations. But if you started going downhill fast we would have."

Puller glanced at the window, where he could see the dusk gathering outside. "The whole thing happened last night?"

Knox nodded.

"So what exactly happened?" he demanded.

"You remember the explosion?" asked Knox anxiously.

"I'm not suffering from memory loss, if that's what you're asking," said Puller. "I saw the det-onation belt around Schindler. We ran for it. We were in the stairwell. The bomb went off and then I was flying through the air. And hit something very hard."

"That would be the wall, Junior," said Robert.

"It felt more like an Abrams tank." He glanced around at the space. "What is this place?"

"Motel room," said Knox.

"So how did we get out of the building Reynolds took us to?"

"Fortunately, your brother and I had made the turn going to the second landing. You got far more of the blast than we did, although we got knocked around too. It's a good thing your brother was there. He carried you out over his shoulder. I never would have had the strength."

Robert said, "I haven't had to carry you that much since you were four years old. And you weigh a hell of a lot more now."

"Cops show up?"

"I'm sure they did. But we managed to get out first." She rubbed his face again with the cloth. "How are you really feeling?"

"Better than I have a right to, I guess."

She sat back and sighed. "Best-laid plans. I've been working undercover on this case for two months, I finally get to who I think is the bigwig, and find out Reynolds suckered me."

"She suckered us all," pointed out Robert. "She obviously trusts no one."

"But I delivered you right to her. I acted my part really well. I almost deafened you to gain her confidence." She touched Robert's arm. "I'm sorry about that. It was an ad-lib. I had to sell that I was really a traitor."

"I understand. And it seems that most of my hearing is back."

Puller now sat up a bit, and she didn't try to stop him. "Why didn't you bring us in the loop *before* we went after Reynolds?" he said, scowling.

She shook her head. "Trying to get you up to speed on the fly right before the op? No way. You wouldn't have been prepped well enough. You would have said something or done something or made the wrong look, and Reynolds is too sharp. She would have picked up on it. I had to let you act exactly how you felt: convinced that I had betrayed you."

"Well, I bought your act," said Puller grumpily. "But you took a risk by not telling me. I might have shot you."

"I had to take that risk. I worked too hard on this sucker. But when I saw Schindler, I was stunned. I didn't figure him for it at all. But there he was." She glanced at Puller. "But it was all a façade. A trick. How did you know?"

"I could see it in his eyes. Up closer they were glassy. And he hadn't moved a muscle."

"He was already disabled," added Robert. "They probably used a paralytic."

Puller said, "Reynolds was obviously testing your loyalty. That's why she moved to shoot Bobby. If you were really on her side, you'd let that happen. You weren't and you didn't."

"So she was able to get me to blow my own cover."

"I'm glad you did," said Robert. "Otherwise I wouldn't be here. I could see the look in her eye. She was going to pull the trigger."

"But why all the shots fired through the window?" asked Knox, who immediately answered her own question: "So Reynolds could get away."

Puller nodded. "It was slickly done, I have to admit."

She sat back and folded the cloth into a square. "This was my only shot to get them, Puller. They're long gone now."

"I'm surprised you got as far as you did with them," he replied.

"It wasn't easy. When we were tipped off about Robert, that he might be innocent, we went back over his case in detail. One thing stuck out for us: Susan Reynolds."

"But how did you approach her?" asked Robert.

"I didn't. I let her approach *me*. We had set up my cover quite convincingly. I was passed over for a promotion. There were certain irregularities in my record, the accusation of a bribe. She could have gained access to this information quite easily. One day she called me out of the blue." She looked at Robert. "I told your brother that we had received an anonymous tip about you. It said that you were innocent and that a co-worker of yours was not the loyal person they claimed to be."

"When did you get the tip?" asked Robert.

"About four months before all hell broke loose at DB and the attempt was made on your life."

"So *that* was the catalyst," said Robert.

Puller interjected, "I think it might have been Niles Robinson. Guilty conscience."

"As I told Puller, unfortunately, we were probably the ones who almost got you killed. We obviously had a leak at INSCOM. Word got out we were looking into your case. We believe that prompted the assassination attempt on you."

"Well, it also gave me the opportunity to escape."

"So we decided to lay a trap for Reynolds. I was with INSCOM. I was possibly damaged goods. I could be helpful to them. It took two months, because she was very cautious. Then she made contact. A phone call, an email, a text. A face-to-face in an out-of-the-way place. Then things started to heat up quickly. I had no idea about the hit at DB on you, Robert. I wasn't in the circle on that one. I already told Puller that. But when it happened and you escaped, Reynolds met with me again. She needed me to be part of the investigation."

"Why not just pull the plug on her right then?" asked Puller.

"Because we might get her but no one else. And we still didn't know what the endgame was. It couldn't just be the murder of your brother. We needed to know what they were after. If we pulled the trigger too soon, we'd never find out what that was."

"So you became part of the investigation," said Puller.

"And from there I teamed with you, which she loved because she was convinced that your brother would seek you out. And the sooner they nailed him the better."

"But why was I so important to them?" asked Robert.

"First, she loathes you. I think you represent for her every promotion she didn't get. Every superior she didn't impress. Every opportunity that went to someone else. She thinks she's smarter than you. And she will do anything to prove it. You were the golden child wherever you went. And when your career carried you to her part of the world, you made a very dangerous enemy. When they needed to get you out of the way before you transferred to ISR, she was more than happy to do it. And that was the second point. They had Daughtrey in hand. He needed to get the job, not you. And we now know he was blackmailed."

"Any idea what they're up to now?" asked Puller. "Reynolds said we hadn't seen anything yet. When she said what they were planning would be memorable, I took the woman at her word."

"That's the rub. Not a clue. I was hoping to learn more about it last night. But she outmaneuvered me. I underestimated the woman, and I guess I overestimated my own cleverness."

Robert said, "Do you think they'll go forward with whatever they're planning?"

"We can't assume that they won't," said

Knox. "In fact this might accelerate their hand."

"But Reynolds can't operate in the open anymore, not after last night," said Puller.

"We haven't talked to the police," said Knox. "They'll eventually ID Schindler's remains through DNA. But I have no idea whose apartment that was, or who was firing the shots through the window."

"And I can't talk to the police, for obvious reasons," added Robert.

"But *we* can, Knox," said Puller.

"It would be our word against hers. We don't have proof. And if they bring Reynolds in she'll tell them about Robert being with us. Then our choice is either to lie or tell the truth, neither of which is a good option if we don't want to go to prison. And knowing her she'll come up with some quite plausible tale that we orchestrated her kidnapping and had a hand in killing a prominent member of the NSC."

"This is ridiculous," snapped Puller. But then he drew a long, calming breath. "If that's the case then we need to focus everything we have on finding out what they're really planning."

"Reynolds has to be intimately involved in whatever it is, because they've taken such great steps to protect her," pointed out Robert.

"That's true," said Knox. "But is it in her official capacity with DTRA, or in her capacity as a spy?"

Puller and Robert looked at her blankly for a few moments. Obviously none of them had the answer to that question.

Knox said, "They only had two motel rooms available. This one and the one next door. I thought you and your brother could have this one, and I'll take the other one."

"I'm going to grab my duffel from the car," said Robert.

After he left, Knox turned to Puller. "She beat me, Puller."

"She kicked my butt too. Again. I'm starting to get a real inferiority complex."

"She took it to one more level. I wasn't anticipating that."

"Then we have to take it to a level *she's* not anticipating."

"But my cover is blown, Puller. We have no way in."

"The three of us will get this done."

"Do you really think so?"

"Without a doubt," said Robert, who had come back in and overheard this part of the conversation.

He put his duffel down and sat on the edge

of the bed. "They gave us some real intelligence without meaning to do so, of course. They thought we'd be dead by now, so my seeing her meeting with Malcolm Aust didn't trouble Reynolds too much."

"Do you think you know why they were meeting?" asked Knox.

"Aust is smart, sophisticated, and rich. But I'm sure Reynolds seduced him. I saw them in the restaurant. It was sexual on his part. It was totally business on hers."

"But what is her business interest in Aust?" asked Knox.

Robert hunched forward. "For want of a better term, Aust is the secret keeper."

"Secret keeper? I thought he hunted WMDs?" said Puller.

"That's part of it. But only part. He's an investigator, an overseer, and an inspector. A confidant. Depending on the situation he will adopt a different role."

"Why would his role vary depending on the situation?" asked Knox. "Like Puller said, his job is to ferret out illegal WMDs."

"Oh, it's actually far more complex than that," said Robert matter-of-factly. "Take Israel, for instance. Their official stance is they have no WMDs. But they're our staunch ally and thus we would never call for an inspection into what they have or don't have. But for strategic purposes we need to know privately what their capabilities are. In steps Aust. Now, Pakistan has nukes. We worry about some of them going rogue because of lax security. The same with Russia. Neither of those countries are true allies of ours, but to call for an inspection of their arsenal is very tricky politically and diplomatically. If an inspection were done with, say, Pakistan, it might turn up locations of WMDs and their security status. If that information were leaked, it could lead terrorists right to the stockpiles, the very thing such an inspection was trying to avoid. Again, Aust is sort of a trusted-by-both-sides intermediary who keeps the system honest, or at least reasonable. And look at Syria. Assad has chemical weapon stockpiles. Under an international agreement he agreed to destroy them. No one with even a grain of intelligence believes that he destroyed all of the stockpiles, for what sane dictator, pardon the seeming oxymoron, would do such a thing? But Aust was sent in to verify what was done. I'm sure he is very good at his job. I'm sure he knows how much Assad destroyed. I'm also sure he knows of other caches."

"But wouldn't he report that?" said Puller.

"He would make an official report, absolutely. That one would be dribbled out to the global media according to the timetable of the powers that be. But there would also be an unofficial report, with limited dissemination, that would tell a different story."

"So the public is kept in the dark," said Puller. "How does that make sense?"

"It makes perfect sense if you want future leverage with someone like Assad or Kim Jong Un or a host of leaders of that ilk. You always hold something back to play later when you need it. Proof that someone like Assad lied and did not destroy all of his WMDs can be very powerful when used later on. It's all in the timing. We still hope for a resolution in Syria that does not involve all-out war. Such intel can pave the way for that."

"But why would Syria allow Aust to know of other caches? They would realize that this would be used later against them."

"That speaks to how good someone like Aust is. He knows places such as Syria like the back of his hand. He has moles everywhere. He can sniff out WMDs. That's why he does what he does. And countries like Syria know this. It's a game that they all play. If the chit is played later against Syria they will respond accordingly. But it buys them time. And it also buys us time to deal with countries like that in a diplomatic, measured way, instead of declaring war and sending boots on the ground. After Iraq and Afghanistan we don't have the stomach or the money for that anymore. But we still have a significant role to play in international affairs. The world expects America to lead. And this is one way we can without committing lives and treasure in vast quantities. It's all about what we know and when we use what we know."

Puller shook his head. "Way above my pay grade. It's why I'm just a grunt toting a rifle."

"Give yourself a little more credit than that, Puller," said Knox.

"But it does come back to Aust," said Robert. "If they need him, then it certainly narrows our search considerably."

Knox interjected, "But what if he's doing so willingly? You said Reynolds seduced him. That it's all about sex on his part and business on hers. But what if he's in on it?"

"And his motivation?" asked Robert.

Knox turned to Puller. "Tell him what you told me before."

"He was the loudest voice that Iraq didn't have WMDs," Puller said. "And we went to war anyway. What if he wants to teach the world a lesson? Particularly America?"

"By helping someone like Reynolds? By perhaps leading her to a cache of WMDs to use against us?" Robert shook his head. "I don't think that's plausible, John, I really don't."

"Well, if it's not then the real answer must be something totally off the wall, because nothing else I can think of makes sense."

Knox said, "We do have one tactical advantage. I've been listening to the news. The authorities are all over that apartment where Schindler was. It was totally destroyed. Apartments above and below were damaged as well. Fortunately, there didn't seem to be collateral casualties. They haven't released Schindler's name yet. They may not have identified him yet. But Reynolds probably thinks we're dead too, our bodies blown to bits in that rubble. If she thinks she's free and clear of us I believe she's going to go ahead with her mission."

"And she might relax her guard a bit," noted Puller.

"Exactly."

"Then we might just have a chance," said Robert.

Puller suddenly stood, a look of intense concentration on his face.

"What is it?" asked Robert and Knox together.

"We need to go somewhere, right now."

"Where?" asked Knox.

"Reynolds's office at DTRA."

"Why?"

"Because I just remembered there was something in her office that might just blow the lid off this whole thing."

65

IT WAS A country house situated between Middleburg and Purcellville, Virginia, originally a horse farm. There were no equines left. It had been purchased for five million dollars, in cash, and was used approximately four weeks out of the year. The rest of the time its owner was traveling the world.

The Range Rover was parked out on the cobblestone motor court directly in front of the double arched front doors. There was a staff to care for the house during the day and a cook at night if needed, but tonight he was not needed and thus the house had only one occupant.

Malcolm Aust was dressed in jeans, a loose-fitting white shirt with the sleeves rolled up, and a pair of black Ferragamos without socks. He wore his wealth easily because he had possessed it all his life. He had not earned a penny of it himself, but he felt his potentially dangerous work as a WMD inspector justified his living in luxury. He was fifty-four years old, but looked younger because he had the money to take care of himself. He exercised, ate only organic, and had his meals prepared by people who knew what they were doing. His mind was nimble and filled with important facts, invaluable confidences, and a sophisticated world strategy that he was dutiful in carrying out.

He walked around the small table that had been set up in the library. It was a wood-paneled room with three walls of books and cabinetry and windows looking out over the garden. Aust liked to be surrounded by weighty tomes, and had written several himself. To his credit, unlike some people with beautiful libraries, he had read nearly all the books on the shelves.

The table had two place settings. The meals themselves were on a side table and under cover to keep them warm. There were two wineglasses on the table. He checked his watch and then uncorked a bottle from his personal stock. This bottle was especially good, and tonight he wanted especially good.

He heard the car drive up. It stopped and he could hear a car door open and then the click-clack of heels on cobblestones.

Aust poured two glasses of wine. Then he

turned and walked down the hall toward the front doors. Seconds later he opened the door and there she was.

She was dressed as seductively as she had been at their dinner. Well, perhaps even more seductively.

Susan Reynolds's smile was warm and coy and intriguingly suggestive. And despite himself, Aust felt a trickle of delight reach from his neck to the base of his spine.

They kissed. She let her lips linger over his. His hand slipped a bit past her waist and gripped her where the flesh was soft. Through the fabric of her dress his fingers slid across the top of her thong underwear.

Apparently the woman was ready to go to the next level tonight.

"Dinner seems a long time ago," said Aust as he pulled away from her and closed the door.

"Much too long," she agreed. "I missed you the moment you left."

He led her down the hall to the library.

When she saw the table set up she exclaimed, "How lovely, Mal."

He took her hand and kissed it. "Matches my guest. Lovely."

She beamed. "If you keep that up I'll think you have intentions."

"Well, let me clear that right up. I *do* have intentions."

"I thought you would be exhausted after all your recent travels. I was surprised you even had time for dinner last night. I was stunned when you called and asked to see me tonight. Stunned, but delighted," she amended.

"All I do is travel. I'm used to it. But this last trip was particularly arduous, I will admit that. I've been back for weeks, but I'm still exhausted."

"Zaire is not an easy place to get into or out of," she noted.

"It is certainly not. But the mission was too important."

"Perhaps one of your most important, Mal, and that is saying something."

"Shall we sit? I've poured out your favorite wine."

Reynolds glanced at the bottle and smiled. "That symbolizes many happy memories for me."

"Then let's hope we add to that list tonight."

They sat at the table.

"DTRA, I know, must be in a terrible state right now," said Aust somberly. "Donovan was a good man. Good at his job."

"It was awful. We're in total disarray."

"And now there is this bombing at an apartment building in D.C."

"I know. I heard about that too. They don't know the cause. There are casualties, but they haven't released any names yet. But I can't think that it's connected to Donovan's death."

"And the work at the WMD Center?"

She spread her hands. "As you just said, the mission is too important. Even if our leader is dead, we have to carry on."

"Of course," said Aust.

"Despite its remoteness, Zaire must have seemed a bit quaint after the violence of Syria."

Aust shrugged. "I've confronted many dictators like Assad. He gets away with as much as he possibly can. He will lie, cheat, and hide."

"So how many chemical weapons does he have in reserve?"

"Susan," he said in a gently admonishing tone."

"I know you like to keep things close to the vest, but no clues?" she asked sweetly.

"Not even for you, my dear. But when the report is officially released you'll get to read every word." He picked up his wineglass and indicated that she should do the same with hers.

They clinked glasses and drank their wine.

Aust wiped his mouth slowly with his napkin. "I must applaud you for drawing the potentially calamitous situation in Africa to my attention."

"Well, our work at the center is all about spotting those types of scenarios and cutting them to the quick, if possible."

"There had been rumors about it being weaponized. But I thought they were simply rumors. How did you manage to get onto it? You never said."

"Through various channels. We have human intel all over the place. Even in remote Zaire. But we only had generalities to go by, Mal. You were the one who tracked it down."

"We might have been a bit late to the party," he said, his brow suddenly creased with concern.

She lowered her glass. "Late? How so?"

"It will be in my report on Zaire, but on this I can give you a bit of a preview." He put down his wineglass and rubbed his forefinger and thumb together.

"I've seen you do that before. When you're very nervous," she added.

He ignored this and said, "I had communicated particulars to you on the target site."

"Correct. And I sent them onward."

"Well, when we got to the target site it appeared that someone had been there before us."

"Who?"

"Unknown as yet." He suddenly slapped his hand on the table, nearly upsetting his wine. "The thing is, Susan, I'm fairly certain we didn't get all of it."

"Have you made this known yet?"

"I don't want to incite a panic based on incomplete information."

"But why can't you be sure one way or another?"

"There was no one at the target site. Just the cache. Where we expected it to be."

"Well, then?"

"I'm very meticulous in my work, as you know."

"Of course you are. You're a legend, Mal."

"The canisters were in an underground bunker. Ten feet down. Dirt floor, concrete block walls and ceiling."

"And no one was there?"

"They had been."

"How do you know?"

"We found two shell casings and traces of blood. Very faint but they were there."

"As you said, meticulous."

"And something else in the dirt too."

"What?"

"We retrieved six canisters, five-foot-tall cylinders. They weighed many kilos apiece."

"I'm sure."

"But in the dirt, you see?"

"Yes?" she said expectantly.

"It was only a faint trace. But it was unmistakable."

"What was it, Mal?"

"Three more canisters. You could just make out the indentations of the bottoms of them in the dirt."

"But they weren't there? Hidden somewhere else, perhaps?"

He shook his head. "We searched everywhere. There was nothing."

"So three canisters might be missing?"

"Coupled with the shell casings and the blood, I think someone beat us to it. And we found some villagers who had seen the canisters being brought in. There were nine of them. They were sure of that."

"But why take only some of the canisters?"

"Perhaps they hoped we wouldn't see the evidence of the others. Or of the possible attack on those who had possessed the canisters."

She sipped her wine. "There has always been talk of the Russians aerosolizing it."

"That was just a rumor. An unsubstantiated

one. I don't believe that the Russians ever managed to do it."

"But why Zaire of all places?"

"Well, that's where the deadliest form originated. An average eighty percent fatality rate. They have science in Africa, Susan. Better than we think. And parts of that continent have become ground zero for terrorist activity. Lots of money is pouring in there, and it's not to build schools or infrastructure. It's to do harm in other parts of the world. Like right here."

"Which was one reason the center was focused on it."

"And pointed me in that direction."

"We had just the barest of intelligence. You did the hard work tracking it down."

"But if someone got there ahead of me? If they took those canisters for their own purposes?"

"It all sounds very ominous, Mal. How can I help?"

In answer, he reached under his chair, slid out a pistol, and leveled it at her head.

"You can tell me who you tipped off, Susan. And what they plan to do with the canisters. And you can tell me right now."

Reynolds didn't even flinch. "That was quite

a segue, Mal. I'm not sure I've seen better. Or worse, depending on one's perspective."

"You were my point of contact at the center. You said you sent the intel on the target site onward. I'm sure you did. I just need to know to whom."

"I have no idea what you're talking about."

"I won't insult your intelligence, so please don't insult mine. Donovan Carter called me the day he died. He told me he wanted to talk about something important. When I asked him what, he only mentioned one name. Yours. He knew we were friends. He knew we were working together."

Reynolds drank some more of her wine. "And what did dear departed Donovan say about me?"

"That he had doubts as to your loyalty. That issues had been raised. That people were making inquiries and forming sound arguments about your possible treachery. That you might have even framed Robert Puller in order to place your own person at ISR."

"He was that specific? And I thought I had been totally exonerated."

"That's highly doubtful, since I believe that you had him killed."

She waggled a finger and gave him a sly look.

"And yet you had dinner with me on the very night he died. Have you no heart, Mal?"

"I didn't want to believe it of you, of course. You have a first-rate intellect." His gaze wandered over her body. "Along with other attributes."

"I seemed to have dressed up for no good reason tonight." She smiled warmly, her eyes crinkling. "Yet I did get your mind to wander, it seems. You have no idea what you're missing out on tonight, Mal. Your timing is absolutely horrendous."

"Stop treating this like a game, Susan! Do you really deny any of what I've said?"

She shrugged. "I can tell you've made up your mind. And I've never been one to waste time, Mal. And I'm sorry. I liked you. I really did."

"You used me to get what you wanted."

"I did. But you see, I only use the ones I really like. And just to clarify, the Russians *did* manage to aerosolize it. A number of years ago. Then the bastards somehow managed to lose it in Africa. Those were the canisters you retrieved. And I thank you very much for your hard work in doing so. It would have been beyond my capabilities, which was why I called on my good friend and fellow START verifier to do it for me."

Aust said forcefully, "Where are the canisters, Susan? You know as well as anyone what damage they can cause. You will tell me right now, or I swear to God—"

She rose. "I need a drink stronger than wine. Is the scotch in the same place?" She didn't wait for an answer but walked over to the cabinet set against one wall, opened the door, and pulled out a bottle.

Watching her closely, Aust kept his gun trained on her. "I want an answer, Susan. If you work with me, we might be able to undo the damage you've done. That will help your cause later on."

She took down a tumbler from a shelf and unscrewed the top of the scotch. "I appreciate the professional courtesy, Mal, I really do. It's rather gallant of you. But I don't need your consideration. I'm sticking with the ones who brought me to the party." She poured out a portion of the scotch into a tumbler and swirled it around.

"So you would betray your own country?"

"Well, I don't see it that way."

"You're an American!"

She turned back to face him. "I don't go by those types of old-fashioned allegiances anymore. They just don't work for me."

He tightened his grip on the pistol. "Listen to yourself. Are you insane?"

"Well, you need to get out more. Because these days everybody's a little crazy."

She raised her glass as though in salute to him.

A moment later a bullet broke through the window behind Aust and slammed into the back of his head. Aust fell sideways off his chair and thudded to the floor.

Reynolds took a sip of scotch and then put down the glass. She didn't look at Aust as she stepped over his body and walked out of the house.

66

THEY HAD OBVIOUSLY left Robert behind when they went to DTRA. Their badges got them into the building and security escorted them to Reynolds's office.

As the guard unlocked her door using his master key he said, "She won't be in until tomorrow morning."

Puller said, "I doubt very much she's going to be in ever again."

He switched on the lights and strode across the room to stand behind her desk. "You remember I said something was off when we left Reynolds's office last time?" She nodded. He picked up the photo he had seen previously when they visited Reynolds here. "Well, *this* was off."

Knox said, "How so?"

He pointed to a younger Reynolds standing in a row of men. "There she is."

"Okay, so what?"

He pointed at some writing at the bottom of the photo. "The caption says this was the START verification team."

"Again, so what?"

He ran his finger down the line of men. "Recognize anyone?"

She eyed one of the men. "That's Malcolm Aust. But we knew he was on the verification team. So you're still suspecting him of partnering with Reynolds?"

Puller ignored this question and said, "Recognize anyone else in the line?"

Knox took the photo from him and went one by one. When she got to the end she started from the beginning and worked her way down it. She paused at one man standing to the left of Reynolds. He was tall, well built, his features sharp and angular, truly a memorable countenance.

"This guy looks familiar for some reason."

Puller had taken out his phone and brought up an image on it. "I snapped this shot off the computer screen at Fort Leavenworth."

When Knox looked at the picture on the screen and then the photo, she gasped. "Omigod, it's him!"

"Ivo Mesic. The 'Croatian' who brought my

brother's would-be killer into DB in the trunk of his car."

"So you believe he's partnered with Reynolds? But why?"

"She's at the WMD Center. They were both START verifiers, which has to do with nukes. She was sucking up to Aust, who hunts WMDs for a living."

"So they're planning something. With a nuke?"

"I don't know. It's not like folks leave nukes lying around."

* * *

As they left the building and got back into the car, Knox's phone buzzed. She answered it, listened, and then said, "Okay, thanks for the heads-up." She put the phone away, looking pale and shocked.

"What is it?" asked Puller.

"Malcolm Aust is dead."

"What?" exclaimed Puller. "How?"

"He was supposed to phone in on a late conference call this evening that originated in L.A. He never did. They sent someone out to his house to check on him when he didn't answer his phone or email. They found him dead. Shot through the head."

Puller said, "That means the plan must be coming to fruition. They're tying up all loose ends."

Knox snapped, "But what *is* the plan, Puller? We don't have a clue. And that means we can't stop it."

"We *do* have clues. We just have to piece them together. And we've got one of the biggest brains in the world to help us."

He jammed down the gas and pointed the car back to where they had come from. Back to Robert Puller.

* * *

They sat around the motel room looking at each other. Puller and Knox had filled in Robert on what they had discovered at Reynolds's office. And also about Malcolm Aust's murder.

"What had he been working on?" Robert asked. "We need to know that, John. That will narrow things down considerably."

Puller took out his phone and called General Aaron Rinehart. The general was in a late meeting, but he called Puller back a few minutes later. Puller gave him a quick sketch of what they had learned and what they suspected.

Rinehart said, "I'll find out, Puller. In the

meantime, I'll make sure everyone goes on high alert. And I'll put all our resources out to find Reynolds and this Ivo Mesic."

While Puller was on the phone Robert was typing away on his laptop. After Puller ended the call his brother said, "His real name is Anton Bok." He spun the laptop around so they could see a page of both pictures and text.

"The START Verification Team from the 1990s. A full accounting with names, backgrounds and photos." He pointed to one picture. "Bok is the third from the left. Right next to Reynolds."

"What's his background?" asked Knox.

"Former military. Former KGB. With the equivalent of a master's degree in biochemistry and a PhD in molecular biology."

"Chemistry and biology," said Puller.

"*Molecular* biology," amended Robert.

"But he also had experience in nukes, otherwise he wouldn't have been on the verification team," pointed out Knox.

"He was probably there more to gather intelligence for Russia than count warheads," said Robert. "And to recruit Susan Reynolds to his side."

"So biology and chemistry are his specialties," said Puller. "What can we learn from that?"

Robert said, "Not all WMDs are nukes. Nukes are tough to get and impossible to make unless you have a large infrastructure and billions of dollars and years to work with. But you have plenty of far cheaper and easier-to-manufacture bioterrorism possibilities. Contaminating the air, water, and food chains. That would also be more in line with Bok's background."

Knox said, "I'm surprised she left that photo out in her office."

Puller said, "She never knew we had latched on to Ivo Mesic at Fort Leavenworth. So she wasn't worried about our making the connection. And remember what her son Dan said about his father? He would kill the guy if he got the chance? I think Susan Reynolds and Anton Bok are a lot more than business partners. She probably got a kick out of seeing his face every day. And who would get suspicious? She has a photo in her office of her days as a START verifier? Perfectly normal."

"You're probably right, Junior," said Robert.

A few hours later Puller's phone buzzed. It was Aaron Rinehart. Puller listened and nodded. He stood. "Rinehart has someone we need to talk to."

"Who?" asked Knox.

"Donovan Carter's second in command."

"What can he tell us?"

"He apparently can tell us what Malcolm Aust was working on."

67

THEY DIDN'T GO back to DTRA as dawn broke. Warren Johnson, the interim director of DTRA, was at a facility in D.C.

Puller drove fast and they pulled into the underground garage in record time. He and Knox were cleared through security and rode the elevator up to the office.

Johnson met them in the lobby. He was a short man, balding, with a thickened nose and eyes partially hidden behind spectacles. He escorted them back to an office, where they sat around a small table. Johnson came quickly to the point.

"General Rinehart was clear that I was to be frank and speak freely with you about all this."

"That would be helpful," said Puller. "I have a feeling that we might be running out of time."

"He's told me of your suspicions about Susan Reynolds. I won't add my opinion to the mix right now. But with Donovan and now Malcolm Aust murdered, it doesn't really matter what I think." He leaned forward. "The fact is, Susan Reynolds was the point of contact for Malcolm for a mission he was performing in partnership with the WMD Center."

"And what was the mission?" asked Puller. "Something to do with chemical weapons in Syria, maybe?"

"No. We were provided intel about a cache of weaponized Ebola-Zaire in Africa."

"Ebola-Zaire?" said Knox.

Johnson nodded. "There are four types of Ebola virus. Ebola-Reston is one. There was a lot of hoopla about that because it involved monkeys and was in a heavily populated area, Reston, Virginia, hence the name. But Ebola-Reston is nonpathogenic to humans. Ebola-Zaire, on the other hand, is deadly to human beings."

"You said weaponized," pointed out Puller.

"We believe it's been aerosolized. Meaning it can be distributed through the air. Up to this point we always believed that all strains of Ebola required hands-on exposure, exchange of fluids, that sort of thing. That made the virus, while still extremely dangerous, manageable under most circumstances. It was rumored that the Russians had aerosolized Ebola-Zaire some years ago, but the trail on that petered out. We thought it a rumor. Until we received this latest piece of intelligence."

"And Reynolds was running your end of the mission? Was she also the source of the intel?"

"That is not clear," said Johnson, with a very troubled look. "But she may well have been. She and Aust went way back. It was her idea to call on him to track this cache down. He was successful." He paused. "With a disclaimer attached to that."

"I thought there might be," said Puller. "What disclaimer?"

"He didn't believe he got it all. At least that's what he confided to Donovan and Donovan in turn told me."

"Why didn't he get all of it?" asked Knox.

"Because he believed that someone had been there ahead of him and taken a portion of the supply."

Knox and Puller exchanged glances. She said, "So Reynolds piggybacked on Aust to get what she needed? He was probably feeding her daily reports. He gets the location of the stuff nailed down and tells her. And she has her team show up first to take some of it."

Johnson held up a hand. "I'm not speculating on that point. But we don't have time to worry about that. We have a major problem if that cache is going to be used."

"I have no doubt it's going to be used," said Puller. "And I would be seriously surprised if it weren't going to be used against us."

"Us?" said Johnson. "You mean in this country?"

"I mean in this area."

"What do you base that on?" Johnson demanded.

"On the fact that Susan Reynolds is here."

Knox said, "Aerosolized Ebola-Zaire. What sort of casualties are we looking at with the amount of virus they might have?"

"Catastrophic in a high-population area like this. If one drop of virus-infected liquid enters the body, it's enough to kill. There is no cure, and really no widespread approved vaccine for humans. As you may know, there's been another outbreak of it in West Africa. Many have died and they have yet to contain it.

"So people exposed to it *will* be contagious?" asked Knox.

"Of course. But the one good thing about Ebola is that, unlike other diseases, it's only *after* you develop symptoms, meaning you are sick and feverish, that you become contagious. However, it is damn difficult to diagnose Ebola because its symptoms mirror so many other types of diseases. Ironically, the best diagnostic tool is one's passport. If you'd been to areas in Africa that have had outbreaks of Ebola, that helps to narrow the diagnostic possibilities."

"But if it happens here?" said Puller. "People could just think they have the flu. And ten days or two weeks pass and they're contagious and they spread it to a lot of other people without even knowing they have Ebola."

"It is quite an unprecedented possibility," said Johnson glumly.

"How much of the stuff did Aust think had been taken before he got to the cache?"

"Three five-foot-tall canisters. Now, that may not sound like a lot, but with the aerosolized Ebola a little goes a long way. And infection through the lungs, which are chock-full of blood vessels that travel the length of the body, is quite rapid."

"What happened to the canisters that he did recover?" asked Puller.

"They were transported to a highly secure facility equipped for dealing with bioterrorism elements. They are scheduled to be thoroughly examined and then they will be destroyed."

"So the examination hasn't started yet?"

"No. These things take time to prep, to make

sure it's done safely. The examination may lead us back to who engineered the weapon. If so, I would imagine severe consequences will follow."

"Could it be the Russians?" asked Knox. "You seem to think that's where this stuff came from."

"It might very well be. And with the state of the world right now, and Russia seemingly raising its imperialistic head again, things might get a little unstable."

"I think they're pretty unstable right now," interjected Puller.

"So would those infected in that way be able to infect others by just breathing on them, or will it require a transfer of bodily fluids, or touching someone else?" asked Knox.

"I can't answer that definitively, because we've never been faced with something like this. I have our people here working on it, but don't expect a fast answer. Scientists aren't wired that way. But, worst case, I think we have to assume that those infected through the air can in turn infect others the same way: a cough, a sneeze. Which means a serious multiplier effect. Thousands. Hundreds of thousands. It would be like a Hollywood disaster movie."

"So canisters that have been aerosolized, like oxygen containers?" said Puller.

Johnson nodded. "Yes. I've seen photos of the ones that Aust found. That's exactly what they look like. And you think they might be deployed somewhere in this area?"

"D.C. is the capital. If you want to make a big statement, where else would you do it?" said Puller.

"But where, Puller?" asked Knox. "There are too many targets to cover."

Johnson said, "Now, many obvious targets have air monitors, which will detect numerous airborne pathogens and also any deviation in the typical makeup of the air moving through a facility. Many significant military installations have them. The White House, DHS facilities—the list goes on and on. If a deviation or specific pathogen is detected, the air system is immediately shut down and a whole host of procedures will kick in, including possible evacuation or even quarantine, depending on what exactly is in the air."

"Well, that's some comfort," said Knox.

"But again, I'm not sure if many of the monitors deployed now could pick up aerosolized Ebola, since we were not aware such a biological agent existed."

"Okay, there goes the comfort factor right out the window," said Knox.

Puller's phone rang. It was his brother. He moved to a corner of the room and filled Robert in on what Johnson had told them.

"Weaponized Ebola disseminated through the air is some serious shit, John."

"So I gather. Our problem is we know it's out there. We just don't know where the target is. And even if we narrow it down to this area—and I could be totally wrong on that—it's still a lot of options. And I don't think they want to go public with this because of the panic."

"Well, I can't say I can blame them on that," replied Robert. "But I have been giving it some thought. And I've made some phone calls."

"You made phone calls?" said a surprised Puller.

"Yeah. Pretending I was you. We sound alike, bro, in case you hadn't noticed. Anyway, I got hold of one guy at Leavenworth, a Command Sergeant Major Tim McCutcheon. He said he had spoken to you before."

"Right. He was the one who told us about Ivo Mesic hightailing it out of there on the day the Ukrainian tried to kill you at DB. Why did you want to talk to him?"

"Because he has records on the Foreign Military Studies program."

"And why does that interest you?"

"Because I think it interested Ivo Mesic. Or Anton Bok, rather."

"I'm not following you, Bobby," said a clearly frustrated Puller. "And I'm running out of time here, so just tell it to me as straight as you can."

"I think Bok was at Leavenworth for *more* than just a way to get my purported killer onto the base. He strikes me as a multitasker who would not waste time sitting in a classroom for a full month. I think he was there to learn what he needed to learn."

"And what was that?"

"His studies included some interesting subjects in the American military world. But one in particular got my attention."

"What was that?"

"A course titled 'American Command and Control: A History of the Pentagon.' The course also included quite a fascinating and in-depth study of the facility itself. Quite in-depth. How everything runs, Junior. From the cafeterias to the HVAC. From the five rings to the BioWatch program."

"Are you serious?"

"I think in the future we might want to be a little more guarded with our information, particularly for those who wear a different uniform."

"Thanks, Bobby."

Knox, who had overheard some of this, rushed over. "What is it?"

Puller was already hammering the number on his phone keypad.

"This is CWO John Puller. I need to talk to General Aaron Rinehart, and I need him right now."

The voice asked him what it was in reference to.

"Doomsday," said Puller. "Just tell him it's about Doomsday."

68

As THEY ARRIVED at the Pentagon it was now early morning and streams of people were heading to work inside the building. Rinehart met Puller and Knox at one of the entrances with members from the Pentagon Force Protection Agency and several men dressed in biohazard uniforms. They had two golf carts with them. Puller took a couple minutes to fill everyone in on what they might be confronting.

"Weaponized Ebola?' said the head of the Protection Agency, a man named Ted Pritchard. "Aerosolized? So introduced through our HVAC system?"

"Yes," said Puller.

Pritchard said, "But we have air monitors all over this place. Exterior intakes, internally placed. The system can detect deviations and foreign particulates. Including Ebola."

"But even if it detects it, people can still be infected by the time the system shuts down," said Puller.

"Where the hell do you think it is?" barked Rinehart.

When Puller didn't say anything, Pritchard said, "We have seven floors, including two below ground, six and a half million square feet, twenty-nine acres, and seventeen and a half miles of corridors. And thousands of people working here. It's not a needle in a haystack. It's a needle in the middle of a freaking farm."

Puller said, "The last time I was here I nearly got run over by someone hauling a cart full of oxygen canisters. Where would they go?"

Rinehart looked at Pritchard. "Do you have the answer to that?"

"The E Ring is where the senior officers have their offices. When renovation work was done it was configured to be sealed off and then piped to carry an emergency backup oxygen system."

"Command and control," said Puller quietly. He turned to Pritchard. "Where is the oxygen supply for this backup system?"

"Let's go."

The Pentagon consisted of five concentric pentagonal rings intersected by ten radial corridors. Its original cost was eighty-three million dollars and the structure had been built in only sixteen months during America's involvement in the Second World War. Though enormous, it was designed so that one could travel between any two points in the building in seven minutes.

In the golf carts Puller and company made it in four minutes. During the ride Puller said in a low voice to Rinehart, "James Schindler is dead."

Rinehart showed enormous self-restraint at this news. "How do you know that?" he said in a low voice.

Puller went on to explain what had happened in the apartment building.

"I heard about that on the news," Rinehart said, shaking his head. "But I had no idea Jim was involved."

"It's going to take a while to ID him," said Puller grimly. "But I was there and I was nearly killed too."

"Reynolds?"

"She was there as well, but got away."

"I want to hear all about it, Puller. But not now."

"Right."

The site of the oxygen supply was on the basement level near Corridor 3. The door to the room was locked. They unlocked it and poured in.

"Over there," said Pritchard, pointing. There was a cluster of oxygen tanks in the center of the room.

"What do we look for?" asked Rinehart.

Puller examined the canisters. "These look like they've been here a while. And they're a different color from the ones I saw. Green, not silver. Can you check?"

Pritchard hurried over to a computer screen built into the wall and punched in a password and then hit some other keys. He read off the screen and turned to Puller. "They were last replaced about two months ago."

"Is there another place where these canisters are kept?"

"No sir."

"But that's not possible. I was here recently and I saw a cartload of canisters. I was almost run down by them."

"Well, they weren't delivered here."

Rinehart grabbed Puller by the shoulder. "Do you think you've read this incorrectly? It might not be here at all, Puller. We could be wasting valuable time."

Knox looked at him. "But you said you saw the cart with the canisters when you were here?"

He nodded and pointed at Rinehart. "You were with me, sir. Don't you remember seeing it? I grabbed you when you stumbled getting out of the way."

Rinehart thought for a few seconds and then his eyes widened. "I *do* remember that. There *was* a motorized cart hauling what looked like oxygen tanks."

Puller turned to Pritchard. "Where would they be going with those?"

"I'm not sure."

Knox said, "Well, it's not here."

They rushed from the room. Puller started walking full bore down the corridor while the others climbed into the carts and followed him. Knox stayed on foot and caught up to him.

"Where are you going?" she asked.

"I'm hoping I see something that will lead to something else."

"But are you looking for anything in particular?"

"Yeah. Another way to disseminate the virus."

"But what could that be if it's not in the air ducts? That's how you deploy an aerosolized bioweapon."

But Puller wasn't listening to her. He had stopped walking and was staring off.

Rinehart leapt off one of the carts and grabbed Puller's arm. "Do we need to evacuate, Puller? It's the damn Pentagon. It'll take time."

Puller wasn't listening to him either. He hustled over to a wall and snatched off a piece of paper that had been taped there. He read down it and then looked over at the group of men.

"You're having a fire drill today?"

"Yes," said Pritchard. He looked at his watch. "In about eight minutes. Why?"

"And you didn't think to mention it!" barked Puller.

Pritchard bristled. "You said the Ebola would be carried through our air ducts. No one mentioned anything about our fire suppression system."

"We don't have time for a pissing contest," snapped Knox.

Puller said, "You have sprinkler systems throughout the building?"

Pritchard pointed to the ceiling. They all looked up and saw a metal sprinkler head. "It was part of the renovation that was taking place before 9/11. Ironically, the part that got hit by the plane had been the first to be renovated. It's the primary reason the building didn't immediately collapse when the jet hit it. We had exponentially strengthened the structure. God

was looking out for us that day, despite everything."

"Well, let's hope he's on duty today too," said
Puller.

"But, Puller," exclaimed Knox. "You can't
deploy an aerosolized weapon through a sprinkler system."

"We just *assumed* that it was aerosolized because everyone said it was. Johnson said they
hadn't even started to examine the canisters that
Aust found. They don't know what's in there.
But you can carry water as well as air inside
canisters. And you don't have monitors on the
sprinkler system, do you?"

Pritchard shook his head. "Water is water. It
comes from a dedicated pipe for the fire suppression system."

"So it's separate from the drinking water?"
said Puller.

"Yes. It only goes to the sprinkler system. It
was designed that way so we wouldn't have to
worry about not having enough water pressure
in the event of a fire."

"Well, maybe today water isn't just water.
And water will actually cover everyone better
then sending it through the air ducts," noted
Knox. She looked up at the sprinkler head.
"The water will go everywhere, contaminate

every surface. Get into every opening in someone's skin or eyes or mouth. It'll be a nightmare. And but for us being here they'd never know they were getting hit with Ebola instead of just H_2O."

Rinehart said, "But how would they tie it into the pipe? And how will they turn it on?"

"The second answer is easy," said Puller. "And maybe the first answer too. When the fire drill starts, an alarm will go off, right?"

Pritchard nodded. "Correct. The alarm will sound."

"And people will have to evacuate?"

"Can we hurry this up?" barked Knox, but Puller held up his hand, waiting for Pritchard's answer.

"No. It would be too disruptive for a simple drill. Folks are supposed to report to certain areas that they would go to in preparation for evacuation. There they'll get a rundown on what to do and where to evacuate in the event of an actual emergency."

"Okay, but the sprinklers won't come on?"

"No, of course not," replied Pritchard.

Puller said, "Well, this time I think they will. The alarm goes off and the water turns on. People would just think it was some mechanical error. Or maybe an actual fire that just happened to occur. Or maybe some electrical short with the fire alarm system."

Knox added, "And lots of them might go home, change clothes."

"And contaminate thousands of more people, who would in turn contaminate thousands more," said Puller. "And the Pentagon would be contaminated for years. It would be unusable. No one would want to come back in here. Have to hand it to these bastards, they did think this through."

Rinehart said, "We have less than seven minutes, Puller!"

Puller grabbed Pritchard by the arm. "Where is the intake pipe?"

"This way! We'll be there in three minutes."

They jumped into the carts and sped off. People walking down the halls turned to stare after them, obviously sensing that something was amiss.

As they drove along Rinehart said anxiously, "People are starting to get nervous, Puller."

"They can be nervous. We just have to stop them from being dead."

"But should we evac—"

"General, for all I know they have eyes on this place. We start a mass exodus and they could accelerate what they're planning. Unless you know of a way to sneak thousands of people out of this building."

Rinehart shut his mouth and stared ahead, his brow sweaty and his eyes full of worry.

When Pritchard unlocked the door to the large water main room, Puller and the others began frantically searching the space. Puller found it, cleverly concealed in some metal framework built around the massive water pipe supplying the sprinkler system. The three silver canisters had been attached to the pipe such that they would feed directly into the water going to the sprinklers.

"How often do they check this area?" asked Puller.

"I'm not sure," said Pritchard. "Probably not that often. There would be no need to more than perhaps monthly."

"Even though there's a fire drill today?" said Knox.

"It's only a drill. No one expects water or the sprinklers to come on. They just want to test the alarms and make sure people follow the evac plan. The alarm control center is located in another part of the building."

"Should we just pull the canisters off?" said Rinehart.

Puller shook his head. "It'll take too long.

And they might be booby-trapped. In fact, I'd be stunned if they weren't."

"What if we cancel the drill," suggested Rinehart.

"It won't matter, sir," said Puller. "I'm sure what they plan to do will happen regardless."

"But if the Ebola virus has been placed in water, maybe it's been diluted," said Rinehart.

Knox said, "Johnson also said that one drop of liquid laced with Ebola getting into the body is all it takes to kill you."

"Where's the water shutoff?" asked Puller.

"Over there," said Pritchard.

They rushed to the corner. Knox saw it first.

"They sabotaged it," she said. "They broke off the lever."

"We can call the water company and see if they can turn it off at their end," said Pritchard.

"Good luck with customer service," said Puller. "We'll all be dead from Ebola and you'll still be on hold listening to a Bee Gees song."

"We have to do something," barked Rinehart. "We've only got minutes left."

Puller kept looking around the space. "The virus can't infect people so long as the sprinkler system doesn't come on."

"But they must have arranged a way for it to

come on," snapped Rinehart. "Otherwise all of this is pointless."

Puller turned to him. "I understand that, sir. But if we find out how they plan to turn on the system and neutralize it, then we can deal with the canisters safely later." He looked at Pritchard.

"Can they activate it remotely, via a computer?"

"No. That would be a bad design if someone could do it remotely when a fire hasn't been detected. It would cause a lot of water damage."

Rinehart had a sudden thought. "But can you disable the sprinkler system remotely? I mean by using the computer controls?"

Pritchard shook his head. "Negative, sir. Again, that's a safety feature. We wouldn't want someone hacking in and disabling the system. Then if a fire did start there would be nothing to combat it with."

Puller kept looking around. "The best way to engage the sprinkler system is to start a fire. Flames and smoke will set off the alarm *and* the sprinklers."

Knox said, "That's obvious enough. But where? Like Pritchard said, this is a really big place."

"Well, it would have to be somewhere that

people didn't frequent. Otherwise, someone might discover it and report it."

Pritchard said, "What if the folks are in the building right now? And they're going to engage it directly?'

"I doubt they would want to be here if they're going to unleash Ebola-contaminated water," said Puller.

"Right. They'd want to be as far away as possible," said Rinehart.

"Just like I would," muttered Knox.

Puller looked at Pritchard. "If the sprinklers do come on, will it be all over the Pentagon? Even if the source of the fire is small or contained in a particular area?"

"The sprinkler system is on zones," replied Pritchard. "For example, because this room houses the water main for the sprinkler system, a fire here will trigger a very large deployment of water, the theory being if the fire knocked out the water supply for the sprinkler system you want to wet down as much of the place as possible before that happens." He pointed upward. "And right above us is the E Ring. Lots of senior people up there. They'd definitely get hit with the water."

Puller kept looking around. "They took a risk bringing this shit in here. But getting to one place is easier than getting to a second place. You risk getting stopped and your whole plan unravels. But this room is the key. A fire here triggers a ton of water like Pritchard said."

"Here?" said Rinehart.

"Yes. If they could go to *one* room to do everything they needed to do, they would probably opt for that."

As Puller walked around the room his gaze drifted upward.

"There," he called out. He was pointing to the ceiling in a darkened corner about forty feet from the water pipe. "Best place to set the igniter is right here where the canisters and water supply intake are."

"We've got two minutes, Puller," warned Rinehart.

"Looks to be a large burn pack," said Puller as Knox joined him. "They probably figured that would be all they needed. It won't reach the water pipe and disrupt the sprinkler system. But it'll have a hot flash point, lots of smoke and fire. And the fire will eventually burn this room up enough that it'll take a long time for them to find those extra tanks. By then nearly everybody and everything in this place could be contaminated."

"Well, rip it down and let's get it out of here," barked Rinehart.

"Sir, when it detonates we're still going to be in this building no matter how fast we push the golf carts. And the blast will still set off the sprinklers wherever we are. We have to disable it *here*. Now."

He slid a pocketknife from his pocket and handed it to Knox. "Get on my shoulders."

"What?"

He spun her around, gripped her hips, bent down, and hoisted her over his head, settling her seated on his shoulders with her legs on either side of his head facing the same way he was.

"Tell me what you see," said Puller.

"A black box with an LED timer."

"What's the timer at?"

"Twenty seconds and counting."

Pritchard said, "Just pull out the detonator from the pack."

Puller barked, "They're not stupid. That'll just accelerate the detonation."

"He's right," said Rinehart, his voice strained. "Shit, we're nearly out of time."

"How many wires?" asked Puller.

"Two. One red, one black."

"Are they both single-strand?"

"The red is a double."

"The dummy, probably. You cut that it accelerates the time to zero, and boom."

"Probably!" snapped Rinehart. "You don't know for sure? We don't have time for probably, Puller."

Puller barked, "Cut the red one, Knox."

"But you just said that was the dummy."

"Cut the red one. Now!"

"Are you—"

"Puller," yelled Rinehart. "We're out of—"

"Now, Knox," shouted Puller. "Do it!"

She cut the red one and closed her eyes.

There was a pop, a fizzle, and everyone held their collective breath.

Knox finally opened her eyes and was staring at a burn pack that had failed to burn. She exhaled and gasped, "Thank you, sweet Jesus."

"Right," said Puller, after he let out his breath too.

She looked down at him from her high perch. "We did it. Mission accomplished."

Puller shook his head. "No. Not so long as Susan Reynolds and Anton Bok walk the earth."

The next moment the fire alarm went off. Thankfully, the sprinklers did not.

69

PULLER SAT IN a chair and stared over at his brother. Robert had been filled in on what had happened at the Pentagon.

Knox sat between them on the edge of the bed. It was dark outside. Rain was falling. Knox's hands shook a bit.

"The sound of the damn rain makes me think about what could have happened at the Pentagon today," she said.

"The biohazard squad managed to detach the canisters from the water pipe," said Puller. "They're cleaning everything up, checking it all out."

"So *did* they change the aerosolized Ebola to a water-based bioweapon?" asked Robert.

"I don't know, Bobby," Puller said wearily, rubbing his face. "They're figuring it all out. The threat has been neutralized, but the problem isn't solved."

"Because of Reynolds and Bok," Robert replied.

Knox added, "Everyone is looking for them. They won't be able to hide for long."

"Don't be too sure of that," said Puller in a cautioning tone. "They've managed to do just about everything they wanted to so far."

"Except kill everyone in the Pentagon," she shot back.

"Where do you think they might be?" asked Robert.

"Well, they don't strike me as the types to just walk away from a fight, especially after we screwed up their plan," said Puller.

"So they hang around to try to do something else. A Plan B?"

Puller shrugged. "A guess would only be that—a guess." He quieted and gazed solemnly across at his brother. "It's time, Bobby."

"Time for what?" said Knox quickly.

"To turn myself in," answered Robert quietly.

Knox shot Puller an incredulous glance. "What? Are you crazy?"

Puller said, "There's no other way, Knox."

She stood. "Listen to yourself. We still don't have proof that he's innocent. They'll put him right back in DB. And this time he won't get back out."

"My brother's right," said Robert.

"So you're just going to waltz in and surrender?"

"Not exactly," said Puller. "Groundwork needs to be laid."

"What sort of groundwork?" asked Knox.

"You ask a lot of questions," said Puller.

"I usually do when I don't get any answers," she retorted.

Robert said, "How do you want to do this, Junior?"

Puller rose. "I'll need a little time to put the pieces together. Stay put."

Knox stood. "I'm coming with you."

"You don't have to," he said.

"I'm quite aware of that. It's my choice to come with you."

"I can plead my brother's case."

She smiled demurely. "I never said you couldn't. But it's always better to have someone with you who can talk out of both sides of her mouth. And suffice it to say, I can."

"You mean *lie*," said Puller.

"I mean present the best case possible using whatever facts or near facts are handy." She held up her car keys. "Let's go."

* * *

After what had happened at the Pentagon, Rinehart saw them at once. Puller spoke for twenty minutes. Then Knox did so for another five.

When she fell silent, Rinehart said nothing. He sat there in his chair, his large hands clasped together and resting on his desk.

More than once Knox glanced at Puller, but he simply sat there watching Rinehart.

Finally, the three-star cleared his throat and said, "I can't say I approve of what you've done, because I don't. You were tasked to bring Robert Puller in, not to work with him. You disobeyed that order."

"I did, sir."

"For that you could be court-martialed. By harboring a fugitive you could be sent to DB."

"I could, sir."

"Where is he?"

"At a motel in Virginia."

"And you say he's been helping you?"

"He was the one who pinpointed the Pentagon as the target. But for him—"

Rinehart interjected, "The virus would have been unleashed. Thousands of people would have died. This country's military leadership would have been decimated."

"All true," said Knox, glancing anxiously at

both men. "I think he's more than redeemed himself."

"It's not a question of redemption," barked Rinehart. "It's a question of the law." He looked at Puller. "You need to bring him in. Right now."

"I'll do so under one condition."

Rinehart gave him a molten look. "You're in no position to lay out conditions, Puller."

"One condition."

"I know what you've done, soldier. You've risked your life to save lives. But you are dancing perilously close to the edge."

"You need to give my brother protection."

"Protection?"

"He can't go back to DB. Not yet."

Knox said, "They're still out there, sir. Reynolds and Bok and God knows who else. They got into the Pentagon. They have spies, it seems, everywhere. They will know that Robert Puller blew up their plan."

"Well, so did the two of you. If he needs protection, so do you both."

Knox looked at Puller. "It might not be a bad idea, at least for a little while," she said.

"And what about Reynolds and Bok?"

"We're going to get them, Puller," replied Rinehart. "We have thousands of agents looking for them. We have every possible way in and out of this country covered. They won't get away." He paused. "I'll match your condition with my own. You two will join your brother in protection. That way you stay safe and we can have time to sort this out. You've done enough."

"I don't like this," said Puller. "I owe these people, sir. I owe them a counterattack with everything I have."

"I understand that, soldier. But the three stars on my shoulders mean I outrank you by a landslide. And you will stand down. Because I order you to. And I'm not in the habit of repeating myself. Do you understand?"

When Puller didn't acknowledge this, Knox grabbed his arm. "Puller, it's the only way. You don't have a choice. You can't throw everything away now. You've fought too hard."

Puller looked away for a moment and then swung his gaze back to Rinehart.

"I understand, sir."

70

GENERAL RINEHART SAT across from Robert Puller at the safe house where they were being kept. It was a three-bedroom house at the end of a cul-de-sac in a Maryland neighborhood that had suffered multiple foreclosures during the economic collapse. That made it isolated, but also more secure. The safe house itself had a perimeter security force and also personnel in the house. A chopper did a pass over the area every two hours.

Rinehart was in uniform; Robert Puller was in jeans and a sweatshirt. Yet the men seemed on roughly equal footing.

Rinehart said to Robert, "I want to believe that you are innocent of all charges, Puller. I don't want to see you go back to DB. But that's not up to me."

"I understand, sir."

Puller and Knox hovered in the background, listening intently.

Rinehart said, "I'll be frank with you. Despite what I've been told you did to avoid disaster at the Pentagon, there is no solid evidence to overturn your conviction."

"I understand that too, sir."

"And yet you turned yourself in?"

"My brother suggested it, and I agreed. It was never my intent to escape and disappear. I had never planned on escaping, but the opportunity presented itself. Once on the outside my goal was to both prove my innocence and then try to undo the damage that the real traitors had wrought."

"Meaning Reynolds."

"Well, she's the only one still left alive. Daughtrey and Robinson are dead. And they were coerced into betraying their country. She did it voluntarily. Then there's Anton Bok, but he's a Russian operative who turned Reynolds."

"It's still hard to believe."

"I take it she didn't show up for work at DTRA?"

Rinehart shook his head. "No, she didn't. Her house is empty. It seems that she's made a run for it."

Puller said, "After we stopped their plot at the Pentagon, that would make sense."

"But that still doesn't prove your innocence."

"No, it doesn't. Not directly. But I hope that there's enough doubt there now to allow for at least a new trial."

"Again, that's not up to me, but I will exercise whatever influence I have to see that that happens."

"I appreciate that, sir," said Puller.

"It's stunning that we would have a spy so highly placed. And that she managed to kill Daughtrey, Schindler, and Carter."

Robert nodded. "She's certainly capable. And she's not acting alone. Bok is also very capable. He was able to secure a position in the foreign military program at Leavenworth. He was able to get an assassin onto the base. I believe that he was instrumental in the plot involving the Pentagon."

"So it's Russia behind this?" said Rinehart.

"It may be that Bok is acting for a third party, but from things that Reynolds told us, I think that he might be working for Mother Russia, yes."

"That would fit in with what they have been doing lately," said Rinehart.

"Exerting a thirst for regional dominance. And if Bok is working for the Russians, that means that Reynolds is too. She's not the grand planner type. But she's good at executing others' plans. I found that out when I worked with her at STRATCOM."

Knox said, "I believe that a military tribunal would acquit you now."

Robert looked up at her. "My escape won't earn me any points, but once I explain why, I would like to think they would understand."

Puller added, "I think a more serious concern right now is making sure you stay alive."

Rinehart looked a little skeptical. "Do you really think they'll try something? I would have to believe they're more likely to try to get to Moscow."

"Having seen Reynolds up close, I would say that the woman hates to lose. And when she does, she will exact retribution. And the simple fact is she hates my brother. You don't want her for an enemy. Just ask her dead husband."

"You really think she had a hand in that?" said Rinehart a little skeptically.

"I think she had both hands and both feet in it," replied Puller firmly.

Rinehart rose. "Well, I will put things in motion. There will be a lot of hoops to jump through, and there are no guarantees."

"I never expected that there would be," said Robert.

After Rinehart left, Puller sat down next to his brother. "It'll work out, Bobby."

"Don't sugarcoat, Junior. We both know how

bad it is. It's all well and good to sit here and talk to Rinehart about things. But judges and lawyers want facts. They want irrefutable evidence to overturn a conviction. And I don't see how we have that."

"Well, there's one way to get that irrefutable evidence," said Puller.

"How?"

"Find Reynolds and make her tell the truth."

"Well, they have lots of people looking for her," pointed out Robert.

"I don't think they'll track her down," said Knox.

"We could find her," said Puller.

They looked at him.

Knox said, "How? We're stuck in a safe house."

"There's one person I haven't talked to," said Puller.

"Who?" asked his brother.

"Susan Reynolds's daughter. She might have a clue as to where her mom is."

"But how can you go and talk to her?" asked Robert.

"By walking out the door and going to talk to her."

And John Puller rose and did just that.

71

PULLER WALKED INTO the clothes shop around closing time. The young woman behind the counter looked up.

"Can I help you? I'm just about to lock the door."

"I called before and asked to see you? John Puller?" He flashed his badge. "You're Audrey Reynolds?"

"Oh, right," said the woman, frowning. "Yes, I'm Audrey. Give me a sec."

She walked over to the front door and hung the closed sign in the window and then locked it. She glanced up at Puller.

"I'm not really sure what I can tell you."

"Nothing too complicated. I've spoken with your brother. Now I'd like to talk to you." He looked around the shop. To him the items all looked designed for very young women who wanted to look borderline slutty. "How's business?"

"Fine," she said. "Look, do we really have to do this?"

"It *is* important," he replied.

She wasn't as tall as her mother and her body was thicker, sturdier. She must take after her father, he thought. Her shoulder-length brown hair rode loosely on her shoulders. Her face was pretty, but she looked tired. She must be, he concluded, after a long day on her feet performing the retail dance.

Audrey sighed. "Okay. Let's at least sit down. I have a little office in the back room."

They walked in there and sat at a small oval table.

"You want some coffee?" she asked.

"No thanks."

She rose, poured herself a cup of coffee from a pot on the counter, and sat down across from him.

"Okay, what do you want to know?"

"Have you seen your mother recently?"

Audrey took a sip of her coffee and said, "About a week ago. We had dinner."

"What'd you talk about?"

"Stuff. Personal stuff. Business stuff. She helps me with this place. We meet from time to time to go over the status of things."

"So she has the financial resources to do that?"

"Look, I'm sure you've checked her out. You know she got an insurance payout when my father was killed. She invested really well. She's not super rich but she doesn't have to worry about money. And she's very generous with me."

"It's a nice shop."

"Thanks. I've always wanted my own business. And I'm really into fashion design. My mom cares about my dreams."

"I understand that she traveled overseas a lot when you were young?"

"That's right. She helped dismantle nukes. Really good work, right?"

"Yes. Very important. So what do you remember about your father's death?"

She looked puzzled at the change in the direction of the questioning. "Why are you asking about that? It was a long time ago."

"Just getting as much background info as I can. It can be a drudge, but it's part of the process."

She nodded and cradled her coffee cup. "Not that much, really. I'd broken my leg. I remember being in a lot of pain. It was really hot. He went out, and then the next thing I knew the house was swarming with cops and FBI agents. My mother got home the next day and took care of everything. Like she always does."

"Have you spoken to her since you last saw her?"

"A couple of times."

"What did she say?"

Audrey blanched. "Look, it was personal."

"Okay, has she ever mentioned to you a man named Ivo Mesic or Anton Bok?"

"No."

"Have you ever seen this man?" He handed her a photo of Bok.

She gazed down at it while Puller watched her closely, looking for any sign of recognition. She handed the photo back. "No, I've never seen this guy. He doesn't look, I mean he doesn't look American. And those names aren't American."

"He's Russian."

"And you're saying my mother knows this guy?"

"She worked with him when they were verifying the reduction of nuclear warheads."

"So you mean when she was doing her *job*?" she said snidely.

"We know that your mother has a cabin in Rappahannock County, Virginia."

She looked genuinely surprised. "I didn't know about that."

"Do you know of any other properties that she has?"

"She has a condo at Wintergreen, the ski resort near Charlottesville."

"You have the address?"

She gave it to him and Puller wrote this down. "Okay. Anyplace else other than the home in Springfield?"

"Not that I know of."

"She ever mention to you any plans to leave the country?"

Audrey stood. "Look, what the hell is going on?"

Puller closed his notebook and stood. "I'm sorry to have to tell you that your mother is a suspected spy."

"That's bullshit! What proof do you have?"

"I'm afraid I can't tell you that."

"Because there *is* no proof."

"No child wants to believe something like this about a parent. But we are investigating her. I wouldn't be here otherwise."

"I don't believe you!"

Puller looked down at Audrey's cell phone lying on the table. "Why don't you try to call her now?"

"Why?"

"Just to check in. Say hello."

"Why, so you can like track the call?" she said accusingly.

"I don't have any equipment with me to trace the call. And you have to stay on the phone for a while to do it. Just say hello and tell her you'd like to see her sometime soon. That isn't a problem, is it, Audrey?"

"It's no problem," she said angrily. "But I don't feel like calling her, okay?"

"Audrey, this is a very serious matter. I don't want to believe that you're involved in this in any way. I just think you're caught in the middle of something that you shouldn't be. I want to help you get through this. So just call your mother. This is not about you. It's about her."

Keeping her eyes on Puller briefly, she slowly picked up her phone and punched in a number.

"Speakerphone, if you don't mind," said Puller.

She hit the button and put the phone down on the table. Puller could hear the phone ringing and then it went to voice mail. Reynolds's voice came on. Puller hit the end button and said, "If you do hear from her, please give me a call." He handed her one of his cards, which she reluctantly took.

"My mother has done nothing wrong!"

"Then she has nothing to worry about, does she?" said Puller.

Tears had started to spill down Audrey's cheeks. "You're a real shit, you know that! You think you can just walk in here and dump all this crap on me?" She looked ready to throw her coffee at him.

"Just call me, Audrey. When you talk to her."

Puller turned and left the shop, got into his car, and drove back to the safe house.

72

SUSAN REYNOLDS TURNED off the tracker device that was connected to the bug she had put on John Puller's vehicle while it was parked in front of her daughter's shop. She had followed the electronic signal to its destination.

Or almost to the end.

She had turned off two streets before Puller, but she had watched the dot on the tracker reach its destination. She drove off and reached the motel where she was staying under an alias. She had changed her appearance and was using cash for her room. She sent off a secure email with the street address of the safe house.

Several hours went by before her phone buzzed. She picked it up. It was Anton Bok.

"I've reconnoitered the area," he said. "It's definitely a safe house. Five exterior security. My heat imager recorded five inside. Probably John Puller, Knox, and Robert Puller plus two interior security."

"That makes *nine* security counting John Puller and Knox," she said.

"Formidable, but not impossible," said Bok calmly. "However, we can leave it. Live to fight another day."

She shook her head and smiled. "Anton, our fighting days are over. But we've had a good run. Over twenty years. The Pentagon obviously didn't work, but just about every-thing else did. It's a record to be proud of. We served our leaders very well. We were the best operatives they've ever had. The idiots never suspected me all those years. Not until now."

"My country is proud, Susan. Very proud of me. And you. And they will welcome us with open arms."

"But there is unfinished business," she said.

"Unfinished," he agreed. "Robert Puller."

"I've grown to detest his brother almost as much."

"Then two birds with one stone," said Bok.

"Three counting Knox. I'm not forgetting her. Private wings standing by?"

"At a moment's notice. We can be in Russia by tomorrow. We have a medal to give you."

"I would much prefer an evening with you."

"We will have many of those. There is a very

nice dacha near Saint Petersburg that will be ours. It has a garden."

"I like gardens. But the recon?"

"The house is at the end of a cul-de-sac. The front door faces straight onto the road. The houses on either side of it are empty. The exterior patrols are staggered. There is a garage so the cars are loaded and unloaded inside."

"And my shooting spot?"

"There is a wonderful site for you. A knoll rises to the west at the very end of the street in the opposite direction of the safe house. They have demolished the house that once stood there, so the sightline is unobstructed. Twelve hundred meters approximately, with a nice angled bullet flight down to the target."

"I've done longer in my sleep."

"As I know. You must be quick about it, though. Getting you out will be the hardest part."

"I don't intend on lingering. It's not like I'll have to shoot them one by one."

"I will be there personally to retrieve you."

"And then off to Russia?"

"And then off to our new life of peace."

* * *

At three o'clock in the morning Susan Reynolds set up her sniper's nest on the knoll after Anton Bok had confirmed that it was clear. From her carrying case she slid out her favorite weapon. It was a Barrett M82, designated in the U.S. military as the M107. This was a specially configured M107, a special-application scoped rifle, which could fire a unique round.

Using this weapon a member of the United States Army had shot and killed an adversary in 2008 from over two thousand meters. The current world record for a combat kill over distance was held by a Brit. He'd killed an Afghan from nearly twenty-five hundred meters away.

Reynolds's shot would be from a much lesser distance, but it still required an enormous degree of skill. And she had the best technology to aid her, including a laser rangefinder, the best long-range optics, a portable meteorological device, and state-of-the-art ballistic-prediction software.

But really she only required her scope and her gun. It literally would be like hitting the broad side of a barn. She had an auto loader to feed ammo to the M107. She pulled out one of the rounds and examined it. The fifty-caliber cartridge had a green tip with a gray ring around it. It was known in the field as a "combined effects" cartridge.

She replaced the round, set up her rifle, lay down behind it, and settled in. The detachable muzzle brake was at the end of the barrel. That diminished the recoil kick. Her rear grip had a monopod socket. The bipod feet were spiked for better traction in the ground.

She powered up her scope and sighted through it. She performed a sweep with the gun, taking in points to the left and right of the target before she swung it back straight and true and focused on the safe house.

The last patrol had passed by minutes before. It was dark inside the house. They must be asleep by now. She could see no silhouettes moving through the structure. Well, they would never know what had hit them.

She exhaled a long breath, got her heartbeat within the acceptable range and her physiological status to cold zero. But really she knew she could hardly miss at this range and with this particular target. Not with the ammo she was chambering.

She fired once and the round flew dead on before colliding with the side of the house. The cartridge was an HEIAP, which stood for high explosive incendiary/armor-piercing ordnance. The fifty-caliber round had a thirty-caliber tungsten penetrator built into it. It could blast through tank armor, brick walls, and concrete blocks. Wood siding and drywall thus did not pose much of a challenge.

The Comp A explosive embedded in the cartridge detonated on impact, taking out the entire front of the house. The natural gas supply in the house ignited on top of it, taking the roof off and catching both empty houses on either side of it on fire.

Reynolds fired again and took out the security van in front of the house. All four wheels lifted off the ground as the van disintegrated. She fired again at the house and another explosion rocked the night. Another wall of the house fell inward. The interior was completely on fire. Another explosion hit the structure, collapsing the brick chimney.

Reynolds waited patiently to see if anyone came running out of the house. If so, they would eat a fifty-cal round directly. It would pass right through them and explode on the other side.

She fired three more times, taking out all the other security vehicles. One landed directly in the middle of the road, blocking access. Flames and smoke covered the ground and pushed upward, filling the night sky like a wildfire run amok.

Since Reynolds could no longer see her targets, she decided she was done for the night. Anyone in the house would be dead. It was a nonsurvivable attack. Now there was only a car ride to the jet and her new life in Russia could get started.

She was just about to get up from behind her weapon when the round slammed into her left shoulder.

At first she was in such shock that she didn't realize she had been shot. The bullet had gone right through her and struck the dirt. Her collarbone was shattered and her rotator cuff destroyed. She was bleeding, but the bullet had struck her with such force that her wound was mostly cauterized and the blood loss was minimal.

Nauseous from the shock of being shot, Reynolds struggled to her feet, holding her useless arm. She looked frantically around to see from where the shot had come. But all she saw was darkness. Leaving her weapon behind, she started to stumble down the path that would carry her to the car where Bok was waiting. Behind her she heard someone coming. She tried to run in the opposite direction, but the person was moving far more swiftly than she could manage.

Reynolds looked back and stumbled over a bush and fell to the ground screaming in pain.

She turned over and looked up.

John Puller stared down at her, his sniper rifle over his shoulder and his pistol pointed at her.

When she saw who it was, she screamed, "I've been shot!"

"I know. I was the one who shot you."

"You bastard. You miserable bastard!"

He ignored this and spoke into his walkie-talkie. "Send a stretcher. Top of the knoll. Got a GSW. Non-life-threatening. No need to rush."

"I will kill you. I swear to God." She tried to kick at him, but missed. She fell back moaning and clutching her arm.

He knelt down beside her. "There's one key difference between the Olympics and combat, Susan. You might have overlooked it." He paused. "In the Olympics, no one is shooting back at you."

73

WITH THEIR GUNS out, Knox and Robert approached the car parked off a back road. The security forces guarding them had fanned out looking for Anton Bok, but Knox and Robert had stayed together and broken off in this direction while the others had headed to other areas. Knox reached the car first and peered inside.

It was empty.

"Look out!" yelled Robert. "On your six."

Knox leapt over the hood a split second before machine-gun fire raked the front of the car, blowing out the front tire and destroying the headlight on that side.

As Knox hit the ground hard on the other side of the car her gun popped out of her hand.

Robert fired at the gunman, but Bok had already taken cover behind a tree. He stepped out and unloaded again, spraying shots at the spot from where Robert had fired. Bark and leaves were blown off trees.

But that was all, because Robert was no longer there.

Bok took up cover once more and then moved to a new spot.

Knox slid on her belly and snagged her gun. She did a turkey peek over the car and fired a handful of shots in Bok's direction.

None of the rounds found their target because Bok was on the move again. He circled around, intending to come at Knox from her exposed flank.

She deduced this and fast-crawled to the rear of the car.

Bok stepped clear of the trees a moment later and raked the car with fire. The tires on that side deflated and one of the rounds struck the fuel tank. Gas started to splash onto the road.

Bok took a moment to reload his weapon.

Robert called out, "Move, Knox! The gas!"

She looked back at him, then at the gas, then over at where Bok had been.

She turned to run as Robert stepped out into the clearing at the same time that Bok did.

Both men fired at the same time.

Bok had reloaded with incendiary rounds. When his round hit the gas tank the Ford sedan exploded.

A small but still lethal chunk of the car came

swirling at Robert. He tried to duck, but the metal caught him in the arm, slicing it open and knocking the gun out of his hand. Staggered, he grabbed his bloody limb and looked around desperately for Knox.

"Knox!"

There was no answer.

He looked across the way as the smoke started to lift. Through the flames eating at the car he saw Bok standing there, his gun pointed directly at him.

"Susan's been shot. She's in custody," Robert called out.

Bok said nothing to this. He walked forward. He fired a round at Robert's feet. And then another. Robert backed away holding his arm.

Bok walked forward. "Then I have nothing left to live for, do I?"

"That's your choice," said Robert.

"I have no idea how someone like you could be so, how do you say, fortunate," said Bok. "Susan was far more talented. Far more dedicated. She cared far more than you ever would."

"For the *Russians*."

"I made her see the light. That was my job."

"And *her* job was not to turn traitor. On that I'd say she failed spectacularly. And, by the way, we totally kicked her ass."

"Your country has had its day. It's time for new world leaders. The Stars and Stripes are done. She could see that clearly, even if the likes of you could not."

"And you think Russia will fill that void?" said Robert incredulously. "You've got a shirtless leader, an economy totally based on fossil fuels, and a military that can't even control its own nukes. Not a recipe for domination. More likely a rapid decline."

Bok stopped a few feet from Robert and then looked to the side. "Tell her that," he said, indicating something with his gun barrel.

Robert looked where he was pointing.

Knox lay in the grass under the trees, the side of her head bleeding. Her breathing was ragged, her chest heaving.

Robert's lip trembled. "You're never going to make it out of here alive, Bok."

Bok said nothing.

Robert said, "You can kill me too. But you just blew up your only way out of here."

"As I said, it doesn't matter to me anymore. Not with Susan gone. We were in love, you know."

"I seriously doubt people as twisted as the two of you could possibly love anything."

Bok raised his gun and pointed it at Robert's head. "This is for Susan."

From the corner of his eye Robert saw Knox slowly sit up, her gun in her hand. She fired. A shot hit Bok smack in the middle of the head. He dropped where he stood.

Robert looked back over his shoulder. Knox's shot had sailed wide of its mark. The other shot had not.

John Puller was just lowering his sniper rifle. At this close range it was a devastating weapon against flesh, bone, and brains.

"And that was for my brother," he said to the dead man.

Behind him came an EMT squad with medical equipment and a gurney. They raced past where Bok lay and over to Knox. Puller hustled over to his brother and examined his bloody arm.

"How bad?" he asked.

"Not bad. I'll make it. Take care of Knox. She's not good."

Puller called one of the EMTs over. The man sat Robert down and started to treat his wound.

Puller sprinted over to where Knox lay back in the grass and knelt down next to her. Two EMTs had already started to triage her.

She looked up at Puller and said, "Did I get him? Did I get Bok?"

"You nailed the prick. He's dead."

She smiled weakly and touched her head. "Hurts like a bitch. Worse than my hip."

"I know. These guys here are going to take care of that."

"Am I going to make it?"

"There is no doubt that you will."

"Are you lying to me?"

"I've never really lied to you, Knox."

She reached out and gripped his hand. "Your brother okay?"

"Good to go. Focus on yourself."

"Hurts like shit."

Puller stared over at one of the EMTs. "Can you do something about that? Like right now?"

The EMT said, "Trying, sir. It's..."

Puller turned back to Knox. "We'll get your mother to come up and stay with you while you recover."

"You don't want to stay with me?" she mumbled.

"I meant all of us. I'd like to meet her."

"I think...I think you'd like her."

"If she's anything like you, I'm sure I will."

"We got her, Puller. This time we got her."

"Yes, we got her. We got them both."

"Hurts like hell, John."

He gripped her hand more tightly. "You're going to be fine, Veronica."

"You're a good man, John Puller. A damn good man."

Knox slowly closed her eyes.

CHAPTER

74

PULLER OPENED THE door, closed it behind him, and sat down at the small table across from her. He dropped the file folder he was carrying on the table.

Susan Reynolds was in an orange prison jumpsuit and her hands and feet were in shackles. Her left arm and shoulder were encased in a cast. She stared impassively across the width of the wood at him.

"How are the accommodations, Susan?" he asked.

"Lovely. Haven't been this comfortable in years."

He glanced at the cast. "The docs have instructions to go easy on the painkillers. They don't want you to get addicted."

"I was sure I had you to thank for that."

"Sorry about Anton. He unfortunately lost his head back at the safe house."

Reynolds simply stared at him.

He opened the folder. "Since I can barely stand to breathe the same air as you, let's get down to it." He slid a document across to her.

She didn't even look at it. "What is it?" she asked in an indifferent tone.

"A confession. A detailed confession not only to what you've done recently but to what you did to frame my brother. All you have to do is sign it."

"And all you have to do is slide it in a shredder after you leave, because I'm signing nothing."

He leaned back in his chair. "You sign the confession the death penalty goes off the table."

"Lethal injection? Bring it on. You murdered Anton. What do I care about living one second longer?"

"I didn't murder him. I shot him before he murdered others."

"Your version of the truth. I'll stick with mine. So your leverage is less than zero, Puller. Kill me. Get it over with. And your brother can go back to rotting in jail. Even with all that's happened now, there is no evidence to overturn his conviction. I'll think about that when they put the needle in my arm. And I'm sure it will bring a smile to my lips as I say goodbye to this miserable world."

"Even though you set him up, framed him? He's innocent. You know that."

She looked bored now. "How many surveillance devices in here, I wonder? Three? Ten?" She said in a raised voice, "For the record, Robert Puller is guilty as sin. He stole classified information. He met with a known Iranian spy. He was working with me to bring down the U.S. government. He is scum. I will testify to this in exchange for a deal that will allow me to live peacefully and quietly in a minimum-security prison *with* the possibility of parole in five years."

She turned back to Puller and smiled tauntingly. "One always has to have a backup plan." She paused, studying him. "You ever wonder where that text came from telling you not to trust Knox?"

Now Puller remained silent, waiting.

"I sent it."

"Why, if you believed she was working with you?"

"Because I didn't really believe it. I don't trust anyone. No one. Except Anton. And I'm very much into divide and conquer. If you two killed each other off, so much the better."

"What was it like to plan your husband's murder?"

She said derisively, "I was in Russia thousands of miles away."

"Yeah, Russia, your adopted country. But I wonder where your boyfriend Anton was?"

"Well, we'll never know, since you murdered him."

"Your son knew you did it. He told me so. He called me after your arrest. Thanked me for bringing him closure."

"Poor Danny was always a little slow on the uptake. And he spent too much time in fantasyland. And he was way too much of a daddy's boy. He has no balls of his own."

"He's an FBI attorney with a very impressive conviction record."

"Do you think I really care?"

"My point is you didn't fool him."

"And my answer would be exactly the same. I don't give a crap."

"Did you orchestrate my kidnapping in Kansas?"

She nodded. "Whether you told us what you knew or said you would stand down, we would have killed you. We were just toying with you. It's the style that counts. Anton and I have a lot of that. Other people would have just shot you."

"Well, your 'style' gave my brother the opportunity to save my life."

She shifted in her seat and used her chin to rub at a spot near her injured shoulder. "I *would* like to know how you pulled it off," she said. "How did you figure we were going to hit the safe house?"

"Dan told me you were tight with your daughter. So I went to see Audrey. I knew she'd call you after I phoned to set up the appointment. You would have tailed me back to the safe house."

"But I blew it up. Incendiary rounds."

"But we weren't in the house."

"I saw you go inside. And you didn't come back out. Anton was watching the back. He would have seen you."

"That safe house has been in the system a long time and consequently has been retrofitted. There's an escape hatch in the back bedroom that leads to a tunnel that in turn leads to a house four doors down. All the houses around there are empty, so it was easy to do. You hit the right house, but at the wrong time, because there was no one in it. The exterior security took the same path. We didn't want to have anyone in harm's way when you opened fire with your *Olympian* sniper skills."

"And your shooting me?"

"I figured that knoll would provide the best

firing line for you. So I waited about a hundred yards away facing that point. When I saw your muzzle flash I waited for you to finish firing and pulled the trigger."

"You're not as good a shot as you think. At a hundred yards I would have nailed my target ten times out of ten." She indicated her casted arm and shoulder. "You only managed to wound me."

"I've killed people from farther away than your shot that night, Susan. And they *were* shooting back at me. But I didn't kill you because I didn't *want* to kill you. I just wanted to injure you. And I did, incapacitating you at the same time."

She scoffed. "I don't believe that."

"I'm a soldier. I do this for a living."

She barked, "Why the hell would you want to keep me alive? You had no problem killing poor Anton."

"I didn't need *poor* Anton alive. But I needed you alive."

"Why?"

He glanced down at the piece of paper still resting between them. "Because I need you to sign this." He slipped a pen from his pocket and held it up. "I even took care to shoot you in your left arm, so you could sign it with your other hand. You're a righty."

"I have no incentive to sign anything. Certainly nothing that would help Robert Puller. He can rot in prison."

There was a TV bolted to one corner of the ceiling. Puller picked up a remote from the table and turned on the TV.

As the picture came on, Reynolds sat up straight.

"What the hell is this?"

Puller turned to look at the screen where Audrey Reynolds was sitting in a jail cell, dressed in an orange prison jumpsuit, sobbing and looking like she couldn't believe what had happened.

"She's been arrested and is awaiting arraignment," said Puller.

"Why?" snapped a stunned Reynolds. "What possible reason could—"

"As a coconspirator in a terrorist plot against the United States," interrupted Puller.

"She had nothing to do with any of this!"

He looked at her disdainfully. "Come on, Susan. You really expect us to believe that the daughter you were so tight with knew nothing? Even a newbie prosecutor could get a conviction on that. She phoned you right after I called her to set up a face-to-face."

"She called me, yes, but she didn't—"

Puller slammed his fist down on the table so hard that a part of the wood cracked. "Shut the hell up! And listen!"

Reynolds froze.

Puller leaned forward. "Here is how it's going to play out, *Susan*. Unless you sign this confession and provide whatever corroborating testimony is required to see that my brother is fully exonerated, you will be tried, convicted, and put to death." He pointed behind him at the screen. "At the same time your daughter will be tried, convicted, and sent to prison for the rest of her life *without* the possibility of parole. Not because of anything she did. Because of you. You are right on the edge of destroying your daughter's life, Susan."

"She knew nothing about any of this! I will testify to that."

"Do you think the higher-ups care about that?" he said. "And she screwed up big-time."

"You mean the phone call? That was nothing."

"We *listened* to the calls. Right, *calls*. Because she spoke to you again *after* I left the shop. After I told her you were suspected of being a spy. She not only enabled you to follow me right to the safe house, but it was clear on the phone call that she knew you were involved in something criminal. And your financing her dream business? A jury would easily believe that it was in payment for her helping you to spy on this country. And maybe even to launder funds. Terrorist funds. Because the Pentagon plan was not an act of war, it was an act of terrorism. And that makes everyone associated with it, American citizen or not, a terrorist. And that means many relevant legal rights go right out the window."

Reynolds's jaw tightened and she looked like she might be sick.

Puller continued, "She might not have known exactly what you and Bok were doing, but that's clearly enough to get her as an accessory to a terrorist act. Her life is over, Susan. Unless you do the right thing by your little girl."

"I...I can't..."

Puller slapped the table once more with the palm of his hand. "Let me just give it to you straight, Reynolds. I came in here principally to get my brother exonerated. But I also came in here to give you one last shot at saving Audrey. I believe she's innocent. And innocent people shouldn't go to prison. Like my brother! But this is a national security case and they are out for blood. You almost wrecked the military leadership of this country! So they are going after anyone within spitting distance of this thing. And that includes your daughter. The government lawyers are right outside that door waiting for your answer. If you don't sign this confession right now this deal goes away forever. And your little girl gets to spend the next sixty years of her life in a max federal prison. And it will be your fault and only yours. And you can take *that* thought to the death chamber with you."

Puller placed the pen on top of the confession and sat back watching her.

Reynolds stared at him for a moment longer before her gaze went back to her daughter on the screen.

"So you're going to coerce me, threaten me into a confession?" she said dully.

"No, I'm encouraging you as best I can to tell the truth. The facts that you will provide to corroborate the statements in the confession will leave no doubt as to your guilt. And if your testimony leads to other spies or traitors being caught, so much the better."

"And you think the Russians won't try to kill me if I do cooperate?" she shot back.

"Solitary confinement in a federal prison, Susan. We're the best friends you have right now. That's the only place they won't be able to get to you."

Slowly, very slowly, her right hand reached out and took up the pen. After she signed the document she looked at him. "You really are a heartless prick."

"That must be why we get along so well," he said back. "Because so are you."

He scooped up the paper and pen, rose, and walked out the door without once looking back.

75

PULLER ADJUSTED HIS tie and then slipped on his jacket. He buttoned it up, made sure every one of his decorations was in the proper place, and then picked up his cover and put it under his arm.

His brother was waiting for him in the kitchen, also in his dress uniform, his cap riding under his arm too. His other arm was still in a sling from the injury.

"You ready, Colonel Puller?"

"I'm still technically a major, Junior. Lieutenant colonel status hasn't come yet."

"Matter of time. Bet you're one of the youngest one-stars in Air Force history."

Robert plucked an errant thread off his brother's jacket. "We'll see. I've got two years' worth of catching up to do."

"You ready to head out?" asked Puller.

"Let's take a minute," said his brother.

Puller was surprised by this. "Not having second thoughts, are you?"

Robert sat down. "No, it's not that."

"What then?"

"Knox told me you talked to her about Mom."

Puller sat down, his features turning angry. "I told her that in confidence."

"Blame me, Junior. After that exchange I heard between you before she staged killing me, I asked her about what had happened between you two."

"Nothing happened," snapped Puller.

"But I take it something *could* have?"

Puller didn't answer right away. "Yes, it could have. But how does that tie into Mom?"

"Knox told me the most memorable moment from that night was your opening up about our mother. Knox had never seen that side of you. She told me it astonished her how sensitive, how loving you sounded when talking about Mom."

Puller said nothing to this. He just stared down at the floor.

Robert said, "I miss her too, Junior. Think about her every day. Wondering if she's still alive. And—"

Puller broke in, speaking forcefully. "And whether it was her choice to leave us?"

"What do you think?" asked Robert.

"I think," began Puller, "that it's one mystery I'll never solve."

Robert put a hand on his brother's shoulder. "Well, now you have me back to talk about it with. To talk about a lot of things. And you don't have to fly to Leavenworth to do it."

"A dream come true, Bobby. To have my big brother back."

Robert rose. "I was thinking the very same thing, little brother. Now let's go do this."

They drove north. Puller parked in the lot and the two brothers walked into the facility together, removing their caps as they did so. They walked down the hall. As they drew closer to their destination Robert slowed.

"Do you really think this is a good idea?" he said.

"Yes. And you did too, apparently, until about two seconds ago."

"I guess I'm just a little nervous."

"Join the crowd. I'm nervous every time I come here. I'd rather take on a convoy of damn Taliban."

Puller nudged his brother's elbow and they kept walking. Puller nodded at a nurse he knew.

She said, "He's up in his chair."

"Does he know we're coming?"

"I told him. Whether it registered or not, I don't know."

She looked up at Robert. "I'm glad you were able to come, sir."

"*Finally* able to come," said Robert.

Both brothers drew deep breaths and Puller opened the door and stepped in. Robert followed.

The door swung shut behind them and the two stood side by side in their pristine dress uniforms.

Across the room, in his chair, sat their father.

John Puller Sr. was dressed differently today. Usually his outfit consisted of a T-shirt and blue hospital scrub pants with slippers on his feet. His white hair was typically in disarray, his face unshaven.

This morning he had been shaved, his hair was combed, and he was dressed in pants and a collared shirt. Loafers were on his feet.

Robert looked at Puller, who was staring in amazement at his father.

"Something different today?" whispered Robert.

"Definitely," replied Puller.

"General," said Puller. "We're here reporting in, sir." He pushed Robert ahead of him. "I brought along a new man today. He'll be reporting in to you regularly now."

Puller Sr. turned to face them, though he didn't get out of his chair. His gaze moved up and down both men's uniforms before coming to rest on Robert's face.

"Name?" said Puller Sr.

Robert glanced at his brother and received an encouraging nod before saying, "Major Robert W. Puller, USAF."

Puller Sr. stared hard at him for a few moments before looking at his other son.

In that gaze, for the first time in a long time, Puller saw recognition. Not just seeing something. Recognition. He stepped forward and said softly, "Dad?"

Robert glanced sharply at Puller. His brother had filled him in on the subterfuge he normally employed with his father. Playing the role of XO to his father's three stars and head of a corps.

Puller took another hesitant step toward his father.

"Dad?"

Puller Sr. slowly rose from his chair. His legs trembled a bit and his knees creaked, but he finally righted himself and stood tall and firm. His gaze left his younger son and went back to his older boy.

He took a few halting steps toward Robert.

The old man's eyebrows were bunched together, the eyes sharp and penetrating. But at the edges Puller saw something he never had before, not even when his mother had disappeared: tears.

"B-Bob?"

When he heard the name, Puller reached out and touched the wall to keep himself upright.

Robert said in a quavering voice, "It's…me…Dad."

The old man crossed the room with surprising swiftness to stand in front of his son. He looked him up and down again, taking in all aspects of the uniform, his gaze coming to rest on the rows of decorations there. He reached out and touched one of them. Then his hand drifted up to his son's face. The hair had not yet grown back, but Robert had divested himself of all the other elements of his changed appearance.

"It's me, Dad," he said firmly. "Back in uniform."

Puller continued to hold on to the wall as he watched this.

Puller Sr.'s hand dipped down to his son's uninjured one and gripped it.

"Good, son. Good."

Then his father let go, turned and drifted back

over to his chair, and slowly sat down. He turned his face to the wall.

Robert glanced at his brother, his features confused. Puller inclined his head, indicating that Robert should follow his father.

Robert walked over, pulled up another chair, and sat next to his dad. His father continued to stare at the wall, but Puller could hear his brother speaking to him in low tones. He continued to watch for a few moments and then stepped outside the room, leaned against the wall, closed his eyes, exhaled a long breath, and tried to fight back the tears.

As he slumped down to the floor, he lost that fight.

76

PULLER STEPPED BETWEEN the graves at Fort Leavenworth until he found the one he wanted. He was once more wearing his dress blues, his cover on his head. The sun was warming and the skies were clear. Big Muddy was flowing hard from all the recent rains. Fort Leavenworth was back to normal. The DB was back to normal, although still missing one prisoner who would never be returning.

It was a pity, thought Puller, that Reynolds had not been sent to the DB to serve her prison term. She was the wrong gender and she was not in the military. She was now currently in a max civilian prison in Texas. She would never be leaving. And he knew it was still too good for her.

He had gone to see AWOL at the kennel and would be taking his cat home with him. The feline seemed happy to see him, although that might just have been the treat he had brought her.

He eyed the sky and then his gaze fell to the tombstone. He knelt down in front of it. That's when the person appeared next to him. He got a good glimpse of her long legs from his squatting position.

He looked up to see Knox standing there. Her skirt was black and short, her legs bare, and her blouse was white and revealing. She held her high heels in her hand. Her bandages were gone and her hair had mostly grown back after the surgery, though it was a lot spikier now.

Puller actually liked the look. It seemed to fit her better. Bohemian. Yes, the woman definitely marched to the beat of her own drummer.

He stood. She gazed up at him and dangled the shoes in front of him.

"Stilettos are obviously not designed for muddy graveyards."

"I can see that," he said, smiling.

"Okay, you summoned me here. You said meet at Thomas Custer's tombstone on this day at this time. And so here I am."

"I appreciate your coming. I didn't know if you would."

"How could I refuse?"

"Can we walk?"

They turned and strolled side by side down the row toward the parking lot.

"I took my brother to see our dad a while back."

"And how did that go?"

"He recognized Bobby."

"Is that unusual?"

"Well, considering he's been calling me XO for the last year or so, I'd say, yeah, it is unusual."

She lightly punched him in the arm. "You sound a bit jealous."

"I am. Maybe more than a bit."

"But that's a good thing, right? I mean your dad recognizing him?"

"The doctors said it was probably only temporary. The shock of seeing him."

"What do doctors know? I say stick with the belief that your dad is still there, Puller. And he may come out from time to time. And when he does, enjoy having him back. And never take it for granted."

He stopped walking and turned to her. "I've come to expect good advice from you."

"Well, I don't often get the chance to give it. It feels nice in a life that is usually centered around deception."

"I can understand that."

There was an awkward moment of silence until she said cheerfully, "So your brother's fully reinstated. Record cleared. His military career can take off like a rocket again."

"Yes. He's excited and scared."

"I would be too. Anyone would be. But you could have said all this over the phone. We didn't have to fly out to Kansas." She added quickly with an impish look, "Now, don't get me wrong. I like graveyards as much as the next girl."

"I thought I'd lost you," he said abruptly, his voice breaking slightly.

She gingerly touched her head. "See, you did lie to me. You said you were *sure* I was going to make it. But I don't hold it against you." She paused and then added jokingly, "And my brain is still all there. Docs assured me. Nothing leaked out. Not like I had any to spare."

However, her look revealed how moved she was by what he'd said.

He drew closer. "Saying things like that are...hard for me."

She touched his cheek, her expression now serious. "I know that, John. Believe me." She ran her gaze up and down him. "You look so handsome in your dress blues. Going somewhere?"

"Maybe."

"Maybe? You don't know?"

"It's actually up to someone else."

"Someone else? Who? Your CO?"

"No. Actually, it's up to you."

She seemed taken aback but drew closer to him. "And how is that?"

In answer he took out two tickets from his jacket and held them up.

She looked at them. "Plane tickets?" She glanced up at him and said in a panicked voice. "Wait a minute. Not to Vegas?"

"No, to Rome."

"Rome?" she said quietly.

"Ever been there?"

"Twice. Probably the most romantic city in the world."

"I have a week's leave. I want to spend it with you. And only you. I want us to get as far away from crime scenes and clandestine ops as is humanly possible. I just want us to be...normal. Just for a week, Knox. And see what happens. Together."

Knox seemed overwhelmed by all of this. She said, breathlessly, "Puller, we really don't even know each other."

"I know enough."

"You know nothing. You only know what I

told you. And as you quite rightly pointed out, I'm a liar."

"Knox, I—"

She gripped his arm. "I can't tell you how flattered I am."

Puller took a step back, his whole body seemed to deflate, and he looked at his feet. "Flattered? Isn't that what women say when their answer is no?"

She used her finger to lift his chin so he was looking at her. "Like I said before, you're a ramrod-straight kind of guy. Honorable to a fault. And my life is…none of that."

"But only the professional side. And only out of necessity."

"I'm not sure there're any distinct lines there, Puller. Not for me. Not anymore."

"I don't believe that."

"Whether you do or not is immaterial. A fact is a fact."

Puller looked down at the plane tickets.

She said, "I hope they're refundable."

He grinned for a second but there was nothing behind it.

"But you might have need of them one day."

He quickly glanced at her. "Why?"

She reached up on her tiptoes and kissed him. "Because you just never know, do you?"

"So where do you go now?" he asked dully.

"Where they tell me to. Just like you."

"Can you answer something for me?"

"What?"

"Why were you crying that day back in Charlotte? Was it because we were talking about your dad?"

She looked down at her bare feet, her toes pushing against the wet grass. "No. Like I said, I had gotten over him a long time ago."

"So what, then?"

She let out a quick breath. "It was because I knew I was going to have to keep lying to you. That I was going to keep on using you."

"So?"

"So before it didn't matter to me. Suddenly it did and it hit me like a train that morning."

"What changed?"

She grazed his cheek with her hand. "I think you know what changed."

He remained silent.

"I *am* human, Puller. Despite what you might have thought. I do…care." She touched his cheek. He clutched her hand, holding on tightly for a few seconds before letting it go.

She said, "Rain check? A big one?"

He nodded. "Yeah, okay."

She ran her gaze up and down him and shivered slightly. "And can I tell you once more how damn fine you look in uniform?" On that, she turned and walked off, swinging her shoes in one hand. She looked back once, smiled a smile that shook him to his knees, and then got into her car and drove off.

Puller watched her go until she was out of sight.

He looked down once more at the plane tickets.

He had never done anything this spur-of-the-moment in his personal life. His whole existence had been rigid, structured, thought out. Whimsy was not part of his wiring. But today all had been based on spontaneity, something he no longer thought he had. He took risks all the time in his professional life. He had taken none in his personal one.

Again—until today.

But Knox was right about many things she had said. They really didn't know each other that well. And maybe her life was very different from his. And maybe it was all irreconcilable.

But he didn't regret what'd he done. For at that moment in his life it had been the thing he wanted above all other things.

She had been the *person* he had wanted above all others. He had never felt that way about anyone before. He wanted her so badly it was actually painful to bear.

He put the plane tickets away in his jacket and headed to his car.

He had gotten his brother back.

And he had lost the woman he believed he could love.

It should have been a wash.

But life didn't work that way, did it?

He took off his hat and climbed into his car.

He sat there staring in the direction of Big Muddy, his thoughts mirroring the murky depths of the river.

Knox had her national security troubleshooting to pursue.

Puller had his criminals to catch.

Maybe one day their paths would cross again.

He put the car in gear.

Until then, John Puller would just keep doing what he did best.

ACKNOWLEDGMENTS

To Michelle, for always going on the journey with me.

To Mitch Hoffman, for always hitting the right notes.

To Michael Pietsch, Jamie Raab, Lindsey Rose, Sonya Cheuse, Emi Battaglia, Tom Maciag, Martha Otis, Karen Torres, Anthony Goff, Bob Castillo, Michele McGonigle, Andrew Duncan, Rick Cobban, Brian McLendon, and everyone at Grand Central Publishing, for all you do.

To Aaron and Arleen Priest, Lucy Childs Baker, Lisa Erbach Vance, Frances Jalet-Miller, John Richmond, and Melissa Edwards, for a stellar job across the board.

To Anthony Forbes Watson, Jeremy Trevathan, Maria Rejt, Trisha Jackson, Katie James, Natasha Harding, Sara Lloyd, Lee Dibble, Stuart Dwyer, Geoff Duffield, Jonathan Atkins, Stacey Hamilton, James Long, Anna Bond,

Sarah Willcox, Leanne Williams, Sarah McLean, Charlotte Williams, and Neil Lang at Pan Macmillan, for continuing to build me to new heights worldwide.

To Praveen Naidoo and his team at Pan Macmillan in Australia, for doing such a spectacular job.

To Sandy Violette and Caspian Dennis, for taking care of me so well.

To Arabella Stein, for being such a good friend and agent. Best of luck in your new career.

To Ron McLarty and Orlagh Cassidy, for your outstanding audio performances. Congratulations on the Audie! Well deserved.

To Steven Maat, Joop Boezeman, and the Bruna team for keeping me at the top in Holland.

To Bob Schule, for doing a particularly superb job on this one.

To Chuck Betack, for keeping me honest on all matters military.

To Steve Jennings, I will never look at DTRA in quite the same way. Your help was invaluable. But I still can't let you win at tennis (sorry).

To auction winners Shireen Kirk, Lenora Macri, and Susan Reynolds, I hope that you enjoy your characters.

To Roland Ottewell for a great copyediting job.

To Kristen and Natasha, for keeping me reasonably sane!

To Lynette and Art, thanks for everything and best wishes to you in Florida.

And to Spencer, for picking up the laboring oar.